WESTERN SHORES

THE COMPASS SERIES - BOOK 4

LISE GOLD

Love has no age, no limit;
and no death.

— JOHN GALSWORTHY

1

Capitola was everything Madison had hoped for. She'd shortlisted a couple of towns and cities before she came here with the intention of finding a home close to her new job in Santa Cruz, but the small town along Monterey Bay turned out to be even more picture-perfect than the photos she'd seen online. The rows of pastel colored beach-front homes behind the creek made for a spectacular view, painted in shades of yellow, turquoise, pink, blue, purple and soft green. Flowers in contrasting colors hung from the windowsills, matching the front doors and the steps. Even the commercial buildings were quaint, adorned with sun-bleached illustrations of beach scenes and vintage artworks. The town felt bohemian, with its small galleries, numerous tarot readers and stores selling hand-crafted jewelry and screen-printed fabrics. Swings and dreamcatchers hung from trees in the front yards that blended in seamlessly with the natural landscape. Capitola wasn't big, but it thrived on tourism in summer and everything she needed was right here; grocery stores, coffee shops, bars, restaurants and most importantly, the ocean.

Today being a weekday and still early, the beach was quiet, but surfers and paddle boarders were already out there. Madison counted seven of them sitting or standing on their boards, waiting for a wave or just chilling out. Already excited at the prospect of going for a morning swim before work, she held up her hand to greet the nearest ones, knowing they might get acquainted soon if she moved here. There were volleyball nets on the beach and the path along the boulevard seemed like a great place to go for a run.

"Are you okay, Mom?" she asked, looking over her shoulder when she heard her mother panting. With each step, her stiletto heels sunk into the sand, making her lose her balance, yet she'd refused to take them off.

"Yes honey. It's just the sand, it's..." Edie, her mother, finally took off her heels and decided to continue barefoot, then. "Why did you have to cross the beach? There's a perfectly good path leading up to the homes around the back."

"I wanted to see what it looks like from here." Madison took her mother's heels and hooked her arm into hers. "And I can't resist a nice beach, you know that."

The one-storey beach front homes that were built up against a hill with palm trees sticking out behind the rooftops, made for a picturesque backdrop. There was only one house for rent along the strip, and she'd been instantly drawn to the tiny pastel pink building with the bright pink front door when she saw it advertised online. The other places she'd viewed with her mother had been nice; more practical and certainly much bigger, but she'd only gone to see them because her mother had insisted that choice was important in order to make an informed decision. Deep down, her heart had been set on the pink house all along.

"Are you sure that's going to be big enough?" Edie asked as they looked up at it. "It's very pretty..." she turned to Madison and let out a chuckle. "...and it certainly matches your hair sweetie, but it looks awfully small and..."

"I don't need much space, Mom," Madison interrupted her. "I'm used to my dorm so this will be a palace compared to college."

"I'm not so sure about that." Edie squinted, shielding her eyes from the sun. The house was standing between a blue house and a yellow bar, called *Western Shores*. "It will be your first home though, and I want you to be comfortable," she continued, clumsily making her way toward the footpath. "You know your father and I would be happy to help you out with something bigger, and there's always your trust fund. You could buy a really nice apartment in Santa Cruz, or we could buy one together. You could always sell it on if you decide you don't want to stay here or if you get a better job offer somewhere else. It will be a good investment for us too, we really don't mind. I'm just not sure if renting is the right way to go for you."

"I know you want me to buy. And I'm grateful to you and dad for helping me out through college, but it's time I take care of myself now. I've been leaching off you guys for long enough and besides, it's only a six-month contract to start with. It's very rare that rentals like this come up and it will give me some time to explore the area. There's no point going through the trouble of buying something if I'm not going to stay, it's too much hassle."

A feeling or nervous excitement took over as they approached the house because it felt so right that there was no way she was going to look any further. It would be a fresh start. A new town, a new job – her first job, and she'd wake up to the sound of the ocean each morning. She fingered her recently dyed pastel pink bob, imagining herself living there. "And you're right. It does match my hair, it's a good thing I changed the color again. Maybe it's meant to be."

"Are you guys here to view the house?"

"Yeah." Madison smiled at the woman who was arranging flowers on the three tables outside the bar next to the pink house. "Are you Ally?" The woman had long dark-brown wavy hair that fell over her shoulders, and she wore a loose off-the-shoulder white top and a short denim skirt underneath her black apron. She was barefoot, which was unusual for someone who worked in hospitality, but Madison figured it was a beach bar, and so the customers were likely to be barefoot too. Turquoise beaded earrings dangled behind her dimpled cheeks as she smiled back and nodded, then wiped her hands on her apron before she pulled a set of keys out of her back pocket and introduced herself.

"That's me. It's nice to meet you..." She narrowed her eyes. "Madison, was it?"

"That's right." Madison shook her hand. "And this is my mother, Edie."

"Nice to meet you both." The silver bangles around Ally's wrist jingled as she unlocked the front door to the pink house and held it open. "Please come in and take a look around." She switched on the lights in the tiny hallway and walked two steps ahead of them into the combined living room and open kitchen area. There was a beige three-seater couch, a coffee table on a cozy Berber rug, and a big bookcase full of art-related books. Right behind the couch was a small kitchen with a refrigerator, a stove, a sink and a breakfast bar with two stools. A separate piece of wood, matching the kitchen surface, had been placed on the bar to use as a cutting board as there was not much space elsewhere. It felt homey though, with lots of plants and striking modern artworks on the walls. "As I told you on the phone, it's very small. I've been renting it out to tourists but with the bar being next door, some of the tenants have been complaining about the noise and leaving bad reviews. It's not terrible in my opinion, but it does get busy during the summer and it's not always easy to get rid of the last customers at night. Quite frankly, I don't have the energy to deal with the complaints anymore." She opened the light blue and white seersucker curtains to the two ocean-facing windows, letting in the light. "As advertised, here's your unobstructed ocean view. The house comes furnished; it's not the fanciest stuff but I've tried my best to make it nice and practical, and you'll have everything you'll need here. If you want me to, I can remove the books and other items of course."

"It looks lovely and I can live with noise," Madison said. "I've come straight off campus so I'm practically immune to it."

"That's that problem solved then," Ally said, looking relieved.

"Is there a yard?" Edie asked, scanning the space for a back door.

"No, but there's a set of fold-up table and chairs in the hallway that you can put outside your front door if you like. That's how I do it. Besides, you'll have the beach, so who needs a yard?"

"Totally agree." Madison followed Ally to the bedroom and noted her mother wasn't sold. In fact, she seemed horrified by how small it was. The big box-spring bed took up most of the room, but there was a decent-sized built-in wardrobe and a small desk in front of the window, framed by the same curtains. A blue oil painting, inspired by the view, hung above the bed and an off-white crocheted dream catcher dangled next to it. "So, do you live in the same building as the bar?"

Ally laughed. "No, there's not enough space there for me and my son. We do live next door though, to your other side in the blue house. It's got a small tower that we've converted into his bedroom."

Edie turned to her. "You own both buildings?" She was clearly surprised to hear that the woman who worked in the bar next door had managed to buy herself multiple properties on such a sought-after strip of coastland. "Is the bar yours too?"

"Yeah, all three are mine, it's a long story." Madison was sure she saw a hint of sadness in Ally's eyes, but the woman turned away from them, making sure to avoid eye contact. "The bathroom is right here." She walked back into the hallway and opened the only other door, revealing a narrow, white-tiled bathroom that was so small that the showerhead was hanging over the toilet.

Madison couldn't help but laugh. "Okay... I don't think I've ever seen that before. At least I can do two things simultaneously, saves me time in the morning."

Ally laughed too. "Yeah, it's small all right. Theo, my son and I brush our teeth in the kitchen sink. I use one of the kitchen cupboards for toiletries and I've stuck a mirror on the inside. You've got to be creative in a place like this. Oh, and I want to be honest with you about the parking too, although you probably figured that out when you arrived. The thing is, there is no parking space around here. This place comes with a guest permit, but you'll have to leave your pickup at the end of the beach road. It's a ten-minute walk from here and it gets really busy in high season. You might have to park it twenty minutes away sometimes during the summer months, so I just want to forewarn you." She shot Madison an amused look. "But the time you save in the shower will make up for that."

Madison's eyes met Ally's and held them for a beat. Her dimples and the few freckles on each cheek were adorable, and the fine lines around her eyes indicated she smiled a lot. She really liked this friendly hippie chick, and she had a feeling they were going to get on. "What's behind there?" she pointed to a silk screen in front of an alcove in the living room.

"Sorry, I almost forgot." Ally folded the screen away. "This little nook here has a washer and a dryer and there's a little space left in case you have a surfboard or something else big you need to stow away."

"It's very small," Edie remarked, unable to let it go. "We've viewed three-bedroom apartments for the same price not far from here."

"You're right. It is small, but if you take the premium location into account, it's actually highly competitive." Ally shrugged. "I understand if you're not interested, it's totally fine. I've got another twenty-six people lined up to take a look at it, but your daughter sounded so nice on the phone that I wanted to give her the first choice."

"Thank you for that," Madison said, shooting her mother a quick warning look. "I'll take it." She had a feeling Ally was bluffing about the twenty-six people, but even if she was, this place felt good and she couldn't wait to move in.

"Really?" Ally arched a brow and grinned. "Are you sure?"

"Am I sure? You're not exactly selling it," Madison joked. "Did anyone ever teach you about upselling? I love it."

"No, I'm afraid not." Ally chuckled. "But I love it here too. I'm just highly aware of the impracticalities, that's all. And there's the price, of course. I know it's not cheap but if you want it, it's yours. I've got the contract ready for you to sign next door."

"Let's do it, then." Madison ignored her mother, who was trying to make eye contact, determined to talk her out of it.

"Don't you want to think about it, Madison?"

"No, Mom. This feels right, I want to live here." Madison's tone indicated there was no discussion to be had. This would be her new home. She'd never touched her trust fund until now, but she needed some of it to pay for the three months' rent upfront. After that, she'd have a steady income from her job.

"Great, follow me." Ally led them back outside and pulled out three chairs at one of the tables outside her bar. She disappeared for a moment after enquiring what they wanted to drink, then came back with a tray of coffees and a pile of paperwork clenched under her arm. "Here's a cappuccino for you, Edie," she said as she put the cup down on the yellow painted recycled wooden table. "And a soy latte for you, Madison." She paused as she put a second cup in front of Madison. "And our new house special for you to try too. It's a beetroot soy latte. I figured it suited you as both your hair and your house are pink now."

"Damn." Madison looked down at the bright pink hot drink with white foam shaped into a perfect wave. "This is art, Ally."

"Wait until you taste it." Ally put down an espresso for herself and placed the tray under her chair before handing Madison the contract.

"It's so good." Madison licked the foam off her upper lip after taking a sip. "It's sweet, but a natural kind of sweet... and it's spicy, which is unexpected." She gave it to her mother to try.

"Hmm... I like it too," Edie agreed. She seemed a little more relaxed than five minutes ago, Madison thought. Or maybe she'd just resigned herself to the idea, knowing there was nothing she could do to change her decision. Madison would do whatever the hell she wanted to do. It had always been that way.

"Yeah, it's like chai but with a little cayenne pepper added in," Ally said. "People who don't tolerate caffeine love it because the spice still wakes them up in the morning." She gave Madison a smug look. "My own invention."

"Clever lady, you are." Madison returned her smirk while she searched for her driver's license in her purse. "Here's my ID."

Ally snapped a picture on her phone. "Twenty-three," she said after calculating Madison's age. "Do you mind if I ask why you're moving here?"

"A job." Madison flicked through the pages of the standard rental contract. She'd looked them up online before she came here, knowing her mother wouldn't be of much help. Her father took care of things like that in their household, and her mother had always been comfortable taking a backseat to her husband's career as a political strategist, sitting around looking pretty, and occasionally decorating houses they purchased to rent out. Not that there was anything wrong with that. She was an amazing mother and she did a lot of great charity work too. Edie was fifty-two now, but because it was hard to guess her age due to the many procedures that she'd undergone over the past twenty years, people often asked them if they were sisters. "My first job, actually, I got my Masters in Marine Biology last year. I'm going to be a research technician at the Marine Mammal Research Center in Santa Cruz. They're starting a tagging-and-tracking program of long-beaked common dolphins next week so my first three months will be fieldwork mostly."

"I see." Ally seemed a little taken aback by that. She stared at Madison for a moment, then cleared her throat. "I know that place very well," she said. "My husband..." She hesitated. "He was the director."

"Really? What's his name?"

"Marcos Santos." Ally lowered her voice as she said his name, and Madison noticed that look in her eyes again. "I meant to say my late husband. He died nine years ago when Theo, our son, was two." She took a deep breath and gave them a smile. "I apologize, this is all a bit heavy considering this is our first meeting and I didn't mean to bring it up but since you mentioned the lab... It was a long time ago though, and Theo and I are okay now."

"I'm so sorry, honey," Edie said, reaching out for Ally's hand. Madison hoped her mother wouldn't start crying and make matters worse. She tended to get very emotional whenever there were children involved in tragedies.

"I'm sorry too." Madison studied Ally, unable to look away despite the serious conversation because she was simply stunning. Her skin was sun-kissed and her long, brown hair, that she was constantly fussing with, shimmered in the sun. She was petite and cute, with a wide, contagious smile that made Madison smile too, each time she looked at her. She wondered about her age, but it was hard to tell. *Mid-thirties, maybe?*

"Thank you, but really, we're okay," Ally said. "Marcos gave me Theo and I feel really blessed with him. He's sweet and extremely clever, he's doing great in school and all in all, he's just a good kid."

"Children are the biggest blessing God has given us," Edie said in a dramatic voice, rubbing a hand over Madison's arm. "You know, Madison used to babysit when she was younger. She's really good with kids if you ever need someone to look after your son."

Madison barely suppressed an eye-roll at her mother, who was clearly sold on Ally now and all on-board with her moving into the pint-sized house. *Jesus, it doesn't take much.*

Ally laughed it off. "I don't doubt your daughter is amazing with kids, Edie, but I'm sure she's got better things to do and besides, I don't tend to get that personal with my tenants." She knocked back her espresso. "But the tenancy package does include a free coffee each morning so I'm sure we'll get to know each other better." She pointed to the section in the contract Madison was reading.

"Free coffee?" Madison looked up at her and grinned. "Where do I sign?"

2

Ally put the contract in her purse and watched Madison and Edie walk away. Madison seemed like a nice girl; warm, funny, confident... Ally suspected she might be a bit of a party girl too. Despite her unusual appearance, she was very pretty, or perhaps attractive was a better word. Her pink, sharp-cut bob, with the straight fringe that ended just above her dark eyebrows and unusually light-blue eyes, were a fascinating combination and she'd certainly stand out here in Capitola. The diamond stud in her nose, the funny little tattoos on her left hand, the black, chipped nail varnish, her rock-band T-shirt and the super short ripped denim shorts baring toned and tanned legs made her look a little rough around the edges. Going on looks, Madison was the polar opposite to her mother, who couldn't have been more polished and looked like she had her own personal stylist. Her zebra printed dress was slightly outrageous, and her high heels had made Ally chuckle as she'd watched them walk up to the bar. Neither the beach or the cobbled paths in town were practical for heels and Ally had given up on them when she moved here.

Even when going on the occasional date, she didn't bother, afraid she'd sprain her ankle walking to the car. She'd warmed to Edie too eventually, even though at first, she'd come across as a little stern under her cosmetic façade. Edie's designer purse screamed wealth, and even the way she walked made Ally think she came from money. She wondered why Madison hadn't chosen to rent somewhere bigger, as she clearly had no problem putting down the three months' rent upfront.

Knowing the money would be in her bank account by the end of the week gave Ally a sense of relief, and frankly she didn't care about the 'whys and wherefores'. The fee for Theo's private tutor was due again soon. Even after skipping two grades in school and joining the Talented and Gifted Program, Theo was still much smarter than the other kids in his class and really enjoyed the math assignments he was given after school twice a week by a retired professor who lived around the corner and who had taken him under his scholarly wing. Besides that, her son needed new clothes too. He was growing so fast that the jeans she'd bought him five months ago were starting to look short on him already.

Theo took after his father, that much had become clear years ago. His tanned skin, thick, curly hair, tall, slender frame and his off-the-charts intelligence... Ally had been a little shocked by his teachers' feedback during her last meeting at his school. She knew Theo was intelligent, sure. But to find out he was still too smart, even after starting high school at eleven, was something else altogether and she often worried about how to move forward with him, especially since he was so much younger than his peers and had trouble fitting in. Shaking it off as she always did, Ally cleared the table and brought their empty cups inside.

The interior of *Western Shores* was a cheerful mix of

vintage and DIY. The high tables and stools, as well as the bar, were made of recycled wood, and Ally had found the two seventies lounge chairs and the mid-century sideboard in the back at a flea market. The barstools were all different but somehow worked really well together after she'd re-upholstered the seats with yellow leather, and the big murals on the wall opposite the bar, that incorporated the cocktail menu, had been painted by Ally too. Although she'd given up on working as an artist a long time ago, she still loved to pour her creative juices into her home and her beloved bar. The back wall was studded with shells that Theo had found for her, sprayed yellow. She'd covered the recycled tins she used as cocktail glasses in shells too, then dipped them in brightly colored paint and resin. The long rows of colorful 'cups' were an eye-catching detail above the bar, and she even sold them on a regular basis. All in all, it looked great and Ally had used whatever she could find to create an inviting space on a minimum budget. A piece of old driftwood served as a coatrack, and an old fishing net was spun across the ceiling, holding hundreds of tiny white string lights. She'd painted the inside of the restroom doors with blackboard paint and had placed boxes with chalk on the basins, allowing her visitors to write on them. Some of the inappropriate messages and obscene drawings scribbled on the doors during late weekend nights often made her laugh when she wiped them clean in the morning.

Ally greeted a group of four local seniors who always came in before ten am. Most customers were retirees during weekday mornings, apart from the early surfers and paddle boarders who just wanted to grab a quick coffee before going to work. After eight years of running the bar, she knew most of the locals by name, and she liked the daily small talk, especially in the mornings when she wasn't busy.

Without asking, she started making the four cappuccinos they religiously drank, and as she frothed the milk, her thoughts went back to Madison. It would be nice to have a long-term tenant again instead of the tourists who came and went. She wouldn't have to bother with the changeovers and with the online bookings that took up a lot of her time. That thought made her smile. Madison seemed like a great girl and Ally had wanted her as a tenant the moment they'd spoken on the phone to arrange the viewing. After meeting her in real life, she couldn't have wished for a better person to move into the pink house. Being young, she'd have no problem with potential noise, and clearly coming from a wealthy family, Ally was sure she'd be able to pay the rent on time too. There was something else that drew her to Madison though, but she couldn't put her finger on it. Perhaps it was the youthful energy in those amazing icy-blue eyes, or the way she spoke so animatedly, reminding Ally of how she used to be herself when she just came out of college.

"Daydreaming Ally?"

Ally looked up from the coffee machine to find her mother-in-law leaning over the bar. "Damn it, I've ruined the milk." She threw in an ice-cube and shook the milk jug, then started over. "How are you today, Ana?"

"Getting old." Ana's reply was the same each morning. "That lady from Louisiana came to look at the house, right? Did she like it? Or was it too small for her?"

"No, it was absolutely perfect for her. She's already signed, and they just left."

"Honey, that's great." Ana slammed a hand on the bar and sighed dramatically. "I'm so glad you won't have to stress about that house anymore. It was way too much for you while you were running the bar and taking care of Theo."

"Yeah, I'm really happy. She seems lovely too." Ally poured the milk foam on top of the espresso in four large cups, creating a clean, white heart-shape on top, then brought them out to her customers. She patted Ana's shoulder as she walked past her again. "What can I get for you today?"

"Oh, I don't know. I've had too much caffeine already." Ana produced a pristine white cotton handkerchief from her pocket and dabbed her forehead. "I think I'll just have a chamomile tea."

"Are you sure you don't want to try that beetroot soy latte?" Ally asked. "It's really good."

Ana laughed. "God, no. Salad in my coffee? That's just wrong."

"It's not salad." Ally quirked a brow, giving her an amused look. She adored Ana, who had stuck around even after her son's death, to help her out with Theo. Without her, she'd never have been able to open *Western Shores*. The hours had been long in the beginning, until she'd finally hired her best friend Devon, who now shared the shifts with her taking over a lot of the late ones so she could pick Theo up from school.

"It's salad all right." Ana nodded toward the selection of herbal teas that Ally kept in a long, wooden box. "Just give me a chamomile tea. And a slice of carrot cake if you've got any. I don't mind eating salad, just don't like the idea of drinking it."

3

"How did the house hunting go?" Ben, Madison's father asked while they were having dinner. Madison and her younger brother Chuck had helped her mother cook dinner after they'd returned from their trip. It was one of the few activities that never led to arguments and so it had become a way for them to spend time together in a peaceful way. Living on campus, Madison hadn't been home more than once a month in the past years, but after graduating and volunteering at a whale conservation program in Florida for five months, she'd moved back home while she looked for a job. Living with her parents again hadn't been that bad; they got along, and she really appreciated the luxury of having a housekeeper and a pool in the back yard. Lafayette wasn't her scene though, and she couldn't wait to be in her new home in a week.

"There wasn't much house hunting." Edie sighed before taking a careful bite of her salmon, making sure not to smudge the fresh layer of red lipstick she always applied before dinner, even if it was just the family around the table.

"We saw two spacious apartments on Monday. They were stylish and practical and very close to the research center, but Madison decided to go for the third house we viewed yesterday morning. It's in Capitola. The place is terribly small and I'm sure she could find something better in Santa Cruz or San Jose, but you know Madison. She does exactly what she wants and there was no way I could convince her otherwise. Ally, the landlady seems nice though, so at least I know she'll be in good hands."

"Mom, I'm right here." Madison widened her eyes at her mother, then turned to her father. "It's gorgeous, Dad. It's small and pink and it faces the ocean."

"Capitola? Don't think I've heard of it." Ben smiled at his daughter. "Well, if you're happy, I'm happy, honey. And if it's such a nice place, you'd better have a guest room ready for us."

"There is no guest room, sweetheart. One bedroom, a bathroom that's smaller than our hallway closet and a combined living room and kitchen, if you can call it a kitchen at all." Edie took a moment and composed herself, reminding herself that this was a special time for Madison. "But Madison is right; it's very charming and it suits her. It seems like a very safe town too."

"That's great." Ben helped himself to more asparagus. "And you're sure you don't need any help, financially?"

"I'm sure, Dad. I already told Mom it's time I take care of myself." Madison gave her father's arm a squeeze. "Anyway, don't worry about me. Worry about what you're going to do with your time when you retire next month. Are you going to volunteer on campaigns again, like you used to in college?"

"I bet he'll be heading straight for a midlife-crisis," Chuck joked. "Dad doesn't know what to do with himself when he's not working. He can't even relax on holiday. I'm thinking brightly colored crocodile-leather shoes, a Harley-Davidson, a guitar, maybe? And let's not forget a hot, young..."

"Your father will be fine, stop teasing him," Edie interrupted her son, knowing exactly what was coming next. "We're going to take up golf, actually. Well, your father already plays, of course, but I'm having lessons at the moment and as soon as I have my handicap, we can go on golf holidays together."

Chuck's beer went straight up his nose as he laughed. "You and golf? I've never even seen you in flat shoes." Madison couldn't help but laugh too, mainly at seeing her father's bewildered expression. He clearly had not been informed about his wife's plans.

"I *do* have flat shoes," Edie argued. "I play tennis, don't I? And now I have golf shoes too. They're very comfortable, actually."

"She does," Madison confirmed. "I saw her leave the house in them last week on the way to her first lesson." She turned to her brother and tried to keep a straight face as she added: "They have tassels."

"Ooh, tassels." Chuck shot Madison a comical glance.

"You'd better watch out young man, or you'll be spending your last month here in the garage," Edie said, but her small smile told Madison she didn't mind him teasing her.

"Hey, wait a minute. What do you mean by 'last month'?" Madison looked from Chuck to her mother and back.

"Oh, you don't know?" Chuck held up his beer bottle in a toast. "I'm moving out. I got an apartment closer to Presley, so I won't have to drive so far to work anymore." He grinned.

"Kristine and Hannah have given me a full-time contract and I'm now officially a chef."

"That's fantastic, Chuck. Congratulations!" Madison leaned in and gave her brother a hug. They were close, but she'd always seen him as the kid in the family and it wasn't until now that she realized Chuck had grown up and was ready to stand on his own two feet, just like she was. After dropping out of several schools, being a pain in the ass at home and finally enrolling in a cooking class, their half-sister Hannah, had suggested he help out at the restaurant she and her fiancée Kristine ran in Presley. Always being the troublemaker in the family, no one had expected Chuck to excel in what he did, but he'd turned out to be an excellent chef with real passion for cooking and he'd surprised them with many spectacular meals during Madison's time back home.

"Thank you. I'm pretty stoked." Chuck took a long drink of his beer and burped, causing Edie to gasp in horror. "Mom helped me find an apartment. I'll be moving into the Hicking building. It's where her friend Darla lives."

"What?" Madison laughed. "But that's still a good forty minutes from Presley, not to mention the fact that it's practically a seniors' building. They have care available on-site."

Chuck shrugged. "Exactly. They offer cleaning services; how could I resist? Besides, I don't care. It's just a place to sleep and it's close to the freeway."

"Chuck is right," their mother chipped in. "It's very practical. And spacious," she added, shooting Madison a knowing look.

4

"Hey, Madison." Ally gave Madison a hug as she got out of her battered old Dodge pickup. "Welcome to your new life." She gestured to the shopping cart she'd borrowed from the grocery store to move Madison's belongings from her pickup to the house. "Thought you might need some help with your stuff when you called. We'll have to make a couple of trips, but we'll get there."

Madison laughed as she started loading boxes into the cart. "Thanks for meeting me here, you didn't have to do that."

"Don't be silly. You've had a long drive; you must be exhausted." Ally took a bag out of the back of the truck and flung it over her shoulder. "This is how Theo and I do it when we go away. Which sadly isn't very often because of the bar," she added. "The grocery store manager is really nice; I'll introduce you to him in case you ever need to borrow one again."

"It's a genius idea. I wasn't sure if I'd be able to find a parking spot nearby since it's Friday, but I got lucky – someone was just leaving." Madison closed her eyes for a moment and inhaled deep. She felt excited and suddenly wide awake, despite the ten-hour journey that had started at four am that morning. "It smells amazing here," she said with a sigh. "The sea breeze... there's nothing like it."

"I'm with you on that." Ally gave her a wide, warm smile and she tucked her hair behind her ears, making her silver bangles shimmer in the sun as her hand swayed. "I've lived here half my life and still, every time I go away, I'm delighted to come home again. I think you'll like Capitola."

"I think I will." Madison closed the truck and pushed the shopping cart, following Ally down the road to the house. The sun was out, drawing the lucky ones who didn't have to work, to the beach. Although early April wasn't quite warm enough for swimming or sunbathing, they were reading, building sandcastles and enjoying picnics. It was a sweet sight, and one she knew would stay with her for a long time to come. The dozens of benches along the beach path were full of people eating ice cream or socializing, and cyclists taking a break, stretching and admiring the view. The sound of their chatter was dampened by the crashing waves and the screaming seagulls flying overhead.

"Here are your keys." Ally handed Madison the key ring to her new home and held the cart so she could open the door. "There's a spare front door key on there and that's it. There's no back door, as you know, but in need of escape, both the bedroom and the kitchen window are big enough to easily climb through. The bedroom window leads into the alleyway behind the house."

"I'll keep that in mind." Madison pushed the cart inside. "Don't worry, I can take it from here and I'll drop the cart back off at the store. There's only one more load to go, I think."

"Are you sure?" Ally stayed hovering in the doorway,

consciously keeping a distance as this was Madison's home now. "Well, I have coffee next door in case you'd like a cup when you're done. Or something stronger..." She held up a hand. "But please don't feel obliged, I don't want to overstep any boundaries."

"No, I'd love that." Madison turned to her and shot her a grateful glance. "I'm just going to have a quick shower after I finish, and I'll see you out there."

"Did you manage to work out the shower?" Ally asked as she put a plate of calamari with lemon wedges and a garlic dip on their table outside *Western Shores* an hour later. "It takes a little time to figure out the logistics." Seventies surf music was playing from the speakers and people were sitting on the low wall in front of the bar drinking cocktails, happy hour in full swing. There was animated chatter and pleasantries were being exchanged, the carefree vibe a prelude to the start of the weekend.

Madison laughed. "I managed. Once you get used to the sitting down part, it's actually quite relaxing." She took the Negroni cocktail, garnished with a twist of orange peel that Ally had made for her, and held it up in a toast. "Thank you, Ally. This is such a nice welcome."

"The pleasure is all mine." Ally held up her rosé and clinked it against Madison's glass. "Devon just took over my shift and I rarely take the opportunity to just sit here and relax." She turned to the open doors behind her and yelled: "Hey Devon, come out here and meet our new neighbor!"

"Is she here?" A handsome man in his late thirties appeared in the door. Devon had thick, dark hair and bushy brows over his brown eyes. He shot Madison a charming grin as he walked over to them and shook her hand. "Well hello, it's very nice to meet you. Madison, right? I'm Devon, Ally's second in command."

"That's right. Devon runs the bar and the kitchen when I'm off, but when it's busy we're often here together. In high season we usually take on a couple of part-timers too, but right now, we can manage between us," Ally said.

"It's nice to meet you too, Devon." Madison noted his other hand was resting on Ally's shoulder and they looked so intimate that she wondered if they were more than just colleagues.

Devon gave her a good glance-over, then looked up as two women entered the bar. "Good afternoon ladies," he said before turning back to Madison. "Excuse, me, I need to take care of our customers but I'm sure I'll see you around very soon."

"Absolutely." Madison sat back again and took another sip of her drink. Despite the long journey, she felt blissfully relaxed after a long shower and now the cocktail, combined with a gorgeous view over the creek and the bay. She was conscious of Ally watching her from the corner of her eye; it was something she'd been aware of ever since she'd stepped out of her truck. It didn't bother her though. Having pink hair, she was used to people looking at her and besides, it gave her an excuse to look at Ally too, because Ally was very pleasant in the looks department. The hem of her oversized khaki colored shirt dress crept up her legs as she crossed them, revealing tanned thighs. "Are you and Devon dating?" she asked, breaking the silence when they were alone again.

"Me and Devon?" Ally chuckled. "Oh God, no. Devon and I are just old friends. We went to college together. But he *is* single in case you were wondering…"

Now it was Madison's turn to laugh. "No, I was definitely

not wondering about Devon's status. I'm gay, so I have no interest in men whatsoever. He seems nice, though."

"Oh..." Ally blushed as she narrowed her eyes and shook her head. "I'm sorry, I didn't realize."

"Don't apologize." Madison gave her a playful wink and dipped one of the calamari into the garlic dip. "Mmm..." she mumbled, taking a bite. "These are amazing."

"Thanks." Ally seemed grateful that Madison had changed the topic. "We only have snacks on the menu, but our customers love our seafood tempura. I'll make you a selection next time." She felt a little flustered all of a sudden and found herself making agitated hand-gestures as she spoke. "That is, if you want to come back here of course. I don't expect you to be our customer just because you're my tenant and..."

"Relax, Ally." Madison put a hand on Ally's arm, making her blush even more. "I've got a feeling you're new to this whole long-term tenant thing, but I can assure you that I don't feel pressured in any way, okay? I'm totally comfortable."

"Okay..." Ally took a long drink of her rosé. "I'm sorry. I don't know what's wrong with me today. You're right. I've never had a long-term tenant and I guess I'm not sure how to behave. I don't want you to feel like I'm pressuring you to be social but at the same time I really want you to feel welcome." She cursed herself for sounding so anxious all of a sudden and was kind of in awe of Madison's chilled and confident attitude.

"Then just be yourself because you're awesome," Madison said. "Besides, we're going to be living next door to each other for at least six months so we might as well get to know each other." She locked her eyes with Ally's and her intense stare seemed to pierce right through Ally. "So, you studied art, huh? That's neat. Did you paint all those great artworks in my house? And that cool mural in the bar?"

"I did. I'm not serious about it anymore, although I used to be when I was young and thought I could change the world with my art. Make a difference, you know..." Ally chuckled. "I'm under no illusion anymore. There are people way better than me in this world, but I enjoy it so I still do some private commissions and you can even see some of my murals in Capitola."

"I saw some awesome ones next to the bank and on the side of the fire station. Did you do them?"

"Yeah, those are mine. I always feel like painting over them when I drive past though; I'm very self-critical."

Madison tilted her head and studied Ally with renewed interest. "You're really good. Don't be so modest, you clearly have a talent."

"Thank you." Ally had never been very comfortable taking compliments, and she shifted in her chair, changing the subject. "So, do you have a girlfriend?"

Madison shook her head. "No, no girlfriend. I've dated quite a lot but nothing serious and right now, I just want to focus on my job." She hesitated. "Are you seeing someone? I mean, after your husband..."

"Nothing serious either," Ally said. "I've also dated a bit over the years, but somehow I've never managed to fall in love again and so I kind of gave up."

"Why would you give up? You're gorgeous and you seem like a really nice and fun person. I'm sure most men would kill for someone like you."

Ally rolled her eyes and giggled. "Thanks for the confidence boost but having a kid isn't exactly a selling point. Not that I would have it any other way," she hastily added. "Theo is the best thing that ever happened to me and..." Her smile widened as her gaze shifted to the beach, from where a young boy came walking up with an older lady. "Speaking of the devil," she said. "He finishes school early on Friday and likes to hang out on the beach while I work."

"Mom, we found some stuff for my aquarium!" he yelled as he ran up to Ally, holding a Ziploc bag. He was tall and skinny with a beaming smile, olive skin and wild, curly, dark hair.

"You did? That's great, Theo. We'll make sure to get them in there today." She gave him a kiss on his cheek. "Do you remember me telling you about our new tenant? This is Madison. Madison, this is Theo, my son."

"Hi." Theo turned to Madison. "So you're living in the pink house now?" His wide grin turned into a chuckle. "You have pink hair."

"I do," Madison answered, immediately charmed by his childlike honesty. "Pink house, pink hair. So, what have you got in there?" She pointed to the bag he was holding.

"Shells." He held the bag open for her to take a look, then took out a small flat stone-colored object with a five-pointed shape on its back and handed it to Madison. "I found a fossil too. I think this is a Dendraster excentricus."

Madison turned the fossil over in her hands, her eyes widening at the realization the boy had the scientific name spot on. "I think you're right, Theo. This is a fossilized sand dollar." She frowned. "How did you know that?"

Theo shrugged. "It's very detailed so it wasn't hard to figure out, but I still have to double-check my book to make sure. How do you know about shells?"

"I'm a marine biologist," Madison said, and smiled when she saw Theo spike to attention. "I know a thing or two, although I'm not specialized in shells or fossils. You seem to be the expert on that."

He chuckled at the compliment. "My dad was a marine biologist too."

"I know, your mom told me that. What else did you find?"

Theo frowned as he looked into his bag again. "Nothing special. Just a bunch of hermit crab shells. Two are still in there so I need to take them up to my aquarium now. Do you want to see it?"

"Honey, I'm sure Madison is tired and..."

"I made it myself," he continued, ignoring his mother.

"Sure. I'd love to see it. Why don't you give me ten minutes and if your mom is okay with it, I'll come and check it out."

"I'm sorry," Ally whispered to Madison. "Theo, you're going to have to tidy your room first, okay? The front door is open."

"I'll do it right now." An elevated pitch ran through Theo's voice as he rushed away from them.

"I apologize. I'll talk to him tonight," Ally said.

"No need, I really don't mind," Madison assured her, then looked up at the older lady who had finally reached their table.

"Ana, this is Madison, my new tenant and now apparently also Theo's new best friend."

"Hi Madison." The lady shook Madison's hand as she stood up. "I'm Ally's mother-in-law, Theo's grandmother. I look after him when Ally works, and I live just up the hill so I'm sure we'll see each other in passing." Ana was tall and elegant, with short, silver gray hair and sharp, intelligent eyes.

"It's very nice to meet you, Ana." Madison caught Theo running into the house from the corner of her eye. "That's one informed grandson you've got there. And son," she added, casting a glance at Ally. "He seems very bright..."

"Yes, Theo is extremely bright for an eleven-year-old. He likes to read his father's old research journals," Ally explained as if it was the most common thing in the world for someone of Theo's age.

"He's highly gifted and a very curious boy," Ana added. "He was always ahead of his peers, but his development seems to have accelerated lately. He's in high school already."

"Right..." Madison took a moment to process the information, then nodded. "Highly gifted, that explains it. How is he getting on in high school? That can't be easy for him, being the youngest one."

"It's not ideal, he keeps to himself mostly. But he loves his homework and assignments and..." Ally shook her head. "Actually, I'm saying all this but I'm not quite sure how he's doing. I've been called in for a meeting with the principal on Monday and I won't deny that I'm a bit anxious about it."

Madison nodded. "I get that. Did he not say what it was about?"

"No, the school assistant called to make the appointment." Ally really did feel anxious each time she thought about it. It was hard having a child who was too intelligent for the school system and too young to make friends in his year.

"Hey, he's a good boy. I'm sure it's nothing to fret about." Ana put an arm around Ally and placed a reassuring kiss on her forehead. "Everything will be fine, Ally."

"I know." Ally shrugged and smiled at Madison. "But hey, no point worrying about that until Monday. Can I fix you another drink while you check out Theo's aquarium?"

She held up her own glass. "I'm genuinely enjoying your company so don't think I'm just being polite."

"Sure, why not?" Madison got up and pointed to Ally's house. "Can I let myself in?"

"Absolutely. The door is open and there's just one tiny room up the stairs so you can't miss it." Ally found herself staring at Madison's behind. Her legs seemed to go on forever and her perky ass swayed when she walked off. She cocked her head, her eyes shifting to Madison's breasts, their ample shape evident in the tight tank top she wore as she turned to open the door. Apparently, she had a little body envy. She snapped back when Ana cleared her throat and arched a brow at her. "Sorry, Ana. Can I get you a drink too?"

"Sure. I'll have a cappuccino as soon as you're done glaring at your tenant."

5

The carrot cake smelled divine and Ally was pleased as she pressed a hand down on it to check if it was cool enough to glaze. She and Devon took turns baking cakes for the café and carrot cake was always a favorite with the locals. A cheesecake was setting in the fridge and the chocolate muffins were already displayed at the end of the bar. By now, baking had become second nature to her, and it didn't take up much of her time anymore. The smell of freshly baked goods in the morning always drew people in and that was important as there was quite a bit of competition in Capitola.

Ally wasn't used to drinking anymore and she had a slight headache from the copious amount of wine she'd consumed last night. Madison had turned out to be great company. She was funny, intelligent and had an energy to her that drew Ally in and made her want to be a part of her world. They'd talked for hours until Devon closed up and even then, they'd stayed in front of Madison's door, finishing a conversation she could hardly recall. Although it was probably the norm for Madison, Ally never had nights like that anymore. She'd lost touch with old friends, being too busy with Theo and the bar, and her social life was limited to drinks with Devon after work and occasional dates that were usually a waste of her time.

She covered the top of the cake with cream cheese frosting and carried it out to the bar to place it next to the muffins. As she started moving the furniture outside, she saw Madison cross the beach in a black string bikini, holding a towel under her arm. Ally tilted her head, following her with her eyes. Madison's thigh muscles tensed as she quickened her pace, then started running toward the shore. Even from a distance, it was clear that she was athletic, and she looked great from behind. *She looks great from the front too.* Ally shook her head and shot back into action mode when she realized she'd been staring at her again. She put down the chair she'd been holding, then concentrated on the rest of the furniture and the flowers, still keeping one eye on her new tenant. It was way too cold to swim, but it didn't seem to bother Madison as she dropped the towel, sprinted in and dove into a wave. Ally gasped at the sight, goose bumps appearing on her arms just at the thought of going into the water this time of year. Again, she forgot what she was doing as she watched Madison swim farther out in a quick front crawl, disappearing under the water only to resurface a few moments later to turn on her back and finally lay still, simply floating while the dozens of pelicans that were out there today surrounded her. They didn't come here very often, but this morning there were more than Ally had ever seen, flocking around Madison as if welcoming her to the beach. She immediately looked down at the flowers she was rearranging when Madison started swimming back to shore and walked out, her pink hair slicked back and her tanned body glistening in the morning sun.

"Incredible, right?" Madison said through short breaths when she reached Ally, who was now trying really hard not to stare at her abs. She had her towel wrapped around her waist and water was dripping down her face. "The pelicans?" she continued when Ally didn't answer.

"Yes, of course, the pelicans." Ally composed herself. "They're not here very often so you're in luck today." She smiled. "You're a good swimmer."

"I bet you're not so bad yourself, having lived here for so long," Madison said, running a hand through her wet hair.

"I'm an okay swimmer but I'm not going in there before July," Ally said pointing to the ocean. "It's far too cold, you're crazy."

Madison laughed. "It's fine once you're in and over the initial shock." She removed her towel and started drying her hair right in front of Ally, putting her spectacular body on full display.

Ally's eyes shifted to her stomach again. "How are you feeling today?" she asked, trying to distract herself as she apparently was unable to look away.

"I feel great, why?" Madison narrowed her eyes and she gave Ally a teasing smile. "Are you hungover?"

"Maybe a little." Ally groaned. "Okay, yes, I'm seriously hungover. I've got a headache and a dry mouth, and I feel really tired, but I see you're as fresh as a daisy." She laughed and shook her head. "God, right now, I wish I was fifteen years younger."

"Nothing an Advil can't fix. I've got some in the house. Want me to get one for you?"

Ally nodded. "That would be great, actually. I'm so not used to hangovers that I don't keep pain meds in the house.

Want to trade an Advil for a slice of freshly baked carrot cake?"

"Hell yeah." Madison eyed the cake at the end of the bar and shot Ally a grin before she turned. "I'll be back in a minute."

Jesus, her ass is so round and... Ally let out a deep sigh, grabbed the remote and turned up the volume on the speakers inside. She rarely looked at women this way. There had been the occasional incident on the beach, when she was fascinated by some of the female volleyball players' bodies, but this was Madison, her new tenant, and she needed to get a grip. Singing along to *The Beach Boys* – her morning clients loved the vintage surf music she played – Ally turned the 'open' sign in the window and switched on the string lights to illuminate the ceiling.

"One Advil coming up." Madison walked in barefoot, wearing a pair of gray jersey shorts and a white T-shirt. She hadn't bothered to dry herself off, and her wet bikini top was showing through the fabric. "Actually, you might want to take two, that will perk you right up." She handed Ally the strip and an additional yellow tablet. "And a vitamin C capsule because you're dehydrated. Take it with lots of water."

"Thanks, Doctor Wilson. You sound like you know your hangover cures." Ally walked around the bar, poured herself a tall glass of water and swallowed the proffered cure-alls. "Coffee with your cake?"

"Yeah." Madison looked up at the coffee menu behind the bar. "Actually, can I have one of those soy beetroot ones?"

"Of course. I'm glad at least someone likes my beetroot lattes. It hasn't exactly been popular since I introduced it." Ally handed Madison a plate and a fork. "Here, help yourself to cake." She looked over her shoulder while she heated beetroot juice, chai spices and cayenne pepper, adding soy milk foam at the end. "What are you up to today? Unpacking?"

Madison shrugged. "I don't know, I don't really feel like unpacking, it's such a nice day. I might just have a wander around and explore town. Relax a bit before I start work on Monday."

"You should." Ally poured the beetroot mixture into a cup and made one for herself too. Hoping she didn't come across as too intrusive, she said: "I could show you around town if you like? A little later today, when Devon starts. I usually disappear to spend time with Theo, and he calls me if the bar gets too busy for him to handle by himself." She bit her lip and winced. "But just tell me if you'd rather go by yourself. You might be sick of me after last night and I won't take offense if..."

"No, I'd like that," Madison interrupted her. "If you don't mind. But what about Theo?"

"Theo can come too. Or he can go to his grandmother's if he doesn't want to join us." Ally took their drinks outside and Madison followed with her cake. "But I've got a feeling he'll be really excited about it. I don't know what it is, but he's completely obsessed with you. He wouldn't stop talking about you over breakfast this morning."

"Really?" Madison smiled. "That's so sweet. Well, I happen to like him too." She groaned as she took a bite of her cake. "This is so good. Did you make this?"

"Yep. Came out of the oven two hours ago."

"You are one talented lady. A great artist, a fantastic baker and you make the best cocktails... what else are you good at?"

Ally rolled her eyes. "Are you always this charming?"

"Yes." Madison gave her a wink and Ally was surprised to feel a flutter in her belly.

"You must be successful with the ladies then." She swallowed hard when Madison held her gaze, a small smile playing around her lips. Was she flirting with her? She couldn't be...

"I do okay," Madison simply said, then changed the subject. "So, we're meeting this afternoon, then?"

"Yeah. Is three o'clock okay for you?" Ally wiped her forehead, suddenly feeling hot and sweaty. "And don't worry if you change your mind and prefer to go out on your own, I don't want to impose."

"You're not. I like you, you're great company." Madison pointed to her feet. "And I like that you're always barefoot. It's cute."

Ally blushed, not sure why she was feeling like a sixteen-year-old. "I like you too. And I had fun last night." She hid behind her coffee cup when Madison gave her that look again and felt relieved at seeing her first customers approach. "Well, I'd better get back to work. I'll see you later."

6

"It's only a small town but at least you'll have an idea of where to find everything. You know, the bank, the post office, the hairdresser, stores, bars…"

"As far as the post office goes, I don't remember the last time I sent a card or a package as I do everything online and the bank…" Madison held up her phone. "All in here."

"To be honest, I don't think the hairdresser will be of much use to you either. There's no chance in hell they'd have pink dye in stock and the boutiques don't exactly seem like your style, so really, I'm not sure you'd even have a reason to venture out here." Ally took in Madison's outfit; the jersey shorts she was still wearing and a black T-shirt with the name of a band she'd never heard of.

"Don't be so quick to judge," Madison quipped, pointing to the third psychic they passed. "I might want to get my palm read or buy a…" She grinned, gesturing to a boutique that sold various tourist paraphernalia. "A rainbow flag for my front door?"

Ally laughed. "Or an inflatable unicorn?" She frowned as she turned to Madison. "Seriously though, why did you choose to move here? I mean, I love this town but it's so quiet and you're young and..."

"Wild?" Madison joked, finishing her sentence. "No, I'm not wild. Sure, I like a drink and I let my hair down when I feel like it, but being close to the ocean beats any city. Besides, I won't have time to party with the new job and I've had enough excitement during my time in Florida."

"Sounds like it's going to be a big shift in pace for you, though." Ally kept an eye on Theo who was zooming ahead of them on his skateboard. "Did you study in Florida?"

"Yeah. I graduated last year and then I volunteered at a whale conservation program there, right after. I figured it would look good on my resume."

"Twenty-three is quite young to have your Masters."

Madison shrugged. "I skipped a year and a half. Not nearly as smart as Theo but I'm good at math and physics, which is why I got the research technician job. The senior scientist on the program was one of my professors at Florida Tech."

"And you don't want to do your PhD?" Ally asked.

"No. Not yet anyway. Academia doesn't excite me for now. I want to be out there, hands-on with the research, not buried in an office writing reports and applying for grants seven days a week. This way, I can still have a life and that's important to me."

"That makes sense. Marcos used to work six days a week too before he finally got the director's role." She looked at Madison intently. "Did you... did you ever have trouble in school, since you were younger than your peers?"

"A little," Madison admitted. "I was quite the rebel, so the older kids still let me hang out with them, even though I was a late bloomer, physically. It drove my mother to the edge when I started smoking at fifteen, just to fit in, so they sent me to a private school in the end. That was better because I didn't have to try so hard." She shrugged. "In my first year I was probably too young to be in college though. The parties, the drinking, the sex…"

"I can only imagine," Ally said. "But you got through it, and you seem to have your head screwed on."

Madison grinned. "I certainly do. It only made me grow up faster, and there's nothing wrong with that."

"No, I suppose not." Ally led them to Stockton Avenue Bridge, which had a wide view over the creek, the beach and the ocean on one side, and the river walk on the other. They followed Theo down to the river path, lined with white wood-fronted houses with flower-filled yards and private docks along the waterfront. It was a busy dog walkers' route and Ally seemed to know everyone they passed, stopping for small talk and introducing Madison to the locals.

It was incredibly pretty, Madison thought, and she'd only ever imagined living in a town like this, where no one was ever in a rush. Friendly smiles and greetings seemed to be an everyday occurrence, with clean air and incredibly fertile soil all adding to the picturesque setting. A lot of people grew their own produce in their yards with pretty plants, vegetables and spices all mixed together, creating a beautiful concoction of color and height instead of the neat rows she was used to seeing in Louisiana. They passed a couple of restaurants, a wine bar, a quaint old mill and finally a bar on a corner where another path led back to the main road. It was called the *Pink Panther*.

"This place might come in handy for you," Ally said.

"Is this *your* favorite hangout?" Madison eyed the building that was painted in the same shade of pink as her house.

"No, I've actually never been in." Ally giggled. "But it's a gay bar so I thought I'd point it out. You know, in case you want to meet women."

"Well thank you, how thoughtful." Madison laughed at her matchmaking efforts. "I actually rarely go to gay bars, but I'm sure I'll check it out at some point."

"You don't?" Ally frowned. "Why not?"

"It's just so easy with the dating apps nowadays and anyway, I kind of lean toward straight women. Madison gave her a rakish smirk. "More exciting but also guaranteed trouble and heartache."

"I can see how that can cause trouble. It's..." Ally stopped mid-sentence when Theo attempted an ambitious trick on his board and fell off. She rushed over to him, but he'd already gotten up again. "Are you okay, honey?"

"Yeah, I'm fine." Theo's cheeks flushed as he got back on his board.

"I think he's trying to impress you," Ally whispered.

"Well, I think he's pretty good for an eleven-year old." Madison quickened her pace to catch up with Theo. "Hey buddy, want me to show you how to do that?"

"Do what?"

"The flip. Wasn't that what you were trying to do? Come here, give me your board." Madison got on the skateboard, hoping she still had the skills. She hadn't been on one in years, but it felt steady under her feet. "Just like riding a bike," she said, smiling at Ally. "You never forget."

Theo watched her as she gathered speed, then kick-flipped the board with her heel before jumping up. The board spun three hundred-and-sixty degrees along the axis before she landed back down on it. She was surprised it had worked so effortlessly but she didn't let it show because apparently Theo wasn't the only one trying to impress someone. "See? It might be easier to use your heel instead of your toe. Try that first."

"Cool." Theo took the board back, skated off and started practicing while Ally and Madison sat down on a bench to watch him.

"That was impressive." Ally crossed her legs and turned toward her.

"Lucky is what it was." Madison chuckled. "It's been a while. I used to be obsessed with my skateboard when I was younger. My mom was mortified because I was such a tomboy, but she got over it eventually."

"Does your family know you're gay?"

"Yeah, they know. And they have no problem with it. My mom can be overly supportive sometimes, like she makes a big deal out of it while it's really not. But I guess it's her way of showing me she loves me and it's sweet, so I don't complain." Madison smiled and locked her eyes with Ally's. "What about your family? Do they live around here?"

"I don't have much family. I'm an only child and grew up with my father; my mother died in an accident when I was four. I don't see my father as much as I'd like to because he lives in Portland, but Theo and I visit him twice a year and sometimes he comes here in the summer. He remarried a couple of years ago and he's happy. I feel closest to Ana, though. She's been like a mother to me since I started dating Marcos. She's great with Theo and she helps me out a lot."

"I'm sorry about your mother," Madison said.

"I was very young, so I don't remember much of her now, but I can relate to Theo and how obsessive he is about his father; I used to be like that myself. But everything fades, you know, and now she's just a very distant memory." Ally cleared her throat. "Enough sad talk. Are you excited for Monday?"

"Yeah, super excited. A little nervous too, but that's normal. We're not heading out on the research vessel until next week, so I'll have some time to familiarize myself with the equipment."

"Nice. Capture and release tagging?"

"No, we'll be using suction cups with DTAGS, which is why we have to go out there every day, retrieve the cups that eventually fall off and attach new ones. I like it because it's non-invasive and it doesn't disturb the dolphins' balance, which is essential in a social study."

"So, it's a social study." Ally sounded genuinely interested, but then she probably was. Having been with a marine biologist for many years, she was bound to know a thing or two herself. "That sounds fun. What exactly is the research about?"

"My team will be studying complex social structures, such as social interactions, group coordination, relationships and same-sex friendships within a single long-beaked common dolphin population which we'll be tracking for four months. Most days, I'll be out on the vessel and some Fridays I'll be at the lab, analyzing the data. It's part of a bigger program, so at the same time, two similar studies will take place in the Bahamas, tracking a school of Atlantic spotted dolphins and in Florida, tracking bottlenose dolphins, so we can compare them." She shifted, resting her elbow over the backrest of the bench and leaned in closer to Ally. For a split second, she saw Ally's gaze lower toward her mouth, and although she was pretty sure it meant nothing, her eyes were immediately drawn to Ally's lips too. They were a natural peachy color, full and beautifully shaped. When she smiled, her top lip curled up just a little. *So kissable.*

Ally's lips parted for a moment, as if she was about to say

something, but she turned to Theo instead, looking flustered as she twirled a lock of dark hair around her finger. "Interesting. I'm familiar with those programs. You'll have to keep me informed; I'd love to hear how it's going."

"I will." Madison narrowed her eyes, observing Theo, who kept tripping off his skateboard. "I'll be right back," she said, then sprinted off to help him.

7

Madison folded the last box and put it aside. Unpacking hadn't been as bad as she thought it would be. Most of her stuff was still at her parents' house because the rental was fully furnished, and she simply didn't need that much in her life. The things that took up most space like her surfboard, her wetsuit and diving equipment were in the back of her rusty Dodge pickup and so she even had some space left in the closets.

She took a step back, inspecting the living room. Although she loved the artworks previously on the walls, she'd wanted to put her own stamp on the house and had replaced them with what she'd brought along. There were some framed photographs on the wall now; one was of herself, Chuck and their older brother Mason. There was also a picture of her and Hannah, her half-sister from London, who she'd only found out existed last year and who she'd gotten to know when Hannah moved to Louisiana after inheriting her estranged mother's house. They'd become great friends and had even been on a short weekend break together with Kristine, Hannah's fiancée.

The rest of the artworks were mediocre but cheerful paintings done by her mother when she was going through an artistic phase, a couple of candle holders, her grandmother's antique lamp and a throw over the couch that had moved around with her forever. It wasn't exactly a fancy house, but it was homey, with its stone crooks and corners, and it felt warm and inviting.

Pleased to finally have gotten the tedious part over with, Madison fell down on the couch. She'd had a great afternoon with Ally yesterday, this morning had been productive, and she felt ready for her first day at work. The clock on the wall told her it was only two pm, and she was feeling like a drink to celebrate settling in. *Maybe Ally will be working.* Madison had no idea why it excited her to see Ally, but it didn't matter. The gorgeous lady next door made her smile and that was enough to make her get up from the couch and venture outside. Besides, it was her last day of freedom. After tomorrow, she'd be a full-time employee for the first time in her life.

"Hey there, Madison." Devon pulled a chair out as soon as she'd closed the door behind her. "Were you heading here?" He held up both hands. "Don't want to be presumptuous."

"I was, actually." Madison laughed. "Thank you." She sat down and studied the menu with snacks, not feeling particularly hungry. "I'd love a cocktail."

"I can do that for you." Devon tilted his head. "What do you feel like?"

"I don't know, surprise me." Madison looked around. "Is Ally not here?" she asked, trying to sound casual.

"No, she's off today. Hanging out with Theo." Devon

grinned. "Sorry, you'll have to make do with me but I can be good company too, you know." He seemed a little disappointed when four hikers approached. "Sorry, rain check on the company but a bad-ass cocktail coming up."

"You do what you've got to do, I didn't come here to be entertained." Madison waved him off with a smile and greeted the people who sat down at the table next to her. Hearing a door open, she turned to find Ally and Theo coming out of the house.

"Hey," she said, her voice a little too eager for her liking as she shielded her eyes from the bright sun. Ally was wearing an olive-green bikini with a matching sarong and had two towels under her arm. She tried her hardest not to stare, and turned her attention to Theo instead, who was dressed in swimming trunks and a T-shirt with a rucksack on his back and a book under his arm.

"Hey, buddy. What have you got there?"

"It's my shell book," Theo said in all seriousness, holding it up. "So I can check the names of the shells I find."

"That's very cool." Madison's eyes met Ally's. "Hey there."

"Hi, Madison. How are you today?" Ally flicked her hair to one side and ran a hand through it, her other hand resting on Theo's shoulder.

"I'm good. Just finished unpacking, it feels like home already."

"That's great. I…"

"Mom, can Madison come to the beach with us?" Theo interrupted Ally. He gave Madison a pleading look, holding up his book again. "We can look for shells together."

"Honey, I think Madison might want some time to herself. She's only just moved in, and she's got a big day tomorrow." Ally nodded toward the bar. "Why don't you go and get a drink for yourself and a bottle of water for me?"

"But Mom..."

"Please, Theo." She waited until Theo had disappeared, grudgingly kicking a stray wine cork on his way. "I'm sorry. Kids... I have to give it to him; he's usually got more tact than the average boy of his age and I've talked to him about tenants and boundaries, but I guess your common interests got him all excited yesterday. I don't want you to feel pressured in any way..." She paused. "But you're welcome to join us, of course. It's not exactly beach weather yet, but the sun is warm and it's really nice in the crook of the bay."

Madison didn't want to overstep any boundaries, but she had the feeling Ally's invite was genuine. "Are you sure you haven't had enough of me yet?" she asked jokingly, just in case. "I feel like I've been taking up a lot of your time already and I only arrived on Friday."

"No, not at all. I'd love it if you came."

"Okay...." Madison hesitated for a beat before she got up from her chair. "I'll join you guys. I haven't looked for shells since I was Theo's age, it sounds fun." She knew she was using Theo as an excuse, but what was the harm in that? Besides, he was a great and interesting kid and she didn't mind hanging out with him at all. Frankly, she was a little surprised at how happy Ally's invite made her. Maybe she was just so used to having company all the time that she needed it. Or maybe she and Ally could become great friends. "Devon, could I have a bottle of white wine instead please?" she asked when he came out to greet Ally. "I'll get two cups from the house."

Devon looked from Madison to Ally and grinned. "Sure. Women in bikinis and wine. Shame I have to work."

"Spare yourself the effort, Devon," Ally said, rolling her

eyes. "Madison isn't interested in men, so you can stop hitting on my tenant." She slammed a hand in front of her mouth. "Oh my God, I'm so sorry, Madison. Did you mind me saying that? I didn't mean to make you feel uncomfortable or out you or whatever it is you call it, I..."

"Hey, it's fine." Madison laughed. "I'm out, I don't care who knows. And I really don't think Devon was hitting on me."

"Honestly, I kind of was," Devon admitted, sheepishly scratching his head. "But you can't blame a guy for trying, right?" He went inside to grab the wine and looked a little embarrassed as he handed Madison the bottle. "Here, I'll make a tab for you, you can pay later. Have a great afternoon, ladies."

"More?" Madison asked, refilling their cups without waiting for an answer. The soft breeze swept through Ally's hair, making it dance around her face as she sat on her towel, hugging her knees. She had serious trouble keeping her eyes off Ally today, especially since she was wearing a triangle bikini. Madison had a thing for those; she loved how easy it was to make them fall off just by pulling at the strings.

The late afternoon turned out to be surprisingly warm, despite the wind and it was nice to just relax and watch the paddle boarders and the surfers, especially with the great company she was finding herself in. Ally was easy to talk to, warm and funny, and she didn't take herself too seriously either. They'd walked around with Theo for an hour until they'd found enough shells to keep him occupied for hours. Now he was sitting to her other side, studying them and asking her a million questions of which most, she didn't know the answers to.

"Are you trying to get me drunk again?" Ally raised a brow and took a sip of her white wine.

"Should I be?" Madison felt her cheeks turn pink, and she shook her head. "Sorry, that came out wrong. I'm not hitting on you, I promise."

Ally laughed. "Hey, I know that. I'm straight and almost old enough to be your mother."

"The straight part is true. The mother thing is most definitely not," Madison retorted playfully. "We're what... max ten years apart?"

"More like seventeen."

"Really? You're forty?" Madison wanted to tell her that she was insanely attractive, but wisely kept those thoughts to herself.

"Yep." Ally scrunched her nose as she looked into the lowering sun. "Big four-o."

"The way you say it sounds like it bothers you."

"Not really." Ally shrugged. "Well, maybe a little bit. Time flies... Sometimes I feel like it's just passing me by, and that something is missing, you know?" She paused. "Of course, you don't know what I mean, you're only twenty-three."

"That's not fair." Madison nudged her. "Just because I'm younger than you doesn't mean I don't know anything or have zero life-experience."

Ally put a hand on Madison's arm, looking regretful. "You're right. I didn't mean to be condescending. Please forget I said that."

"It's fine." Madison wasn't sure why it bothered her so much that Ally had said that, but it did. She wanted Ally to see her as an equal, quite possibly for all the wrong reasons, but still... The hairs on her arm rose at the touch of Ally's hand. It was warm and soft, and she fought the urge to take it in her own.

"So, tell me, how do you chat up women?" Ally asked playfully, changing the subject after a silence. "I'm not making fun of you, just curious about how it works." She shot a sideways look at Theo, who was lining up his shells in perfect rows of four and marking them with Post-its. "Don't worry. He gets so engrossed in his shells that he won't even hear me say the words 'chocolate ice cream'."

Madison noted that Theo did indeed not react and chuckled at his unbreakable concentration. "It's pretty much universal, isn't it? Men or women, it makes no difference. You like someone, you try to make them like you back." She continued when Ally didn't answer. "For example, if I saw you lying here, I'd ask you if you needed help with your sunscreen. Then I'd have an excuse to talk to you *and* touch you at the same time."

"Now that's a strategy," Ally said before taking a long drink of her wine. "What if I turned down your offer?"

Madison noted she looked a little flustered and decided to continue, partially to get back at her for the age comment, and partially because she simply couldn't help herself. "You wouldn't. You'd be so confused as to why a woman would be so bold as to ask you that, that you'd instantly agree." She shrugged. "It's how it works. And then I'd make sure to give you the best massage of your life while rubbing sunscreen all over your back and down the sides of your body. I'd tell you how incredibly beautiful you are and..." She hesitated, not sure if she was taking it too far. "Finally, you'd give me your number and I'd take you out on a date."

"Okay..." Ally fanned her hand in front of her face for comical effect and downed the last of her wine, but Madison could tell she was more than a little affected by her words. "Sounds like straight women are your thing indeed."

"They are, but I've never had any long-term success with that strategy," Madison said in a self-deprecating tone. "I did well with the ladies in college, but they all went back to their boyfriends in the end."

"Who went back to their boyfriends?"

Madison almost jumped up when the question came from Theo's lips, telling her he'd been listening to them all along. "Nothing, Theo, just some friends I was talking about." She looked at Ally for help when Theo didn't seem satisfied with her reply.

Ally winced. "Theo sweetie, Madison is gay. It means she likes women instead of men."

"Oh." Theo chuckled. "I know what that means. Some girls in my school kiss. It's gross."

"Right..." Ally looked like she was breaking out in a cold sweat. "God, I sometimes forget he's too young for that school in certain ways," she said, lowering her voice, then added: "I honestly thought he was lost in his shells."

"My mom isn't gay because she was married to my dad," Theo then stated matter-of-factly. He held up a long, orange shell that resembled a screw. "I can't find this one, Madison. Can you help me? It's a turret but I'm not sure what kind exactly."

"Of course, let's have a look." Madison regretted her flirty comments like there was no tomorrow now and was grateful for Theo's question. She picked up his book and flipped the pages, avoiding Ally's gaze. She would not make that mistake again.

8

Ally had trouble relaxing. She'd been pacing around the living room since Theo had gone to bed, doing nothing in particular and couldn't work out why she was feeling so restless. Perhaps it was the upcoming meeting with the principal tomorrow, or maybe it was the fact that she couldn't seem to stop thinking about Madison. The latter was ridiculous because there was no reason for her to be preoccupied with her tenant, other than that maybe she was desperate for a female friend. That thought made her feel sad, realizing she didn't really have any good friends left, apart from Devon. It was refreshing to have open and honest conversations with a woman again and, despite their age difference, they really clicked. She worried she might have claimed too much of Madison's time, but then the enthusiasm to hang out had seemed entirely mutual and their chemistry natural. Of course, Madison was new here and she didn't know anyone. Things would likely change once she found her way and made friends of her own age and that was fine. For now, Ally appreciated the companionship and especially the fun she'd had in the past few days because it had made her feel alive again in a way she'd never expected she could. She hadn't felt depressed or sad in the past years but flat, yes. It wasn't as much boredom as a lack of stimuli. Things were always the same here; not much ever changed. The people, the scenery, the seasons, the tides... Ally loved Capitola but as a single mother, she sometimes longed for someone to stir things up a bit and Madison's arrival was obviously doing just that.

Was it her though, or had Madison also been a little flirty? Ally felt another flutter in her belly, and she instinctively reached for the bottle of red wine on the kitchen counter and poured herself a glass. Pacing back to the couch again, she sat back and pulled her feet up underneath her, picked up a magazine from the coffee table and randomly flicked through it without registering much. No, of course Madison hadn't been flirting with her. That would be crazy. She was in a different league entirely; she was young, very attractive and she didn't have a single responsibility or a care in the world. *Why am I bothered anyway?* It wouldn't make a difference whether she'd flirted with her or not. *Then why can't I stop thinking about her, God damn it!*

Ally took a sip of the wine, then decided she'd had enough alcohol for the weekend and put the glass back down with a deep sigh. The feeling of unease, excitement, and she hardly dared to admit it – desire – tugged at her like an old friend reminiscing. Although it had been many, many years since she'd felt it, she recognized the sensation all too well and she knew then that she found herself on dangerous ground.

"Fuck," she muttered to herself. It was still there, digging its way up, after silently lying dormant for decades. That one night in college, when she'd let go of all her inhibitions and given into her deepest cravings under the influence of vodka and God knows what else she'd drank or smoked... She had been a curious and free-spirited person then but hadn't thought about it in a long time, and despite the foggy haze that blurred her memory of the beginning of that night, she remembered everything that had happened toward the end of it. Every look, every touch, every sound that came from Abigail, the English art student she'd shared a room with. *So soft, so sensual and oh so passionate...*

They'd clicked over music at first. That had turned into dancing, and Abigail, who was an out-and-proud lesbian, had joked about one thing leading to another and said that Ally should try everything at least once in her life. Ally had known what was about to happen. She'd known where their 'friendship' was heading that night and she'd gone along with it, curious and willing to explore. It was only ever one night and although Abigail had been her guilty pleasure, Marcos had become the love of her life shortly after. Ally realized she'd been just like the girls Madison had described. *They all went back to their boyfriends in the end.*

Yes, that was her; there was no excuse. A sudden misgiving for how she'd treated Abigail then came over her. The girl had been in tears when Ally had told her she was going on a date with Marcos, but Ally had never given it a second thought after that; she'd just assumed that was the way things went in college and that Abigail would move on, eventually finding someone who was like her. But she knew better now, and she knew she'd hurt her, just like Madison had been hurt.

Allowing herself to give into her erotic fantasies for a moment, she closed her eyes and imagined her and Madison together, like she'd been with Abigail. Entangled, passionate, focused only on each other as if the world around them didn't matter.

Ally had been madly in love with Marcos, but she'd never felt the physical passion with him that she'd felt that night with Abigail. Nothing had ever come close to it. It hadn't mattered much because she knew he was the man she wanted to start a family with and grow old with, and they were truly happy together. She looked up at their wedding photo on the wall and smiled as a tear trickled down her cheek. They'd wanted another baby after Theo but then Marcos had fallen ill and eventually, she'd lost him a year later. Now, being a single mom to one was more than enough and she had no desire for a brother or sister for Theo, especially now that she'd passed forty.

Yawning, and deciding it was time to call it a day, Ally got up, cleared the coffee table and brushed her teeth in the kitchen sink. She went to her bedroom, removed her clothes in front of the mirror and stared at her reflection. Ally never took the time to look at herself, to really look but tonight, she felt an urge to do so. The non-matching underwear made her cringe. Her bra had once been white but was now a grayish shade from washing it with dark garments, and the blue panties were so old that she couldn't even remember when she'd bought them. Not dating had made her a little complacent in the looks department, at least when it came to what was underneath her clothes. The last time she'd worn nice lingerie was three years ago, and that was also the last time she'd had sex. Not because she'd particularly felt like having sex, but because she'd been worried that it had been too long, and she'd wanted to check if everything still worked. She'd wanted to see if she could bring back the desire and sensuality she used to feel but most of all, she'd longed to feel wanted again. The man she went on her second date with back then had been handsome and kind, but the chemistry just wasn't there, and so the night had been a little disappointing and she hadn't gone there since.

Ally ran a finger over the fine lines around her eyes and squinted. They didn't normally bother her but being around Madison reminded her that she wasn't getting any younger. The stretchmarks from her pregnancy and the C-section scar were highlighted under the bright light above her, and she reached for the dimmer to turn it down. She took off her bra, cupped her breasts and lifted them, turning to the side as she studied herself. Sure, her breasts weren't in the position they used to be in but all in all, she wasn't entirely unhappy. Her figure was still trim from standing on her feet all day and apart from the few gray hairs that she hated with a passion, she looked okay for her age. Her next birthday was something she'd rather not think about because each year, it reminded her of how little changed in her life. She'd go for dinner with Ana, Devon and Theo – not because she felt like celebrating but because it was expected of her. The same restaurant on top of the hill, where she and Marcos got married, the same conversations. After a couple of drinks, Ana would get melancholic and start talking about how sad it was that Marcos wasn't there with them and, with all the best intentions to lighten the mood, Devon would order more alcohol. Feeling restless, she crawled under the covers, thinking that perhaps she would just skip the celebrations altogether this year; it would save her worrying about it.

9

"Did you get settled in okay? Find somewhere to live?" Tom, the principal investigator and senior scientist of the team Madison would be working with, asked as they returned to Madison's desk after introductions to the team and a tour of the building. Madison had her brand-new security lanyard in one hand and a coffee in the other, taking everything in with great enthusiasm. Her desk was in a corner, next to shelves of ROV's and equipment, ranging from cameras to satellite tags, sensors, and hydrophones to record vocalizations. There was also a computer, a bunch of screens, an old printer and a pile of files at the end of her desk that she had to get through by the end of the week.

Madison would share the room with five others; an engineer, an admin, a marine operations manager and two junior scientists. Tom had his own office in the dry lab down the corridor. She knew how lucky she was getting this job. The job market was highly competitive in her field, especially along the West Coast, and she still wasn't sure why he had picked her over the dozens of other candidates who'd applied.

"Yeah. I'm renting a place in Capitola. One of those colored miniature houses along the beach. Ally Santos's house, actually. She told me that Marcos, her late husband, used to work here."

"Ally, huh?" Becks, the marine operations manager said, looking up from her desk. She was in her fifties, Madison guessed; voluptuous with short, blonde hair and square, black-rimmed glasses. "Haven't seen her in a while. We kept inviting her to socials, but she never came. Must have been hard for her to come here after his death. How is she?"

"She seems fine." Madison smiled at the older woman who had gotten her the coffee. "Theo, her son is eleven. He's highly gifted."

"Being Marcos's son, I'm not surprised." Becks said, then waved a hand at Tom. "Sorry for the interruption."

"That's okay, Becks." Tom turned back to Madison. "I never had the pleasure of meeting Marcos Santos, as I've only just started myself, but I know the houses you're talking about." He pulled another chair to her desk and sat down. "So, you're right by the beach. Nice job on finding that. I live here now, in Santa Cruz. My wife and kids insisted on being by the beach too when we moved here, but they've had to settle for the harbor. We have a boat there so if you ever want to borrow it, just let me know. It's available to all team members." He chuckled. "It's not like I have much time to use it myself."

"Thanks, I'll keep that in mind. Although I expect to be pretty busy myself."

"Yes, you will be. I'm confident you'll be the perfect addition to our team. Knowing you from college, I was aware of your strengths, and a math and physics genius like you is exactly what we need. As you already know, your general day-to day activities will involve conducting tests and experiments, gathering, interpreting and recording research and data, maintaining the computers and lab equipment in here as well as on the research vessel, and you'll also be in charge of quality control and preparing samples. In the coming months though, you'll be doing fieldwork most of your time." He smiled. "And that's exciting, right? I expect all reports on my desk each Friday by five, and this week, I need you to prepare all the equipment for next week and get familiar with the reports on previous studies in the same field, although I'm pretty sure you've read them all already. I also need you to do a couple of test runs with our research vessel; I'll email you the captain's details so you can arrange it with him. Any questions?"

Madison shook her head. "No, I'm on it." She knew Tom was a very, very busy man and didn't want to take up more of his time. Her team members seemed nice and she would catch up with them to fill her in on anything she wasn't sure about.

"Excellent." Tom looked pleased with her positive attitude and turned on his heel. "I'll be buried under paperwork in my office in the coming days but let's catch up on Friday."

"So, you two already knew each other?" Becks asked after he'd left. "Tom only started two weeks ago so he's new to all of us."

"Yeah, he taught me at Florida Tech. I always liked him and kind of looked up to him." Madison took a sip of her coffee. "He's a good guy. To the point, a little serious and very intelligent."

"So are you, I've heard." Becks laughed. "Intelligent, I

mean, since you're the youngest member in our team. Not the serious part."

"Not so serious, no." Madison laughed too. "But I'm very serious about this job so I promise I won't let you guys down." She looked at the pile of folders, then at all the equipment and swallowed hard, feeling completely over-whelmed.

"I know you won't." Becks rolled her chair over to Madison's desk. "I've been here for twenty years and I've seen many people come and go so I know it can be a little much, being thrown in at the deep end like this." She put a hand on Madison's arm and squeezed it. "I'm going to give you a head start and walk you through our procedures step by step, okay?"

Madison sighed in relief, grateful for the kind woman's offer. "Thanks, Becks. That would be awesome."

10

"Thank you for coming in, Mrs. Santos." Mr. Peterson, the principal, shook Ally's hand, then gestured to the chair on the other side of his desk. As opposed to the stuffy and dark principal's office Ally remembered from her youth, Mr. Peterson's office was clean, white and free of clutter. Two big windows let in plenty of light and the three tall plants in pots next to a designer chair in the corner of the room and the modern artworks on the walls even gave it a personal touch. It suited the charming dark-haired man in his late forties, who was dressed casually in jeans and a gray sweatshirt, and Ally understood then why the other mothers were swooning over him.

Ally was grateful for the nearby high school Theo had moved to at the start of this year. It was friendly, with a strict anti-bullying policy and open-minded teachers. That was important to her as Theo was a little different to most boys his age and had trouble fitting in. Always fully engrossed in his books and science projects, he didn't seem to mind not having friends at his new school, but Ally knew it wasn't healthy for him to only hang out with her, Ana and Professor Browne, his private tutor, either.

"It's not a problem. Please call me Ally."

"Then please call me Jack."

Ally sat down and waited for him to pour her a coffee from the pot between them. "Thank you, Jack. God, I needed this," she said, taking a sip and almost burning her mouth on the scorching hot brew.

"Long day?"

"Yeah. I run a bar and it opens early." She hesitated, brushing a lock of hair away from her face. "And I can't deny that being called in for a meeting with the principal had me tossing and turning too."

"There's nothing to worry about, Ally," Jack assured her. "Theo is doing great, if anything, too great." His face took on a more serious expression as he continued, rolling up the sleeves of his sweatshirt. "He's highly intelligent, which can be a blessing as well as a curse for a boy his age, and I'm worried this school may not be able to accommodate his needs anymore, which is why I asked you to come in and meet with me. The thing is, when we assessed Theo last year, we thought our high school would be a good fit for him. He had no trouble doing the initial tests, but now I believe the increase in homework and study material has accelerated his development. Mrs. Simpson, his biology teacher, was hardly able to correct his latest assignment on ecology, as she spent hours checking his facts. They were all correct by the way." He gave Ally an amused look. "She informed me that the assignment was close to professional standards and admitted that the twenty-four flawlessly spelled, albeit slightly child-like phrased pages, were a little above her intelligence level."

"That makes sense." Ally smiled, feeling proud of her

son. "Theo's obsessed with his father's research. My late husband was a marine biologist; he probably copied the format from one of his old reports." She sighed. "You're right, I've noticed the change in him too. I don't have the ability to answer most of the questions he asks me and if the school can't help him either... well, what can I do? We can't possibly make him skip another year? It would be really hard on him socially."

Jack nodded and cleared his throat. "Yes, Theo does have more potential than any of us are able to develop, so I've done some research. I'm sure you're aware of the GATE? The Gifted and Talented Education Program administered by the California Department of Education?"

"Yeah, I've looked into it." Ally bit her lip. "But the nearest school is in LA and we'd have to move if he went there. I'd have to sell my business, our house..." She sighed. "Find a new job..."

"Yes, I was talking about The Seymour Institute for gifted youth in LA." Jack nodded and pursed his lips, taking his time to continue. "It's a great school, and he could potentially slot right into a class with children of his own age and level. It's private and costly but I think he will thrive there. He's well-adjusted here but seems lonely and bored and that's my main concern. It's great that he's got a focus, being so interested in marine biology, but the other ninety percent of the time is wasted on him as he already knows the material handed out in class. He's simply too much ahead of everyone else, including his teachers and they've told me he tends to zone out a lot in class. It's common for extremely intelligent kids to become depressed if they're not challenged enough and I'm worried that will happen if we don't do something about it now."

"I understand. It's hard enough to entertain him at home

sometimes." Ally bit her lip, the worrying feeling in her stomach tightening. She was immensely proud of Theo for being so smart, but she knew there was no school nearby that catered to kids like him. "So, what do I do?" she asked, dreading the answer. It wasn't just the distance that concerned her, there were the school fees too and they were sure to be substantial. They were getting by fine financially, because she'd rented out the pink house during summers, but there was never much left at the end of the month. Marcos had left her some money, but throughout the years she'd needed it for repairs and to set up the café so she would have long-term security.

"There's an option for funding and grants to help with the cost of education and board," Jack said, wincing at Ally's shocked expression. "I asked them to send over some information for you to look at. Theo would have to do some tests first to see if he qualifies but if this is something you'd consider, I'm hopeful he'll be accepted. The board group has Friday afternoons off so the kids can go home on weekends if distance permits."

"What?" Ally's hands were shaking as she took the information pack from him. LA was a six-hour drive and the idea was simply unacceptable. "No," she mumbled. "Absolutely not. Theo needs me." She started feeling angry at Jack for even suggesting it. "He's eleven years old for God's sake. How could I possibly let him be so far from home on his own? He needs me."

"I know." Jack gave her an understanding nod. "But it would be really good for Theo to be around like-minded kids, so he can learn and be himself in an environment where he doesn't feel like the odd one out."

Ally sniffed, unable to stop tears from welling up. "Do you really think he feels that way?"

"He's a loner and that's no surprise. He's much younger than his peers, yet no one here can level with him. They don't bully him, we would never allow that, they just don't understand him, and so he's mostly ignored."

"So you think I should just send him away?" Ally's voice went up a notch, desperation seeping through it now. It would change everything in their life and worst of all, she'd be all alone again. Remembering what it used to be like after Marcos passed away, she told herself there and then that she could never let Theo go. Loneliness had almost suffocated her daily, and she knew she wouldn't be able to go through that again. Theo had been her rock, and although he was still young, his intelligence meant that they were able to have surprisingly adult conversations at times. If he wasn't going be there anymore… She knew that thought was selfish but most of all, she just didn't want him to be alone. He was too young, and he needed her after losing his father.

Theo hadn't suffered from depression or severe grief – he'd been too young to understand what had happened back then. But he did carry an unhealthy obsession with his father, which told her that no matter what, it was still fresh in his mind somehow. And how could it not be? The kid had a photographic memory. He needed her, and that was that. "No," she said again, then put the brochures back on Jack's desk and stood up.

Jack got up too and followed her to the door. "I'm sorry, Ally. I didn't mean to upset you."

"It's fine. I just can't do this now." Ally turned to him in the door. "I know you have my son's best interests at heart, I apologize for my outburst."

"Wait." Jack handed her the pack and put a hand on her

shoulder. "Just read it and have a think about it, or let Theo read it. Please."

11

lly felt a strange sensation ripple through her belly when she saw Madison walking toward the house. She straightened her apron and checked her hair in the reflection of the window, then rolled her eyes at herself for even doing so. Why was she so worried about what Madison thought of her? What was she doing having a silly crush on someone way younger than her and a woman no less! She must be having some idiotic midlife crisis she decided, and shook it off. Madison looked great though, dressed in jeans and a white T-shirt that hugged her in all the right places. With her purse and her black blazer dangling from one arm, she smiled as she neared.

"Hey, how are you?" she asked, lingering at her front door.

"Great. How was your first day at work?"

"It was fun, actually." Madison put the key ring back in her purse and walked toward Ally instead. "Nice team and it was good to see Tom, my PI, again. Becks, the marine operations manager, is a lovely woman too; she told me she used to work with Marcos and she says hi."

"I remember Becks, she's great." Ally smiled. "I'm glad you enjoyed it. First days can be overwhelming."

"Yeah, it was a lot to take in, I'm feeling a bit drained. This week we're planning the project, so we'll be in the lab mostly, then starting from next week I'll be out at sea."

"Hmm... Let me guess, seven am start?"

Madison nodded. "Yup. Guess that means my party days are over."

Ally laughed. "In that case, can I get you a drink while you still can?"

"Actually, can I have a soy beetroot latte with extra cayenne? Maybe that will wake me up."

"Of course. To go?" Ally asked, not wanting to be presumptuous.

"No, I'll have it here. It's a nice evening and I've been inside all day." Madison sat down and looked up at Ally. "Want to join me? It doesn't look like you're overly busy, unless..."

"Sure," Ally replied, a little too quick for her liking. "Monday evenings are always quiet. Devon had a long shift because I had to go to Theo's school, so I've only been here for about an hour and haven't spoken to anyone since I started." She fiddled with a lock of her hair, then realized she was staring and quickly straightened herself. Madison was glowing; her eyes twinkling and her cheeks rosy from the sun she'd caught over the weekend. Her pink bob was straightened, her fringe ending just above her dark eyebrows, resulting in a fascinating mix of natural beauty and edgy style. "Well, I'll get the drinks, I'll be right out." She walked around the bar and shot herself a warning look in the mirrored wall behind the liquor bottles. It was silly, the way she felt like she was a teenager all over again each time she saw her enchanting new tenant, and she tried to keep her trembling hands steady as she poured soy milk into the metal jug.

"On the house, to celebrate your first day," she said with a beaming smile as she put a larger-than-life coffee cup if front of Madison. The cup had been a present from Ana, but being highly impractical, she'd never used it before.

"Jeez, this is like a soup bowl." Madison laughed as she picked it up with both hands and took a sip. "Thank you. But you don't have to do that, I want to pay for my drinks."

"I know, but I want to. It's been a big day for you." Ally stirred some honey through her mint tea and sat back. "So, no regrets?"

"None whatsoever." Madison wiped her upper lip, removing the foam that had gathered there. "What about you? How was the meeting with the big scary principal?"

"The big, scary principal was nice, actually. But the conversation was a little heavy. Turns out that even now, Theo's still too bright for his school and his teachers, and Jack Peterson, the principal, suggested I should consider sending Theo to a private school for gifted kids." Ally slumped back in her chair, feeling deflated just talking about it. "He told me Theo is becoming bored and can't level with the other kids in his class, and that this new school might give him the chance to hang out with like-minded kids and teachers who can help him thrive and who are able to bring out the best in him. But the thing is... it's in LA." She wiped the tear that trickled down her cheek. "I'm sorry. I shouldn't spill this on you, especially not right after your first day in your new job, and... Fuck. Now I'm crying."

"Shhh..." Madison walked around the table and put her arms around Ally from the back, hugging her tight. She wasn't sure if she was crossing boundaries, as they had only known each other for a few days, but Ally seemed to relax in her grip. "It must have been a big blow, news like that. LA isn't just around the corner."

"Yeah. I don't want him to go. I can't send him away, can I?" Ally took hold of Madison's arms and pulled her closer against her. "He's too young, he needs me. But on the other hand, I'm worried he'll get bored if he stays here and I don't want to hold him back or not have him reach his full potential..."

"I get that. Have you asked Theo what he wants?"

Ally sighed, her eyes glistening as silent tears ran down her face. "No, I haven't. He's too young to make decisions like that."

"But he's highly intelligent and as you said – way ahead of kids his age." Madison shook her head against Ally's. "Actually, forget what I said, I'm overstepping here. I know nothing about your situation, and I know nothing about being a mom." She let go and looked at Ally, who was staring ahead of her, the low sun framing her face. "But I will tell you one thing. Theo seems to know just as much about marine biology as I do, and I've studied my ass off. He's just a kid. It's not intimidating but I get it when you say that it might be a waste of his potential not to let him explore his passion."

"You're probably right." Ally composed herself and wiped her cheeks. "I don't want to hold him back, but I don't want to lose him either."

"I understand this is difficult," was all Madison could say. Frankly, she didn't know anything. She barely knew Ally or Theo. Still, she'd felt an instant bond with them, a familiarity that however strange, seemed entirely logical. "If you ever want to talk," she continued, "I'm here for you, okay? And I had fun with Theo yesterday, I really mean that. Your kid's super interesting, fascinating even. If you want me to talk to him, just let me know and I'll be happy to help."

"Thank you." Ally cast her a grateful glance and chuckled. "Look at me. You've just moved in and I'm bugging you with my private life already. I promise you, I'm not normally like this. It's just that hearing something like that... It feels like my whole world is giving way underneath me all over again. Maybe because I know deep down that it's best for him, or maybe I'm scared I'll lose him because we'll never be on the same level intellectually..."

"Hey, you're his mom. Intelligence has nothing to do with love."

"I know." Ally sniffed. "But the way he interacts with you... it's like he lights up. That doesn't happen with me. He tries to explain things that he gets excited about, but it all sounds like another language to me and I have no idea whether to pretend I understand or to be honest because I don't want to disappoint him. I'm supposed to teach *him* things, not the other way around."

"You're looking at this the wrong way, Ally. Theo and I just happen to have a common interest." Madison pulled Ally into her arms again, sensing she hadn't been hugged in a very, very long time. "If it makes you feel better, he's way smarter than me too. I could never keep up with him if we discussed other topics. I mean, if he wanted to talk history I'd be seriously fucked. I only just passed on that." She smiled when Ally giggled through her tears. "And if he wanted to talk about literature, I'd be even more fucked because I can barely spell my own name let alone read the classics."

Now they both laughed at her playful cussing, and Ally let go of Madison then. Although she missed the contact immediately, she reminded herself of boundaries. Yes, it felt nice to be held by Madison, but the only thing between them was a growing friendship, nothing more.

12

———

"Hey, Mom." Madison wedged her phone between her shoulder and her ear while she removed a ready-made meal from the microwave. "What's up?"

"Nothing much, sweetie. Just wanted to check how your first weekend in your new home had been. And your first couple of days at work, of course. How was it?" Edie paused. "Are you looking after yourself? Eating healthy?"

"The job's been great. A lot to take in, but I'm getting there, and I have a good feeling about it. And of course I'm eating healthy, I always do," Madison lied, tearing the top off her vegetarian lasagna. She didn't normally buy store-made meals, as she didn't like all the waste they involved, but she hadn't had much time to cook this week and getting take-out every night was too much fuss. "Anyway, why the concern? It's not like I didn't live on my own when I was at college. What's the difference?"

"Oh, there's no difference, I know that. It's just that I got so used to having you at home again and now I'm worried that you'll lose all the good habits you've been building up while living with us. I know it's silly. You're twenty-three and I shouldn't even be having this conversation with you."

"You're right. You shouldn't, but it's sweet of you to worry. How was your golf lesson today?"

"Not bad. I managed to hit the ball." Edie laughed. "What about you? What have you been doing other than starting the job?"

"I spent Saturday and Sunday afternoon with Ally and Theo, and I unpacked." Madison didn't mention she'd had drinks with Ally on Friday too, because even to her it seemed unusual that they'd seen so much of each other and she didn't want her mother to think there was something going on.

"Good. I like Ally, and I'm glad you'll at least have some kind of mother figure in your life while you're living there."

"A mother figure?" Madison almost chocked on her first bite as she sat down on the couch, because Ally was as far from a mother figure to her as she could possibly imagine. In fact, hearing her mother say that made her feel sick, especially as she'd spent a substantial amount of time staring at Ally's legs over the last couple of days. "Hey, that's just crazy. I haven't been living at home for the past six years apart from recently and I'm pretty sure I can cook my own dinners and find my way to work and back without motherly supervision."

Edie was silent, and Madison knew her mother was rolling her eyes on the other end of the line. "You know what I mean, Madison. She seems lovely and caring. And we've exchanged numbers so I can call her to check how you are if you don't pick up for days on end like you do sometimes."

"Oh God, don't. Please don't, Mom." Madison put her meal on the table. For some reason, their conversation had taken her appetite away. "That's not healthy and you know it. Are you getting antsy because Chuck is moving out?" She suddenly felt sorry for her mother as she said it out loud. "Because it's okay to feel upset about that. But the healthy way to deal with your last child flying the nest would be to start looking for other hobbies, other things to focus on, not befriend your children's landlords. And convincing Chuck to move into Darla's building? I'm still not over that shock to be honest with you."

Edie chuckled, clearly caught out. "Okay, I admit, I like to have him close by but it's not just that, it was a great deal. The price was very reasonable, and the apartment is spacious. Chuck can pay us rent and we have a great investment. There's even a gym in the building and you know how Chuck likes his work-outs."

"Sure. Chuck will be joining the seniors' Zumba classes on Sunday afternoon. And then he'll keep them up all night when he brings girls home. Four nights a week," Madison added. She smiled at the silence that followed because she could almost hear her mother's brain turning frantically now. "You hadn't thought about that now, had you, Mom?"

Everyone in the family knew Chuck was a ladies' man. Hell, everyone in Lafayette knew it. It just wasn't something they openly discussed anymore, after he'd dated several of his parents' friends' daughters and broken their hearts one by one.

"That's not true. Chuck is growing up too, Maddie. I'm sure he'll behave now that he's got a responsible full-time job and his own place to take care of."

"Of course he will," Madison said in a semi-sarcastic tone. "Chuck is..." She let it go when she caught a glimpse of Ally walking by her window. She hadn't seen her in the past three days, coming home late, after Devon had taken over

Ally's shift. Without thinking, she rushed over and hid behind the curtain. "I'm sorry, Mom. I have to go, there's someone at the door. I'll call you soon, okay?"

She felt a little foolish for sneaking behind the curtain, for sure, but seeing Ally stretch and roll her shoulders as she looked out over the ocean was totally worth the risk of getting caught. Her tank top crept up and Madison could see the tanned skin of her back above the edge of her long, flowing skirt, billowing in the wind along with her hair that fell below her shoulder blades. She was barefoot, her silver ankle bracelet shimmering in the last light as she hiked up her skirt and walked farther out, until the water washed over her feet. She looked like she belonged there, ethereal and graceful as she walked along the shore. *Perfect.* The pull to go outside and talk to her was strong, but by now Madison was worried her interest was getting obvious and so she decided to stay inside and finish her work instead. With everything being new to her, there was a lot to catch up on and she wanted to be done before the weekend.

Just as she backed away from the window, Ally took off her top and tossed it behind her in the sand. Madison snapped to attention and took a seat on the armrest of the sofa, still half hiding behind the curtain while Ally lowered her skirt, leaving her in a turquoise bikini. She smiled as she tilted her head and stared at Ally's ass, remembering she'd claimed it was too cold to swim. One careful step at a time, Ally walked in, jumping in the cutest way each time a wave hit her. She was clearly determined though, and started running, then dove in, disappearing under the water for a moment. A soft gasp escaped Madison when she resurfaced and ran her hands through her hair, slicking it back. Why did her landlady have to be so God damn stunning? It was distracting in the best of ways, especially now that she had the perfect view of her, her hips swaying as she waded back out of the ocean toward the beach. Then, Ally's gaze focused in her direction and, although she was too far away to see her in the window, the light was on and Madison realized she'd be able to see her shadow.

"Fuck." Slowly, she backed away, then dove down onto the couch and turned on her back, covering her face in her hands. "Fuck," she muttered again. She'd been caught and now there was nothing she could do but own it. With a groan, she shot up, grabbed a towel from the hallway cabinet and opened her front door when Ally passed.

"I see you got over the cold," she said, leaning against the doorpost. Although she tried not to sound too flirty, it came out a little more playful than she'd anticipated as she handed Ally the towel.

"Oh, thank you." Ally chuckled, looking a little shy as she wrapped it around her waist. "Not sure I actually got over it, but it feels great now that I'm out." She dropped her clothes onto one of the chairs in front of the bar. "I didn't plan on going in; you must have inspired me the other day."

"Nice." Madison winked. "Let me know and I'll come with you next time."

"I will." Ally dried her hair, then secured the towel back around her chest. "I'll wash this for you tonight."

"No rush, I have more." They both lingered, not sure how to continue the conversation. "Is Theo sleeping?" Madison finally asked. She wanted to invite Ally in, but she was in her bikini and was probably ready for a shower.

"Yeah. At least I think he is." Ally's eyes met Madison's for a beat and there was that look again that made her doubt everything she knew about Ally. It could have easily been mistaken for shyness, but Madison was pretty sure it was something closer to curiosity. She'd seen women look at her like that before and the thought she could be right about her hunch, that Ally might be a little interested in her, made her weak in the knees.

"I know he reads under the covers with his flashlight," Ally continued. "But he doesn't have trouble waking up in the morning, so I just pretend that I don't know." She shrugged and lowered her voice. "I can't blame him; I used to do it myself all the time."

"Me too." Madison smiled. "Be grateful he's reading scientific journals up there. It could be a lot worse."

"You're right." Ally looked down at her bare feet. "Well, I'd better go and have a shower. Thank you for the towel."

"No problem, I'll see you around." Madison stepped back in the door opening but didn't go inside before Ally was at her own door.

She looked over her shoulder and smiled as she opened it. "Yeah, I'll see you around."

13

"Honey, can I talk to you for a moment?"

"Sure. What's up?" Theo looked up from his breakfast, a hint of worry flashing across his face. It broke Ally's heart when she saw it. Despite his age, he was always concerned about her. Although she made them breakfast in the mornings, he always made her first coffee of the day, exactly how she liked it. Ally loved their mornings together. They talked about mundane topics, in contrary to after school hours, when Theo wanted to discuss his homework assignments that were tailored to his level and way over her head. Mornings were simple. *Did you sleep well? What did you dream about? How do you want your eggs?* And then there was his sleepy face and his tousled hair that she adored. In the mornings, he was a kid, her kid, and the kitchen was their comfort zone.

Over time, the kitchen had lost its sad appeal after Marcos's death. Instead of reminding her of what was missing in their life, the empty stool had now been claimed by Theo and it made Ally happy to sit next to him in the mornings. She'd painted the wooden cabinets yellow and decorated the kitchen with ivy plants that hung from the ceiling in crocheted baskets, and Theo's detailed drawings of shells, crabs and oysters covered the fridge, held in place with colorful magnets.

She sat down next to him at the tiny breakfast bar, buttering a slice of toast. "I spoke to Mr. Peterson on Monday. Don't worry, it's nothing bad," she quickly added in an attempt to put him at ease. "He says you're doing great."

Theo shrugged. "It's easy."

"I know it's easy for you, honey. Do you like school?"

Again, Theo shrugged. "Don't know," he said, keeping his eyes fixed on his scrambled eggs.

Ally didn't want to ask him if he had made any friends, because she already knew the answer to that. She'd asked before and it had clearly upset Theo. He never brought anyone home and rarely got invited to birthday parties, when he was, she had a feeling it was because the parents had put together the invite list and not the child. "You see, I'm so incredibly proud of you for being so smart..." she hesitated. "Just like your father. And Mr. Peterson, well, he told me about this school for kids like you. For gifted kids."

Theo looked up now, curiously. "What school?"

Ally reluctantly handed him the information pack. She knew it would be much easier just to let him read it. He was a very fast reader and would understand it word for word.

"Why are you upset, Mom?"

Ally wiped at her eyes. "I'm not upset, sweetie. I just don't want you to think that I want you out of the house. Because I really don't. The reason I'm a little sad is because the school is in LA, and you'll only be able to come home on weekends. Honestly, I don't want you to go, but Mr. Peterson highly recommends the school and I thought you should take a look at it so you can decide for yourself." She was surprised to see Theo eagerly scroll through the brochures and leaflets, biting his bottom lip the way he did when something caught his interest.

"They have sixty percent individually tailored learning programs," he said, clearly fascinated that such a thing even excised. "And they teach Mandarin."

"Mandarin?" Ally frowned. "I didn't know you were interested in learning Mandarin."

"Yeah. I did a free YouTube course and I've been listening to a Chinese podcast on my laptop. I think I understand it a little now, but I can't write anything yet. It would be so cool to learn." He flipped through to the next page in the brochure. "And they have a basketball court!"

"They have all kinds of fun stuff. There's a cinema and a pool too."

"And a lab!" Theo's voice went up a notch.

"Yes, it's a great school. But as I said, it's not that I don't want you here. If it was up to me, you'd live with me forever."

Theo chuckled at that. "No one lives with their parents forever." He looked up at Ally. "Don't worry. I don't want you to feel alone, so I won't go."

"No, Theo, it's not like that. If it's just me you're worried about then please don't. If this is something you might want to do, then think about it. There will be children like you, kids who are really intelligent. You'll have common interests and most of them will be your age."

"Kids like me?"

"Yes, like you." Ally swallowed down the lump in her throat. The hope in Theo's voice almost killed her because it was clear he was hungry for friendship. "If it's something you might want to consider, we'd have to take a trip there first because you'll have to do some tests. Mr. Peterson can arrange that for us." She ran a hand through his hair. "But you don't have to decide anything right now. Think about it and you can talk to me or to Mr. Peterson about it whenever you want, okay?"

Theo nodded. "Okay." He finished the last bite of his breakfast and got up after looking at the clock. "We have to go."

"I know." Ally got up too and grabbed the car keys while Theo packed his rucksack. When they rushed outside, she almost crashed into Madison, who was just about to go to work.

"Good morning guys."

"Good morning," Ally caught herself staring at her legs in the skimpy shorts as she greeted her back. Why was she so obsessed with her tenant's body?

"We're prepping the boat for next week," Madison said, noticing Ally was glancing at her casual outfit. "Might as well get a tan, right?" She turned to Theo. "Do you need a lift to school, buddy?"

"Thank you, but I was just about to take him."

"But I'm literally passing his school. Franklin High, right?" Madison shrugged. "I honestly don't mind, and it will save you the drive."

"Are you sure?"

"Yes!" Theo's face lit up and he seemed fully on board with the idea. "Can Madison take me? Please?"

"All right then. If you really don't mind… thank you." Ally handed Madison the second coffee that she'd poured into a take-out cup. "At least take this. I'll make myself a new one."

"Thanks!" Madison took the cup, waved and walked off with Theo in tow.

Ally laughed when she heard Theo ask: "Do you have a cool car?" And then she laughed even harder at Madison's reply: "No buddy, I definitely don't have a cool car."

14

"Have a great weekend guys, I'll see you on Monday." Madison jumped off the boat, onto the dock and made her way to her old, red, busted-up pickup truck that was parked along the pier. Her mother had been ecstatic to see her truck disappear from their family driveway after complaining that it ruined the 'front yard appeal'. With that, she meant that the big truck blocked their fancy cars and the golf cart she loved to have on display for all the neighbors to see. It just wasn't a good look and Edie liked things to be pretty and perfect. Madison however, had been over the moon when she'd found the monstrosity of a vehicle online for only two-thousand dollars. It was big enough for her equipment, and to her mother's horror, she'd even thrown a mattress in the back so she could take a nap when she was on the road.

It had been a good first week and she felt confident that they were all set for their first venture, and that they would find the school of dolphins on their first day. She'd seen them during the two test runs, in the same place at the same time. Apart from Becks, the team had been a little apprehensive around her at first, mainly due to her age, she suspected, but as the days had passed and she'd gotten to know them better, they'd thawed as they'd realized she knew exactly what she was doing.

Her phone indicated she had messages, and she leaned against the driver's door, scrolling through them. There were several notifications from a dating app she'd signed up to last night in bed, more out of curiosity than a serious desire to go on a date. She smiled, feeling a little smug at the volume of hits she'd received, with no less than seven women asking her out and another twelve complimenting her on her looks and sending flirty messages. She clicked through their profiles, kind of excited at the idea that they all claimed to be gay, available, single and within close proximity. Her attention spiked at the profile of a woman with shortish hair and a warm smile. She seemed sporty and stylish, and although she wasn't Madison's type, she looked like she could be good fun. The message said: *'Hey! I'm Pat. I see you live in Capitola. Love your pictures and your profile, I surf too. Want to meet up for a drink in the Pink Panther?'*

"Why not?" Madison mumbled to herself as she typed a message back. *'Sure. When do you want to meet?'*

'How about tonight?'

The prompt reply took Madison by surprise, then she saw that Pat was online. *Fuck.* Now she'd expect an answer back right away. For a split second, her mind drifted to Ally, and she almost felt like she was doing something wrong. Rolling her eyes, she shook it off, knowing there was no point waiting for a straight woman to magically show interest in her. *'Tonight is fine,'* she typed then. *'See you there at nine?'*

'Perfect. It's a date.' Pat disappeared offline before Madison had time to change her mind and she was left

baffled, wondering how she'd gotten herself a date in under thirty seconds. *What the fuck just happened?*

She got into her truck and started driving home, mulling over what to wear. The ocean was to her left, the sun bleeding into it as it lowered itself behind the horizon. Madison hadn't been familiar with Northern California until she'd moved here, and the sheer beauty of the landscape took her breath away each time she ventured out. The shoreline held spectacular rock formations, alternated with the most magnificent secluded beaches. There was so much to explore, and she was looking forward to doing just that during her time here.

The parking fairy had blessed her today, and she found a spot near the village entrance, next to a boutique that sold hand-made jewelry. She passed the small Capitola Historical Museum, and waved at the old lady who was knitting on the porch, walked underneath the old rail road that was overgrown with vines, then turned onto Main Street and greeted the owner of the surf shop where she'd been in to buy a pair of new shades. She liked the air of endless summer in the area, and the laid-back attitude and slow pace of life. Dogs were welcome everywhere here, and most of them were exceptionally well-behaved, strolling next to their owners off the leash, or even taking themselves for a walk. People were very friendly, she'd noticed, but it wasn't the superficial kind of fake enthusiasm she'd so often encountered on previous road-trips through California. Capitola seemed to have a sincere sense of community, with a welcoming and open-minded attitude, and Madison wasn't used to that. Instead of talking about the weather, people asked how she was settling in, and wanted to know if she'd visited one of the many beaches they were clearly very proud of. Going on her unconventional looks, she'd expected some peculiar looks at first, but there had been none of that and she was starting to realize that everyone was a little different here; perhaps a bit more spiritual and focused on the environment rather than on possessions and wealth. The houses were pretty but not big or extravagant, the cars mainly hybrids, and the businesses were sustainable. There was no trash on the beach or the streets, little waste in the sense of plastic bags or packaging, and a lot of people carried their own reusable coffee mugs and water bottles with them.

Being environmentally conscious herself, Madison felt like she fitted right in and she couldn't have picked a better place to live. During her time as a volunteer in the whale conservation program in Florida, she'd seen the impact of human waste on the ocean first-hand. Madison lived comfortably and didn't go to extremes, but she made sure to buy biological and eco-friendly products, carried canvas grocery bags, cups and bottles with her, and tried to limit her carbon footprint as much as she could. It made sense that Ally was the same, with her late husband having worked in the same field and living in a community where people cared, and she liked that about her. But then again, there were a lot of things she liked about Ally. Her contagious smile, her lips, her intense, dark eyes, her laugh, her body, the way she dressed; feminine and with a hippie vibe, the sound of her bangles when she moved, always in a relaxed pace, her face raised toward the sun, and often barefoot. She liked the way Ally interacted with Theo, the warmth and love that poured out of her each time she looked at him, the way she talked to him like an equal, never in a condescending high pitch like so many other mothers did. She loved spending time with Ally too, because she was sweet, creative and interesting and she didn't even know it.

Nearing the rows of colored houses, Madison cursed herself for thinking of Ally yet again. If she was going on a date, she'd have to put her out of her mind and even if she wasn't meeting a woman tonight, she still had to stop picturing her naked or imagining what it would be like to kiss her each time she saw her. Quickening her pace, she slipped inside before she got distracted by thoughts of the alluring brunette again.

15

"You look nice. Got a hot date?" Ally joked as she let her gaze roam over Madison's cute pastel pink top that matched her hair, and her low-cut skinny blue jeans and Converse. She felt that strange pull of attraction again and ignored it, but her eyes widened when she saw a blush creep onto Madison's cheeks. *No, she doesn't...*

"Actually, I do." Madison shook her head and chuckled. "Nothing special, just a Tinder date. I figured I might as well get to know a few people if I'm going to be staying here for a while and the thing with dates is... nine out of ten times, you're better off as friends and that would be fine too. Unless she's an awful person," she added, nervously laughing again. "But she comes across as a nice woman on her profile, so we'll see."

"Tinder, huh?" Ally was surprised at the sensation of a sharp punch to her gut. Surely it wasn't jealousy? It couldn't be, that would be ridiculous. She forced a smile and said: "I've tried it a couple of times myself. I ended up deleting the app." *Damn it, now I sound bitter.*

"I take it the whole experience wasn't a success then?" Madison grinned. "You know, for every decent person, there are about thirty perverts, crazies and catfish out there. At least that's what the statistics say. You just need a little luck in finding the right one." She tilted her head and looked Ally up and down. "I wouldn't think you'd have trouble meeting someone nice though; you're smoking hot, so I imagine you'd have a lot of guys to pick from." Her smile widened when Ally seemed flustered. "Don't be shy, it's a compliment, you should take it."

"Thank you. I'm actually not used to getting compliments anymore. Guess I forgot how to react." Ally fiddled with a lock of hair, twirling it around her finger. "So, what's the lucky lady's name?"

"Pat." Madison shrugged. "Must be short for Patricia."

"Or Patrick," Ally joked but then suddenly sobered when she realized she secretly hoped she was right.

"Could be. You never know with these online profiles. But let's hope my date's a woman as her profile says. Plus, she wanted to meet in the *Pink Panther*, so I guess that does rule out straight men on a mission to turn a lesbian."

"Right." Ally politely laughed. "In that case it probably is a woman." She shuffled on the spot and forced herself to stop fiddling with her hair. "Thank you for dropping Theo off at school by the way."

"It's not a problem. I enjoyed his company in the car."

"I'm sure he did too. He wouldn't stop talking about it when I picked him up. Anyway, I won't keep you." Ally waved Madison off as she turned and walked back into the bar. "Go. Have a great night. I hope she's everything you hoped for." She rolled her eyes at her lame remark as she disappeared around the corner and hid behind the bar. It was still quiet, but she knew it would get busy later. Already a group of cyclists were making their way to the terrace and she wished she had another couple of minutes to herself. Without thinking, she reached for a bottle of tequila and poured herself a shot. It wasn't something she made a habit of, but the fact that Madison was going on a date had thrown her a little, and that annoyed her. *What's wrong with me? And what's this weird obsession with her?* It wasn't as much an obsession as a curiosity, Ally knew that. Was it just because she knew Madison was gay? Because she was most definitely gorgeous, charming, interesting and smart. *And she's also seventeen years younger.* Knocking back the tequila, Ally decided to get a grip and get over whatever this crazy infatuation was. There was a tray of snacks behind the bar that she'd prepared earlier in case Madison came over for a drink, and she felt foolish for assuming her cute neighbor would rather spend Friday night on the terrace with her landlady than go out and meet people of her own age. She picked it up with a sigh and brought it out to the group that was getting seated outside.

"Happy Friday, snacks on the house," she said, smiling. "What can I get you all to drink?"

"Thank you. Now that's a nice gesture." As soon as the man had said it, his face pulled into an expression of surprise. "Ally."

"Mr. Peterson. I mean Jack," Ally said, correcting herself. "I didn't expect to see you here."

"Well, I don't normally come out this way, but someone told me this was a great little bar and so we decided to try a different cycling route this time."

"Glad you did. Welcome to *Western Shores*." Ally turned to his friends, who ordered a beer and Jack ordered one for himself too. "Cycling and beer, huh? Is it just me, or is that a contradicting combination?"

Jack laughed. "We're no fanatics. It's more of a social thing and anyway, it only took us thirty minutes to get here, so it can hardly be classed as exercise." He hesitated. "Where's Theo?" he glanced at his watch. "Oh, he must be in bed."

"Yeah." Ally pointed up to the little tower on top of the blue house. "That's his bedroom up there, so he can call me whenever he wants."

"Really? You live there?" Jack looked up at the house. "Love the color. I love all of the houses here, actually. Must be nice working right next door." He cleared his throat as he locked his eyes with Ally's. "Just so we're clear, I wasn't checking to see if you'd left him home on his own or anything like that... I know you're a good mom and...."

"It's fine," Ally interrupted him with a smile. The way Jack was looking at her, she got the impression he was fishing as to whether she had a significant other, and she wasn't sure how to feel about that. He was a handsome man who was good with kids, thoughtful and put together. The moms who swooned over him outside the school gates had told her he was a widow too, after his ex-wife had died in a car accident, three years ago. They were about the same age, and with Theo, he would get her like no other. "No need to explain, I know you didn't mean it like that. I'll go get your beers." She rushed inside and once again, hid behind the bar.

"Thank you, Jack. You really didn't have to do that." Ally pulled the chain through the chairs and tables Jack had piled up in front of the bar. While his friends had cycled back home, Jack had stayed to keep Ally company until the last customers had left and they'd talked about Theo and Jack's daughter Sally, who was three years older than Theo. It had been nice to talk to someone who understood what it was like to be a single parent, and how it felt to lose the most important person in one's life. Jack was funny, charismatic, handsome and deep down, Ally knew she'd read the signs. Jack liked her and he seemed like a great guy. For the past two years she'd been dating, searching for anything even close to someone like Jack, but now she found herself having no interest whatsoever. She just wasn't feeling it. *Why?*

"It's not a problem, I'm enjoying this," Jack said, bringing his empty bottle inside.

"Yeah me too." Ally smiled at him from behind the bar as she finished cleaning the coffee machine. "So... are you cycling back in the dark?"

Jack laughed. "I have lights so it's safe. And I only had three beers, I'm sure I can handle the short journey." He hesitated, then leaned in over the bar, locking his eyes with Ally's. "Maybe we should do this again, when you're not working. I'd love to take you out for dinner if you're free someday next week."

"Oh..." Ally stopped what she was doing, looking a little caught. Really, she should feel excited that Jack was asking her out, yet she couldn't make herself feel that little bit of extra enthusiasm to return his flirty gaze because her mind was consumed with Madison, out on her date. It was almost midnight and since she hadn't come home yet, Ally begrudgingly concluded that she was having fun and that the date was hugely successful. That bothered her more than it should. The woman was making her crazy and it had to stop. It was silly and childish, and she really had to get over herself, because this was real life. She had a son and a business, and she was not supposed to be pining over graduates. Even less so over a female graduate who was out on a Tinder date tonight.

"Sure," she heard herself say. "Dinner would be lovely, I'm free on Monday."

16

On her way to the *Pink Panther*, Madison checked Pat's profile again. Going on a date with a woman had never seemed like a big deal before, but now that she was living in a small community, it seemed like the biggest fucking deal in the world. If the date was a disaster, there was a big chance she'd bump into the woman again somewhere, and if the date was fun, she'd have to think very carefully whether she wanted to take it further or not because she had a feeling 'casual' was not something many people did around here. What if they really did like each other but it didn't work out? What if Pat lived around the corner?

Despite her hesitation and mild panic, there was no real reason to back out though, and it had been a while since she'd had some action, or even flirted with a woman. *Apart from Ally,* she reminded herself. But then again, that was just playful interaction and besides, it really was about time she stopped going after straight women. Finally, everything was coming together for her, and living an adult life now, she should probably start behaving like one too. Still, she couldn't seem to shake off the look in Ally's eyes when she'd told her she was going on a date. For a split second, she'd flinched, then quickly painted on a smile. By now, Madison knew Ally's smile all too well and that last smile hadn't been entirely genuine. Was it just her imagination, or was there something between them? Even if it had been a flash of jealousy, Madison didn't think Ally would actually go there with a woman and who was she to even consider competing with a deceased loved one, especially since he was the father of her child, which complicated matters even more. Marcos had clearly been the love of Ally's life, and perhaps Ally wasn't ready to open herself up to others yet, even though it had been over nine years.

Strolling along the canal and lost in her own thoughts, Madison realized she'd already reached the *Pink Panther*. A little apprehensive to go in, she took her phone out of her purse, pretending to be texting someone while she staked the place out in front of the window. It was surprisingly busy, but then it was a Friday night, and she silently cursed herself for even agreeing to go on the date now because it seemed pretty daunting to go in. *What am I doing here?* She'd rarely been to gay bars. There weren't any in Lafayette where she grew up and living on campus it had been just been too easy to flirt with girls, usually with success but little commitment. Everyone was curious at some point, and she'd obtained a reputation as a player amongst her fellow students. Madison wasn't really a player though. The girls she'd 'dated' just never stuck around because in the end, they were straight. And so, she'd moved onto the next and the next and the next... And now, she had no idea how to date actual lesbian women. Women who were willing and available for a potential long-term relationship, not just for a drunken night.

She looked inside but couldn't see anyone who resembled Pat. There were mainly men in the bar, apart from a handful of women on the dance floor.

"What are you doing out here, honey? It's far too windy to be lingering outside." An elegant blonde woman wearing a stylish pantsuit and high heels regarded her before lighting a cigarette. She took a long drag, then turned back to Madison, blowing smoke out in her face while she gave her a curious glance-over. "Well, aren't you a cutie? If I was into women, I'd be all over you. Are you new to the area?"

"Yeah. I just moved here last week." Madison put her phone back in her purse and smiled. Studying the woman curiously, she realized she might be trans.

"Nice. You look like you could spice things up a little around here. I'm Chelsey by the way." She shook Madison's hand. "Are you here by yourself?"

"I'm supposed to meet someone, actually. Pat. Do you know her?"

"Oh, Pat!" Chelsey fluttered her obviously false eyelashes. "Yeah, she's inside, corner end of the bar. She stubbed out her cigarette and beckoned Madison to follow her. "Well come on, honey, I'll introduce you. And let me make you one of our famous strawberry margaritas; you look a little nervous." She winked. "No need to be, we're all very welcoming here and Pat's a nice girl."

P at wasn't blonde, Madison noted. In fact, she had no hair at all as her head was shaven. Although Madison wasn't a big fan of that look, being more into feminine women, she kept an open mind and smiled at the woman who turned on her stool when she followed Chelsey inside. Pat was also a lot shorter than Madison had imagined her to be, but her smile was dazzling and her eyes a fascinating shade of green.

"You must be Madison." Pat stood up and gave her a kiss on her cheek, then gestured to the stool next to her. "Thank you for agreeing to meet me."

"Thanks for the invite." Madison nodded to Pat's glass. "What are you drinking? Can I get you another one of those?"

"I'm good. But I'm buying you a drink." Pat said in a self-assured manner. "What do you want?"

"She wants a strawberry margarita, is what she wants," Chelsey chimed in, making the decision for her. "Trust me."

Pat laughed and leaned in closer, her elbow resting on the bar. "I guess that's what you're having then. There's no arguing with Chelsey." She took a sip of her beer and gave Madison an approving look. "You're stunning. I'm excited to be in your company tonight."

"Thanks. You look great too." Madison wasn't feeling any kind of attraction at all, but that was fine because Pat seemed like a nice woman, even though she was turning the charm up a little too high. "Is this your local?"

"Yup. Come here every weekend."

"And after tasting this, so will you," Chelsey interrupted them again as she put an enormous cocktail with two straws in front of Madison.

"Okay... I'm glad I can walk home." Madison grinned. "Because I'm not sure what state I'll be in by the time I finish this."

The evening turned out to be fun, and Pat was great company. They talked about the best places for food and drinks in the area, Pat told Madison about her job as a veterinarian and Madison shared stories about her first week at work. Not until half an hour into their date, did they realize they would be on the same research vessel twice a week. Pat had been recruited as one of the veterinarians to check animal welfare during the tagging procedures and the coincidence had been celebrated with more drinks. The *Pink Panther* got even busier after ten pm, when karaoke night kicked off and Madison found herself downing one shot after the other. When she went outside with Pat, who wanted to smoke a cigarette, she felt like the world was spinning around her. She'd drank way more than she should have, partially because of initial nerves and partially because she had no idea how to break it to Pat that it wasn't going to go anywhere, despite the fact that they were having a great night. Thankfully, it was Pat who broke the silence as they sat down on the bench in front of the bar.

"Hey, I know this isn't going to work out, but I'm still having a good time with you."

"Oh…" Madison let out a sigh of relief and laughed. "Yeah, there's no chemistry, right?"

"Not much…" Pat cocked her head and regarded Madison. "That, and the fact that you've mentioned your landlady about six times throughout the night. Ally must be some woman."

"Really? Have I really talked about her that much?"

"You don't even know it, huh?" Pat looked at her in surprise. "Straight women crushes… we've all had them. And you've got it bad, girl. The way she plays with her hair, her dark eyes, her laugh…" She put on an exaggerated swooning tone. "I get it, you like girlie girls and I'm not one of them, but most of all, you like someone called Ally who has a son and runs a bar and…"

"Oh God, please stop." Madison interrupted her, holding

up a hand in mortification. She tried to recall their conversations through her foggy haze and realized that she had indeed mentioned Ally quite a few times. "Damn it," she muttered, feeling frustrated with herself. "I'm sorry, that's really uncool. I had no idea I kept rambling on about her."

"Hey, it's okay." Pat laughed. "Now that the awkward conversation is out of the way; do you want to go back inside? Sing a song with me?" She grinned. "I already requested one, so you'd better help me out."

"Absolutely. But I need water first; I don't want to fall off the stage." Madison smiled. She was so glad they'd moved to the friend zone that she wanted to hug Pat "I have to warn you though, it will be the worst singing you'll ever hear in your life."

"Perfect, I'm looking forward to it." Pat stood up, held out a hand and helped Madison up. "Come on, Maddie. Let's bless these lovely people with the performance of our lives."

17

The knocking started softly, then grew into a louder banging, and Madison wasn't sure if she was dreaming or if the noise was real. She groaned when she realized someone was at her door, then raised her fingers to her temple and slowly sat up in bed. It had been a late night at the *Pink Panther*, with way too much alcohol. She vaguely remembered singing with her date, then remembered having a conversation about Ally, and she felt blissfully relieved that nothing had happened with Pat. Unable to remember her walk home, she checked her purse on her nightstand. Everything was still in there when she searched for her phone and realized it was eleven am. Looking for her robe, she stumbled naked across the room, and when she couldn't find it, she grabbed a coat instead.

"Who's there?" she asked in a crackled voice, peering through the peephole in the door.

"Duh! It's me, Theo!" The boy's voice shouted back at her. "Do you want to come to the beach with us?"

Madison shook her head and laughed as she opened the door. "Hey buddy. What did you say? Something about the beach?" She rubbed the sleep out of her eyes and realized it was funny that even in her hungover state, seeing him genuinely made her happy.

Theo grinned sheepishly, then laughed and pointed at her coat. "Did you sleep in that?"

"No, I did not." Madison raised a brow. "Want to come in? Just give me a minute, I have to get dressed first."

"Theo!" Madison heard Ally's angry voice and stepped outside to see her stomping toward her son. "Theo, I told you not to bother Madison." When she saw Madison in the doorway, she stopped and gave her an apologetic look. "I'm so, so sorry he woke you up. This will never happen again, I promise."

"Hey, it's fine, don't worry about it," Madison said, then turned back to Theo. "But you have to listen to your mom." She relaxed her face then, unable to hide her amusement because Theo looked mortified. "As I said, just give me a minute to get dressed and I'm all yours."

"Please, Madison, you don't have to do this." Ally looked Madison over and tried to suppress a chuckle.

"What?" Madison raised a brow, pretending she had no idea how ridiculous she looked. She guessed her hair was sticking out on all sides and she probably had mascara stains under her eyes too. The thigh-length summer coat was zipped up to under her chin and underneath, her bare legs were sticking out, only one foot covered by a sock. "What's so funny?"

"Nothing." Ally shook her head in amusement. "You go back to bed, I apologize again for my son. He knows better." She shot Theo another warning look.

"No, wait... I want to come to the beach with you guys. Really, I do. Theo asked me if I wanted to come and I'm taking that as an official invite." She shot Ally a challenging look, then they both burst out laughing.

"Okay then. Take your time, you know where to find us. I'll bring you some breakfast, you look like you could do with something solid to line your stomach."

"See, Mom? I told you she'd want to come." Theo hopped from one foot to the other, ignoring Ally as she quickly maneuvered him away from the door.

Madison gave him a wink and grinned, feeling better already.

H alf an hour later, she stepped outside, barefoot, heading for the beach. She'd taken a quick shower and was dressed in a bikini and a pair of denim shorts, her towel propped under her arm along with a bottle of water. She really needed to hydrate. Despite her hangover, she felt surprisingly chirpy, and she knew deep down seeing Ally was the main reason for that. But even spending time with Theo was a great prospect, now that she knew him a little better, and she couldn't deny that the boy was growing on her.

Madison's heart started pounding faster when she spotted Ally and Theo among the other beach goers, reading a book together. They were such a cute pair. Her eyes roamed over Ally's body from a safe distance, indulging in her subtle curves, sparsely covered by her bikini – a black one this time. Making sure to walk extra slow, so she'd have more time to take her in, Madison mulled over her conversation with Pat, now that everything was slowly starting to come back and into focus. Pat had been right. She hadn't been able to stop talking about Ally, and she made a mental note to send her a message to apologize. It was downright cringeworthy how she'd managed to lead every conversation back to Ally, as if she was all she wanted to talk about.

"Hey guys." She folded out her towel, then dropped her bottle of water in the sand. "What are you doing?"

"I'm learning Mandarin," Theo said in all seriousness.

"And I am too, I guess," Ally added with a comical grin. "Ni Hao! How was your date?"

Madison sat down next to them and shrugged. "It was great. No chemistry whatsoever but a good night, nevertheless." She could have sworn she saw relief in Ally's eyes. "Pat was a woman, thank God," she continued with a wry smile. "And she was intelligent and funny but not my type physically although she was attractive, I suppose. We had a lot to drink as you can probably gauge by the state I'm in this morning and it was a late night. But other than that... no spark, nothing." Of course, she left out that she'd mostly talked about Ally during her date. "How was your night? Busy at the bar?"

"Mom was talking to Mr. Peterson," Theo said, looking up from his book. "I think Mr. Peterson likes her."

Madison watched Ally shift uncomfortably, frowning as she took the book from him in an attempt to get his full attention. "Honey, how do you know I was talking to him?"

"I was watching you from my window." Theo chuckled. "He told his friends he was going to ask you out."

Ally looked more than uneasy, but she didn't comment on it.

"Are you going out with Mr. Peterson?" Madison teased, although she wasn't sure if she wanted to know the answer. "Isn't that the principal?"

"Yeah, he's the principal." Ally rubbed Theo over his shoulders. "I know you've only just had breakfast but why don't you go and ask Devon for an ice cream? We just got a new delivery of Ben & Jerry's." She waited until Theo had sprinted off, then turned back to Madison. "Jack, the principal, came over for a drink with his cycling buddies. They left and he stayed behind and helped me close up the bar." She paused. "And then he asked me out for dinner, and I said yes but..."

"But?"

"I'm not really feeling it."

"Right." Madison's lips pulled into a smile as she leaned back on her elbows. "Why not? Just not your type?"

Ally stared ahead, pondering over it. "No, it's not that. I guess he would be my type." She shook her head. "Honestly, I have no idea why I'm not interested." She caught Madison's eyes and held them for a beat, as if she wanted to say something but was afraid to do so.

Madison nodded. "Just because he's Mr. Perfect doesn't mean you should feel like you have to date him. Call him, tell him you've changed your mind. And if he's really as nice as you say, maybe you could become friends."

"I don't think friends was what he had in mind." Ally reached into her bag and handed Madison a *Western Shores* take-out box. "Anyway, here's the breakfast I promised you. I hope it makes you feel a little more alive."

"You really didn't have to do that." Madison took the box and felt the hairs on her arm rise as their fingers brushed. Ally took in a quick breath at the fleeting contact and Madison was sure by the way she trembled that she felt something too. Unable to resist, she placed a hand on Ally's arm, craving more. "Thank you."

"It's fine, I like making breakfast; it relaxes me and..." Ally's voice trailed away as she looked down at Madison's hand, then raised her gaze to meet her eyes. They stayed like that for a moment, until Ally finally continued. "And I wanted to apologize for Theo waking you up and..."

"I've got my ice cream!" Theo announced his return by enthusiastically landing in the sand next to them and then giving them a big chocolate-covered grin. "Can we go look for shells now?"

"That was fast. Madison hasn't had breakfast yet, honey. Why don't you go ahead; we'll meet you at the wharf in a little while." Ally gestured toward the old wooden steps that led up to the fisherman's wharf and waved him off.

Madison opened the container with scrambled eggs, avocado and salmon, and felt like hugging Ally when she handed her a thermos with coffee and a fork too. "You're an angel, this is amazing. Want some?" She held the fork out for Ally, who shook her head.

"No, I had breakfast with Theo." She smiled sweetly, then as if realizing she was staring again, she quickly averted her gaze to Theo, who was running under the wharf, scanning the sand. "Do you have any kids in the family?"

"No, not yet." My older brother is in a long-term relationship, but he's also married to his career and my younger brother is way too wild to even think of starting a family. He dates a different girl every month, and to my mother's horror, he's dated most of her friends' daughters too. I also have a half-sister, who I only got to know last year, when she moved from the UK to the US to reconnect with her roots. Her mother was married to my father a long time ago, and then her mother passed away... It's a long story, I'll tell you about it sometime. Anyway, Hannah, that's her name, she moved here to be with Kristine, her girlfriend, and if anyone would have a kid soon, my bet would be on them. And then there's me. I love kids, but I'm single and not in that headspace yet..." Madison bit her lip, immediately regretting what she'd just said. "I mean, it's unlikely that I'll date someone and adopt or conceive a child with them anytime soon, but I'm totally open to dating people with kids... That's what I meant, I think." *Oh God, could I be any more obvious?*

"It's okay, you don't need to explain yourself. You've just started your first job, life's exciting right now. You should enjoy your freedom while you still can," Ally said it in a light-hearted tone. "Because believe me, having a kid is great but there's a lot you have to give up. And I mean, a lot."

"Theo seems pretty easy," Madison said. "I think he's great." She really, really liked Ally and if there was any chance Ally might be the slightest bit attracted to her, she didn't want her to think Theo would be a problem to her.

"He is. He really is an easy boy. But my God... now that we're thinking of applying for the school in LA, there are a whole lot of other things to worry about." Ally shrugged. "Like how I'm going to pay for it all if he gets in and wants to go. I've just found out he's not eligible for a grant because I own multiple properties."

"So you've talked to him about it?"

"Yeah. You were right. It's up to him in the end. He seems really excited about the idea and it broke my heart to see his face light up at the mention of meeting kids of his own age."

"I'm sorry. It must be hard for you to even consider sending him away, even if he really wants to go."

Ally scrunched her nose and mustered a smile. "Well, it is what it is. We'll go visit the school first and then take it from there." She took the empty box back from Madison. You were hungry, huh?"

"I was, and I feel a lot better now. I'm not used to drinking shots anymore. It's been at least..." Madison laughed. "Actually, it probably hasn't been longer than six months, but still…"

Ally laughed too. "Well, apart from Friday night with you, it's been about thirteen years since I drank a lot. I have the occasional shot of tequila, but never more than one."

"Wish I'd been that clever last night." Madison looked at Ally, who produced a bottle of sunscreen from her bag and started applying it to her shoulders and arms. "Want me to put some on your back?"

Ally's eyes widened as she looked at Madison, then burst out laughing. "Is this one of your tricks you were telling me about?"

"Hey, I said your back, not your breasts," Madison joked. "Well? You know you're going to burn without a T-shirt on…"

"Actually yes, thank you." Ally chuckled. "I usually ask Theo but he's a little distracted right now."

"Good. Because I promise you, I'll do a much better job than Theo. I'm thorough, you see," Madison added with a chuckle. "I take sun-burn prevention very seriously and I've got bigger hands. Feels much nicer too." She felt a flutter of excitement when Ally turned around and lay down on her stomach, and suddenly, the silence hung thick, like an impenetrable wall had been erected between them. As much as they were comfortable not speaking, she knew this was different as she watched goose bumps appear on Ally's tanned back before she'd even touched her. Maybe it was just the wind, but it was getting warmer now, and she wasn't cold herself. As she put the lotion in her hands and placed them on Ally's shoulder blades, she could feel a shiver run through her. Ally's skin felt so smooth that Madison had to refrain from turning it into a massage instead. It was only a slap of sunscreen after all, not an excuse to grope her. When she heard a soft moan escape Ally's lips though, she put more pressure on her back and circled her thumbs down along her spine. She squirted more lotion into her hands, then went to work with Ally's shoulders, kneading them harder this time before slowly moving down to her lower back.

"Is it wrong if I say that feels really, really good?" Ally asked with an embarrassed chuckle.

"You like it?" Madison shifted her attention to Ally's waist, curling her fingers around her curves as she slid them back up underneath the back string of her bikini, making sure to stop just before she reached the sides of Ally's breasts. Ally's back was pretty much covered now, but Madison felt reluctant to take her hands off her. "Want me to stop?" She asked, lowering her voice.

Ally didn't answer straight away, as if she was processing the question that was more loaded than they both let on. "I wouldn't mind if you continued for a bit longer," she finally answered. "If *you* don't mind."

Madison bit her lip at her answer and shifted slightly so she had better access to Ally's back. She wanted to straddle her, to run her hands all over Ally, feel her breasts, her ass, her thighs, her... She let out a slow breath, then shook her head and continued, kneading her back in slow and sensual motions. Ally shifted her hips and it made Madison wonder if it was turning her on. She was just contemplating whether to strum her fingers over the sides of Ally's breasts, when Theo's voice interrupted their moment.

"Madison, look what I found!"

They both shot up, looking way more guilty than they should. "That's gorgeous, Theo." Madison reached for the large, brown, ear-shaped shell that was pearlescent inside. "You know what this is, right?"

"It's an abalone shell," Theo said. "They're really strong. Mom uses them as snack bowls for the bar."

"That's right. I've seen that; they look very pretty." Madison stood up and put an arm around him. "If there's one, we might be able to find more. Want to go and have another look with me?" She held out her hand to help Ally up. "Are you coming?"

Ally nodded, looking flustered as she got up too, then lowered her gaze to their entwined hands before quickly letting go.

18

"Can you give me a hand here, Ally? Ally?" Ally shot up when Devon nudged her shoulder. "What the hell is wrong with you, woman? You've been in your own world for the past three hours and we've got a full house!"

Ally shook her head and refocused on the line of people waiting to order drinks. Every seat was taken, and Devon had put out some standing tables so everyone would be able to put down their drinks. Being a Saturday, the crowds were to be expected, but they hadn't anticipated it to be quite so busy. The popular playlist was on and *Western Shores* was filled with happy people, the sound of laughter and animated chatter ringing though the air. The vibe was great, and normally Ally thrived on shifts like these, but today, it all passed her in a haze. "Sorry, just a bit tired, that's all."

"Tired my ass. Does it have anything to do with that principal you're going out with? Have you been daydreaming too much?"

"Fuck... Jack," Ally muttered. She'd been meaning to call him to cancel their date but after Madison's massage at the beach, she'd been in a strange state, unable to do much else but recall the feeling of her strong hands on her back. Not only had it felt incredibly good, it had also awoken something in her, a desire that had thrown her completely and now she wasn't even capable of performing simple tasks like fixing drinks anymore. "What can I get you?" she asked the first person who looked at her, writing down the order so she wouldn't forget.

Devon had called her during their walk on the beach while they were looking for abalone shells with Theo. A group of twenty tourists had come in, some kind of family get-together, and he needed help at the bar and in the kitchen as the bar was already pretty full to begin with. To Ally's relief, Madison had offered to stay with Theo, because she didn't like to have him in the bar while she worked.

They hadn't really talked after the deliciously sensual backrub and that bothered her. Instead, they'd walked side by side in silence, only using Theo as a means to communicate. She should have joked about how long it had been since she'd been touched but she hadn't and now she was afraid her silence had given away the fact that Madison's skilled hands had turned her on like crazy. Perhaps Madison wanted more too, though... That thought made her quiver and as she looked down, she saw the overflowing glass of Coke in her hand.

Devon took the glass from her and rolled his eyes. "You know what? I think I can manage now; most people seem happy. Why don't you go sit down for a moment and I'll give you a shout if I need any more help." He brought his mouth closer to Ally's ear, sounding amused as he lowered his voice: "By the way, you're not off the hook; we'll talk about Mr. Peterson later."

· · ·

"There she is." Several hours later Madison opened the door to let Ally in. "Busy shift?"

"Yeah. But Devon can handle it now." Ally walked into Madison's living room where Theo was sleeping on the couch.

"Well, I made us some pasta, so he's had dinner, and we watched a movie together."

"I can't thank you enough." Ally winced. "I said I'd never call on you to look after Theo and here I am. I'm so, so sorry. I would have normally called Ana, but she's playing poker tonight and it's the highlight of her week. It's not fair to you though, to be childminding on your precious day off, especially when you started the day with a hangover."

"Hey, it's fine, we had fun together." Madison paused, her eyes searching for Ally's. "And I had fun with you too. Thank you for this morning."

Ally's breath hitched, and she took a step back, preventing herself from doing what she really wanted to do, which was put her mouth on Madison's and kiss her senseless. It was silly, she knew that, but it didn't stop her from thinking about it. "I had fun too," she whispered. There was an awkward silence, and just as Madison was about to open her mouth again, she walked over to Theo and gently nudged him.

"Theo, honey, wake up. We're going home."

Theo mumbled something, then turned his back to her.

"Come on, Theo." Ally thought about lifting him, but knew he was too heavy for her to carry up the stairs now.

"I can take him," Madison said, bending forward and lifting Theo over her shoulder without waiting for an answer. "We walked a lot. Must have really knocked him out."

Ally laughed at how Madison carried Theo like a bag of potatoes, holding him by his legs in front of her chest while he continued to sleep. She opened the door for her, then opened her own front door to let Madison in and walked ahead up the short flight of stairs to the little tower where Theo's bedroom was. "Thank you," she whispered when Madison put him down gently.

"My pleasure." They stood there for a couple of beats, facing each other until Madison finally cleared her throat and smiled. "Well, I'd better get home myself. I'll see you guys soon."

"Yeah. Are you around tomorrow or next week?" Ally didn't want to sound too eager but realized she did as she followed Madison down the stairs.

"I've got long days, so I probably won't be home much, and I need to be in the lab tomorrow as I'm a little behind."

Ally nodded forcing down her disappointment, lingering in the hallway. She didn't want Madison to go yet, but she had no excuse to ask her to stay. "Nice. I'm sure you'll enjoy being on the water all day." She hesitated. "I'm waiting to hear back from the school in LA. If they're on board with Jack's report, we can fly over the coming weekend and Theo can take the tests the Monday after. I'm working all day tomorrow too, so we might not see each other for a while..." The words hung in the air between them, and she was sure there was a trace of sadness in Madison's expression.

"Okay... I hope it all goes well. Will you let me know?"

"Of course. I'm sure I'll speak to you in the meantime." Ally's gaze shifted to Madison's perfectly shaped lips and instinctively, she inched a little closer, drawn to her as if she had no control over her actions. She noticed a brief flinch in Madison's eyes, and immediately regretted doing so.

"I hope so," Madison whispered, backing away toward the door. "If not, have a good week."

At that very moment Ally wished the ground would swallow her. Had she been too full-on? She was a fairly confident person, but whenever she was around Madison, she second-guessed her every move. Was it obvious that she wanted to kiss her? Madison clearly wanted to leave. Had Ally misread the signs? She wasn't sure of anything anymore but mustered a smile as she opened the door for her. "Yeah. You too. Have fun at work."

19

"**A**re you ready?" Pat took the pair of binoculars Madison handed her.

"Yes Ma'am." Madison tugged at the cord on her life vest, tightening the waistband.

"Good. So am I. It's nice to be back on a boat, I like these projects." Having been involved with similar studies in the past, Pat already knew some of the existing team members and seemed at ease in the group that counted eight today. "So, what's going on with Ally?" she asked as she stood and scanned the waters before her. They were looking out for the pod of dolphins that came to feed along the coast of Monterey most mornings. They would tag a couple of them with suction cups, then monitor them for as long as they could until the suction cups fell off, which was usually between four and twelve hours. The new method was a less invasive way of tagging marine mammals without disturbing the pod or the individual animal, as they didn't have to capture them, but it also meant they had to come out here every day and repeat the tagging over and over. Madison didn't mind that at all; she loved being out at sea, and even though it was only day one, she knew she'd never grow tired of the tranquil bobbing of the vessel once the engine was switched off, the breathtaking view over Monterey harbor and the endless North Pacific Ocean.

"Nothing much, we've become friends." Madison looked through her binoculars from the bow, keeping her eyes on the west side of the boat while Pat, standing next to her, focused on the front and Ravi, one of the junior scientists, scanned the east side. Three others were standing on the stern, doing the same and Tom, who was experienced with tagging, was sitting on a bench in the middle of the boat, checking the DTAGS on the long sticks that he would use to secure the suction cups onto the dolphins as soon as they got really close. After a couple of practice demonstrations and onboard training, Madison would take over so he wouldn't have to be here every day. Pat was only required to be present to monitor animal welfare and safety during the procedures, but she liked to get more involved and knew the process better than Madison did.

"And you're sure she's not even remotely interested in anything more?"

"No, I'm not sure. Yesterday was…" Madison lowered her voice so Ravi wouldn't hear them. "It was strange. I'm pretty sure we had a moment when we were on the beach together yesterday morning and last night, after she picked Theo up from my house, I was convinced she wanted to kiss me. There was something in the way she looked at me…" She shrugged. "But I could have imagined it."

"Wait a minute. You thought she wanted to kiss you and you didn't do anything?" Pat laughed. "What's wrong with you?"

"Nothing. I just wasn't sure and besides, she's Ally. She's straight and even if she's not entirely straight, I don't want to mess things up with her. I mean, flirting is one thing, but there's also Theo to think about…"

"Yeah, the kid… And she's got you looking after him already?" Pat chuckled.

"It wasn't like that and I don't mind. I actually like Theo a lot."

"So the fact that she has a son isn't a problem to you?"

"No, not at all. But it does make things more complicated." Madison narrowed her eyes when she thought she spotted movement in the distance. "She's also older than me and more settled. I guess I just want to think things through for once and I want her to take me seriously."

"Maybe she's not looking for complicated. Maybe experimenting with a woman and having a bit of fun is exactly what she wants." Pat shot her a sideways glance. "How much older are we talking?"

"Seventeen years."

Pat gasped. "Damn. And that isn't a problem to you either?"

"No, why would it be?"

"I don't know… I could probably think of a million reasons."

Madison shook her head, continuing to focus on the movement ahead of her. "Ally's a great person and I'm insanely attracted to her, so the age thing doesn't bother me." She wasn't sure why Pat thought it was such a big deal but then again, maybe she wasn't thinking straight because Ally seemed to have that effect on her. Their moment in the hallway last night hadn't left her mind for a waking second and despite her trying to do the right thing, she knew kissing Ally was all she wanted. "I don't want to fuck it up," she continued. "But you're right; maybe she just wants to experiment. I hadn't thought of it that way." Ally didn't strike her as the casual type but then again, she didn't know her that well. After being single for so long, she could imagine Ally had her needs, and living next door to a lesbian who was clearly attracted to her, it wasn't unimaginable that she might have ideas she wouldn't normally entertain. "Guys, I think I have eyes on them," she said a little louder, pointing to the spot in the far distance.

Pat and Ravi both turned to check and agreed with her. Grateful to end the conversation that had brought up more questions than she was willing to deal with right now, Madison raised her voice and shouted: "Ten o'clock!"

20

"The principal is here for you," Devon called into the storage room in a teasing tone.

Ally looked up as she threw her apron in the laundry basket. "What? Fuck!"

Devon frowned, studying her. "Ally, he's at your front door with a huge bunch of roses and besides the fact that you're not there, you're not even dressed yet."

Ally's heart sank to her stomach. "I forgot to cancel. Fuck, fuck, fuck." She looked to Devon for help, but he just shrugged, clearly confused.

"Why would you cancel? I thought you liked him. You've been all dreamy lately and..."

"It's complicated." Ally interrupted him, shaking her head. "Can you please go back out there and offer him a drink or something? Say I'll be out in five minutes? Fuck," she cursed again. "Now I have to go."

Devon nodded. "Sure, I can do that. But I don't get why you've changed your mind. Has he upset you in any way? Because if he has, I swear I'll..."

"No, no. It's not that. Jack's a great guy." Ally rubbed her temple. "I just forgot to cancel, and I haven't even arranged a sitter for Theo." She took a deep breath and gave Devon a pleading look. "Please just keep him busy for a little while, I need some time to collect myself." She waited until Devon had left, then closed the door behind her and stared at her reflection in the broken mirror above the sink. She hadn't been herself since Saturday, constantly torn between a state of embarrassment and arousal. She'd almost kissed Madison. Almost. The pull she'd felt at being so close to her was something she'd tried to push away, but her mind kept going back there. What was up with Madison anyway? One moment she was flirting with her, the next, she couldn't get away fast enough and that was starting to confuse her.

Theo had been late for school, she'd dropped at least six glasses and she'd even forgotten to empty the till last night. But worst of all, the date with Jack had slipped her mind entirely. Sweet, handsome Jack, who was now waiting for her with flowers, and she felt terrible for that. She looked around in a frenzy, searching for something to wear other than her *Western Shores* branded work T-shirt, and spotted an old checked flannel shirt hanging from one of the hooks on the door. It was creased, but at least it was clean, she thought, sniffing it before she slipped it on and rolled up the sleeves. The shirt was way too big for her, she figured it was Devon's, but she managed to make it work by tying the shirt-tails into a knot at the waist. It would have to do and besides, she had no desire to impress Jack with her looks.

Dread enveloped her and made her silently groan when she walked out and saw Jack was dressed up, wearing nice jeans and a crisp, white shirt. He was clean shaven and gave her a wide smile, holding up the flowers for her.

"Ally. You look wonderful."

"Ehm... Thank you," she stammered. "You didn't have to

do that." She ignored Devon, who was eyeing up her half-baked outfit.

"Yeah, nice shirt," he said with a grin, then got up from the chair opposite Jack and offered it to Ally.

"I'm so, so sorry," she continued as Jack stood up and gave her a kiss on her cheek. "Theo's sitter has literally just cancelled so I won't be able to go out, I'm afraid." She gave him an apologetic look and shrugged. "I would have called you had I known sooner, but she literally called a minute ago. Maybe we could have a drink here with some snacks? I really am sorry you came all the way here before I could catch you."

If Jack was disappointed, he didn't let it show. "Hey, don't worry about it, Ally. Sure, we can stay here. Is Theo home?"

"Yeah, he's in his room but he's had dinner already, so I'll just..."

"Mr. Peterson!" Theo interrupted her, waving down at them from his tower window.

"Great," Ally muttered. "Now he's going to tell the kids at school that his mom was hanging out with Mr. Peterson again." She rolled her eyes and chuckled.

"Hey Theo!" Jack waved back at him, ignoring her remark. "How are you?"

"I'm learning Mandarin," Theo said with a grin. "Are you taking mom out?" He yelled it so loud that other patrons around them laughed as they turned their heads to look at Ally and Jack.

"Mandarin? You'll have to come into my office tomorrow and teach me some phrases." Jack blinked at him. "Not that I'd understand any of it." He cleared his throat. "But to answer your question; your mom and I are just having a drink together, that's all."

Theo narrowed his eyes and tilted his head. Studying his

mother's outfit, he clearly decided that there was no romance involved as his mother rarely made this little effort. "Okay," he yelled. "I'll come in tomorrow after math!" Then he retreated and closed the window.

"So, I have some good news," Jack said after Devon had brought over their drinks. "The Seymour Institute is happy for Theo to come over and do the tests next Monday. "I mean, it's good news if that's what you want for him. It's totally okay if you've changed your mind of course," he added.

Ally took a couple of deep breaths as she let his words sink in. "Okay, that is good news, I suppose. Theo wants to go check it out. He seems really keen on the idea and if that's what he wants..." She took a sip of her wine. "I can't say I'm happy about him potentially going to a boarding school, but you were right when you said there's no way his potential can be developed here, and in the end, I want the best for him."

"We all want the best for him." Jack gave her hand a squeeze. "I'll let them know and set it up for next week if that still suits you."

"Yeah. Next week is fine. I kind of scheduled it in already, anticipating they'd be impressed by his grades and preliminary IQ test." She looked up at Jack and chuckled. "And now he's learning Mandarin just for fun, I mean, isn't that insane?"

"Not to him. Theo needs mental stimulation so it's only natural that he goes through obsessive phases, seeking new challenges. Right now, it's Mandarin, next month it might be physics. But The Seymour Institute will pick up on the things that he loves and where his true talents lie. They'll be able to develop his already extensive knowledge in marine biology too, meaning he might be one of the biggest names in the field one day, should he continue to show interest in the subject." Jack looked a little uncomfortable as he continued. "I know the school fees might be an issue. I checked, and they provide a grant for one child each year so it would be worth applying for, but taking into consideration that you have three properties in your name, I doubt they'll even consider it."

"Yeah, I already looked into that." Ally sighed. "But I'll make it work one way or another." She looked over at the pink house. Madison wasn't home from work yet. She missed her more than she liked to admit and found herself constantly checking the beach road, looking out for her. "I could always sell one of the buildings." It wasn't what she wanted because deep down, her and Marcos's plan of converting at least two of the three buildings into a spacious home was still very much alive. But for Theo she would do anything and if that meant selling the pink house, then that was what she would have to do.

"I know you will." Jack nodded. "You're a great mom, Ally."

Ally smiled at him. "And I have no doubt you're a great dad."

"We're not doing so bad, are we?" Jack held up his beer before he took a sip. "I'd say we're very well suited, you and me."

Ally looked down at the table, worried he'd get carried away if she wasn't honest right away. "You know, Jack... I don't think I'm ready to date yet." She knew it sounded silly since she'd been single for nine years, but she had no idea how to break to him that she had a mad crush on a much younger woman who seemed to overshadow everyone else in the universe. *Damn you, Madison.*

"What was that all about?"

"What was what all about?" Ally opened the till and removed most of the big notes, then placed them in the safe underneath.

Devon gave her a skeptical look. "You know what I'm talking about, Ally. The principal. Jack. The nice guy who adores you and now all of a sudden, you seem to have no interest in him whatsoever." He continued to stare at her when Ally looked away.

Ally leaned back against the counter and crossed her arms in front of her. She couldn't hold it in any longer; she had to tell someone, or she was worried she might go out of her mind. Before she had time to think it through, she said: "I have a thing for Madison. I mean, I have a crush on her." Her face flushed as Devon's eyes almost fell out of their sockets. "I haven't felt like this since... well, never, I guess. I think about her all the time and it's so physical and distracting that I have trouble concentrating on anything at all."

"Are you serious?"

Ally nodded slowly, running a finger over her lips in an unconscious gesture. "I want to kiss her so badly it hurts. It's madness, I know. It makes no sense and I certainly didn't see it coming."

"You..." Devon said, still not quite believing what he was hearing. "But you're... you're straight, right?"

Ally shrugged. "Not right now, apparently. I had a fling with a woman back in college, but I've never had feelings for any other women since, so I just put it down to a one-time-thing." She gave him an earnest look, deciding to be completely honest. "It was amazing though, physically speaking."

"Really? Why didn't you tell me? We were already best friends back then."

"I'm not sure. I met Marcos only a couple of weeks later, so I just parked it and didn't really think of it until now."

Devon walked around the bar and took Ally in his arms, sensing that she needed a hug. Ally held onto him in return, fighting back her frustration.

"I don't know what to do with myself, Devon. I feel all kinds of weird and amazing and confused and..." She rested her forehead against his shoulder. "She's much younger than me; this free-spirited person with pink hair who likes surfing and skateboarding. She's just getting her life together and I have Theo and the bar... It makes no sense and it won't work. I know it will never work."

"You don't know that," Devon said. "All kinds of people end up together, even the most unlikely pairings. Saying that, I don't find you two so unlikely, now that I think about it. The way you interact together... it's natural and it seems like the two of you have fun when you hang out." He chuckled. "Apart from the fact that she's a woman; I can't deny that you surprised me there. So, you really like Madison, huh? You seem pretty shaken up by her."

"I do." Ally stepped back and covered her face in her hands, hiding her blush. "But I don't know if it's purely physical or something more. I haven't had sex in a very long time and..." She shook her head. "Oh God, why am I even telling you this?"

"Because I'm your bestie and you love me." Devon reached for the bottle of tequila and poured them both a shot. "Here, drink this, it might calm you down." He shot her an amused smirk. "Jesus Ally, you're all over the place. If you don't mind me saying, you're looking like a woman who's a hot mess right now."

"I know." Ally knocked back the tequila and slammed the glass down on the bar. "What should I do?"

"I don't know. If you think this is just a physical thing, it might not be that complicated. You could have hot steamy sex and get it out of your system. Does Madison feel the same?"

Ally shrugged. "She's flirty, but I think she might be flirty by nature. I haven't seen her around other women, so I have no way of knowing. The other night, I really wanted to kiss her, and I think she sensed it." She bit her lip as a frown appeared between her brows. "But then she left... That means she's not interested, right?"

"Hey, don't ask me about women." Devon chuckled. "I've dated more women than I've had shots of tequila and I still don't understand them." He poured them both another shot and scooted one in Ally's direction. "Why don't you just talk to her? Isn't that the advice you women always give each other?"

"That's easier said than done. I think I'll just ignore my raging hormones and wait until this phase or whatever it is passes." Ally let out another huff of frustration and downed her second shot. "And can we please pretend we never had this conversation? No teasing, or this will be the last time I ever tell you something private. I know what you're like when you..."

"Hey, you know I can't resist an opportunity to embarrass you," Devon joked. "But I promise I'll do my best."

21

Madison rushed home on Friday, hoping to catch Ally and Theo before they left for LA. Although they'd exchanged messages, they hadn't really spoken, and she'd found herself missing Ally. She scanned the other cars parked along the beach road as she got out of her pickup but didn't see Ally's white Chrysler. Disappointment settled in the pit of her stomach, and she let out a deep sigh while she dragged her bag home.

The week had been great. Fieldwork was what she thrived on, and especially now that she was getting to know her colleagues better, it was fun being on a boat all day, despite the long days. But Ally had been on her mind a lot, especially their moment in the hallway. Why hadn't she just kissed her when she'd been given the chance? She sure as hell wanted to. It had left her craving Ally even more and here she was yet again, crushing on a straight woman. With the emphasis on woman this time, because Ally was most certainly not a girl and that was one of the things that attracted Madison to her.

Ally was her own person, both confident and content

with her life. She had her shit together unlike most girls Madison had dated in college. Well most of her shit, anyway, as Madison wasn't sure about her sexuality. Did Ally really like her that way or had she misread the signs and was she just lonely and in need of company? And if she was, why wouldn't she give Jack a chance? Was she simply curious about being with a woman? Madison had no desire to be used as a means to sexual exploration again, and the fact that she was falling for Ally made her realize she had to be careful and protect herself because whatever was going on between them could very well be short-lived.

She was pulled out of her thoughts by Devon, who came out of the bar and waved at her.

"Hey Devon. I've missed them, haven't I?"

"Yeah, they left early; Ally wanted to beat the traffic." Devon looked her over with a hint of curiosity. "Why? Do you need something?"

"No, I just wanted to say goodbye and wish them luck." Madison shrugged and sat down on the terrace in front of *Western Shores*. "But it's fine, I'll see them next week." She couldn't help but notice the odd look on Devon's face. Was he trying to suppress a grin or was that just his natural expression? She hadn't paid enough attention to him to know for sure. "Can I have a soy beetroot latte with extra cayenne, please?"

"Gross. You too now?" Devon grimaced. "Did you have a good week at work? Haven't seen you around much," he said, raising his voice as he walked inside to make the latte.

"Yeah, it was great. Interesting," Madison said, leaning back and sticking her head around the corner. She didn't feel like elaborating; her brain was too tired to explain what she did all day without using scientific jargon.

"Interesting..." Devon repeated as he rummaged around

by the coffee machine. "Well, I'll tell you something interesting. You know Mr. Peterson, the principal of Theo's school?"

"Uhuh." Madison frowned, not liking the mention of his name. "He asked Ally out, right?"

"Yes, that's right. Well, he was at her door this week. All dressed up, flowers in hand, ready to pick her up and guess what? She'd forgotten all about it. Instead of running inside, getting changed and asking Ana to look after Theo, she put on one of my old shirts, which made her look like she was in the middle of a spring clean, then used Theo as an excuse not to go. They had drinks here instead while snacking on deep-fried food and she didn't even make an effort."

"Oh." Madison was unable to stop the corners of her mouth from pulling up into a smile because she couldn't deny she'd been a little jealous. "She's probably just not interested in him. Can't force something that's not there, right?"

"No, I guess not." Devon came back and put the coffee down in front of her. "But Ally's been acting strange lately, that's all I'm saying. Daydreaming, forgetting stuff, dropping things..." He crossed his arms in front of his chest and gave her that weird stare again.

"Okay..." Madison's pulse started racing as the thought struck her that it might have something to do with her, but she forced herself not to get her hopes up. "She's been a little stressed about Theo's school situation. It might just be that," she said, trying to sound casual.

"Yeah, it might be that. Or it might be something or someone else." Devon winked. "Anyway, I'll stop gossiping about my boss now and start serving my customers. Enjoy the weekend, Madison."

"You too." Madison narrowed her eyes as she watched him disappear inside. He was definitely acting strange, like he was trying to get a reaction from her. Had Ally told him something? There was nothing to tell unless... Well, unless Ally shared the same feelings.

Madison scrolled through her messages from Ally. They weren't flirty in the slightest, but there had been a lot of messages back and forth, she realized then. Way more than friends would normally exchange. The last message from Ally read: '*If I don't see you before we leave, have a great weekend. Come by the bar on Tuesday night if you're back in time. Can't wait to catch up.*'

Madison wanted to send something back but decided to wait until she was able to think of something funnier or more interesting to say than just a '*Sure, can't wait to catch up either.*'

She sat back and sipped her latte, thinking it was kind of boring here without Ally. The terrace was full, but she didn't really feel like making new friends tonight. She contemplated calling Pat, but she'd spent the whole week with her already, and she was pretty sure Pat would have a hot date tonight, since she'd been on her dating app for hours each day during the time she wasn't on stand-by. Her phone rang then, and Madison smiled when she saw it was Chuck.

"Hey Chuckie-Chucks. How's my little brother? Have you moved yet?"

"Hey sis. Yeah, mom and dad moved me yesterday." He paused. "And mom stayed over to help me unpack while I was working so I'm already settled in."

"You mean mom did everything?" Madison heard him laugh and knew she was right. Their mother still fussed over Chuck as if he was a new-born sometimes.

"Kind of. But you know what she's like. She loves to help."

"And you love to be helped," Madison retorted, unable

to keep the sarcasm out of her voice. "Are you working tonight, or will you be able to enjoy your newfound freedom in peace?"

"No. Hannah's in the kitchen, I've got two days off."

"Nice." Madison took a sip of her spicy drink. "Any plans?"

"Nothing special. Just dinner." Chuck was silent for a beat. "With Darla."

Madison laughed so hard then that her drink went up her nose and she needed a moment to compose herself, gathering napkins to clean up the mess on the table and her T-shirt, although she was sure the red stain would never come out. "You're going for dinner with Darla? Why?"

"Why not? She's nice."

"But she's mom's friend and triple your age. What could the two of you possibly have to talk about? I mean, it's not even the age-thing so much," Madison corrected herself, remembering she was swooning over someone seventeen years older herself, "but Darla is the polar opposite to you. She's this overly-sophisticated older lady with prize poodles and you're... well, let's be honest, you're a twenty-year-old party animal who burps and farts." She grinned. "Unless you're hoping she'll do your laundry for you or clean your apartment because believe me, that's not going to happen. She's got cleaners, and with a whole string of rich ex-husbands, I don't think she's ever lifted a finger in her life."

"Of course I don't expect her to do my laundry. Darla's actually really good company." Madison was surprised that Chuck seemed offended by her joke because normally, he'd go along with it. "Anyway, don't tell mom I'm hanging out with her, she might get the wrong idea." He cleared his throat. "So, how are things with you? Can I come and visit soon?"

"Yeah, I'd like that. I only have one bedroom though, so you'll have to sleep on the couch."

"I'm okay with that. Are you dating anyone, though? Because I don't want to listen to my sister…"

"Jesus, Chuck, stop it. No, I'm not dating."

Chuck laughed. "Great. Then we'll have to go on a night out together, it's been forever. I can be your wingman, find you a hot chick."

Madison rolled her eyes. "Sure. And I'll find you a hot chick too."

22

"You did well on your tests, Theo." Mrs. Vargo, the director of The Seymour Institute handed Theo a copy of his test results, then gave one to Ally. The friendly lady had shown them around campus while Theo's test results were being processed, and now she had just picked them up from the administrator's office. She was in her sixties, Ally guessed. Wearing a floral dress, a woolen button through cardigan and big round glasses low on her nose, framing friendly brown eyes, Mrs. Vargo looked nothing like a director, but more like a slightly frumpy librarian.

"Thank you." Ally flipped through the pages of what seemed like terribly complicated data, then settled on the last page, where it showed an average score of ninety percent accuracy in Theo's answers over the different subjects. "What does that mean, ninety percent?"

"It means he qualifies. We start accepting at seventy-five percent." Mrs. Vargo gave Theo a warm smile. "You're a very clever boy. Someone will talk you through your results in detail later, if you'd like that."

Theo frowned as he studied his score too, then nodded. "What did I get wrong?"

"You didn't get much wrong at all," Mrs. Vargo said. "The questions are really, really hard and you're not expected to know everything. No one knows everything, right? And there were a lot of different subjects."

Ally gave Theo a hug and a kiss on his forehead, sensing his frustration. She had a hunch it was the first time he'd gotten things wrong in a test and could tell he was disappointed in himself. "You did great, honey. I'm so proud of you."

Mrs. Vargo waved her hand to call a boy over. Although he was a lot shorter than Theo, he looked like he was about the same age. "Tej, this is Theo. Theo, this is Tej, one of our students. I'm sure Theo would like to rest his brain a little after four hours behind the computer, so Tej, if you don't mind taking him on a tour and showing him the student's recreational spaces..."

"Sure. Want to see the gaming room?" Tej asked, turning enthusiastically to Theo.

"There's a gaming room?"

"Yes, there is," Mrs. Vargo said. "All educational games, of course, no Warcraft or whatever else it's called," she added. "I need to talk to your mom for a moment, is that okay? We'll be right over there if you're looking for us." She pointed to a set of gray couches in the corner of the lobby.

"Sure." Theo looked excited as he sprinted after Tej, who had already disappeared around the corner.

"He seems to like it here already," Ally said, following him with her eyes through the glass divider. The boys were having an animated conversation by the looks of it, and she couldn't remember a time she'd seen Theo interact like this with another boy his age.

"Most of our students do." Mrs. Vargo shot her a sweet smile. "Some get homesick and, in those cases, we tend to try it for another month, giving them the chance to properly settle in. If they're still unhappy, we'll send them home. At their age, you can't force it but I'm sure you're aware of that. It only works if they're here willingly." She made them both a coffee from the machine next to the couches and handed one to Ally as they sat down. "Our students are from all over the world, but we only speak English here and expect our students to speak English among each other too. That way, no one feels left out."

"That's nice. Ally took a sip of her coffee and felt a little overdressed as she crossed her legs and looked down at her feet. She hadn't known what to expect, and so she'd opted for the black suit and heels she hadn't worn in years. Most teachers just wore jeans though, and the kids, both boys and girls, were dressed in black slacks, white polo shirts and bright blue sweaters. No ties, no blazers, no pleated skirts, and she liked that. "What's the study program like? And what about their free time? How much freedom do they have outside school hours? Theo loves to be outside and he loves the beach so I think he would miss that."

"Good questions." Mrs. Vargo handed her a leaflet. "The classes run from nine to five, Monday to Thursday and Friday is only half a day so the students can go home for the weekend, if home is close enough. Some of our students, like Tej, tend to stay here during the weekends as his flight home would be too long and we have special arrangements with his parents so they can be more flexible with visiting him, or he can go home for longer periods from time to time. Although most classes are group led, the individual is central in our program so sixty percent of Theo's homework and assignments will be tailored to him. Unfortunately, we're not that close to the beach but we do have substantial grounds and we organize excursions twice a month for those who want to go to a museum, a national park, a farm or anything else that might interest them, and the students get to vote on what activities they do." She pointed to the second floor where the canteen and the recreational areas were located. "Theo will have breakfast, lunch and dinner with the live-in students in his year each day and is expected to make his own bed and get dressed and showered himself each morning. Of course, the laundry is done for him and things such as toiletries are also provided. He'll sleep in one of the dorms I showed you, with no more than five other boys. Apart from the sleeping and shower arrangements, boys and girls are not separated but they are kept under strict supervision to ensure they don't mingle in inappropriate ways, if you know what I mean."

Ally laughed. "I don't think that will be a problem with Theo. He has no interest in girls whatsoever."

"You'll be surprised." Mrs. Vargo laughed too. "Once children fall into an environment where they can truly be themselves, they often start exploring other things, like their sexuality for example." She shrugged. "It's just a natural development but we make sure to educate them as best as we can in an open-minded and safe way. The students are aged between twelve and sixteen, apart from one girl, who is eleven, and Theo, if he joins us, although I can see he's turning twelve this summer before the new schoolyear starts. We make exceptions sometimes as some kids are more mature for their age and have no problem being away from their parents. There's a communal cinema room where age-appropriate movies and box sets are played at night, a gym where all sorts of classes are taught, a tennis court and, as mentioned earlier, we even have a gaming room, where all games are allowed as long as they're not violent. Unfortunately, we can't allow pets as some children may be allergic but if Theo wants to have an aquarium, which I believe you told me is his pride and joy, then we can allow that as long as he takes good care of it himself. For those who like to explore music, there are classes available at night, and most instruments are on site to borrow."

Ally smiled. "It almost sounds too good to be true, and I must say, I'm getting a really good vibe from the Institute and the people who work here. But what if he gets lonely or wants to call me?"

"If Theo truly is homesick or upset for some reason, we'll allow a phone call of course, but in general our live-in students have a video call with their parents or primary care givers once or twice a week. Mobile phones are not allowed, to the dismay of our older students." Mrs. Vargo chuckled. "They all have the same parental controlled laptop with access to the study material and informative websites. There is strictly no access to Netflix or other movie sites. News yes, gossip, no. We have to draw the line somewhere. There are also several councilors who are available around the clock if he wants to talk, and of course, they can always come to one of the teachers, or to me."

"Okay... Ally had to admit she was feeling less apprehensive now that she was here and had spoken to some of the teachers and Mrs. Vargo. The other students were nice and polite but still seemed like they were able to be themselves and if she were to trust anyone with her son, it would be these people here, who she could see were doing everything in their power to create a sense of community and a home away from home for children like Theo. "Well, if Theo wants this, then I'm willing to try, but the fees are extortionate for someone like me," she said with regret.

Mrs. Vargo gave her an understanding nod. "Yes, I'm aware that the costs are challenging. Most parents have commented on the fees, but if you look at the specialized staff we have here; the teachers, the supervisors, the councilors, security staff, the cleaners, the canteen crew and the night watch alone, we have a lot more staff than the average school... then add up study materials, the campus, you name it... We try to make it as affordable as we can. Unlike twenty years ago, when institutes like this were more likely to receive applications from kids coming from wealthy families, times have changed and that's great. Schools pick up on the intelligence levels of their students nowadays and they're more proactive." She handed Ally another leaflet. "That's why we have very lenient payment plans. Our financial advisor is available five days a week if you have any questions. And there are the grants, of course, but from what I've gathered you're not eligible, unfortunately."

"Okay...Thank you." Ally glanced over the leaflet, then put it in her purse. After two weeks of sleepless nights, she felt like she could breathe again. She'd been so nervous about the visit, but it truly was a great place and if she sold the pink house, she'd be able to make it work financially. "If Theo decides he wants this, when can he start?"

"I suggest you enroll him in our summer program, which starts in June, when the school year ends. It's eight weeks of fun learning, less serious than the regular classes throughout the year, and it's a great way to test if he likes living here without having to commit to a whole year financially. It's very popular, so I suggest you let us know sooner rather than later if you're interested. If after the summer program you both decide this school is right for him, we'll sign him up for the school year."

"Great. I'll think about it and let you know as soon as

possible." Ally smiled. She liked the idea of a test-period as it was less definite.

"Excellent. In the meantime, you can contact the management team with any additional questions you may have." Mrs. Vargo stood up. "Shall we go and see what the boys are up to?"

23

"Hey buddy! How was LA?" Madison asked, ruffling a hand through Theo's thick, dark hair. She smiled at Ally when she opened the door further. "Sorry I'm late, we didn't dock until seven." Butterflies hit her core at the sight of Ally, who was wearing a yellow sundress that accentuated her slim waist and her breasts. God, she'd missed looking at her.

"The school was really, really amazing. And we went to see the Hollywood sign and Universal Studios too!" Theo was in his pajamas, looking adorable and completely overexcited. "Can I stay up late now, Mom?"

"Sure. I suppose that's fine just this one time." Ally ran a hand through her son's hair and took a step back. "It's nice to see you again. Come in, I'm sure Theo is dying to tell you all about our trip."

Madison put her hand on Ally's wrist, stopping her when she was about to go inside. "Actually, I was hoping he could tell me about it in the pickup. One of my colleagues just called to inform me that something is happening on Sunset State Beach, and I think Theo would love to see it.

And you too of course," she added, lowering her voice as her smile widened. She just couldn't help it; Ally made her happy. "I know it's late and that Theo is supposed to be in bed soon, but I promise you, it will be worth it."

"Okay…" Ally gave her a curious look.

"What is it?" Theo was already putting on his boots.

"You'll have to wait and see." Madison winked at Ally. "Well, come on. You too. It's twenty minutes from here, you can catch me up on everything as I drive."

It was dark by the time Madison pulled over in the deserted parking lot. She wasn't sure how to get down to the beach as she couldn't see much, but Ravi had already seen the truck coming and waved at them with a flashlight.

"This way, guys. Follow me." He turned to them as they walked down a narrow sandy path. "You must be Ally and Theo. I've heard a lot about you. I'm Ravi, Madison's colleague. I live just a little farther down and saw something on my way home." He paused half-way down the path from where they could look onto the beach. "Thought you'd all like to see it."

Madison, Ally and Theo all stopped in their tracks as they suddenly came face to face with a bright blue glow shimmering over the surf, stretching along the coastline as far as the eye could see.

"What in the…"

"They're bioluminescent algae, Mom," Theo said in an excited voice. "It's called algal bloom."

"That's right," Ravi said. "And some people call it red tide. Madison was right; you're a smart kid. Want to go down, get closer?" He turned to Madison and held up his camera. "I think I've got enough pictures for tonight. Will you be okay getting there and back up? Here, take my flashlight."

"Thank you so much, Ravi." Madison shot him a grateful look. Growing up in Louisiana, she'd never seen red tide firsthand, and she was mesmerized by the intensity of the neon glow. When they continued down the path, following Theo, Madison realized she'd taken Ally's hand. It had been an unconscious gesture, and she panicked at first, unsure if it was too forward. But Ally's slender fingers curled around hers, taking a tighter grip as they descended the last steep part of the path. Her heart started beating wildly in her throat and her stomach fluttered like crazy. She felt Ally's hand trembling and for a moment, she almost forgot why they were there.

"Mom, can I have your phone to take pictures?" Theo asked.

"Sure, honey. But just don't wade in, okay? The tide is too strong." Ally's voice sounded shaky as she handed Theo her phone. She turned to Madison when she let go of her hand and something passed between them then, Madison was sure of that.

Ally looked so incredibly beautiful tonight that she had trouble taking her eyes off her. Her oversized cardigan hung open over her summer dress, her long hair was blowing freely in the wind, and her dark eyes had a luminescent intensity to them Madison hadn't seen before as she sat down in the sand, patting the space next to her.

"Thank you for taking us here," she said softly. "It's the most spectacular thing I've ever seen, and Theo is beside himself."

Madison sat down too and scooted a little closer, so their arms touched. She smiled as she watched Theo take pictures. "Have you ever seen this before?"

"Once, a long time ago. It wasn't as widespread as this, though. As you probably know, it's not uncommon along the coast here. There have been sightings in the past years, but I never took the effort to drive out at night. I should have, seeing Theo so excited, now. It's incredible."

"It's perfect." Madison missed the contact of Ally's hand already and now that she knew Ally wanted to hold her hand too, she was tempted to enfold it once again. Just as she reached out, Theo came walking back to them.

"Why is it called red tide when it's blue?" Ally asked. "Or is that a silly question?"

"No questions are silly. How about you answer that, Theo?" Madison looked up at him.

Theo was still holding up the phone, snapping away. "It's because the dinoflagellates produce toxins that make the water look red during the day. When their conditions are right, they multiply like crazy and so you get a big red strip when it's light but in the dark, like now, they light up in the waves when they're moved around." He looked to Madison for confirmation.

"Spot on, buddy. I couldn't have said it better myself. Some of the toxins are poisonous though, so it's best not to go in the water when you see a red tide," she added. "But they're not always bad for humans."

"Have you seen this before?" Ally asked.

Madison shook her head. "No, I grew up in Louisiana, and even in college during the years that I visited beaches at night, I've never come across anything like this. It's not as rare as it used to be though, possibly due to climate change."

"A beautiful disaster," Ally said with a sigh. "I worry about the ocean."

"Yeah, me too." Madison blinked, almost blinded by the

flash when Theo turned the phone their way and took a picture of them. "Hey, what are you doing?"

"Nothing. I just wanted a picture of you and mom to take to LA with me."

Madison's eyes widened in surprise. "Theo, that's so sweet." In a reflex, she reached for Ally's hand, and they exchanged a smile as he took another one. She felt genuinely touched by his words, and knew she was going to miss him too.

"Why don't we take a picture of the three of us, then? If front of the bloom," Ally suggested, gently squeezing Madison's hand.

"Yes!" Theo gave Ally her phone. "You'll have to turn off the flash though, otherwise you won't be able to see the dinoflagellates." Ally and Madison laughed at the complex word that rolled off the eleven-year-old boy's tongue as if it was nothing and turned around, making space for Theo in the middle.

"I'm going to take a moment and appreciate the fact that my son still wants pictures taken with me," Ally said and chuckled as she held out the phone and took a couple of pictures of them. It was dark and blurry, but their faces were visible in front of the neon blue phenomenon that was glowing in the background.

Theo studied the picture and smiled. "I like it."

"Me too." Ally leaned into Madison as she looked up at the sky. "Oh look, there's a full moon tonight, I forgot about that. We might have to stay a little longer now, it will be even more amazing with the moonlight shining over the blue shore when the clouds clear out of the way. Are you cold Theo?"

Theo didn't answer as he was already sprinting away from them again, taking more pictures from a different angle this time. He looked so fragile, Madison thought, with his pajama pants tucked into his boots and an oversized coat covering his skinny frame. "I think Theo is fine. Are you cold?"

Ally shook her head, then laughed when she realized she was shivering. "A little."

"Good thing I packed this, then." Madison opened the backpack she'd brought and took out a fleece blanket. She wrapped it around both of them and pulled Ally in closer. Ally rested her head on her shoulder in return and let out a contented sigh. Neither of them said anything as they watched Theo from a distance, but Madison could feel Ally's breath quickening and her own pulse raced at their closeness. The evening was bewitching, and as the sky turned darker, the moon took center stage, its imposing presence lighting up the sand. The beach looked like it was covered in tiny diamonds, and the horizon behind the blue glow was glistening too. She was so aware of Ally's body against hers, so aware of every breath she took.

Ally snuggled closer. "Is it weird if I say this is incredibly romantic and special?"

"No, I think it's romantic too." Madison hesitated. "I'm not sure if I should tell you this but I feel incredibly attracted to you." She felt Ally tense up at her words and she was afraid she'd scared her.

"You are?" Ally asked in a whisper.

"Yeah." Madison lowered her voice too. "Very much. And maybe I imagined it, but I get the feeling it's not entirely one-sided." When she turned to look at Ally, she knew she'd been right. Their eye contact was electric, the energy between them shifting to an entrancing pull. Arousal coursed through her, and she took in a quick breath when Ally put a hand on her thigh.

"You didn't imagine anything," she whispered. "I really, really want to kiss you." Her hungry eyes dropped to Madison's lips and she licked her own in an unconscious gesture, tilting her head slightly.

"I want to kiss you too." Madison felt Ally's breath on her mouth, her body heat under the blanket and the simmering chemistry that made it impossible to resist her anymore. She craved her like nothing she'd ever craved before and needed to feel her so badly that her body ached. She leaned in, lightly brushed her lips over Ally's and let out a soft moan. Ally moaned too, as she shivered against her. They were both aware of Theo in the distance and knew they couldn't take it any further. *Not now.* It would be so easy to part her lips and claim her mouth, Madison thought. To take Ally's face in her hands and kiss her like she'd never been kissed. She wanted to push her back in the sand and make love to her right there, in front of the dazzling blue spectacle. Fantasies of Ally's naked body, glistening in the moonlight took over her mind but they were ripped out of their moment when Ally heard Theo calling her name.

"Fuck." Ally moved back, looking flustered, her breathing ragged and fast. "We can't do this right now," she whispered, squeezing Madison's thigh before turning her attention to Theo. "Yes, honey?"

"You have to come and see this from up close. The sand lights up when I step on it!"

"Really? Well, I'd love to see that. Let's have a look." Ally slid the blanket off her shoulders and stood up.

Madison walked to the shore with them but didn't take Ally's hand this time. They would have to be very careful with Theo around and their near kiss had given her a wake-up call. She laughed when Theo raced ahead and started running back and forth over the wet, algae-covered sand.

Each time he put his weight down, the sand around his boot lit up, the light spreading around him like an electric field. The footprints behind him were still illuminated too, creating a path of neon glow. She took a couple of pictures and a video of him, thinking he would probably want to use it for one of his school projects, and when she looked over her shoulder, a field of sparkling blue crystals had appeared where they'd walked.

"Here, use this to write your name," she said, handing him a piece of driftwood. She filmed him while he did and felt happy to see the big grin plastered over his face when his name lit up the sand.

Ally scooped up some of the sand in her hands and watched it come to life, glowing when she opened and closed her fists. "It's like magic... So mesmerizing."

"Yeah, it is. Make sure to wash your hands when you get home, just in case," Madison said. She turned to Theo, who had written her name in the sand now. "I have a couple of test tubes in my rucksack if you want to take some of the algae water and sand home to study under your microscope. There are some gloves in there too." She was glad she'd come prepared as she watched him sprint toward her backpack and blanket like an animated puppy.

"You're amazing. Thank you for being so good with him," Ally said in a soft voice. They were facing the ocean, watching the water sparkle as the waves crashed against a couple of lonely rocks behind the blue shoreline. The back of their hands brushed between them; their touch more electric than all the footsteps in the sand combined.

"I can ask Ana to have Theo over for a night," Ally said then, lifting her head to meet Madison's eyes. There was no doubt as to what she meant by that and Madison could only nod. "He loves staying at his grandma's house."

Madison bit her lip as she lowered her gaze to Ally's mouth again. "Okay." For some reason, she couldn't think of anything else to say, because she apparently had a one-track mind now.

"Maybe you could come over for dinner?" Ally continued, giving her a flirty smile.

"Dinner would be nice." Madison put her arm around Ally's waist, figuring Theo would see it for an innocent gesture between two friends. "Will you have dessert too?"

"I was especially thinking of dessert, actually. All kinds." Ally chuckled. "It's been a while since I've had dessert."

"Nice. Desserts are my favorite. I like to take my time with them." Madison continued to tease, grateful that Ally wasn't able to see her blush in the dark. She looked angelic in the dim light, with the glow of the moon reflected in her dark eyes, her bottom lip glistening, so sensual and inviting... She looked as aroused as Madison felt, and the idea that they'd be alone soon was almost too much to handle. They heard footsteps behind them, and Ally turned back to face the shore, taking deep breaths as she pulled herself together.

"Is Friday good for you?" she asked, smiling at Theo who was carefully scooping sand into one of the test tubes.

"Friday is perfect." Madison gave Ally's waist a squeeze before she stepped away. She wasn't sure what was happening between them and she had no idea how Ally really felt other than that she wanted her, physically. Either way, she knew she would never say no to Ally. At the worst, it would be a beautiful disaster.

24

"Thank you for carrying him upstairs again," Ally said. Theo had fallen into a deep sleep in the back of the truck and Madison had lifted him out and put him in bed, placing his test tubes on the nightstand next to him. "And thank you for a great night."

"The pleasure was all mine." Madison turned at the door and for the second time, they found themselves lingering in the hallway. But tonight was different because Ally knew that Madison wanted her too. Their conversation at the beach had changed everything; in a good or a bad way was yet to be determined, but now was not the time to over-think things. It had set something alight, fueled a need that was growing by the second and suddenly, Friday seemed like lightyears away. She wanted Madison and she wasn't willing to wait. Ally's pulse quickened when Madison slowly licked her lips, and she took a step closer. The need to be near her overshadowed any fears or doubts she felt, and the fiery look that passed between them was enough to make her breath hitch. When Madison noticed her reaction, she closed the distance between them, pushing Ally up against the wall.

"What do you want?" she whispered, her mouth almost on Ally's.

Ally felt Madison's chest against her own, heaving up and down fast. Her eyes were so full of desire that Ally had to swallow hard before she was even able to answer because Madison made her feels things she hadn't felt in years. Here was this young woman who had come into her life without warning and swept her off her feet. Their chemistry was undeniable, but she had no idea when or where it had started. All she knew was that it was impossible to fight, and for once, she just wanted to enjoy the ride, do whatever the hell felt right without overthinking things or worrying about the consequences. "I want you to kiss me," she finally whispered back through quick breaths. "I need you to kiss me, Madison."

Within a split second of uttering the words, Madison cupped her neck and pressed her lips hard against Ally's. Ally froze for a beat as her body went into high alert, all her nerves bundling into a raging ball of fire deep in her core. The physical impact of the kiss was so unexpected that she forgot to breathe as she laced her hands into Madison's hair, pulling her closer. The need she felt, the want, was like nothing she'd ever experienced and everything around her faded into a blur. Theo sleeping upstairs, the noise from the bar, the fact that she was kissing a woman... Madison parted her lips and their tongues met in a wild dance, making them both moan and sink into each other's embrace. There was no tenderness, no careful exploring. Just pure lust running through their veins.

Needing more, Ally ran her hands down Madison's back and slipped them underneath her T-shirt, raking her hands over her back like she'd been dying to do all night. She'd fantasized about this, but the reality was so much better than her dreams. Madison's lithe body leaning into her own, the heat from her skin under her fingers, the way Madison kissed her with such urgency that Ally's knees started to give way underneath her.

When Madison reached under her dress and cupped her ass with both hands, Ally bucked and moaned louder. Encouraged by her need, Madison squeezed her cheeks hard as she pulled Ally's hips tighter against hers and wedged a thigh between her legs, putting pressure against her throbbing center. The simple act was so possessive and sexy that Ally thought she might climax there and then. Marcos had always been patient and tender when they made love; he had never taken control like this, and she realized she loved it. She wanted Madison to ravage her, to do whatever she wanted with her.

Pulling out of the kiss to catch her breath, she whispered: "I want you." Her heart was beating out of her chest and her body was on fire. She was so turned on that she could barely think straight, the delicious ache between her legs dominating her mind. When she looked up to meet Madison's eyes, Madison took a step back and shook her head as if waking up from a trance. She ran a finger along her lips, her gaze wildly confused as she steadied herself against the door. Then she slipped her hands into the back pockets of her jeans, restraining herself from reaching out again.

"Jesus, Ally. I want you too. Like you have no idea, but..." She nodded toward the stairs and lowered her voice. "Theo is sleeping up there and I'm not sure if this is the right time. What if he hears us?"

The word 'Theo' woke Ally up too, then. "Damn it.

You're right." She tried to calm herself down, but it seemed impossible as she was trembling all over, her body screaming out for Madison. "You're right," she said again, then straightened herself and ran a hand through her hair. "I'm supposed to be the responsible one here, I guess I got carried away."

"Me too." Madison shifted on the spot, reaching for the doorknob. "I should go, or this will get out of hand because believe me, I want you so badly that I can hardly keep away from you. But it's not a good idea for Theo to wake up and find you in the hallway making out with your neighbor..."

"I know," Ally said, the reality of what they were doing finally sinking in. "Go." Scared of what she might do if she came closer again, she remained where she was, leaning against the wall as Madison opened the door. "So, I'll see you Friday?"

"Yeah. I'm looking forward to Friday." Madison was about to leave, then changed her mind and walked back to Ally. She gave her a flirty smile, ran her fingers through Ally's hair, kissed her hard and reached for her ass again, but this time her hand crept inside Ally's panties, leaving her squirming in her grip. Pushing herself up against her, she deepened the kiss. Her hand travelled from Ally's ass over her hips, up to her waist, hiking up Ally's dress, then she stopped and pulled away abruptly. "Sorry, couldn't help myself." She turned and walked out of the door, leaving Ally breathless in the hallway.

F*uck*. Ally let out a sigh and sank down onto the floor. She traced her hips and her waist, where Madison's hands had been only moments ago and shivered, closing her eyes as she tried to keep every detail of the kiss alive.

Madison's lips, so soft against hers. She'd forgotten how good it felt to kiss a woman, how it flared up this boiling, raging lust inside her that could only be satisfied with one thing: more. Her tongue, her breath, her voice; raspy and sultry, her arousal seeping through it. Her touch that melted her from the inside out, the way she'd held her; not sweet and gentle but all-consuming and possessive, fueled by a feverish need. She'd never been kissed like that. Ally was still buzzing, her hands and knees shaking as she leaned back against the wall and stared into nothing. She hadn't expected this; what their intimacy would do to her, physically. A thrilling glow settled in her core, longing, lust, yearning tugging at her. A couple of deep breaths helped steady her violently beating heart, but she knew nothing could stop the ticking time bomb that was her raging desire. Madison had pressed the button, set in motion what was sure to be a roller-coaster of sleepless nights, steamy fantasies and physical cravings, and it wouldn't subside until she gave into it. She stretched her legs out in front of her and slouched further down, knowing she'd be here for a while as she recovered. Friday couldn't come soon enough.

25

"Thank you for starting at four." Ally shot Devon a grateful look as she took off her apron and made herself a coffee to take home. Frankly, she'd rather have something stronger, her nerves crying out for a stiff drink. But it was a little early in the day for alcohol and she wanted to keep a clear head before her dinner with Madison.

"Hey, you're the boss; I just rock up when you ask me to."

"Well, it's raining, so hopefully it will stay quiet tonight. I won't be available, but if it does get busy, just ask one of the regulars to help out and offer them free drinks in return. We're not supposed to, but it won't hurt just this once."

"I'm sure I'll be fine," Devon reassured her. "What are you doing tonight?"

Ally didn't dare look him in the eyes and poured the coffee extra slow, concentrating on filling it up right to the brim. "Just dinner."

"Just dinner... with who?" Devon poked her in the ribs, teasing a grin out of her. "Is it Madison?" Ally shook her head and tried to keep a straight face. "Yes, it is," he continued. "I knew it. Look at you, all giddy and excited."

"Shut up and stop being so nosey."

"Who's looking after Theo while you're getting it on with the hot girl next door?"

"Ana," Ally said, then rolled her eyes, realizing she'd given herself away. She really wasn't thinking today, but Devon was right; her face spoke for itself and there was no point denying her plans. "But she doesn't know I'm seeing Madison," she quickly added. "I told her I was going on a date, so whatever you do, don't tell anyone, okay?" Ally had known Ana would welcome the excuse of a date with open arms, as she wanted her to move on with her life more than anything. And it kind of was a date; she *was* having Madison over for dinner, after all. Whatever they did after dinner was private, and Ana didn't need to know everything, especially when it came to Ally's sex-life, or rather the lack of one. *Until tonight.* She shivered at that thought as a rush of arousal spread out from her center. It was all she could think of now and although she knew it was probably a bad idea, she wanted it more than her rational brain could talk her out of. "Seriously, this stays between us."

"My lips are sealed." Devon pretended to zip his mouth closed and looked her up and down. "What are you wearing? Do you want to borrow my checked shirt? It's still dirty from the last time you wore it and it might even be a bit creased if you're lucky."

Ally laughed. "No, I think I'll be fine without your shirt tonight. I'm not wearing anything special; she's just coming over for dinner at my place." That was a lie, of course. Ally had done little else than think about what she was going to wear, and she'd even driven to the department store to buy new lingerie yesterday. A delicate champagne colored set with laced edges. It had cost more than she'd spent on herself in a long time but the way it made her feel when she'd tried it on in the dressing room was worth every penny.

"Nothing special or nothing at all?" Now it was Devon's turn to laugh at his own joke. "So... do you think there's a chance of a little action?" He wiggled his eyebrows. "A kiss, maybe? Because Madison clearly likes you too. She was here last Friday, and she seemed terribly disappointed that you'd already left for LA."

"Oh God. You didn't say anything, did you?" Ally's eyes widened in horror.

"Of course I didn't. I may love to tease you, but I still have integrity." Devon smirked. "At least some." He put on his apron and stuck a notepad in the pocket, then started making coffee for himself when Ally moved out of the way.

Ally looked around to make sure there were no customers nearby, then shot him a smug look. "Actually, we've already kissed." Normally, she wouldn't be so open with Devon, but he knew how she felt, and she simply loved saying it out loud because it was the most exhilarating thing that had happened to her in a long time.

Devon's mouth fell open as he stared at her. "You did not!"

"Uhuh." Ally couldn't stop smiling now. "And yes, I know she likes me too. At least in the physical sense. I don't think she's after a relationship of any kind, especially not with someone who's seventeen years older and comes with a kid, but I don't want that either. I figured I need some action in my life and this is what I want right now. Nice and simple."

"Nice and simple my ass," Devon repeated as he arched

a brow. "Trust you to pick your tenant who will be living next door for at least another five months to have 'nice and simple' with. But you know what? I'm happy for you. You always put others first and it's about time you started thinking of yourself. Live a little."

"Yeah, I think so too." Ally sensed an underlying worry in Devon's tone. "Hey, I know the tenant thing isn't ideal, and neither is the age-difference or the fact that I have a son. But we're friends first, and we're both adults; we can talk about it." She pointed an accusing finger at him. "And don't you dare make an ageist joke. She's mature for her age, we can handle this."

"I know; I didn't mean it like that." He pulled her in for a hug and placed a kiss on her forehead. "It's really good to see you like this, Al. So... I don't know..." He paused. "Cute? Vulnerable? It's endearing that you're totally out of control."

"I'm so not out of control." Ally gave him a slap on his chest and picked up her coffee cup. "I'm going. Good luck tonight." She walked out of *Western Shores*, aware that she was in fact, completely out of control. Since Tuesday night, her life had been in turbulence. She'd been even worse at work, forgetting just about everything, from basic things like ordering coffee beans to buying toilet paper. Thankfully, she had Devon and thankfully, it had only been three days since she'd last seen Madison, because time had crept by at a snail's pace and she wasn't sure if she could wait any longer. The terrace outside was quiet and she was grateful for the rain, leaving the bar near-empty for now. It smelled incredible every time it rained, as if the ground had some magical element to it that came alive when wet. It smelled fresh and earthy, rather than salty, the vegetation on the hills around Capitola village breathing in relief. It hadn't rained in a while, but Ally could see from the dark clouds on the horizon that it wasn't over yet. A storm was brewing, and it might get pretty spectacular tonight. She smiled to herself as she opened her front door. But then again, there were more spectacular things about to happen, and the storm was the last thing on her mind.

26

"Come in, you're going to get wet." Ally opened the door wide and quickly closed it again when rain started pouring in. The weather had taken a turn for the worse, with strong winds and showers leaving the beach deserted. "At least Devon will have an easy night."

"He will. No one in their right mind will go outside tonight, believe me." Madison pushed past her in the narrow hallway, all too aware of their physical closeness. Should she have kissed her? Hugged her? Suddenly, everything that had seemed so natural before was now immensely complicated and she found herself overthinking everything she did. Catching a whiff of Ally's perfume, a flutter ran through her core, and a flashback of their heated kiss started attacking her mind as if she had no control over it. *Breathe, Madison.* She'd tried not to think of the kiss in the past days, to put her job first, but that had proven hard. Now that they were in the same room again, the chemistry between them sizzled, and she allowed herself to indulge in Ally's subtle curves under her thin strap dress, her bare feet, legs and shoulders on display. "It smells amazing in here."

"Great. I hope it tastes good." Ally pulled her hair behind her ears and gave her a quick smile as she walked back into the open kitchen and focused on the food she was preparing. "It's nice to see you again," she said without taking her eyes off the cutting board. Madison could tell she wasn't the only one who was nervous, and that put her a little more at ease.

"You look amazing," she said, coming up behind Ally. She put her arms around her waist and felt the muscles in Ally's abdomen tense as her breath quickened.

"Thank you. So do you."

Madison knew Ally was just as turned on as she was, and if it had been anyone else, she would have slammed her against the counter and kissed her hard. She would have lifted her dress and made her come over and over, right there in the kitchen. Not that she'd been very subtle in the hallway the other night; she'd been so hungry for Ally that she hadn't been able to hold back. But tonight, she wanted it to be special, and so instead she kissed her softly on the cheek and stepped back, leaving Ally breathless, steadying herself against the counter. Anticipation was the best fore-play, and Madison wanted her to be so ready that by the time she held her in her arms she would melt into a feverish puddle.

She walked around, taking in the interior of the blue house. Although she'd been here a couple of times, she hadn't gone farther than Theo's bedroom and the hallway. Ally's house was cozy, and not much different from the pink house in layout, just a little wider and with the extra tower, where Theo slept. A soft yellow throw covered the corner couch that stood on an Aztec-looking rug and there was an impressive collection of cacti; some big in pots on the floor and some smaller on the sideboard against the side wall.

There were lots of photographs on the walls, of Ally and Theo, Ally and Marcos's wedding, and a couple of them as a family when Theo was still young.

"Your husband was a handsome man," she said, studying the wedding photo. The Latin American man was tall and well-built, his face open and friendly. He had a protective arm around Ally, who looked incredibly happy, dressed in an off-the-shoulder white wedding dress, her hair adorned with little white flowers.

"Yeah, he was." Ally composed herself, grabbed a bottle of white wine from the fridge and took two glasses out of the kitchen cabinet. "We were so in love. Initially, I took the photographs off the wall after he died. I couldn't bear to look at them, but as Theo grew older, he started asking questions and he wanted to see pictures, so I put them back. I like having them there now. It makes me feel he's still here somehow."

Madison followed her with her eyes as she poured the wine and put the glasses down on the breakfast bar. There was no dining table as the small space didn't allow for that, but the bar was the perfect place to sit down and talk while Ally was busying herself with the food. She looked incredibly cute in a yellow and white polka dot summer dress, and the toenails of her bare feet were painted a soft pink. Ally was one of those women who never tried hard. She was just her stunning self, with a minimum of make-up and nothing contrived in the way she dressed. She noticed Ally's hand was trembling as she took a sip of her wine. It was only to be expected as she may have been the first woman Ally had ever kissed, and she didn't think there had been many men after Theo's father either. She was shaky herself just from the light kiss and the sensation of brushing up against her cheek.

"Do you want me to set up on the bar?" Madison asked, noting she was being unhelpful. She got up and took the two bamboo placemats sitting on the counter, then searched for cutlery in the drawer without waiting for an answer. "These okay?"

Ally turned around and they were suddenly face to face in the small kitchen.

"Yeah. Those are fine," she said, her eyes hazy and full of need as she glanced at Madison before turning back to the pan.

Madison stood there for a moment, so thrown off her game by how Ally had just looked at her that she forgot what she was doing. This woman was making her crazy in all the best ways. She took a deep breath and put their plates and the cutlery on the bar. "Want me to light these?" She pointed to the three candles in the holders.

"Sure, I like having them on at night." Ally added boiling water to couscous in a bowl and used a fork to fluff it up. "The food is pretty simple, but I figured you'd want something fresh rather than your usual microwave meals." She drizzled sea salt and olive oil over a salad and finished pan-frying two marinated salmon steaks.

"How do you know about the microwave meals?" Madison asked, impressed by how fast and efficient Ally was.

"I saw you come home with a pile from the grocery store." Ally shot her an apologetic glance. "I promise you I'm not a stalker, it's just that I can see everything from my window and..." Her voice trailed off as she focused on plating the food.

"Hey it's fine, no need to explain. I forgot my shopping bag and I don't like to use plastic ones. Not that the microwave meals are much better; but I found some with biodegradable packaging." Madison paused. "And yes, this really is a nice change, so thank you. I don't bother to cook when it's just me, I don't see the point."

"I get that." Ally put their plates on the bar and sat down next to her. "Well, you're always welcome to have dinner with me and Theo." She smiled, but Madison could tell there was something she needed to get off her chest. Despite the unmistakable pull between them, Ally seemed hesitant, like her mind was constantly turning something over in her head, anxious to offload what was troubling her.

Madison leaned in and tilted her head to one side. "Ally, why don't you just tell me what's bothering you? If you've changed your mind, it's fine."

"No, it's not that." Ally swallowed hard, arousal flaring up in her eyes again. "I think you know it's not that." She took a small bite of her salmon and chewed slowly while she thought about what to say. "I think we need to be clear that whatever happens between us needs to stay casual."

"Hmm..." Madison licked her lips and smiled, trying to put her at ease. "I can do casual. Want to elaborate?"

"Well... what bothers me is not so much the fact that you're a woman, although admittedly, it's a little out there for me. It's that we're both at entirely different stages in our lives. I have a child and we..." Ally waved a finger between herself and Madison. "We're almost a generation apart, so I'd say that all in all, this is a pretty bad idea. Also... my body is not like yours. I'm older and..."

"Hey, don't say that," Madison interrupted her. "All the other stuff; fair enough and you might have a point there, although I disagree myself... But you're gorgeous, Ally. I love looking at your body."

"I might still look fine to you now, but what about in ten years' time?" Ally shook her head then and gave a self-mocking smile. "Sorry, I'm getting way ahead of myself here, this is ridiculous. I guess what I'm trying to say, is that this can't be anything more than sex, because it would never work long-term."

Madison nodded. She wasn't sure if she agreed, but the word 'sex' coming from Ally's mouth was enough to set her on fire and she knew then that she'd go along with anything Ally wanted. "I get that you have to think that way. You have Theo, and so it's only natural that you're likely to think things through more than people without kids. And yes, it would probably be confusing for him, especially now, with so much change going on for him already." She paused. "So yes, casual is good, and Theo won't find out from me, I promise."

"You're fine with it?" Ally narrowed her eyes. "You told me you were sick of being used by straight women and it seems to me that that's exactly what I'm doing so..."

"I know I said that," Madison interrupted her. "And that's another reason to keep it casual. At least we both know where we stand." She knew deep down that she probably felt more, but nothing was going to stand in her way of a night with Ally, and that included her feelings. Surely, she'd be able to compartmentalize how she felt if she tried? Set it aside and deal with it later? She shot Ally a teasing look. "Although I'm not convinced that you're entirely straight."

"No, me either." Ally's eyes darkened as they locked with Madison's. "That kiss... It seriously messed me up and even just sitting here next to you is doing things to my body I didn't know I could feel. So no, I'm definitely not entirely straight. I've..." She hesitated. "I've been with a woman before, a long time ago."

"You have?" Madison grinned. "Let me guess... in college?"

Ally sighed and buried her face in her hands. "Yeah, I know it's such a cliché. I was one of those girls. Her name was Abigail and when I met Marcos, I forgot all about her. It was only one night, but I've felt a little guilty over it lately."

"I'm sure she got over it." Madison placed a hand on Ally's thigh and saw her take in a quick breath as she tensed up. Knowing her touch had such an effect on Ally caused a twitch between her legs.

"Yeah. I'm sure she did." Ally paused. "I'm glad we talked about this, I needed to get it off my chest." The electrifying tension between them was now growing to alarming proportions and Madison was desperate to pull her in and kiss her. Ally's glistening lips were parted, her dark eyes hazy and she was breathing fast, looking incredibly aroused. She licked her lips in an unconscious gesture, and Madison knew that they were in for a long night.

"Dessert?" Ally asked then, suddenly getting up from her barstool. "I'm not really hungry and by the looks of it, neither are you."

"I'm sorry." Madison gave her an apologetic look. "It's really delicious but I have trouble eating when..." Her voice trailed away.

"I know. Me too. However, I seem to recall you saying that desserts were your favorite thing and that you liked to take your time with them." Ally cleared their plates and walked over to the kitchen, looking like she needed some breathing space.

Madison followed her with her eyes. "I can always find room for something sweet. Can I help?"

"No, you just go and make yourself comfortable on the couch. I'll bring it over."

27

Ally put their plates in the sink and opened a box containing two slices of chocolate cake she'd brought over from the bar. When she looked over her shoulder, she saw Madison refilling their wine glasses. Barely able to contain her feelings of excitement and the arousal that was making her weak in every limb, she placed each slice on a small plate and added forks before walking back into the living area on shaky legs. Why hadn't Madison kissed her properly yet? She was worried she'd interrupted their flow by starting a serious conversation but then again, she was also glad she'd brought it up.

"Do you like chocolate?" She asked.

A small smile grew on Madison's lips. "I do. Are you sure you want to have dessert with me?"

"Never been more sure of anything," Ally said in a near whisper. When she handed Madison the cake and sat down next to her, Madison took her legs and lifted them onto her lap. It was enough to make her squirm, and she almost dropped the cake as Madison placed a warm hand on her bare calf. Her heart started racing, any uncertainty melting away. In need of something to focus on, she took a bite of her cake, not hungry in the slightest or even feeling like eating cake right now.

"So, you know when you asked me how I chat up girls?" Madison said in a flirty tone.

"Uhuh." Ally looked into her eyes and despite her nerves, couldn't help but smile. "I experienced you in action on the beach; I was impressed. Got any more of those moves you'd like to show me?"

Madison grinned. "Well, it just so happens that you have some chocolate on your lip."

"Do I?" Ally held her breath when Madison leaned in, took her face in her hands and slowly licked the tiny traces of chocolate from her bottom lip. The touch of her tongue made her moan, her hips shifting restlessly on the couch as she felt herself getting wet. She loved how Madison took control, flirted with her, made her feel desired and sexy.

"There, that's better." Madison licked her own lips as she put her cake down on the coffee table, her mouth still close to Ally's.

Ally's insides were doing somersaults and she felt dizzy from the move that was so incredibly erotic that her whole body was screaming out for more. "Are you sure there's nothing left?" she asked, putting her cake down on the table too.

Madison looked down at her lips again, her breathing heavy against Ally's mouth. "Actually, now that you mention it..." She inched closer again and repeated the motion until Ally gasped, parting her lips. The kiss that followed was sensual and sexy, slow and deep. Madison's soft lips felt amazing, and the overwhelming sensations that stirred in her core made her ache between her thighs. They both let out a soft moan as their lips melted together, their tongues engaging in a passionate dance.

Ally laced her fingers through Madison's hair and pulled her on top of her. Feeling her weight and the heat of their kiss was like nothing she could have prepared herself for, and when Madison shifted her thigh between her legs, Ally thought she might explode.

"Fuck." Her breath hitched when Madison moved her mouth to her neck, kissing and sucking at her sensitive flesh. "That feels so good." Hiking up Madison's T-shirt, she slipped her hands underneath the fabric to rake them over the warm skin of her back.

Madison's breath was against her ear, fast and ragged. "Do you want me to stop?"

"No, God no!" Closing her eyes, Ally gave into all the delicious sensations she felt everywhere. Her body was on fire, and she wanted more. So much more.

Madison lifted her head to look at her and moved a hand under Ally's dress, running it up the outside of her thigh, teasingly slow. For a fleeting second, Ally became highly aware of the fact that she was being intimate with a woman again. The way Madison smelled, her softness, her touch, her hair that felt so silky when she ran her hands through it... Yes, it was different, but different in the best of ways. Ally shifted her hips to give her better access and met Madison's eyes that studied her every reaction as she continued up along her waist, toward her breasts. Her lips were parted, pulling into an almost invisible smile each time Ally reacted with soft gasps and moans. She realized Madison loved watching her then, and that turned her on ever more. The warm hand skimmed the bottom edge of her bra and disappeared underneath, Madison's exploring fingers finding her hard nipple.

"Oh God, that's..." Ally didn't get to finish the sentence as Madison's mouth took hers in a deep kiss that erased every last bit of brainpower and left her with nothing but her senses. It was so right, so perfect, so earth-shatteringly good. Every part of her body craved the woman who was now strumming her thumb along her nipple and kissing her like they were the last two people left on earth.

"I told you I like to take my time with dessert," Madison said in a low and teasing tone when she pulled out of the kiss to give Ally time to catch her breath. "I take my dessert eating very seriously."

"I can tell," Ally whispered, struggling to get words out. "I like it. A lot."

"Then maybe you'd like to continue this in the bedroom? I think I need more space for what I'm planning on doing to you."

Ally felt a pool of desire settle between her legs, and she was almost certain Madison knew it. "Yeah. Bedroom sounds good." She waited for Madison to get up and took her hand when she held it out.

"You're trembling." Madison gently stroked her hand. "Are you sure you're okay?"

"Believe me, I'm trembling for all the right reasons." Ally walked ahead of Madison, leading them back through the hallway and into her bedroom.

"It's nice," Madison said, looking at Ally's bed more than anything. The walls were painted a light gray, the wooden floor white-washed, and long, dark curtains framed the window. Ally's new bedlinen, that she'd also bought with tonight in mind, was white with a thin gray stripe woven through, the few personal touches such as candles and towels matching the colors in the simple room with only the big bed, an antique desk and a white-washed closet making up the furniture. She smiled when Ally closed the curtains and turned on the string of colored lights hanging over the curtain rails. "Very cute, just like you."

Ally blushed when Madison walked up to her. She knew she was too old for colored lights in her room, but she liked the cozy glow they gave off and had decided to leave them there after the previous Christmas.

"Thank you." The hairs on her arms rose when Madison fingered the cotton fabric of her dress.

"Can I take this off?"

"Please." Ally felt her chest rise and fall quickly, her pulse racing. Her heart was beating so fast that she could feel it everywhere, and when Madison reached for the hem, slowly lifting it, she let out the breath she'd been holding, deciding this was it. *No turning back now.* She raised her arms, allowing Madison to take it off.

Madison's lips parted as she took Ally in. Her champagne colored lingerie set, bordered with lace against her tanned skin, her slender frame, her small breasts, the curve of her waistline and her hips... "You're so, so beautiful."

Ally shook her head. "I'm forty and I've had a child. I'm..."

"Stop." Madison lifted Ally's chin, making her look up at her. "You're beautiful, Ally."

"Thank you," Ally said hesitantly before letting out a faint sigh. "So are you. You're stunning. Not just now... I thought that the first time I saw you." She slipped her fingers under Madison's T-shirt, marveling at the soft, warm skin and the tight abs against her hands. Touching Madison felt even better than she'd imagined and despite her nerves that were back tenfold now, she wanted all of her. Tracing her waistline, she moved her hands up to her breasts. When she skimmed her fingers over Madison's bra, feeling her nipples harden, her breath hitched, and a flash of arousal shot to her center, making her clit twitch. "I want you," she whispered, slowly taking off Madison's T-shirt. She shivered at the sight of Madison's toned arms and full breasts, covered by a simple black bra. Ally had seen her in a bikini but being here together in her bedroom was something else entirely. She could smell her, feel her heat, sense her need.

Madison ran her hands through Ally's hair and down her neck to her shoulders, hooking her fingers under her bra straps. "Can this come off too?"

Ally nodded and closed her eyes as Madison slid the straps off her shoulders, then reached around her to unhook her bra. She heard a soft gasp as it dropped to the floor, the sound of Madison's desire giving her a push of confidence to take her bra off in return. Ally stared at Madison's breasts, taking in their fullness, the goose bumps on her flesh, the hard, pink pebbles that she was dying to touch. Madison seemed entranced by her near-naked body too, biting her lip as she inched closer to kiss her. The moment they came together was the moment Ally knew that this was what she'd been craving ever since that first time with a woman in college. It had always been good with Marcos, and she'd loved him so much that the sex hadn't even mattered, but Madison's skin on hers, her feminine curves and her soft moans took intimacy to a whole new level, flaring up her most private fantasies that she'd ignored for years. She let Madison guide her to the bed and lay back, quivering when she took off her shorts and covered her with her warmth. She kissed her, more persistent this time, reacting to Ally, who pulled her in and wrapped her legs around her thighs.

"Touch me," Ally whispered. "I need you."

Madison looked down at her and shot her a teasing smile. "Be patient now... Trust me, it will be worth it." She shifted onto her knees and kissed her way down Ally's neck, then moved her mouth to her breasts. When her tongue twirled around one of her nipples, Ally arched her back, her chest shooting up as a throaty groan escaped her.

"Oh God, yes..." She weaved her hands through Madison's hair, and then her other breast was devoured, before Madison moved down over her ribcage and her belly. Ally was unable to lie still, almost losing it with anticipation. Warm breath on her inner thigh made her grasp the bedsheets, her hips bucking as Madison took hold of her panties and slid them down her legs. She then deftly spread Ally's legs and blew over her aching center, drawing a loud cry from her mouth. Ally's hips rose again as she felt Madison's tongue on her swollen folds. She liquified into a pool of wonderful sensations, shattering waves of pleasure hitting her one after another. Madison's tongue on her clit brought her to the brink of exploding, and she groaned when she pulled back, the loss of her touch denying her the orgasm she so badly needed. "Please don't stop."

"I'm not stopping..." Madison crawled up to meet her eyes. "I just want to see your face when you come because I've been fantasizing about it for weeks." She steadied herself on her elbow, ran a hand along Ally's cheek and moved her other hand down, slipping it between her legs.

Ally's eyes widened and she gasped when Madison carefully entered her, then added another finger, moving deeper. She could tell by the look in Madison's lust-filled eyes that she was thriving on making her feel this way. She lost all sense of her surroundings, drawn into Madison's eyes as she filled her up and started fucking her slowly, moving her body, her hips thrusting against her thigh in the same rhythm as her hand.

Ally's body moved in time with her actions, never taking

her eyes off Madison's face as the pressure in her core started to build again. Madison's fingers curling and pushing inside her caused a warm tingling to spread out and when she thrust into her once again, hitting a spot Ally didn't even know was there, her muscles started clenching around Madison's fingers and she reached for her face. Moaning loudly, she was thrown into a climax of enormous proportions, soaring into oblivion. The force of it made her body shake all over, but whatever Madison was doing to her, she didn't stop, drawing out every last bit of pleasure until Ally finally crashed underneath her.

"You look like you enjoyed that," Madison said with a satisfied smirk, placing soft kisses on Ally's forehead and temple.

"I think that's an understatement," Ally whispered through short breaths. Her eyelashes fluttered against Madison's lips as she slowly regained control of her body, and to her surprise, she felt tears trickling from the corners of her eyes. Unsure of why she was crying, she wiped them away and smiled.

"Are you okay?" Madison looked down at her and kissed another tear that rolled down.

"Yeah. I'm great, actually. I don't know why I feel so emotional though, it's..." She sniffed. "I just haven't felt this good in a really long time."

"Come here." Madison rolled off her and pulled her tightly into her arms. As Ally let her hold her and she buried her face against Madison's shoulder, she felt a little concerned because already, this didn't feel casual anymore.

. . .

Ally finally wriggled herself out of Madison's grip. She had no idea how long they'd been lying there making out in each other's arms, with the storm raging outside, but it was pretty spectacular now with regular, loud thunder clasps, followed by lightning flashing through the curtains, lighting up the room. Madison's mouth on hers was pretty spectacular too, and the sound of the wind hurling and the waves hitting the cliffs reflected her inner turbulence. A glance at the clock told her it was midnight, but she felt wide awake, arousal keeping her on high alert. Each kiss, each touch was so intense, and she loved the feel of Madison's skin against her own.

She wanted to make Madison cry out, the way she'd done to her, over and over tonight, but nerves and hesitation had kept her from touching her where she wanted to touch her most. Now that she had gotten used to the feel of her body though, being with Madison was like a drug and she wanted more. Everything had been so much simpler in college, back then she had been braver, young and carefree. That was a time when even Ally had believed that the world was at her feet and that there was nothing she couldn't do.

"You know, I may not be an expert at this," she said in a soft voice. "But I want to make you feel good too."

Madison smiled. "Just so you know, I don't expect you to be an expert at anything and I certainly don't want you to do something just because you feel you have to. We can just lie here and kiss." She arched a brow. "You're a very, very good kisser by the way."

"Thank you. So are you." Ally grinned. "You're good at many things." She rolled over, opened her nightstand drawer and took out her vibrator. "But since this is our first time, I'm going to cheat," she said, holding it up. "Ever used one before?"

Madison bit her lip as her eyes darkened. "Not in a long time."

"Then let me," Ally whispered. She crawled on top of her and straddled her, pushing her center against Madison's who immediately shifted beneath her. She could feel her heat through her panties as she leaned forward, kissing her slowly and sensually, her hips moving, grinding down on Madison. She loved the smell of Madison's hair and her skin and inhaled the scent of something floral and sweet as she trailed her lips down her neck to her breasts. For the first time, she allowed herself to really explore them, to feel them under her fingers and her tongue. They were perfect in every way, she thought, as she traced the curves on the side, then cupped them, skimming her thumbs over her rosy nipples.

Madison's reaction made her smile. The noises she made, her ragged breathing, the way she rolled her hips against her wetness... Ally loved everything about it and the need to taste her was so strong she had to force herself to slow down, because she wanted this to last. Her mouth lowered to one of her nipples, and she barely skimmed the hard bud with her tongue, teasing until Madison arched her back, begging her to take it. She parted her lips and closed her mouth around it, her tongue caressing the sensitive spot. It made her hungry for more, dying to taste every inch of her. Moving her attention to her other breast, Ally's hands started leading a life of their own, sliding up and down Madison's body, exploring her curves, caressing her. It was as if suddenly everything had fallen into place and making love to Madison was an everyday occurrence, completely natural and satisfying. She embraced the moment, slipping into a trance-like state in which she stopped thinking. She was only her body as she raised herself and rolled her hips, throwing her head back in ecstasy.

Madison moaned and took Ally's hips before moving her hands to her ass. "You have no idea how sexy you are when you move like that," she said, cupping Ally's breasts.

Knowing she was turning Madison on aroused Ally too, and she started feeling more confident, powerful even.

Madison's stomach was toned and hard under her fingers, her muscles tensing as she traced them. She moved back between Madison's legs and looked down at her black panties. It was the only piece of clothing left between them, and it needed to come off. Hooking her fingers underneath the waistband, she hesitated for a moment, then pulled them down, her breath hitching when she saw Madison's glistening wetness. Seeing her desire brought up a carnal craving to consume her, and Ally pushed her legs apart and settled between them, her lips parting as she bent forward to run her tongue over her throbbing center. Madison's aromatic juices were the sweetest, the most perfect flavor she'd ever tasted, and the arousing sensation against her tongue and her lips made her quiver. She pressed her mouth harder against her swollen sex and gave into it wholly, completely, as she grabbed her hips.

"Fuck, yes!" Madison screamed as Ally ran her tongue up and down, smiling against her sensitive skin. Ally could feel she was on fire and heard her moan when she licked her clit while taking the vibrator from the mattress. Madison cried out again, lifting her hips to meet her strokes that grew quicker. Ally's tongue trailed down, circling her entrance and when she entered her, Madison grabbed her hair and groaned in pleasure.

"Fuck Ally, that's amazing."

"Oh yeah?" Ally sounded pleased with herself as she repeated the action, taking a tighter hold of her hips, spreading her legs farther and darting her tongue inside her again.

"Fuck..." Madison clearly didn't know what to do with herself, and when Ally switched on the device and placed it on her clit, she almost shot off the bed. "Don't... stop." She could barely speak through her short breaths, frantically bucking her hips.

Holding the vibrator in place, Ally entered her with her tongue again, loving the feel of Madison's hand in her hair, pulling her closer against her. It was arousing her no end, making her squirm in pleasure and she knew she could do this forever because there was nothing more beautiful and satisfying than making a woman come.

Another loud cry sounded through the room before she felt Madison's walls contract around her tongue. She drank her in, closing her eyes as she pulled her as close as she could, her face buried between Madison's legs. It felt magical to be so incredibly intimate, to make another woman explode with delight. She kept the vibrator where it was, until Madison lay spent beneath her. Then she switched it off, tossed it on the floor and crawled back up to kiss her.

"Jesus, where did you learn that?"

"Nowhere," Ally whispered, looking up. "Just a fantasy I had."

Madison wrapped her arms and legs around her and kissed her back with so much conviction that to Ally, it felt like they were one and the same person, their limbs entangled, and their bodies and mouths locked like they were glued together. "That was amazing," she mumbled against Ally's mouth after she pulled away to catch her breath.

Ally nodded against her forehead. "Yeah, it was." She grinned. "I could do that all night long."

"Okay..." Madison smiled as she cocked her head and studied her. "So I take it you're not weirded out? Because I won't deny that crossed my mind before I came here tonight."

"Not weirded out at all. More like, obsessed now." Ally laughed. "Seriously, this is incredible. You're so soft and sexy and..." Her hand traced Madison's hip and reached for her ass. "Curvy," she finally settled on. "So feminine but also so strong."

"Well, I am a woman..." Madison's teasing smile faded, and she cupped Ally's cheek. "But I feel the same and we have all night." She lowered her voice and smiled as she whispered: "You're perfect."

Ally brushed her lips against Madison's, realizing that she hadn't felt this happy in years. "Your right, we have all night," she said as she trailed her fingers seductively down Madison's body.

28

"Mom!" Loud banging on Ally's door woke Madison up. She took a moment to gather her bearings, then shot up when she recognized Theo's voice. "Mom! Wake up!"

"Hey, Ally," she whispered, nudging her softly. "Theo's at the door."

Ally turned to her and smiled, then her eyes widened in panic when she heard her son. "Fuck. Fuck, fuck, fuck." She jumped out of bed and put on a robe. "Wait here, don't come out," she whispered, wildly waving her hands around. Then she opened the door and shouted: "Hey honey, I'll be right there."

Madison rubbed the sleep out of her eyes as she stayed in bed and listened to the muffled conversation in the hallway.

"Were you still sleeping, Mom?"

"Ehm yeah. I thought I'd have a slower start this morning since you were with grandma and I didn't expect you back yet."

"Oh…" There was a pause. "I forgot my book; I need to get it from my room. Grandma is taking me to the beach."

"I'll get it for you. Wait, Theo…"

Madison heard footsteps in the hallway and crawled under the covers, wishing she could make herself disappear. Neither she nor Ally had set an alarm after falling asleep around three in the morning. Their night had been incredible, but now she was worried it might turn into a nightmare. If Theo decided to go into the bedroom and saw her, he'd not only be confused, but probably feel betrayed too, knowing they'd been lying to him. Luckily, the footsteps continued past Ally's bedroom and up the stairs.

"Got it!" she heard him yell, before he ran back down.

When the front door opened again, Madison let out the breath she'd been holding and threw the covers off. *Thank God.*

"Good. Now you go have fun with grandma. I'll see you later." There was a long sigh after the door closed, then Ally came back in, looking flustered. "For a moment, I thought he was going to come in here. There's no reason why he would, I just panicked, I guess." She leaned against the doorpost, composing herself as she held onto her chest, then walked to the bed and let herself fall down next to Madison.

"Yeah, me too." Madison turned to her and took her in her arms. "But he didn't." She pulled Ally in closer. "How are you? I mean, after last night…"

Ally looked at her and smiled. "I'm good." She shrugged. "I feel a little weird I guess, if I'm entirely honest. Not because of the sex, but because I haven't woken up with anyone since Marcos, so it's just a little strange. But good too," she added, placing a soft kiss on Madison's temple.

"And I feel excited and..." she chuckled. "Extremely satisfied."

"Good." Madison laughed too as she pulled at the tie of Ally's robe, releasing it. "I'm not sure if the definition of 'casual' includes morning sex, but if you're willing to blur the boundaries just a little, then I think we could have a lot more fun before you start work."

"Oh yes, work..." Ally looked at the clock on her nightstand and shook her head. "It's Saturday, I'm supposed to open at eight." She shivered when Madison slid the robe off her shoulders and ran a hand over her breasts. "I have fifteen minutes," she said through ragged breaths, then moaned when Madison moved her hand between her legs.

Madison's breath hitched when she felt how wet Ally was, and rolled on top of her, desperately wanting more of what could only be described as the best sex she'd ever had. They'd given all of themselves for hours, and their bodies seemed to fit seamlessly, like they were made for each other. She knew from experience that it was rare to find something like this, something so physically perfect. There was more of course, but she didn't dare go there.

Ally took her wrist and stopped her then as she gave her a flirty smile. "Wait... let me text Devon, see if he can open up for me. I think we might need a little more than fifteen minutes."

"Okay, I really need to go now." Ally sat up in bed and ran a hand through her tousled hair. "I'm worried Theo will come back and I have to go help Devon. It gets busy on the weekends and it's almost lunchtime." She looked regretful as she turned to Madison. "Hey, I know we said this was casual but..."

"But what?" Madison felt her hopes rise at Ally's words. Ally wasn't even out of the door and she missed her closeness already. They'd made love non-stop, unable to keep their hands off of each other, and passion and arousal were still coursing through her veins like an unstoppable force. The daylight hadn't changed anything; they were still wallowing in a continuous rush. Ally looked sexy with her robe half-open as she pulled a towel out of a drawer and searched for clothes.

"Well, maybe we could do this again sometime... soon?" she bit her lip and shot Madison a cheeky grin. "If you want?"

"Yeah, I want," Madison joked back. She jumped out of bed too and gathered her clothes. "I'd like that very much. Anytime you have an evening to yourself." She winked. "I'm right next door, so just knock." Her clothes were on in no time, and she slipped into her shoes, tucking her socks in her back pocket.

Ally's smile told her that she liked that idea. "Great. To be continued, then." She paused, shifting on the spot. "I ehm... I have to take a really quick shower. Are you okay letting yourself out?"

"Sure. Go." Madison walked over to her and playfully slapped her behind, then pulled her in for one last kiss. She made sure to make it count, sneaking her hands into Ally's robe over her waist and her breasts. She wanted Ally to think about her today; to crave her until their next time. "I'm going home to have a shower too." She felt Ally's eyes on her as she let go and headed for the door.

"Good morning, Cupid." Madison jumped at Devon's voice. She'd opened the door quietly, scanning the front of the house first, but just as she closed it, Devon appeared on the terrace. "Busted," he said, lowering his voice as he walked up to her with a smirk on his face. "So, you're the reason Ally couldn't open up this morning…"

"It's not what you think." Madison gave him a strained smile as she tried to sound casual. She was painfully aware of her unwashed face and her hair that was sticking out at all angles. Her T-shirt was only half tucked into the waistband of her jeans on one side, and she hadn't bothered to tie her shoelaces since she was only going next door anyway. She also had a feeling one of her socks was hanging out of her back pocket. There was no point trying to come up with an excuse, because he'd never believe her, looking like this. Despite Devon's self-satisfied look, she felt immensely happy and proud, as if she'd just kissed the prettiest girl in school.

"Okay, whatever you say." Devon tilted his head and looked her up and down once more, shielding his eyes from the sun. "At least you'll have the shortest walk of shame in history." He laughed at his own joke, then gave her a wave. "You have a great day, Madison."

Madison shook her head and laughed too. "Thank you, you too, Devon. Ally will be right there in a few moments."

29

"Could you possibly give me any more grief for this?" Ally put the last cups and plates into the dishwasher after the lunch shift. She'd never intended for the bar to become a dining venue because the kitchen was way too small for that. Their snack menu of simple but fresh finger food had become so popular though, that it had just naturally evolved that way. It was busy, and despite her serious lack of sleep, she felt energized and was chirpy way beyond her usual demeanor.

"I'm not giving you grief; I'm just making fun of you." Devon slapped the dish towel he was holding against Ally's behind. "I haven't seen you this dreamy in... well, never actually." He grinned and quirked a brow. "So, you're officially into the ladies now, huh?"

Ally rolled her eyes as she walked back into the bar with Devon on her heel. "I'm not into anything, it's just casual." She looked over her shoulder and shot him a warning look. "And you have to promise me this goes no further, okay? I don't want Ana or Theo to know."

"You don't want Ana to know what?"

The sound of Ana's voice made Ally's skin crawl, and she looked up, coming face to face with her mother-in-law, who was standing in the doorway. "Ehm..." Her eyes shifted from Ana to Devon, then to the ceiling as if somehow magically, a reasonably sounding answer would present itself.

"Don't worry, Theo's at home getting something from his room." Ana gave her a curious look and raised herself onto one of the barstools. "So, what's the big secret?" Then she shook her head and laughed. "I'm just kidding, Ally. I don't need to know everything; you know I'm not like that. Come on, how long have we known each other... Almost twenty years?"

"I know." Ally swallowed hard. "It's nothing bad or serious, I promise."

"It's nothing bad indeed, I can tell from the way you've been glowing lately. Did you really think I hadn't noticed? I know you've met a man and that's okay. You need to move on, stop living in the past and make new memories. Marcos would have wanted that for you." Ana nodded toward the coffee machine. "Now get me a cappuccino, I'm almost passing out from caffeine withdrawal."

Ally chuckled in relief and grabbed a cup from the shelf beneath the coffee grinder. She was grateful for Ana being the way she was. Although the wonderful woman she'd grown to love so much always kept a respectable distance when it came to Theo's upbringing and never interfered in her private life, she was always available to help out with her grandson, and provided a sympathetic ear when Ally needed one. She'd been Ally's rock throughout the years, and so Ally felt like she owed her an explanation. Filling the portafilter with freshly ground coffee and locking it into the espresso machine, she gave Ana a smile and said: "Yes, I have met someone. And it's been really nice but it's nothing serious and it never will be. That's why I didn't want you or Theo to know."

"Well honey, whether it's serious or not, you look happy and that's the most important thing right now. Just look after yourself, okay? Don't get sucked in too deep in something that has no future."

"I won't," Ally said, concentrating on the milk. "You know, Theo and I talked a lot about The Seymour Institute this week. I'm going to enroll him in their eight-week summer program to see how he likes it."

"I know, he told me all about it." Ana took the cappuccino Ally handed her and smiled when she noted the foam had been poured into a perfectly shaped heart. "He seems excited about it."

"He is excited. I've rarely seen him so animated and engaged as when we were there, visiting."

"And how do you feel about it?" Ana asked.

"I'm not sure." Ally shrugged. "I'm happy for him and immensely proud of him of course, but I feel bad for putting him in a boarding school and I'm going to miss him so much that I hardly dare think about it."

"Yeah, me too." Ana's eyes glimmered with emotion. "But they'll give him a real head start in life." She took Ally's hand over the bar and stroked it. "How about the money?"

"It's very expensive. Theo's not eligible for a grant because of my properties, so I've decided to put the pink house up for sale. That way, we won't have to worry about money. I just need to find the right time to tell Madison that I might have to break her contract and that she needs to find another apartment if the sale goes through quickly. I'm not looking forward to that conversation."

"Goodness." Ana took a moment to process what Ally was saying. "I know how much you love that house and how you've been dreaming of expanding... If there was any way I could help you out financially I would, but..."

"I know you would. But it is what it is, and I count myself lucky to at least have a property to sell. I've already spoken to a realtor and she thinks it will be gone in no time, with this being a sought-after prime location."

"I have no doubt." Ana took a sip of her cappuccino. "Well, it seems like you've got it all figured out." Despite the cheerful tone in Ana's voice, Ally knew that just like her, the woman would be heartbroken when Theo left. She hadn't had an easy life, bringing up Marcos on her own while working three jobs after her husband had left them without warning. "He seems quite keen on your new tenant, by the way. He talks about her a lot."

Ally felt her cheeks flush at the mention, and she heard a chuckle coming from the kitchen, where Devon was cleaning the deep-fat fryer. "Yes, Madison is great with him, and as far as a tenant goes, I couldn't have been luckier. I told her she didn't have to hang out with him just because she lives next door, but I think she genuinely likes to. They share the same interests; Madison is a marine biologist."

"Just like Marcos, I've heard that too. Theo said she took you guys out a couple of nights ago, to see the red tide. That must have been incredible for him."

"Yeah, he loved it. I had a great time too, actually." In need of distraction, Ally poured herself a sparkling water, barely able to look Ana in the eyes.

"Sounds like you've made a new friend, I'm happy to hear that. How old is she anyway? She must be quite a bit younger than you."

Ally almost choked on her water and when she heard Devon laugh again, she decided she was going to kill him as soon as Ana left. "Twenty-three, I think. I'm not sure," she said, knowing exactly how old Madison was. She steadied herself against the bar and felt a little hopeless thinking of their age difference again. No matter how great last night and this morning had been, they would definitely have to keep it casual.

30

"Tom, you wanted to see me?"

"Yes," he said, without looking up from his laptop. "Just give me a minute." It was Friday and most of the team had gone home for the weekend. Tom – who had tagged on for the day – and Madison were the only two people left on the vessel, tying up loose ends after an already long week. Madison was just finishing downloading the data from the DTAGS they'd retrieved, when Tom had mentioned he wanted to speak to her. The meeting couldn't have come at a worse time, as she was dying to get home and spend some time with Ally and Theo.

They'd seen very little of each other this week. Madison left before *Western Shores* opened in the mornings, and when she came home, Ally was either working or indoors with Theo. She didn't want to disturb them after eight, afraid to wake him up. She'd been in the bar once, while Ally was there, but it wasn't the same, with people hanging around, listening in on their conversations.

She sat down on the bench opposite Tom and helped herself to a beer from the cooler. "Want one?" They always had some with them on Fridays, but the team generally seemed keener on getting home than staying behind for a drink.

"Absolutely." Tom closed his laptop, took the beer Madison handed him and held it up in a toast before taking a long drink. "Ah, that's better." He wiped the sweat from his brow before sitting back, stretching his long legs out in front of him. It was unusually warm for May, and Madison felt clammy too, now that they were docked.

Sipping her beer, she waited patiently for Tom to start talking, but he seemed in no hurry. Although she couldn't think of anything in particular, she was worried she'd done something wrong. Why else would Tom want to talk to her? "You usually don't come out on a Friday. Is everything okay?" she asked.

"Yes, everything is excellent, I just needed a break from my office and wanted to see how you were all doing. I'm happy with the progress we're making and I'm very pleased with your work ethic and your initial reports." He smiled. "And... I've actually got a proposal that might interest you."

"Okay..." Madison was all ears now; a serious talk of the positive kind so early on into her career was almost too good to be true. "Tell me."

"One of my colleagues, the PI on our sister study in the Bahamas, called me yesterday."

"You mean Dr. Munroe?" Madison asked. She'd been liaising with Dr. Munroe's research technician since she'd started, sharing early findings.

"Yeah. Abe. He asked me if I could spare someone from my team to help out there for two months." Tom held up a hand. "Just so we're clear, I thought of you; not because I'm unhappy with your work here, but because you're the only one on the team who's interchangeable, so to speak. It's easier for us to find a part-time freelancer to take over from you here, than it is to find someone in Bimini, so I thought it might excite you to go out there and help." He took another sip of his beer. "They started a little earlier than us and Abe's research technician will be leaving the team due to a re-scheduled operation, so you'll only be there during the last two months of the study. Meanwhile, Becks can send you through our daily data and you will continue to analyze it, alongside your work in Bimini. It's a lot, and you'll have to work long days while you're there, sometimes six days a week, but it's doable. So, what do you say Mads, are you up for an adventure?"

Madison smiled as she let it sink in. The Bahamas was an exciting prospect indeed, and the chance to be part of the study on both locations was an opportunity of a lifetime. "It sounds amazing, I'd be honored," she said. "When would I have to leave?"

"In about seven weeks, so you'll have more than enough time to prepare. You won't need to worry about living arrangements as they'll have an apartment for you." Tom seemed pleased with her enthusiasm. "After you're done, you'll slot right back into my team, of course."

"Fantastic, count me in." Madison's smile widened. "Not only would it make her work even more interesting, but she'd be working in a tropical environment and the remote posting would look great on her resume.

Tom finished his beer and stood up. "Well, I won't keep you any longer. Enjoy your weekend. I'll email you more information in the coming weeks." He started packing his things. "How's that kid you were talking about, a potential marine biologist I believe you said?"

"Theo's good. He's starting at The Seymour Institute in LA soon."

"That's very impressive. Are you and his mom dating?"

"No, we're not." Madison swung her bag over her shoulder and felt a little sting at her own answer. "Just friends." She pointed at Tom's bag. "Need some help with that?"

"No, you go, it's not heavy." Tom waved at her. "I'll let Abe know you're in."

31

"Is he sleeping?" Madison opened the door to Ally and let her in.

"Yeah. I told him I'd be here if he needed anything, but he was so tired after your skateboarding session that I don't expect him to wake up until the morning."

"Good. It was fun." Madison watched Ally's hips sway as she walked into her living room. God, she was sexy. She was wearing a cream colored loose knit sweater over a pair of blue denim shorts, one shoulder bare and showing a black bra strap. Again, Ally was barefoot; she didn't seem to bother with shoes when she wasn't working or in town, and Madison loved that about her. "I'm glad I bought that skateboard for myself. I never thought I'd actually get back on it, but I think I might be hooked all over again."

Ally laughed. "And I never thought I'd be turned on by someone on a skateboard at the age of forty. You look hot when you're doing that spinning thing, you know..." She tugged at Madison's white tank top, inching her closer as she sat down on the couch's arm rest.

"You think so?" Madison arched a brow and leaned in

closer, brushing her lips over Ally's. "Then it's a good thing we're finally, alone again," she whispered. "I've been looking forward to fucking you all week."

Ally's breath hitched at her salacious words. "Me too." She pulled the hem of Madison's top up, wanting to take it off.

"Wait." Madison grabbed her wrists and stopped her. "I really need a shower. It's been a long day and after the skate-boarding..." She tilted her head and gave her a flirty wink. "So, why don't we have one together?"

Ally's eyes widened. "Are you serious?" She pointed in the direction of the shower. "You can barely fit one person in there, let alone two."

"That's the whole point." Madison pulled her back up and slid her hands over Ally's ass as she brought her mouth to her ear. "Small space, lots of steam, soap... Nice and slip-pery as I slide my hands up the inside of your thighs..."

Ally shivered, a smile playing around her mouth as she forced her hand inside the waistband of Madison's shorts, pulling her against her hips. "It doesn't sound so bad when you say it like that. You seem to have a way with words and can be very persuasive." She let go and followed Madison to the shower while she watched her take off her clothes on the way, leaving a trail of garments behind her on the floor. Ally followed suit, ridding herself of her shorts and sweater and finally, her lingerie.

Thoughts of having Madison naked and to herself again had been distracting her all day and now that they were here, she was physically aching for her. They hadn't planned it but the moment they were face to face after Madison came home from work, was the moment they both knew they wanted each other badly. It wasn't just a casual treat anymore. It was a drug, something she needed, and she'd sprinted over as soon as Theo had fallen asleep. There had been no invite from Madison's side, no communication between them while Theo was present, just a mutual understanding to continue this crazy and delicious thing they'd started a week ago at the earliest opportunity. And here she was, already on fire, her fuse waiting to be lit.

Madison turned on the shower. "You know what the best thing is about this tiny bathroom?"

"What?" Ally's eyes darkened as she looked over Madison's body. She was so at ease with her nakedness, loose-limbed and confident and simply fascinating to watch.

"It's great for sex. All kinds of sex." Madison sat down on the closed toilet seat under the running shower, then patted her lap. "Come sit here."

Ally locked the door as Madison leaned back with her elbows on the tank, water running over her face, shoulders and breasts. Sexy didn't begin to describe her athletic yet feminine body, glistening under the running water. Ally sat down on Madison's lap and leaned back against her, her eyes fluttering when the warm water caressed her skin. Madison's hard nipples were poking into her back as she embraced Ally.

"I like the mirror," Madison said in a husky voice, referring to the mirror that was attached to the inside of the bathroom door, opposite them.

"I thought you might like it," Ally muttered, her lips parting as she watched greedy hands enclose around her breasts and thumbs skimming her nipples. Intense arousal flared up at seeing herself like that, being seduced by a woman.

"It's a shame it will be misted in no time." Madison rested her chin on Ally's shoulder and bit her lip as their eyes locked on their reflection in the mirror. "I like to watch you; you're so incredibly hot." She licked her lips as she spread her legs apart, pulling Ally's legs along with them.

Ally gasped, adrenaline coursing through her at seeing them like that. The simple act had her so turned on that the water trickling between her legs felt like a vibrator against her center, and she bucked her hips and threw her head back against Madison's shoulder, breathing fast. Their image blurred as the small space steamed up fast, only faint flesh colored silhouettes against a white background meeting her eyes now.

"I think you're going to like this," Madison whispered against her ear, then kissed her way down her neck and back up, while caressing her breasts. Her lips lingered on Ally's earlobe, biting it gently. It made her moan, and she bit again, this time drawing a cry from Ally's mouth.

Ally sensed Madison liked being in control, and she loved surrendering to her, because it made her feel beautiful and wanted.

"But first, we need some soap," Madison continued. Her voice was low and teasing as she squirted some shower gel into her hand, pushed Ally forward a little and rubbed it over her back with long and deliberately slow strokes. She took her time, making sure not to miss a single inch.

When Ally leaned back again, Madison's breasts felt slippery against her skin, each movement delightfully intimate as she rubbed herself against her, her clit twitching at the sexy sensation. "That feels so good."

"I'm not done with you yet." Madison took the bottle of shower gel and poured a generous amount over Ally's breasts, making her shiver when the cold liquid hit her warm skin. She started rubbing it over Ally's breasts and belly, moving up and down with both hands until it started foaming.

Ally let out soft whimpers as Madison's slippery fingers raked lightly over her nipples, then lower, over her belly and her thighs. By now her legs were trembling with anticipation, waiting for the skilled hands to move where she wanted them most. Her head was still resting against Madison's shoulder, her cheek against her neck. She could feel the vein pumping there, fast like her own heart. After years without real intimacy, it was overwhelming to feel so much again, to give herself to someone else and succumb to her physical needs with more abandon than ever. It was liberating, and their encounters felt like a precious gift; a spark that had fired her up, making her remember and feel things she'd forgotten about. Her body was alive again, her mind constantly consumed with arousing thoughts. And all because of Madison, who had come into her life only by chance.

A thrilling spasm ran through her when Madison's hands focused on her thighs, their movements perfectly symmetric as they brushed down to her knees and back up, then caressed her inner thighs, inching up teasingly slow. Just as she was close to Ally's burning flesh, she eased away again, massaging her thighs until Ally was squirming in her lap, begging her with quick breaths and moans. "Please," She muttered.

"Please what?" Ally could feel Madison's lips pull into a smile against her ear. She didn't wait for an answer and moved her hands inward, then finally ran her fingers through Ally's swollen and oversensitive folds.

Ally buckled in ecstasy as she cried out and reached for the back of Madison's head behind her, lacing her fingers through her wet hair. Almost delirious after the relentless teasing, she arched her back, spread her legs wider and let out a throaty moan as Madison's fingers moved to her clit. "Fuck, yes!"

"You like this?"

"I do," Ally said through ragged breaths.

"What about this?" Madison moved her hand down and entered her slowly with two fingers, pulling her tighter against her with her other arm around her waist. "Is this good?"

"Oh God..." Ally groaned at the feeling of Madison's fingers filling her up. She was so close already and she wanted it to last. Madison went deeper, then pulled out of her just a little before she started fucking her fast, the palm of her hand rubbing her clit at the same time.

"Jesus Madison..." Ally's eyes fluttered closed as she braced herself for a shattering climax, her hands fisting Madison's hair. Sensations of the best kind took over her body and she bucked her hips, crying out as she lost herself.

Madison held her and kissed her temple while she finally fell into a state of blissful relaxation. The soothing warm water, Madison's touch and the tender sensation of her lips drew a sigh from deep within her. "You're amazing," she whispered, and took another moment before she stood up and turned around, then straddled Madison. She wrapped her arms around her neck and kissed her, slowly at first, then hungrily. Madison moaned, rolling her hips, and Ally could feel her need coursing through her. Pulling out of the kiss, she shot her a flirty look and picked up the bottle of shower gel. "I don't know why I was so skeptical about this shower idea of yours; it's genius." She tilted her head and locked her eyes with Madison's, who looked like she was about to explode with lust. "But now it's my turn to get you clean."

32

"Good morning." Madison grinned as she saw Ally sitting on the terrace with a coffee, reading the newspaper. "You're looking very chilled. Did you sleep well?"

Ally chuckled and gave Madison an amused look. "I did. I had the most wonderful shower last night; it really relaxed me." She gestured to the towel under Madison's arm. "Are you going for a swim?"

"I am." Madison glanced at the table next to Ally, where three people were drinking coffee. She didn't know them, and she sensed from Ally's playful flirtation that she didn't either. "My muscles are a little sore, also from last night. I may have been sitting in the same position for too long, so I thought I'd get some exercise in." Ally laughed out loud now, and Madison had to use all her willpower not to walk over and kiss her. She looked perfect sitting there in her denim skirt and an off-the-shoulder white linen top under her apron; serene and happy, relaxing in the morning sun as if she had all the time in the world.

"I see you're not busy. Can I join you for a coffee after my swim?"

"Of course. It's only eight, so I don't expect anyone else just yet." Ally turned back to the beach, shielding her eyes from the sun. "The pelicans are back again. Even more this time."

Madison narrowed her eyes, then frowned in confusion at the sight of hundreds of them. She'd been so distracted by Ally that she hadn't heard the screeching noise, which was hard to miss, and she wondered how she'd slept through it. "Look at that... I've never seen so many of them, anywhere." She marveled at the sight of the big, brown birds, flapping and gliding in unison, diving into the water, then gulping up their prey on the surface. "There must be something going on, I'm going to check it out." She crossed the beach and smiled when she got closer, noticing little heads sticking out of the water, too. There were not only hundreds of pelicans, but also dozens of sea lions, seemingly feasting on the same thing. She turned around and waved Ally over, who excused herself to her customers before running up to her.

"What's up?" Ally looked surprised too, when she spotted the sea lions. "Oh my God, I didn't see them with the sun shimmering over the water. That's incredible, we never get sea lions here."

"That's what I thought. This is so cool." Madison watched them swim and play while they feasted on the phenomenal amount of small of fish that had appeared in the bay overnight. She waded in, making sure not to get too close to the sea lions. Although they were generally friendly, they were still large, unpredictable animals. "They're anchovies," she said, looking down at the silver-colored fish swimming around her legs. "I don't know how they ended up here, but they've certainly made for a feast." She pursed her lips as she waded back. "Or, the pelicans may have driven them here, into the shallow bay. They hunt in groups and often swim in a 'U' shape, flapping their wings on the water and driving the fish to where they want them. But so many fish... that's unlikely."

"Clever woman, you are." Ally winked. "I may go in myself and get some anchovies before they're all gone."

"That shouldn't be hard with the amount you've got here." Madison put an arm around her as they watched the sea lions frolic and glide through the water. She knew she was blurring the lines as this was supposed to be casual, but she just loved to be around Ally, and it was almost impossible to keep her hands to herself. Ally didn't seem to mind though, leaning into her.

"I'd better go get Theo from his bedroom. He's going to love this."

"You might want to call Devon too. Word spreads fast about a phenomenon like this and if the beach starts to fill up with people coming to see the sea lions today, then the bar will be really busy too."

"You're right." Ally took Madison's hand and squeezed it as she turned to go back. "I take it you're not going for that swim, then?" she called over her shoulder.

Madison shook her head and laughed. "I'd better not. I'll call the coast guard to come and put some signs up to prevent people from going in."

B y six pm, the storm of people had finally subsided, and Ally sat down for a break in front of the bar. There had been locals, hordes of tourists, specialists and even a couple of news channels checking out the rare occurrence. She and Devon had served drinks non-stop, and they'd just run out of food. Devon was pleased as he'd made more tips than the whole of last week combined, and Ally was happy because... well, just because she was. She watched Madison come back from the beach, with Theo running after her, carrying a bucket.

"Mom, I got you fish!" he yelled, holding it up.

Ally felt warm inside at the sight of them. Madison had planned to spend the day on the beach to watch the spectacle, and she'd offered to hang out with Theo, who was beside himself with excitement. "You got me fish?" She laughed when he handed her the bucket full of anchovies. "Thank you, honey, that's actually really useful right now. I'll hand these over to Devon so he can prepare them, and I might even give you some pocket money for your effort."

"No need, I made lots of money today." Theo grinned as he pulled a huge pile of dollar bills out of his pockets.

"Where did you get that from?"

Madison winced and shrugged. "He never asked for it; people just tipped him naturally and who was I to stop them?" She chuckled and gave Theo an amused look. "He started throwing random information at people about pelicans, sea lions and anchovies. They were fascinated, and then more people joined in. I swear, it was so funny. Everyone was asking him questions and he knew all the answers. You're even going to be on the news, aren't you, buddy?"

"Really?" Ally didn't know whether to compliment him on how he'd earned the money or not, and she could tell by the look on Madison's face that she wasn't entirely sure about it either. "Well, we're going to have to watch that later, then. Well done, honey."

Theo looked immensely proud of himself. "It's on at

eight," he said. "And I want to go back tomorrow, the sea lions might still be there."

"I'm sorry," Madison said when he ran up to his room to put the money away. "I swear I wasn't encouraging him to take money from strangers, it just happened."

"I know. I imagine they were pretty impressed." Ally shrugged it off. "I can't exactly ask him to play dumb either, so it is what it is." She looked down at the bucket in her hand and laughed. "I'll take these to the kitchen. Want to watch the news together at eight?"

"For sure." Madison blew her a kiss when she was certain no one was watching. "Theo and I will make us some food."

33

"I had a really great weekend. Thank you." Ally closed the door to *Western Shores* and turned the sign on the door to 'closed'. "And thank you for your help with Theo and..." She gestured to the bar. "With this. You really don't have to do this."

"I like to help." Madison smiled as she carried the last crates with empty bottles to the storage room. When she came back behind the bar, Ally had switched off the music and it was blissfully quiet. The nightcap she'd gone in for had only been an excuse to see Ally again, but she'd had a fun night and gotten to know some of the locals better. "Those sea lions have brought you booming business two days in a row now. Let's hope they stick around for a while," she joked.

"They sure have. We've made more money this weekend than we have in the past three weeks combined. Never mind the sea lions, we've been serving tempura anchovies non-stop, it's becoming a *Western Shores* specialty." Ally made a Negroni for Madison and poured a glass of rosé for herself. "Last night, Theo asked me why he wasn't allowed to get me any more anchovies, so I had to explain that I can't have him running back and forth with buckets because it will look like I'm putting an eleven-year-old to work." She laughed. "And then I also had to explain that he couldn't accept any more money from people, especially not with journalists lurking around because he's not legally allowed to work. Of course, that was followed by a discussion about charging people money for his knowledge versus earning money as tips, and he was way better with his arguments than I was, so I finally gave up, figuring he's got school this week so at least I won't have to worry about it."

Madison laughed too. "Being a mom must be hard sometimes."

"Believe me it's getting harder, especially now that he knows he's smarter than me." Ally took a sip of her rosé. "Anyway, enough about me. Are you busy next week?"

"Yeah, I'll probably get back late most nights." Madison clinked her glass with Ally's and took a sip. "You?"

"Apart from my usual hours, only two late shifts on Wednesday and Thursday, so not too bad. Come by the bar for a drink if you have any energy left after work..." Ally winced then, as if she'd said something she shouldn't have. "Or don't," she hastily added. "I don't want you to feel like you have to because we're..." Her voice trailed off. "Hell, I don't even know what it is we're doing."

Madison flinched at Ally's words, noting her frustration, and she wondered if just like herself, Ally was getting sucked into their 'casual' relationship way deeper than they'd originally planned. She'd tried to keep an emotional distance, but it was hard when all she craved was to be with her. "Hey, are you okay? Do we need to talk?"

Ally closed her eyes and let out a deep sigh. "I don't know. I just feel... confused, I guess."

"That's okay. I know that this is probably just a phase for you, so I won't be offended if you've changed your mind. You can tell me; I won't freak out on you." Madison inched closer and put an arm around her waist. She cast a glance outside, aware that people could see in.

As if reading her mind, Ally took the remote from the bar and switched off the lights, leaving them with only the faint light from the refrigerator under the bar. "No, no it's not that. I mean, realistically – yes, it might be a phase. No pun intended, but I have no way of knowing right now as I can't seem to think straight when you're around. But the main reason that I'm a little anxious is because I haven't felt like this in a long time... It's so physically and emotionally overwhelming that honestly, it's a little scary."

"I know what you mean." Madison gave her a sweet smile. Hearing those words coming from Ally gave her hope that maybe there was something more in it for them – perhaps a future? "Would it help if I said it's scary for me too?"

"Really?"

"Yeah." Madison paused, then decided to be completely honest. "I'd be lying if I said I didn't have feelings for you. I really, really like you, Ally." It felt terrifying to say it out loud, but with it also came relief. She knew there were a lot of things they hadn't told each other in order to keep their emotions out of it but maybe it was time that they let their walls down. "And actually, now that we're sharing, I wanted to talk to you about something else. Tom asked me to go to the Bahamas for two months to help out on a sister study there. It's an awesome opportunity and I've accepted the offer. I just thought you should know, considering our circumstances."

"Oh wow, that sounds amazing, I'm happy for you."

Ally's tone was a little overly enthusiastic. "I don't want you to feel like you have to run this past me, though. I mean, I really like you too, but we're not dating, and you don't owe me anything." Ally looked like she regretted saying the harsh words as soon as they'd left her lips, but she didn't take them back.

"Right." Madison nodded, unsure how she should feel about Ally's response. Why was she talking about physical and emotional connection one moment, then pretending nothing was going on the next? "I'm aware of that, I just thought you should know. Anyway, it's not for a while. I'll be leaving in about seven weeks."

"Great." Ally hesitated. "I actually wanted to ask you something... Have you been on any more dates since the last one?" She shook her head, clearly regretting that one too. "I'm sorry," she said, waving a hand. "Is that an insanely possessive question to ask?"

Madison frowned in surprise. Ally was sending out so many mixed messages that she was having a hard time keeping up. "Dates?" She shook her head. "Of course not. I wouldn't sleep with you one night and then go on a date with someone else the next. That's crazy, why do you even think I would do that?"

"I don't know, I just assumed you... Since this is casual between us..." Ally seemed taken aback by Madison's fierce reaction. "Never mind, forget I ever asked."

"Well, I'm not like that." Madison cocked her head and narrowed her eyes. "Have you been on any other dates while we've been seeing each other?"

"God no." Ally chuckled nervously. "I could never do that if I'm sleeping with you; casual or not."

"Glad we're on the same page, then." Feeling curiously relieved, Madison leaned over the bar, letting out the breath she'd been holding. She didn't like the idea of Ally dating anyone else at all, and it then dawned on her that she wanted Ally to herself, the thought of somebody else touching her seemingly abhorrent. Why was Ally so scared of them getting close? Was she simply protecting herself or was she really convinced this was a bi-curious phase? Madison's instinct told her that their night and shower together had affected Ally in more ways than one. She was also pretty sure that whatever side of the sexual scale Ally was on, she was in fact, attracted to her. And what was wrong with enjoying their mutual attraction as much as they could? "Can I take you out on a date?" she heard herself ask before she'd had time to think it through.

"You want to take me out on a date?"

"Yeah. When was the last time you went on a fun date? The one with Jack obviously didn't work out..."

Ally thought about that. "Hmm, yes, I still feel a little guilty about that. But to answer your question, my last fun date was twelve years ago, maybe? It must have been the last time Marcos took me out. After that, dates have been few and far apart, and none of them were particularly good." She studied Madison as if trying to work out if she was serious. "A date is kind of official, don't you think? I'm not sure if that's a good idea..."

"How about a casual date then?" Madison decided she wasn't going to give up that easily.

"What does that look like?"

Madison shrugged. "Let's see... fast food? Drive-thru maybe? Then go to a rap concert or a strip club?" she joked. "Pretty sure there's nothing romantic about that." She was happy to hear Ally laugh again and as soon as it had come, the awkwardness between them faded.

"Or a shooting range? The cemetery? A family-function,

maybe?" Ally suggested, joining in with the fun. "You could bring your mom?"

Madison clapped her hands together, highly amused by Ally's suggestions. "Sure, that can be arranged. How about Friday?"

"You really are serious about this, aren't you?" Ally took off her apron and threw it in a corner with the rest of the laundry. She was still a little reluctant, but Madison could tell her resolve was crumbling.

"Not about my mom but about the date, yes, I'm serious. How about Friday at six? Wear something practical. Nothing sexy like you're wearing now, obviously." Madison's gaze darted to Ally's bare legs in the short denim skirt she was wearing. The low-cut white *Western Shores* T-shirt with rolled-up sleeves was a nice touch too, showing off her cleavage and toned arms.

"Come on, this isn't sexy. It's my work outfit." Ally arched a brow and shot her a flirty smile. "And I can't believe I'm agreeing to this, but Friday is good. I'll ask Ana if Theo can stay over again." She held up her glass in a toast. "Here's to the most unromantic, most casual date in history. I'm looking forward to it."

"Me too." Madison clinked her glass against Ally's and gave her a playful wink. "Maybe Devon will let you borrow his shirt again."

Ally was in stitches now, holding onto her belly as she couldn't stop laughing. She tried to compose herself and fanned her face with her hand. "I can't believe he told you that embarrassing story."

"Glad I can make you laugh." Madison smiled as she pulled Ally toward her, and she felt a stir when she saw something other than amusement in her expression. There was no doubt about the electricity that sparked between them; it happened every time they were alone. Madison licked her lips and lowered her gaze to Ally's mouth. "Do you want to go somewhere?"

Ally took in a quick breath, her heaving chest telling Madison that she did. "Believe me, I'm all for it, but I need to go home. I don't want Theo to wake up and not know where I am."

"Of course, I wasn't thinking." Madison hesitated for a moment, then stepped back. She finished her drink and put their glasses in the sink, cursing herself for being so selfish. Even after all the time they'd spent under the shower and in bed together, her hunger for Ally hadn't subsided one bit. She looked around for anything else to clear, then folded up two empty cardboard boxes from the coffee delivery and held them up.

"You can put them in here." Ally opened the door to the storage room. When she followed Madison in, they were face to face, the sexual energy between them almost palpable. "Fuck, I want you so badly," she muttered in frustration. "Why do you have to look so damn good in that shirt?"

Madison stared back at her, puzzled as to why Ally was so into her old denim shirt that was hanging open over her white vest top. Deciding she didn't care that they were in the bar, she took off her shirt, and dropped it to the floor before pushing Ally against the door. She kissed her hard, moaning as Ally parted her lips to let her in. Their hungry mouths clashed together, their hands roaming underneath each other's clothes, seeking skin. Ally started pulling up Madison's top, but her action was interrupted as Madison reached under her skirt and slid her hand over her panties, cupping her center. She smiled when Ally let go of the fabric, suddenly out of control as she gasped against her mouth.

Breathing heavily, Ally placed her hands on Madison's chest gesturing for her to stop. "I hate to kill the mood but I need to speak to you about something really important. Can we go outside and have a drink on the terrace?"

Madison looked at her as if she'd lost her mind. "Are you serious right now?" She tilted her head, fire still sparking in her eyes as she reluctantly removed her hand away from the heated wetness between Ally's thighs. "I was just about to fuck you on that freezer over there, but I guess it can wait if it's important." She winked, picked up her shirt and opened the door for Ally.

Ally straightened her skirt and ran a hand through her hair before they took their drinks outside and sat down on the wall in front of the bar. It was dark and quiet, the town asleep apart from two young people on the beach, making out.

Madison put a leg on each side of the wall, facing Ally. She was still so turned on that she couldn't stop thinking about finishing what they'd started. She scooted closer and leaned in to kiss Ally's cheek, then ran her lips down to her neck, sucking at her flesh.

Ally giggled and stopped her once more. "Cut it out, Madison," she whispered. "People can see us here and besides; you might not want to do that after I've told you what I'm about to tell you."

At that, Madison sat back, suddenly serious. "What is it?"

"I have to sell the pink house." Ally figured it was best to just spit it out. She took a deep breath and stared ahead at the ocean and the starry sky, avoiding Madison's eyes. "I have to sell it in case Theo wants to go to The Seymour Institute after he's done the summer program there. I won't be able to pay for it if I don't."

Madison was quiet, pursing her lips. "You're selling the pink house," she repeated.

"Yeah. I don't want to but it's not like I have a choice." Ally turned to her and looked regretful as she put a hand on her arm. "I'm so sorry. I'll sell it with you as a sitting tenant so you can remain there for the rest of your contract but after that it won't be mine anymore and there's a good chance the new owner might want you out."

"Okay..." Madison nodded. The news was disappointing to say the least, but she didn't let it show. She knew Ally had no choice, and if it meant Theo would get the education he deserved, it was the right thing to do. "I understand," she said. "You do what you need to do. I mean, of course I was hoping I could stay for at least another six months or a year once my contract ended, but I totally understand." She mustered a smile. "It won't be hard to find something else, so please don't apologise."

"Thank you for being so understanding. Would it be okay if we arranged the viewings while you're away?"

"Of course. I'll make sure to leave it tidy."

Ally nodded. "I told Theo this morning and he was upset that you'd be moving out." She sighed. "I'm sad about it myself because I love having you next door and I know you like it here too. It's an unexpected turn of events for both of us, I suppose."

"Sad but necessary." Madison didn't want to think about leaving, so she ran a hand over Ally's cheek, leaning in to kiss her instead. Ally let out a soft moan and wrapped her arms around Madison's neck in return, sinking into the kiss. Despite what they'd just discussed, their actions got heated again and Madison was forced to pull away, conscious that someone might see them. "This sucks," she continued, a small smile playing around her lips. "But God damn it, it doesn't stop me from wanting you right now, so maybe we should go back into that storage room."

Ally chuckled and shook her head. "You're so bad."

"I am." Madison shot her a cheeky grin. "Well?" she asked, sliding a hand under Ally's top.

Ally stood up, pulled the keys from her pocket and dangled them in front of Madison, as she shot her a flirty look. "Of course I want to go back in. All I can think of now is you and me on top of that freezer."

34

"Looks like things are going well with your girlfriend," Devon said, nodding to Theo and Madison, who were skateboarding on the small strip of concrete between the houses and the beach.

"She's not my girlfriend." Ally shot him a warning look. "It's not like that, we're just friends... you know... with a little extra thrown in."

"Friends with benefits?" Devon titled his head, studying Madison. "She's hot, kind, funny, intelligent... And she's great with Theo."

"Yeah, she is, isn't she?" Ally said, failing to notice the dreaminess in her own voice.

"And you know what?" Devon continued. "I don't even think she hangs out with him to get into your pants... I think she genuinely likes that little troublemaker." He winked, indicating that he was joking.

Ally slapped him playfully with her dish towel and turned back to the coffee she was making. "Be careful who you joke about. The way it's going, my son might be President one day, so you'll want to be on his good side." She watched Theo smile proudly when Madison clapped and gave him a high-five after a successful flip. He should have been in bed by now but when he'd spotted Madison coming home at seven, he'd begged Ally to stay outside for a little longer. Madison had seemed happy to entertain him, and from the look on her face, she was enjoying herself too. Ally tried to ignore the warm and fuzzy feeling it gave her, watching them together. Theo had never really had a father figure in his life. Devon was always here for him, of course, and he loved him. But he wasn't paternal in the slightest, and he'd never entertained the idea of going outside to spend time with Theo unless she asked him to look after him. Yet here was Madison, this young, tomboyish woman, who shared his interests in the ocean, had taught him how to do tricks on his skateboard and who played catch on the beach with him whenever she had a free moment. Theo loved their interactions and that scared Ally, because Madison wouldn't be here forever. She had the world at her feet right now; no commitments, immense talent, she was super intelligent and had a job she loved passionately. It was only a matter of weeks before she'd be gone again. She might even get a better offer in the Bahamas and stay there, anything was possible. Although Ally was worried that, like Theo, she was getting far too invested, she was enjoying herself too much to break it off. There was going to be pain; she knew that. But maybe it was worth it.

"Hey, would you be able to start early again tomorrow?" She asked Devon. It's not a problem if you can't, but I'd like to pick Theo up from school and spend some time with him since he's staying over at Ana's."

"Of course. Three pm okay?"

"Yeah, that's perfect." Ally turned away from him but

knew she wasn't off the hook and groaned when she heard him chuckle.

"Another date?"

"It's not a date."

"Sure." Sarcasm was dripping through Devon's voice. "She's not your girlfriend and it's not a date. It's nothing, right?"

Ally let out a deep sigh and stared him down, ignoring his question. "What are you still doing here anyway? Aren't you supposed to be on a date yourself tonight?" She held up Devon's empty beer glass. He always had one after his shift but today, he'd been sitting here for over two hours, and that was unusual. "Do you want another one?"

"Sure, why not? She cancelled on me so I might as well stick around for a while longer."

"Wait... the woman cancelled on *you*? I don't remember a time someone ever turned you down." Ally laughed. "Apart from Madison, of course."

"And you." Devon shot her a cringing grin.

"Yeah, but that was twenty-two years ago and as soon as I said no, you asked my best friend, so that doesn't exactly count."

Devon chuckled. "True. Anyway, she didn't turn me down, we've just postponed the date. She was busy."

"Okay. What's her name?"

"Chelsey. We haven't actually met yet, we've just been chatting. A lot," he added.

"So that's why you've been on your phone so much late-ly..." Ally poured him another beer. "And I take it she's not online now because she's busy? And you like her even more because she's not all over you and permanently available like most women you date." She put the beer down in front of him and arched a brow when he didn't answer. "Is she local?"

"No, she lives in Rio Del Mar, but she works around here somewhere. Won't tell me where, though."

"Mysterious, I like her already," Ally teased. She waved at a couple who sat down outside and grabbed the drinks menus. "Well, I'd better get to work. To be continued."

35

Madison felt a little on edge as she got out of her pickup on Friday. The thought of having the whole weekend to herself with Ally right next door did funny things to her body, and the prospect of a date even more so. She'd replayed their heated moments over and over in her mind, still not quite grasping how it had come to the point where Ally consumed her thoughts twenty-four-seven.

The casual date she'd planned for tonight would, of course, be nothing but super romantic because how could it not be? Ally was amazing and she deserved the world. Madison was pretty sure no one ever took care of Ally the way she looked after everyone else, and she wanted to change that. She'd picked up a bottle of wine and a food hamper on her way home and had planned a sunset picnic on the beach in Santa Cruz, followed by drinks over a flamenco concert on the pier. A bunch of talented street musicians were there every Friday night, and she'd stopped by and talked to them the night before, making sure they'd be there. Madison had no idea if Ally liked the sound of Spanish guitars but there was only one way of finding out.

Looking back, Ally had been on her mind for weeks, even before they realized they had mutual chemistry. Apart from the instant sexual attraction, she'd felt a genuine interest and admiration toward the sweet, hard-working and undeniably beautiful mother. But now, their intimacy had awakened something that was entirely new to her. It was a constant longing for her, a constant need to be with her, or to be close. The flutters in her core, the dreams, the thoughts... She was falling for Ally and she was falling hard.

Madison stopped in her stride as she walked up to the house, carrying the hamper when she spotted someone who looked suspiciously like her mother, sitting at a table in front of *Western Shores*, with Ally. Her heart sank in her chest when she realized that the woman wearing the red seventies-style pantsuit and the long, blonde wavy hair was indeed Edie. No one put as much effort into her appearance as her mother did. *God, no, please. Not tonight...*

"Madison, honey!" Edie stood up when she saw her approach. "Surprise!" Her bright-red lips pulled into a beaming smile as she ran up to Madison and gave her a long hug. "There you are. I was waiting for you to get back from work. Thought we could spend the weekend together."

"Mom, it's so great to see you," Madison stammered, not wanting her mother to know she'd rather lose a finger than cancel her date with Ally and spend the weekend shopping together. "When did you get here... and how?"

"I just got on a flight, then took a taxi here." Edie chuckled. "Look at your face! I knew you'd be excited to see me. You know, when you told me I should start doing more things for myself, I figured you were right. So, I came here for a little break. Girls weekend. How about that?"

Madison didn't have the heart to tell her mother that she'd clearly misunderstood the message; that her whole point was for her to stop obsessing about her children and find something else to focus on. So, she smiled back and gave her a kiss on the cheek instead. "It's great to see you, Mom. Really nice to have you here. And you look..." Madison looked her up and down. "Very glamorous as always."

"Thank you, honey, I dressed up for the occasion." Edie straightened her outfit that was more suited to a private party in Saint-Tropez than something to be worn on a family beach. "Ally and I have been catching up over coffee, it's been so nice."

"I see you have." Madison's eyes met Ally's, and in that moment, she wished the ground would just swallow her. She was pretty sure her mother hadn't been here very long yet, as Ally looked like she was dressed up and ready to go out on their date, looking gorgeous in a cute navy dress and leather sandals. She was clearly uncomfortable too, crossing and uncrossing her legs until she eventually stood up.

"Hey Madison." Then she turned to Edie, deciding that apparently, that was all she had to say. "Well Edie, it was lovely to talk to you, but I have to go and do some stuff in the house now. Devon can fix you some snacks if you like."

"Devon can certainly fix you some snacks," Devon said as he came out. "And you Madison, have a very, very captivating mother."

"You charmer." Edie giggled like a schoolgirl and patted his arm. "Thank you, Devon, but I think we'll be fine. I'm taking Madison out for dinner." Edie regarded Ally, and Madison dreaded her mother's next words as she knew exactly what was coming. Edie meant well, she always did. "Would you like to come too? My treat." She waved her purse at Ally and winked. "Or rather my husband's."

"That's very kind of you to offer but I'm good, actually. I have food in the house and you two should spend some quality time together."

"Nonsense." Edie was not a woman used to hearing the word 'no' and would not accept it from anyone. "Devon told me earlier that Theo is spending the night at his grandma's house, and Madison and I would love your company. Right, Madison?"

Madison didn't think it could possibly get any more uncomfortable, her mother saying all the wrong things and insisting Ally go for dinner with them. Ally looked like she was about to run off too, her eyes nervously shifting from Edie to Madison as if begging her for help to get out of the awkward situation. But what could Madison do? She couldn't exactly dismiss the invitation and she desperately wanted to spend time with Ally.

"Of course. It would be great if you'd come along," she heard herself say before giving Ally an apologetic shrug. She dropped the hamper on a chair and saw the corners of Ally's mouth curl up into a small smile as it hit her what Madison had planned.

"Excellent. Shall we meet you here at seven?" Edie rubbed Ally's shoulder as if they were best friends already. "I've made reservations at a very nice restaurant in Santa Cruz and someone told me they have flamenco music on the pier there on Friday nights. Sounds fun, right?"

"Yeah, I also heard about the flamenco musicians," Madison said. "I was already planning on checking them out tonight so that's a great idea, Mom." Her eyes met Ally's and they both let out a chuckle, realizing that Edie had hijacked their date. God, maybe she was more like her mother than she liked to admit. She caught Devon's grin before he turned to tend to the next table and knew he would be in trouble with Ally.

"Sure." Ally's smile grew as she had no other choice than to give in. "Let's meet at seven."

36

"I see you went along with my family function idea for our date," Ally joked, shooting Madison an amused glance as they followed Edie to the main road to meet their taxi. The woman was remarkably fast as she tottered along in her high heels. "Good choice and definitely the least romantic choice of the options we discussed."

Madison chuckled. "I'm really sorry about this. I obviously had no idea she was going to show up."

"But you were planning on taking me to see the flamenco musicians?"

"Yes, and a sunset picnic." Madison hooked her arm into Ally's and pulled her close.

"That's so romantic." Ally gave her arm a squeeze. "I think I would have loved that."

"Rain check then?" Madison arched a brow and shot her a smile. "Because as much as I love my mother, having her here is not exactly my idea of a date. And as much as it's awkward for you, it's awkward for me too so let's just try to get through this as best as we can." She kept her voice low so her mother couldn't hear her. "You look stunning by the way."

"Thank you, you look very nice too" Ally said in a soft voice. "I know you didn't plan this, and I'll do my best tonight, as long as you stop looking at me like that because it's turning me on."

"I'm not sure if I can promise that." Madison licked her lips as she looked down at Ally's mouth. "But I'll try my best."

W *hat have I gotten myself into?* Ally managed to smile and keep the conversation flowing, but inside she was in turmoil. She'd been unable to sleep much for weeks, because she kept lying awake, fantasizing about Madison, and she was a little disappointed they wouldn't get to spend the night together.

The situation was nothing short of ridiculous. She had a crazy crush on Madison, who was way too young for her, and now she was sitting at a table with Madison and her mother of all people, who couldn't be more than ten years older than herself. To say she was uncomfortable was an understatement. Ally was a mom with responsibilities, Madison was a carefree girl who was likely to move away after her six-month tenancy was up. She liked to skateboard, had tattoos, wore a diamond stud in her nose and sported shocking pink hair. She'd already had her first offshore job offer, and the chances of her sticking around in Capitola while the world was her oyster were extremely slim. But Madison was also very, very good in bed and despite trying to convince herself that they were completely incompatible, Ally was insanely attracted to her.

There were so many things going through Ally's mind. Was

she into women now? She'd always been happy with Marcos... Was she bisexual or just bi-curious? There was also this strange guilt that bugged her. It was hard to rationalize as she hadn't done anything wrong, but deep down, she felt like she'd cheated on Marcos. She hadn't felt it before, on the few occasions she'd kissed someone after a date, but now she did. The other dates hadn't meant anything to her, and she'd forgotten about them the next day, after deciding she had no feelings for the men in question. With Madison though, she hadn't been able to do that. And then there was Theo, who was getting pretty attached to Madison. That was a potential problem too, but then again, he might be okay once he started summer school and made friends of his own. Her eyes kept darting to Madison's lips as she spoke, and their intense eye contact was electric. *Don't even go there,* she told herself. *Not tonight.*

"Any preference for wine?" she heard Edie ask, waking her up from her steamy thoughts.

"Oh no, I like anything. You decide." The restaurant on the wharf in Santa Cruz was one of the most exclusive ones in the area but she guessed that to Edie, it was simply part of her everyday life. The woman was lovely, there was no doubt about that, and Ally had to admit that she'd had a really nice conversation with her before Madison arrived, even though it had been highly awkward from her side as her mind couldn't get over the fact that she'd had sex with her daughter on top of a freezer at *Western Shores* only last Sunday.

"Ally likes Chablis," Madison said cheerfully. "Or rosé."

Ally smiled, impressed that Madison remembered. "It's what I normally drink yes, but it's more out of habit and anyway..."

"Nonsense, Chablis is an excellent idea," Edie interrupted her. She smiled, her heavily injected lips stretching extensively. She had no crow's-feet or any other signs of emotion on her face except for a sparkle of excitement in her kind eyes. Ally could tell she'd had quite a bit of work done, but the woman still looked dazzling, nevertheless. She seemed like a caring, pleasant person who never apologized for who she was, and Ally really liked that about her. Despite the plastic façade, there was a very genuine woman in Edie ... "That will go great with the lobster. And how about some oysters and scallops to start with?"

"Yes, let's do that," Madison agreed and winked at Ally. "If dad's paying..."

After the starters, Ally noticed herself loosening up more. Seeing Madison unfazed by the situation helped, and she was having fun now. Edie was full of great stories and hugely entertaining with her slightly naïve outlook on life. Ally guessed she'd been brought up with a silver spoon in her mouth, yet she was very involved with charity work and genuinely cared about some great causes. She'd also picked up new hobbies lately, but none of them had turned out to be a success so far.

"And so I went to golf practice with your father for the first time but he doesn't seem very interested in playing with me..." Edie rambled on as she gestured for the waiter to refill their glasses.

"Maybe dad just needs his own time with his golf buddies," Madison came to her father's defense. "It's his time away from home, and he's got his own set of friends he loves to hang out with. Maybe you should find people who..." She grinned and paused, searching for the right words. "Play at your own level? Maybe some other newcomers to the sport? How about Darla?"

"Darla isn't interested in sports. She thinks exercise is bad for you."

Ally laughed. "How can exercise be bad?"

"I don't know. She claims it makes her stressed and causes premature aging." Edie rolled her eyes. "Anyway, I'm going to check out that new mindfulness center that opened in Lafayette. They do yoga classes among other things so I might find something that interests me there. I'm just a little bored, I guess. It's been awfully quiet in the house since Chuck left."

"I can relate to that," Ally said, giving her a knowing smile. "I'm dreading Theo moving to LA for the summer. Maybe I should find myself some distraction too." She blushed as soon as she'd said it, avoiding Madison's eyes. Madison had certainly been more distraction than she could handle but of the good kind, nevertheless.

"How about men?" Edie asked, chirping up. "Are you not dating? A gorgeous woman like you shouldn't be single, Ally. Especially now that you're in your forties. You need someone to take care of you and..."

"Mom, we're not in the middle ages. Ally is a happy independent woman," Madison interrupted her mother.

"She's right, I am." Ally took a bite of the scallops that were perfectly caramelized, paired with a creamy root and horseradish mash and glazed micro vegetables. It had been years since she'd been to a fine dining restaurant, and although she didn't care much for it in general, it was really nice to indulge in the great service and fabulous food. The view over the bay was stunning from the terrace where they were seated, comfortably warm under the heaters. "I've been on dates, but I just haven't met someone I can see myself spending the rest of my life with. It's hard with Theo; I don't want to introduce him to people who might disappear from his life again."

"Of course, I understand that. But surely, it's going to be a little easier, when he'll be away during the week?" Edie tilted her head, regarding Ally as if she was some rare species that she admired. "You really are quite something. Have you had any work done?"

"Work?" Ally shot her a confused look.

"Yes, facial work. You know, fillers, Botox, chemical peels?"

Ally felt like laughing at the question, then realized that Edie was being serious and shook her head as she tried to keep a straight face. "No, I haven't. Just a whole lot of sunscreen."

"Hmm... Well, it's a shame we live so far away, we have a couple of handsome bachelors at our country club," Edie said, again in all seriousness.

"It's nice of you to think of me, but believe me, I'm quite happy on my own."

"Of course, I apologize if I was being intrusive." Edie chuckled. "I just like to play matchmaker. I'm quite good at it too, you know." She winked and turned to Madison. "And what about you, sweetie? Have you met some nice girls whilst you've been here?"

Madison sighed and sunk deeper into her chair. She didn't like her mother using the word 'girls' and she didn't like her talking to her in that motherly tone when Ally was around either. It only emphasized how much younger she was than her table companions, and it bothered her that Ally might think she was too young for her.

"Women, Mom. I'm twenty-three, I don't date girls. And no, there are no women in my life, I've been too busy with work." She bit down on her lip, considering her words when she saw Ally flinch just a little.

"Are you sure about that? I know that look." Edie quirked a brow. "I'm your mother, I can tell when there's someone on your mind. I saw it the moment you got back from work. Don't think I didn't see that picnic hamper you brought back either." She gasped and covered her mouth with her hand as something struck her. "Good Lord, did I ruin your date night? I didn't even think of that... I should have called first to check with you instead of just showing up unannounced."

"It's fine, Mom," Madison reassured her. "And yes, if you must know, I was going on a date, but I have no idea where it's heading and there will be lots of opportunities to take her out again, so don't worry about it."

"I hope you at least called her to let her know you couldn't make it?" Edie looked terribly guilty now.

"Of course I did. Can we talk about something else now?"

"Sure, sweetie. Is it someone from work?" Edie continued her interrogation.

Madison kept her eyes fixed on her plate, suddenly unable to take another bite. She imagined Ally feeling just as uncomfortable as she did but didn't dare look at her. "No, it's not." She shook her head and took a long drink of her wine, emptying her glass. "As I said before, I don't want to talk about it, maybe some other time."

37

"So... you going to the Bahamas, Ally selling the house, that's all big news." Edie sat back and regarded Madison. "Are you finally going to tell me about this woman too?" she asked, choosing her words carefully, making sure not to use the word 'girl'.

"Nope," Madison said matter-of-factly. She thanked the waiter who brought out their coffees and turned her attention to the view from the café on the Monterey Marina Wharf. Sea otters were playing between the boats tied to the docks. There were dozens of them, and the cute creatures kept making both her and her mother laugh. Madison had been passionate about sea otters ever since she'd volunteered at an otter sanctuary in her first year of college. They'd matched up orphaned pups with surrogate moms, who would raise them until they were old enough to be released back into the wild. She knew her mother, who had never seen marine mammals in the wild, would like it too, so she'd taken her on a tour along Monterey Bay, stopping off at various beaches and wharfs to see sea lions, seals and sea otters.

Since she'd moved, she hadn't had much opportunity to explore the area and there were so many gems along the Northern Californian coast. So many places she'd like to take Ally. Of course, they'd hadn't had much opportunity to walk around, with her mother being limited by her high heels, but she imagined herself and Ally hiking along the shore one day, kissing at every opportunity. Maybe she'd buy a boat so she could take Theo on trips... She shook her head, ridding herself of the wishful vision of Ally and her living a happily ever after. "Did you know sea otters use tools?" She asked, changing the topic.

"I did not know that." Edie narrowed her eyes, knowing exactly what her daughter was doing, but going along with it anyway. "Tell me about it."

Madison took a sip of her coffee, glad to be off the hook. "They use sharp rocks or empty shells to open the shells of snails, crabs, mussels, sea urchins and such. Sometimes they use them for other things too, like grooming." She smiled as she watched two otter pups wrestling. "And you know what's really fascinating? They tend to have their favorite tool that they carry with them under their armpit for when they need it. Sometimes, they hold onto it their whole life. Basically, it means they get attached to things."

"That's fascinating indeed."

"It is." Madison continued before her mother could get another word in, most likely enquiring about her love life again. "The mother and pup also hold hands while they're sleeping so the pup won't drift off, or the mother will wrap the pup in kelp and use that as an anchor. And sometimes, couples or friends hold hands too. It's incredibly cute to watch."

"How adorable. You've always been full of interesting

facts." Edie sighed. "I'm sure your new love interest is thoroughly impressed by your great academic knowledge too."

"You're incredible..." Madison was baffled by how her mother was always able to lead a random conversation right back to where she wanted it. "I told you, I don't want to talk about her."

"See? There's that look again." Edie tilted her head and patted her cheek, letting Madison know she was blushing. "Oh boy, you've got it bad. Come on, spill. I promise I won't tell anyone."

Madison groaned, knowing her mother would never give up unless she gave her something. They'd always been able to talk about everything and, although her mother was pretty open-minded, she wasn't sure how she'd react to the Ally situation. "Okay, okay." She held up a hand and paused, taking a deep breath. "But you're going to have to keep your opinions to yourself, promise?"

"Promise." Edie held up her hand too, and crossed her middle and index finger, her eyes wide with excitement. "Well?"

"It's Ally," Madison blurted out. She waited until the news sank in and watched her mother's eyes narrow in confusion. "That's why I said I have no idea where it's heading. She doesn't usually date women and she's really cautious because of Theo and..."

"Ally?" Edie fell silent for a beat. "The Ally, we had dinner with last night? Your landlady?"

"Yeah." Madison noticed she was stirring sugar cubes through her coffee, even though she didn't like sugar in her caffeine. "I really, really like her, Mom."

"Oh." Tension grew at the table while Edie frantically started stirring her coffee too. "But she's straight and much older than you. And as you already mentioned, she has a son."

Madison shrugged. "I'm not so sure about the straight part anymore, but yes, she's older than me. Who cares? And Theo's a great kid; I like him."

"Who cares?" Edie's voice rose to a shrill pitch and she looked at her as if she'd lost it. "Madison, I have no problem with Ally. I think she's an admirable woman. Not only an impressive business woman but wonderful in every way. But I don't want either of you to get hurt and that's exactly what will happen here."

"Why? Why is it such a problem? I don't get it, I seriously don't." Madison's tone was defensive as she sat back and crossed her arms in front of her chest.

"Well, for starters, Ally has only ever been with men, am I right?"

"Yes, apart from one night in college. But people can be fluid."

"I know that, sweetie but it's very rare for people to discover that so late in life. What if this is just an experimental phase to her? What if she's just looking for some excitement in her life? It must be quite monotonous living in such a small town, seeing the same people every day, doing the same work, never getting away much... Maybe she's just going with it because it excites her today. But what about tomorrow, when she wakes up and realizes it's been a mistake, that she'd rather live a traditional life with a man who can be a father to her son? What then?"

"I can be there for Theo just as well as any man can."

"Can you? It's not even about gender. You're twenty-three, Madison."

"That's a bullshit argument and you know it. You had Mason when you were twenty-three."

"You're right." Edie took a deep breath and looked up at Madison, finally meeting her eyes. There was a glimmer of emotion in her gaze as she nervously worried her lip, searching for the right words. "But I want so much more for you. You're talented and young, and you have your whole life ahead of you. Having a child is a huge responsibility and it would tie you to this little town, for at least the coming seven years. Even when Theo goes away to boarding school, he'll still need a stable place to come home to. What if you decide this life is not for you after all? Have you even considered that? From what I've heard the boy really likes you and he'd be heartbroken if you left."

"What if, what if... Theo doesn't need to know we're seeing each other, not for a long time. I don't want to think that far ahead yet because whatever is going on between us, it's still in the early stages."

"But you have to think ahead!" Edie slammed her hand on the table. "Even if you choose not to tell him, Theo will find out at some point. That boy is observant, and people talk, especially in a small town. He might get hopeful that his mother is finally happy with someone or he might bond with you, if he hasn't already." She hesitated. "Or... he might not be able to accept that his mom is gay. It's his mother after all, and it's unlikely he's ever considered the idea of her dating a woman. It might ruin his relationship with Ally."

Madison was very quiet then, knowing her mother had a point. Still, what she felt for Ally was too strong to dismiss, too overwhelming to ignore. They'd only known each other for six weeks but it felt like a lot longer than that. "I'm crazy about her," she mumbled. "It's not just going to go away."

Edie's expression softened, and she put a hand on Madison's. "I'm just worried. For all of you, okay? And I know you've had enough of my 'what-ifs' but I'm going to tell you one more thing anyway because I want you to think this through carefully before it escalates. You're twenty-three now, but what happens when you're thirty-three and she's fifty? You might want to go out, but she'll probably want to stay home. What if you want a child of your own, but Ally feels like she's past the whole child-rearing phase and wants time to herself? Do you even have anything in common? I'm sure you'll have different tastes in music, movies, you name it. Not to mention that later on, you might want to have sex, but she might be going through the menopause and have no interest in that. And what if you're forty-three and she's sixty and starts experiencing health problems? You might not be able to go on certain holidays together or go for long walks or even relate to each other anymore. Age-difference can be a terrible strain on a relationship. Darla…"

"Please leave Darla out of this," Madison said in a sharp tone. "Darla is nearly sixty and only dates young boys who have no brains so don't you dare compare us to Darla and her toy boys." She huffed. "Besides, age doesn't define life-style anymore and everyone goes through menopause. I will too; it's not a big deal." It felt ridiculous to even think that far ahead but deep down, Madison knew there was at least some truth to what her mother was saying. She'd acted on impulse, physically craving Ally so much that all the rest had faded into the background. She'd thought about these things sure, but not to the extent that her mother was apparently able to lay out in detail within a matter of minutes.

"Just think about this carefully, okay, sweetie? That's all I'm asking." Edie took her hand. "I'm sure Ally is considering all these things too, and maybe that's why she's holding back. You just need time to process this because right now, you're both high on dopamine and believe me; it will wear off, even though you think it never will. And then, all you'll be left with is each other and how compatible you are may define the success of your long-term happiness together."

Madison gave her a small nod. "Sure. I'll think about it. Now, can we please talk about something else?" She shot her mother a pleading look and decided to get back at her for killing her vibe. "Has Chuck told you about his date with Darla yet?"

38

"Are you alone?" Ally mouthed, scanning the premises for Edie as she took off her apron. She'd been so desperate to see Madison that she'd forgotten to take it off in the kitchen before she left.

Madison got up from the chair in front of her door, her face immediately lighting up. "Yeah. She left for the airport a couple of hours ago." She pointed to the apron that was visibly covered in stains, despite it being black. "Looks like you had a busy day."

Ally nodded. "Yeah. Ever since the sea lions we've become popular for our anchovies." She chuckled. "The difference is that now I have to order them from the fishermen at the wharf and they don't always have them. But it's calmed down, and Devon is closing up for me." Conscious of her customers, she refrained from grabbing Madison by her waist and pulling her in. Besides, Theo would be back any minute with Ana, who had taken him to the mall just outside town. "Can I join you until Theo gets back?"

"Of course, sit down." Madison offered her own chair, then went inside to fetch the other chair and a glass.

"Drink?" She held up a jug with lemonade and poured Ally one without waiting for an answer.

"Thanks." Ally took a long drink. "This is delicious." She looked Madison over, appreciating her outfit, or rather the lack of one. She was wearing a pair of skimpy shorts and a crop top that only very few people could pull off, her tan skin glistening with sunscreen. "Did you have a good time with your mom?"

"Yeah, it was fine." Madison tried to sound positive, even though the past two days had been hard, with her mother refusing to give up on the topic of her and Ally. "She means well, you know, but she needs to learn not to show up unannounced. I took her on a tour along the coast to avoid getting lured into shopping malls or booked in for a mother-and-daughter facial."

Ally laughed. "I would have guessed shopping is her thing. She's nice though; I like her."

"I told her about moving out of the pink house and about us." Madison regretted it as soon as the words were out. "I mean, I didn't say it was anything serious, because it's not, right?" she hastily added, knowing that was a big fat lie, at least from her side. "Just that I really like you." She could tell by the shocked expression on Ally's face that she'd made an error of judgement by telling her. "And maybe I shouldn't have, I'm sorry. Her interrogation tactics are just so... persuasive."

"It's fine." Ally shrugged. "Devon knows too. I just had to tell someone and he's always around... it's hard not to talk about something when you think about it all the time."

Madison relaxed a little, knowing Ally had confided in someone too, although it didn't surprise her. "I figured he knew. He basically spelled it out when he saw me coming out of your house the other morning."

"Right... of course he did. Devon doesn't do subtle." Ally looked worried as she continued. "So, what did your mom say? You know, about us... I imagine she wasn't delighted with the idea and I can't blame her; there are a lot of things that have been bugging me too." She cast a glance over Madison's legs. *But they haven't stopped me from wanting her.*

"You're right. She had a lot to say about it," Madison admitted. "Even though she really likes you." She reached out over the table and brushed her hand over Ally's. "Do you want to tell me what's been bugging you? Because you keep saying that you're not sure whether this is a phase and that's fair enough. But what we've got going on seems mutually passionate to me and so I feel like you're hiding behind that excuse for other reasons."

Ally fidgeted with her hair, avoiding eye contact. It kept surprising her how mature Madison was, how intuitive when it came to her feelings. "Okay..." She didn't care if Madison was a woman; she wanted her more than she'd ever wanted anyone and that was enough to know she could be attracted to her for the rest of her life. "It's not the 'gay' thing," she said, making quote marks in the air. "You're right, that's not my main concern. My main concerns are other things, the biggest one being our age difference. Seventeen years is a lot." She paused. "And Theo and your future and your heart and mine – we could both get hurt really badly."

"I know. And I hear you." Madison looked up. "Technically, I get that you have a problem with our age difference. You might think I'm too immature for you and yes, my mom summed up a million reasons why it could be a problem too. But it doesn't feel difficult, right? It doesn't feel complicated or problematic. It feels natural and easy and fun." She leaned forward, lowering her voice. "And passionate and romantic."

Ally's lips pulled into a smile. "Yes, it does feel passionate and romantic, and you make me feel alive. I love that." She hesitated. "My issue with our age difference is not so much the seventeen years, but the fact that you're twenty-three. I don't want you to waste the best years of your life in a small town when you have opportunities to travel the world for your career and live in exotic places, experience extraordinary things and be the best you that you can be. If we were both ten years older, it would be a lot easier for me to accept."

"Then it can only get better. You'll like me even more in ten years' time." Madison crossed her arms and shot her a smug smile, although she didn't feel entirely confident. "And I'm not dreaming of exotic places or adventure, my work excites me and there are plenty of opportunities along the coast here. And yes, I'll probably be sent away for my job for two to three months every now and then, but I adore Capitola and I'd love to make this my home. Trust me, I know what I want."

"I'm not sure if you can really know what you want at twenty-three," Ally argued carefully, her voice soft. "Even though you might be sure of this now, you might change your mind in the future. As I said, I have to be careful, both for myself and for Theo."

"Come on, that's bullshit, and you know it." Madison jutted her chin. "You were what, nineteen when you met Marcos? You clearly knew what you wanted then. And as far as Theo goes, I love spending time with him. Even if you decide you only want to be friends in the end, I'd still take him to the beach or go skateboarding with him. We're buddies; I'm not just going to drop him."

Ally was silent because she simply couldn't argue with that. Madison seemed to have a solution, explanation or an answer to everything, and she was, admittedly, very mature for her age.

"I'm sorry. I really don't want this to turn into an argument, but you're the one who doesn't know what she wants, not me. And that's fine; I'll give you all the time in the world and we can keep this casual if that's what you need." Madison stretched her leg under the table, running her bare foot along Ally's calf. She raised an eyebrow and shot her an enigmatic smile when she saw her shiver at the contact. "But you still owe me a date."

At that, Ally chuckled, and the tension between them melted. "Okay, you've got it." She made sure to wipe the dreamy smirk off her face when she heard Theo calling from down the road. "Let's try again next Friday. Without your mother this time."

39

"This okay with you?" Edwina, the realtor asked when Ally came out to look at the sign her assistant was putting up next to Madison's window.

"Yeah, that's fine." Ally took a deep breath and mustered a smile. "So, you said you have high hopes for this property?" She handed them both a coffee, then looked up at the sign. It was strange seeing it outside her own house.

Edwina nodded and gave her a reassuring smile. "Most certainly. It's small but the view... priceless. You never know what you're going to get for these beach-front properties but what I can tell you is that I'm confident we'll get the asking price. And if we're lucky they'll start bidding way over that." She pushed her chest out and took a wide stance on her heels, resting her hands on her hips. Her broad shoulders were accentuated by the shoulder pads in her black pantsuit jacket that was way too warm for the time of year.

"Let's hope they do." Ally regarded Edwina, stepping back so she wouldn't strain her neck while trying to look her in the eyes. The woman was so tall that she only came up to her chest. What was it with realtors and power dressing?

"Well, this is one of those must-have places; it's iconic for the area and someone who wants to be part of the colorful living in Capitola won't have size on top of their list." Edwina flicked through her paperwork and pulled a page out of her file. "Last time one of these came on the market was six years ago, so I think we'd better brace ourselves." She handed it to Ally.

"Seven-hundred-and-fifty thousand?" Ally swallowed hard. "For one of these?"

"Yup. And that was six years ago." Edwina gave her assistant a thumbs-up. "Looks good, Lara."

"Jesus." Ally had to admit, she felt a little less sad knowing she'd be able to pay for Theo's school and have some cash left over to do work on their own house after the sale. There would also be the flights back and forth every weekend, but at least she wouldn't have to worry about that now. "My tenant will be gone for a while. She's leaving at the end of next month on a job assignment, so it would be great if we could arrange the viewings during that time."

"No problem." Edwina checked her file again. "And after that she only has a month left on her contract, I see. Any chance you could just convince her to move out sooner?"

"No." Ally furrowed her brows, unsure why the thought of asking Madison to leave early upset her so much. She didn't think Madison would have a problem with it; she would have to look for something else anyway, so it would probably be easier for her to do that now. Getting three month's rent back if she was going to be away would be a pretty sweet deal too, but Ally didn't like the idea of not having her around for the last month. "That's not an option," she said, her tone indicating that there was no discussion to be had.

"Very well, as long as she leaves it tidy and doesn't have a problem with us letting ourselves in, then that should be fine." Edwina held out her hand. "Thank you for the coffee. It was nice to meet you, Ally. Our photographer and stylist will be in next week and we'll have your house up on our website shortly thereafter."

"Thank you." Ally turned to Lara, who was pulling her long, auburn hair into a ponytail. "And you."

Lara gave her a short nod and a smile and stared up dreamily at the pink house. "I wish we could afford it." She sighed and picked up her toolbox. "It's so cute; I'd love to live here."

"Maybe one day, babe." Edwina gave Ally a wave and put an arm around Lara as they walked off. It was only then that Ally realized they were a couple. She tilted her head, studying the two women until they disappeared around the corner. Imagining herself and Madison like that, she wondered what it would be like, being openly gay in her own small community. Would they get strange looks? Would there be gossip? Capitola was an open-minded village but being a bar owner, most people knew her. She shook her head and reminded herself that their relationship was only casual and there was no need to worry or to contemplate their future. She headed back toward *Western Shores* and as she looked over her shoulder and took in the 'for sale' sign again, a deep sadness settled in her core. Yes, it was necessary, and yes, it would give her peace of mind and relieve her of a huge financial headache, but she never thought this day would come. Her eyes stung, and she quickly wiped at the tear that fell, knowing the pink house would belong to someone else soon.

"Honey, are you okay?" Ana asked as she came up behind her.

"Yeah, I'm fine. It's just..." Ally pointed at the sign, currently unable to speak due to the lump in her throat that threatened to make her break out into sobs any moment.

"I know it hurts." Ana rubbed her shoulder. "I know you and Marcos dreamed of converting all three houses and living here forever. But things have changed, and you have to move on. For your sake and for Theo's."

"I know." Ally sniffed. "I guess I just thought I could keep this all, somehow. I love this place and I love our life here. It's so small, but just knowing we could expand our living space into the pink house one day made it worth it."

"You're never going to move on if you stay here." Ana sat down at one of the tables and beckoned for Ally to sit down next to her. "I know you loved my son very much, and that this is your way of honoring him, keeping your mutual dream alive. But you're not going to meet someone if you stick around in Capitola and hold onto the past. And as much as I'd like you to stay for selfish reasons, because I do really consider you my daughter, you have to start thinking about what you want out of life. Have you considered moving to LA if Theo starts school there after the summer program?"

Ally nodded. "Sure, it's crossed my mind, but this is our home. It's a great place for Theo to grow up, and I have *Western Shores*. If we moved to LA, we could never afford a place by the beach and that's what he loves most. I'd have to sell the bar, find a new job and let's face it; I've studied art and have no experience in the trading world, so what could I possibly do?"

"It doesn't matter what you do, you'll make it work. Your life might be here, but love is out there, Ally. It's not easy to meet someone in a village. You're still very young, so don't make the same mistake I did."

"It's not the same, Ana. I'm not looking for love and despite what you might think, I *have* moved on. I just don't want to move away from here. The people, the beach, the storms, the light..." She took a deep breath. "Do you remember when I first moved here with Marcos? I wasn't convinced at all. I'd always dreamed of life in a big city, but I kept telling myself it wouldn't be forever. That it was just for Marcos's career. And then it grew on me and now... now this is my home, my one certainty in life. I love my bar and I love the small community, so don't take my reluctance to move as just a hint of nostalgia"

She looked out over the beach and thought of Madison for the millionth time that day, wondering if she was thinking of her too. "And as far as dating goes, well... I've met someone who has truly turned my world upside down but..." Her voice trailed away as she fixed her gaze on the horizon.

"But?" Ana asked, her expression both hopeful and worried.

"But, it's Madison."

Ana gasped. "No... Madison your young, pink-haired lodger?" She was silent for a moment, then shook her head. "No, no, no."

Ally sighed at her entirely predictable reaction. "She's not going to be my lodger for much longer but yes, she is a lot younger than me."

"And a woman," Ana added in utter shock.

"Yes, and a woman. Believe me, that part has not gone unnoticed." Ally felt herself tremble, a little afraid at her boldness. It was one thing telling Devon, but it was another thing telling her mother-in-law. She'd wanted to keep it quiet, and she had no idea why she'd told Ana. Still, she couldn't help but smile because each time she said Madison's name out loud, she felt warm inside, not to mention aroused beyond imagination.

Ana stared at her for what seemed like an eternity, but the anticipated stream of questions and judgmental opinions Ally was bracing herself for, never came. Instead, she kept shaking her head as if she couldn't quite believe it.

"Aren't you going to say something?" Ally asked tentatively. "Aren't you going to ask me if I've lost my mind or tell me it's a terrible idea?"

Ana shrugged. "Honestly, yes I do think you've lost your mind. And yes, I think it's a terrible idea. But is my opinion going to make you change how you feel?"

"No."

"Well then..." Ana's eyes narrowed as she lost herself in long forgotten thoughts. "I had some lovers myself over the years, after Marcos's father left me," she finally said. "None of them were meant to be, but they made me happy in the moment, and sometimes that's enough." She tilted her head, hesitating before she spoke again. "But saying she's turned your world upside down is quite a statement."

"Yeah, she has." Ally pursed her lips and sighed. "But I also know that it's utterly absurd and that it would probably never work, so I'm trying to keep my heart out of it."

"And Theo," Ana added. "Make sure to keep him out of it too because this is just a phase and you're not thinking clearly."

40

"Hey, I thought we said nothing romantic," Ally joked, but her beaming smile gave her away as she took the bunch of lilies from Madison and walked into the kitchen with them.

"They're not red roses, they're white lilies," Madison argued, grinning back at her.

"Yeah but white lilies are my favorite flowers. How did you know that? Did Devon clue you in?" Ally put them in a vase, arranged them until she was happy with how they looked and inhaled deep against the white aromatic petals. "Mmm..."

"You look sexy sniffing flowers. You're so into it, it's a delight to watch." Madison laughed when she saw Ally's cheeks flush and continued: "But then everything you do is sexy."

Ally wrapped her arms around Madison's waist and went up on her tiptoes to kiss her. She smelled so good, even better than the lilies, and she looked irresistible in a pair of faded jeans, a white T-shirt and the denim shirt she'd commented on a few nights ago. "Where are you taking me?"

"That's a surprise." Madison pulled her in and kissed her back. "But don't worry, my mom's not coming this time." She took a step back conscious not to get carried away again because tonight was not about sex, she told herself. It was about their date and it was about to get super romantic. "Are you ready?"

"Yeah, I guess so. Unless I need to bring something?"

"No, nothing. Just your beautiful self." Madison knew she was laying the charm on a little thick, but she couldn't help herself. Ally made her want to say all those things to her and she meant them. "Come on, I'm driving."

"Oh nice. Are we having dinner by the pier?" Ally asked fifteen minutes later when they parked up at the Santa Cruz Marina.

"Not quite." Madison walked around the truck and opened the door for Ally, then took her hand when she got out. "You know, you don't have to hold my hand if you're uncomfortable with it," she said when they stepped onto the pier and she noticed Ally looking over her shoulder.

Ally gave her a shy smile. "I'm not going to lie; it feels strange to hold your hand in public. I've never done that before." She tightened her grip. "But I like it."

"Are you worried what people are going to think?"

"Maybe a little," Ally admitted. "You and me... come on, you can't deny that we'd draw attention if there were people here. Everyone looks at you when you come home from work, and for all the right reasons, don't get me wrong. Your hair color and those icy-blue eyes..." She took a moment to indulge in them and flutters immediately took over her belly. "I'm not complaining; I love looking at you, but we don't exactly blend in."

"I didn't think of it that way." Madison let go when they reached the end of the pier, where Tom's boat was docked. She'd prepared everything earlier so she wouldn't have to carry all her stuff along and had been impressed by how nice it was. She'd expected an old fishing boat, but instead, it was a recreational speedboat with a white gloss exterior and walnut and white leather finishings. "Well, if it makes you feel more at ease, there won't be any people where we're going." She smiled when she saw Ally's face light up.

"Are we going on a boat trip? I thought you were taking me here for a picnic."

Madison laughed. "It's pretty here, but not date-worthy, especially not when it comes to you." She blew Ally a kiss, and they took off their shoes before she helped her onto the *Katherine*. "Tom let me borrow his boat; it's pretty neat, right?"

"It's very cool." Ally walked around and took in the boat. A walnut table and two benches with blue and white cushions were on the aft, and there were another four built-in seats at the stern. The small, covered cockpit had two comfortable seats too, the instruments and surrounds polished to perfection. It was clear that the boat was cleaned more often than it was used, and Madison reminded herself she'd made the right decision by not pursuing a PhD. Tom had teased her about the string lights that she'd secured around the benches and yes, it was a little sappy, but all in all she was pretty pleased with how it looked. There was wine sitting in a cooler she'd brought along earlier and she'd put a blanket on the bench in case they felt cold later.

"Make yourself comfortable." Madison felt proud when she saw how impressed Ally looked.

"Aww... did you do all of this for me?" she asked as she sat down on the bench. "This is so sweet." Her face gave off a radiant smile. "Not exactly casual though, is it? In fact, it might be the most romantic thing someone's ever done for me."

"Don't be too quick to judge. Who says we're not going fishing?" Madison joked. "You wait here; I'll be right back; I just need to go and pick up our dinner."

"This feels like a good spot." Half an hour later, Madison switched off the engine, leaving them in blissful silence.

"It's perfect." Ally followed her out onto the deck, where they sat down and opened a bottle of rosé to go with the food that Madison had picked up from one of the restaurants along the pier. She was silent as she filled their glasses, amazed by the view. To their left was Santa Cruz, the rides from the amusement park on the boardwalk and the restaurants and bars lit up in an array of bright colors against the evening sky. On either side of the boardwalk high sea cliffs rose from the ocean, making for a fascinating contrast. Even though they were only ten minutes out, they seemed so far away from everything. There was no noise but the sound of the ocean and the few seagulls that had followed their boat. To their right was the horizon where the sun was setting; orange around the low sun, running into a gradient of rich purple in the sky.

Madison checked something on her phone, then put it away. "I followed the coordinates a colleague gave me, so we might see humpback or gray whales. They're known to be around here, but then again, we might have missed them. Either way it's nice."

"It's very nice." Ally's smile grew, and she looked a little emotional as she continued. "I can't believe you went to all this trouble."

Madison ran a hand through Ally's hair and gave her a soft kiss on her cheek. "Well, since my mom already stole our last date, I had to think of something else. Tom was kind enough to offer the boat." She opened her bag and handed Ally a spoon she'd brought and a container with the cioppino from the restaurant. Then she took some candles out of her bag, lit them and placed them in glass holders, before switching on the lights. The soft glow lit up the boat's deck, creating a dreamy atmosphere.

"Mmm..." Ally inhaled above the container and started stirring the hearty stew filled with fresh seafood. "How did you know I loved cioppino?"

"Devon told me. I was digging for information when I got a moment alone with him. I figured it was fine as he knew anyway. He was really helpful, telling me about all your likes and dislikes before he became completely intolerable, cracking one indecent joke after the other."

"That's Devon for you. He just can't help himself; he's been teasing me relentlessly." Ally laughed. "But he's got his eye on someone too, so I'm patiently waiting for the right moment to get back at him. It's only a matter of time." She closed her eyes as she swallowed a spoonful of the fish stew and chewed on a plump mussel. "So good."

"You're right; it's really good. I've never had this before." She looked up from her food when she heard a splash in the distance and gasped, barely able to contain her excitement at the sight of a humpback whale.

"Oh my God." Ally instinctively reached for her hand when another one appeared, a cloud of steamy spume spouting up as its head rose out of the water.

"It's a female; she's large," Madison said, goose bumps appearing on her arm when the whale leapt out of the water in front of them, causing a huge splash. "I've seen whales breaching on a couple of occasions, but they never cease to amaze me." They sat there, mesmerized by the spectacle, the larger-than-life barnacle-covered creatures rising and spouting moist, warm air from their blowholes every three minutes or so until dusk settled, and they disappeared out of sight.

Madison couldn't help looking at Ally, who was so into the whales and her food that it was adorable, and it was then that she noticed she had tears in her eyes. "Hey, are you okay?"

"Yeah. I'm fine, better than fine. I don't think I could have planned a more perfect date if I'd arranged it myself, it's just that..." Ally took a moment to collect herself. "You're so incredibly kind and thoughtful and romantic and attractive and..." She shook her head. "And every time I try to tell myself not to get too invested you do something wonderful like this and make it really, really hard for me not to yearn for something more."

Madison swallowed hard as she continued to stare at her. Ally's ravishing face was glowing in the candlelight, her big, dark eyes looking into hers with such earnest. She hadn't expected to hear those words as Ally had been very clear about boundaries but hearing them said aloud made her so intensely happy that she almost cried herself. "I adore you," she said without thinking. "I really do. I love everything about you, everything that you do. I love how you make everyone around you smile, how great you are as a mom, how you look, how you move, how you talk, how you think, how you dress, how you laugh..." She paused and decided to be entirely honest as she'd probably crossed the line anyway. "And I love how you make me feel. I don't want to lose that."

Ally's lips parted; her gaze puzzled as if she couldn't quite believe what she was hearing. She was quiet, and Madison didn't want to say anything else either, afraid she'd made a fool of herself. Long moments passed, until Ally wiped at her eyes and finally spoke. "I love everything about you too," she said softly. "And I don't want to lose this either, but let's be realistic; this probably won't last; you're only twenty-three."

"How can you be so sure about that?" Madison scooted closer. "How can you know if you won't even try?" She tilted her head, regarding Ally, who was clearly torn. Despite what she'd said, Madison could see she was letting her guard down tonight. Ally's voice and the emotion in her eyes were evidence of something special, something bigger that was growing between them despite their mutual attempt to not let that happen. For her, it was already too late; she was head-over-heels in love with Ally. "Why can't we just go with it? See where we end up? Take each day as it comes. None of us can see into the future. I promise I won't hurt you and I won't hold it against you if you decide that in the end, it's not what you want. After you've given it an honest try," she added. "It's all in your hands. Please, just give me a chance." Madison never thought she'd be begging, but here she was, desperate for anything Ally was willing to give her.

Again, there was a long silence, but this time Ally slowly let her shoulders drop, releasing some of the tension between them. Madison could almost feel it melting away as her expression softened, the seriousness in her eyes fading a little. "I want to." She bit her lip and shrugged. "But I'm scared."

"I'm scared too. It is scary to open up to someone and it's

been a long time for you." Madison's lips pulled into a hopeful smile and she took Ally's hands into her own, knowing that deep down, she wanted to give in. Ally just needed to have faith, despite their age difference, and despite Theo and everything else she used as an excuse.

"Okay." Ally nodded and entwined their fingers, then lifted a hand to kiss the back of Madison's hand.

"Okay?" Madison's smile widened. "As in yes, Madison, I want to date you?"

Ally chuckled. "Yeah, I guess that's what I want if I'm totally honest with myself. I love spending time with you, and I suppose..." She hesitated. "Well, maybe I should give you the benefit of the doubt."

"Thank you." Madison leaned in and brushed her lips over Ally's. "Thank you." She kissed her and ran her hands through Ally's hair again.

Ally let out a soft moan and pulled her in closer. "But Theo can't know," she mumbled against Madison's mouth. "Not yet, anyway."

"He won't find out." Madison parted her lips, deepening the kiss until they were lost in each other once again. It was different this time though; not hungry and rushed, but tender and slow, as if they both realized they had all the time in the world now. A sense of calm and wonderment came over her, and she felt happier than she had in a long time. Although they were only fleeting thoughts, a lot of things went through her mind as they made out in the dusk. Their first meeting, the way she'd instantly fallen in love with the house, the strange pull she'd felt toward Capitola without ever having been there and her instant connection with Theo... Somehow, it felt like they were meant to meet and be here together tonight, as if the stars had aligned and everything was falling into place and was starting to make sense.

The sun had disappeared, and soon the Big Dipper was twinkling overhead, the moonlight reflected in the quiet ocean. Madison knew she'd always remember this moment and although she wanted to tell Ally all that and more, their kiss was too magical to interrupt.

41

"That was quite possibly the best date in history." Ally took Madison's hand as she climbed onto the Capitola pier, which was a short walk from home. "Are you sure it's okay to keep the boat here?"

"Yeah, it's totally fine. I'll just take it back on Monday." Madison jumped after her and took her hand as they walked back. "I'm glad you had a good time. I did too."

"I can't say I've ever been dropped off at home in a boat before. It certainly beats a cab." Ally leaned into her and let out a contented sigh. She was still on a high from their date. They'd seen whales, kissed, eaten delicious food, drank wine and then talked for hours while watching the stars, wrapped up in a blanket together. Then there had been an even steamier make-out session and as a result, she was all hot and bothered.

"Do you want to spend the night together?" Madison asked, clearly thinking the same as they crossed the beach together.

"I do." Ally was grateful that Madison couldn't see her big grin in the dark because right now, she couldn't think of anything she'd rather do than getting undressed together. It was after midnight and Capitola was asleep, apart from one bar along the beach, where the light was still burning. She could see the staff members gathered around a big table, having a drink before going home for the night. *Western Shores* was closed, the outside furniture neatly stacked up next to the door. "I hope Devon's gone home already," she whispered, narrowing her eyes as they neared.

"Looks like it; it's dark in there." Madison noted she was tiptoeing in the sand, which made no sense at all, but she sure could do without him catching them on their way home, especially since they were walking hand in hand and looking all loved up. "No wait, I think I can see someone sitting at the bar. Two people," she added.

"Two?" They reached the concrete path in front of the buildings and when they sneaked past the bar, Ally stopped and tugged at Madison's hand as she looked in. "Oh my God," she whispered. "He's having a drink with a woman. I wonder if it's the one he's been messaging with." She pulled Madison along so they wouldn't be in plain sight, then looked in again.

"Ally, don't spy." Madison tried not to laugh but it was hard as she watched Ally getting all excited. Unable to fight her curiosity she finally gave in herself, and gasped when she realized who Devon was talking to. "It's Chelsey."

"Yes, Chelsey! That's her name, I forgot." Ally turned to Madison, hating that she felt a hint of jealousy. How did she know her? Chelsey looked gorgeous with her long, blonde hair cascading down her back and she had an amazing figure, hugged by a simple black dress. "Do you know her?" She hoped the question came out as casual as she'd intended it to sound.

"Not very well, but I've met her."

"Where did you meet her?" Again, Ally could kick herself for sounding possessive already. "Never mind, it's none of my business."

Madison grabbed Ally by her waist and pulled her in as she leaned back against the wall. "Are you jealous?" she teased.

"No. But you have to admit that she's very attractive and..."

"She just started working in Capitola recently," Madison whispered, before shooting Ally a grin. "At the *Pink Panther*, that's where I met her."

"Right..." Ally tilted her head and frowned. "But she's straight, right? Devon seems so into her."

"Chelsey's trans," Madison said. "It's no secret, but maybe Devon didn't know before they met." She nodded to Ally's door. "Come on, let's go; I don't think he wants anyone to see them. He's probably not ready; maybe that's why they're hiding in there."

Ally's eyes widened. "What? That woman is trans? No..." She cast one last glance inside before Madison dragged her away from the window. "Wait... are you telling me that that gorgeous lady in there is or was a man?" she asked after she'd closed her front door behind them.

"I think she identifies as a woman, so she won't like you calling her that."

"I'm sorry, I didn't mean it like that. It's just the last thing I expected from Devon, that's all. They've probably been in there talking for a while, so that's a good sign, right? I've rarely seen him so... I don't know. He seemed really into her when he told me about her, and he hadn't even met her yet. That's very unlike him. Devon's usually all about the sex." Ally walked to the kitchen, taking a moment to process what she'd just seen and heard, her expression still baffled when she opened the refrigerator door. "Do you want a drink?" She closed it again when Madison shook her head. "Best not to mention we've seen them, huh?"

"Best not. He'll tell you in his own time. Or maybe it won't go anywhere." Madison cupped Ally's cheek with an amused look on her face. "Are you telling me that you've just agreed to date a woman, yet you're shocked that your friend is dating a trans woman?"

Ally chuckled and leaned into Madison. "Hmm... I did agree to date you, didn't I? But then again, you can be very persuasive." She kissed her seductively, pressing her hips against Madison's "It feels weird to say it out loud."

"Yeah?" Madison slipped her hands under Ally's dress and ran them up her thigh, leaving a trail of goose flesh where her fingertips had been. "So, would it be weird if I called you my girlfriend?"

"A little bit," Ally admitted, gasping when Madison's hands continued under the fabric of her panties, cupping her ass. It was incredible how a simple touch was like a switch, turning her on in a split second. Only Madison could do that. "But I like it." She started pulling the hem of Madison's T-shirt up, but Madison surprised her by bending forward, taking hold of her legs and picking her up, throwing her over her shoulder.

"Good," she said, laughing when Ally let out a cry of surprise. "In that case, I'd like to take my girlfriend to the bedroom."

42

"Pancakes!" Theo shouted as he ran into the kitchen.

"Good morning to you too." Ally laughed as she pulled him in and gave him a kiss on the top of his head. She was glad they'd managed to wake up earlier this morning, giving Madison time to go home before Theo came back from Ana's. "Are you hungry?"

"Yeah." He sat down at the breakfast bar and drank the glass of milk she put down in front of him.

"Did grandma not want pancakes?"

"No, she said she'd had enough of me." He chuckled. "Just kidding. She was going to the charity bake sale at the church."

Ally shrugged cheerfully. "Well, more for us, then. And I'm not working until later tonight, so I thought we could do something fun together." She smiled at him. They only had one week left before she had to drive Theo to LA to attend The Seymour Institute's summer program. Devon had agreed to work some extra hours and she'd hired a part-timer from an agency so they could have some quality time together.

"Did someone say pancakes?" Madison yelled from the hallway after letting herself in. She was freshly showered, wearing a pair of navy jersey shorts and a white tank top over her bright blue bikini. Ally had trouble taking her eyes off of her and almost forgot to flip the pancake until she smelled something burning.

"Madison!" Theo's face pulled into a grin when he saw her come in. "Are you having breakfast with us? Can we go skateboarding? And then go look for shells?"

"Dude." Madison high-fived him and leaned against the counter, eyeing up Ally who was still wearing her robe. "I have an even better idea and I think your mom will like it too." She paused for effect and ruffled a hand through his hair. "How about paddle boarding? It's really still on the water so it's a perfect day for it."

"Yes!" Theo shrieked. "Paddle boarding!" He slapped his hand on the bar, then stopped and frowned. "But we don't have one. Mom threw it away because it was really old."

"But I have one, and we can rent a second from the wharf for your mom."

"Can I go on yours, then?"

"Sure you can. You've got a life vest, right?"

"Paddle boarding sounds fun." Ally placed the first pancake onto Theo's plate and held up the pan for Madison. "Want one?" She'd already asked Madison if she wanted to spend the day with them and it had been Madison's idea to rent a board. Despite living on the coast, she couldn't remember the last time she'd been out on a board, and she was looking forward to it.

"I do." Madison took the pan from her. "But you sit down and enjoy your coffee, I'll make the rest."

"Okay." Ally sat down next to Theo and sighed in delight. "How nice to not have to make my own breakfast for once. Are you sure you know how to?" She laughed when Madison made a show out of ladling the batter into the pan and twirling it around like a pro. "Never mind, I see you've done that before."

"I used to make them for my study club members in college on Wednesday nights because they're cheap to make and everyone loves them." Madison flipped the pancake up in the air, then caught it on the other side. "It's about the only thing I can make." She winked at Theo. "Good thing I really like pancakes."

Ally felt warm inside watching her. It was normally quiet in the mornings, with her and Theo having a sleepy conversation over breakfast, but Madison's presence made everything lively and fun. She held out her plate so Madison could slide the pancake onto it and watched her spoon more batter into the pan, turning the heat up.

"More?" She asked Theo.

"Yes!" He grinned. "I want ten."

"Ten?" Madison put a hand on her hip and raised an eyebrow. "Are you sure you're going to be able to eat that many?"

"No, he won't." Ally stole the last piece of his pancake and laughed when his eyes widened. "But I will."

The sun gave the bay a peaceful silver shimmer as they bobbed on the calm waters, just past the wharf. Although they were quite a distance out, Ally felt safe with Theo being on Madison's board. He was wearing a wetsuit and a life vest and Madison was a great swimmer, so she didn't have a care in the world and was enjoying the sunshine and their conversations as they watched the fish beneath them. Theo loved to identify each variety and tell them what he knew about them, and Madison filled him in on the things he wasn't sure about.

"Ever seen any sharks around here?" Madison asked.

Ally laughed. "Oh God, don't ask me that, now I'm going to be frightened having my legs in the water."

"There won't be any sharks right now." Theo sounded pretty sure of himself as he said it. "The water's not warm enough yet, but there might be sharks in late July or August."

"Right." Ally sighed. "That's a relief, thank you for that." She turned to Madison. "There have been rare sightings, but no attacks in the past twelve years, at least not in our bay."

"There might be sharks in LA."

"Probably, but you'll be at school."

"Yeah kiddo, you won't have any time for shark-watching. Have you guys decided when you're leaving for LA yet?"

"I was thinking Saturday." Ally put her paddle on the board as she was drifting next to Madison. "We're driving because we need to take enough things to cover his eight week visit and I thought Sunday might be cutting it a bit short with the long drive."

"We're going to stay in a hotel," Theo added excitedly.

"You are?" Madison took him by his waist and shifted him back onto the middle of the board. "That's cool. Have you ever stayed in a hotel before?"

"Only once, when mom and I went to San Francisco."

Ally shook her head and rolled her eyes. "Hearing him say that makes me realize how little we've been away since it's been just him and me. The only times we take a trip is when we visit my father nowadays. Having a bar kind of ties you down, so it will be nice to go somewhere for a change, even though I'll be a little sad that he's leaving." That was an understatement, as she was dreading saying goodbye, but this was only the summer program so it was best not to be too dramatic around him as he felt guilty already for leaving her.

"Do you want to come?" Theo asked, looking at Madison over his shoulder.

"No honey, Madison needs her weekend to rest, she works all week," Ally said, giving Madison an apologetic shrug. "What did we say about not asking before you've discussed things with me?"

"But you're working all week too, and you're going."

"Yes, but I'm your mom. I want to make sure you're okay." Ally's eyes met Madison's and she almost broke out into laughter when Madison shot her a begging look, her bottom lip jutting out. Did she really want to come? She frowned, pointing at her, making sure Theo didn't see their sign language. When Madison nodded, she held her gaze and smiled.

"I wouldn't mind... I could come along, help you out with the drive," Madison said then, knowing Ally would be okay with it. "We could leave on Friday or on Saturday, make a road trip out of it. Unless you want quality time together, I completely get that."

"No, come along. We don't need quality time," Theo assured her.

"Oh, we don't?" Ally joked. "All right then, if you say so..." The idea of a trip with her son and her new favorite person in the world seemed almost too good to be true. She loved how Madison slotted into their life so seamlessly without even trying. Truth be told, she wasn't entirely at ease about their 'dating' yet, but Madison's words last night had convinced her to at least be open to the idea and to go with the flow. When Theo was around, they were just friends, and that was perfect. And when he wasn't around...

Ally shivered, remembering last night, after Madison had carried her into her bedroom. Her eyes darted to Madison's toned stomach and her long legs, dangling over the edge of the board and she knew there was no question about her sexuality anymore. She just couldn't seem to stop lusting after her, using any excuse to touch her, however casually. "How about late Friday afternoon, then? After you come back home from work?"

Madison blew her a kiss, making Ally weak in all her limbs. "Friday is perfect. I'll make sure to have my bags packed."

43

Ally zipped closed the last of Theo's bags. He didn't need many clothes as he'd only be away five days at a time, but the Institute had sent her a long list of things for her to pack, including gym and swim wear, basic white T-shirts, underwear and socks, pajamas, boots, coats, and his favorite books and games.

She was leaving with mixed feelings, because she was happy for Theo, who couldn't wait to start the summer program. Not once had he seemed sad about the idea of leaving home, and he'd been in a great mood this morning, knowing it would be his last day there for a while. Ally would have some time to herself during the week now to go out or just relax, and she'd tried to see that as a positive but still, it wouldn't compensate for how much she'd miss having him around every day. It was a new beginning for them both though, and she told herself not to be dramatic about it.

She was glad Madison was coming with them, as it would distract her from the inevitable and put her in a better mood, which would eventually help Theo with saying goodbye too. The only thing that had bothered him was leaving his mother behind and she didn't want him to worry about her.

The rattling sound of a shopping cart being rolled toward her front door brought a smile to her face. She heard Theo's voice, and then the sound of Madison's laughter.

"We're ready when you are," Madison said with a beaming smile when she opened the door. Theo was sitting in the cart, eating an ice cream.

Ally chuckled and shook her head at the sight of them. Madison had an ice cream in her hand too and handed her the half-eaten chocolate-covered cone.

"Here, I thought we could share."

"Thank you." Ally blushed as her eyes met Madison's. "Well, we'd better start loading this up, then. Are you getting out, Theo?"

"No, you can just pile it on top of me." He grinned.

"All right, then," Ally said with a sigh. He'd been boisterous since he'd come back from school, but Ally wasn't going to argue with him now. "Let me get the bags and then we need to go say goodbye to grandma."

Ally had insisted on driving today as Madison had never been along the Big Sur before. They had just passed Carmel-by-the-Sea and were turning onto the Big Sur Highway 1 that ran all the way along California's central coast. Although it was early evening now, it would still be light for a while, and anyway, it was much better to drive with the worst tourist traffic out of the way. In fact, it was the perfect time, she realized, as the sunsets were incredible here. She remembered coming here with Marcos on romantic picnics when they were younger, but the trip down memory lane didn't hurt like it usually did when she thought back on their time together. It was just a dear, distant memory, that made her smile as she cherished driving with the wind blowing through her hair.

"My God, it's so incredibly beautiful here," Madison said as she caught her first glimpse of the unspoiled coastline. She was looking out of the open window, her arm hanging over the door, catching the wind, just like Theo was doing in the back. "I didn't expect this, I really didn't."

"Yeah, it's very pretty, right? I thought you'd like it." Ally looked to her right and decided the view of Madison next to her in tight jeans and a white T-shirt was equally appealing, but aware of Theo sitting in the back, she didn't speak her mind. Instead, she turned down the volume on the radio because the sound of the roaring ocean seemed more fitting than pop music. The views that came into sight after each winding turn were mesmerizing, the ocean below them rough, with high waves splashing up against the rocky cliffs.

"I can't believe I've been in Capitola for ten weeks and yet never driven here before." Madison inhaled deeply and looked almost emotional as she stared out over the resplendent coastline. To their left were the green Santa Lucia Mountains with wildflowers and trees sticking out above patches of mist. "It's so raw and remote, wild and untamed..." She turned to Ally and put a hand on her thigh, then looked in the rearview mirror. "Can we pull over somewhere along this road?"

"Of course. There will be lots of places to pull into soon."

After a forty-minute drive and comments left, right and center from Madison, who was about to explode with excitement, Ally's smile widened when she saw the Bixby Bridge.

The concrete, open arched structure over the Bixby Creek's steep and crumbling cliffs looked as iconic as she remembered.

"Wait... I know this." Madison's eyes narrowed as she took in the view. "I feel like I've seen this before."

"It's only the most photographed bridge in the world. You've probably seen it in a commercial or TV show or something," Ally said. "I love it. Crossing it takes me back in time." She stopped herself then, not wanting to talk about Marcos with Theo in such close proximity. Any mention of him tended to make him ask questions for days on end and this time, she wanted it to be just about the three of them. "Back in time..." She gave a wistful sigh as she said it. "You must think I'm so old."

"No, I don't." Madison shot her an amused smile. "I think you're... wait..." Distracted by the scenery, she took a picture of the bridge and the creek in front of the mountains rising from the ocean, the water crashing up against them. The sight of the dramatic terrain gave her goose bumps, and she turned off the radio entirely to experience the full effect before she continued, choosing her Theo-proof words carefully. "I think you're very nice and pretty. And funny, that too, but not old."

"Yeah she's old," Theo shouted from the back. "She's much older than most moms at school."

"Thanks for your vote of confidence, Theo." Ally stopped the car in one of the pullovers after the bridge and looked at him over her shoulder. "Get out of my car," she joked, giving him a playful slap on his knee.

Theo chuckled as they got out, stretching and inhaling the pure sea air. The temperatures were going down as the sun lowered, and the breeze was strong but pleasant.

"I don't need to tell you why they call this Hurricane

Point." Ally tucked her hair behind her ears as they walked toward the edge of the cliff.

Madison was holding onto her hair too, the pink locks blowing wildly in the gusts of wind that seemed to come from all sides. Instinctively, she grabbed Theo's arm as she looked down. Although there was a low barbed wire fence, it was so steep and deep that it made her stomach drop. "Be careful, buddy." It was breathtaking though; the thin strip of golden beach, the turquoise ocean running into the creek, and sea otters floating on their backs in the kelp below.

"Can we go and see the sea otters?" Theo asked excitedly.

"There's no way we can get down there," Ally said, but she knew there would be more mammals on the beaches further down the road, that were going to be more accessible. She took note of Madison's hand around her son's arm and felt a warm and fuzzy sensation at how protective she was over him. "I suggest we go to Pfeiffer Beach. We can get down there and watch the sunset. It's not so far from the campground we're staying at tonight and then I won't have to drive in the dark."

"Nice! Are we camping?" Madison seemed about as excited as Theo today, and Ally loved her youthful enthusiasm that drew her in and made her feel animated herself.

"Not in the literal sense. I've booked a cabin, but it should be fun." Everything was planned with Theo in mind and she now regretted not having taken more trips with him while they'd had the chance. She'd become so complacent in her life, falling into a predictable rhythm of running the bar and being a mom at home that she'd failed to think outside the box and plan things that were a little different and fun for them both. From now on, she'd make more of an effort, she told herself. Maybe they could go abroad for a couple of weeks over his holiday once she'd sold the pink house, expose him to different cultures and places that would inspire him. Maybe even China, since he was so into learning Mandarin. And maybe even with Madison…

The path down to Pfeiffer Beach was steep and narrow, and they carefully made their way down with Theo walking in the middle. They'd pulled over many times during the short drive, stopping off to take pictures of the coastline and the thick redwood forest that was now over-taking the hillside.

"Unbelievable." Madison let go of Theo's hand when they reached the crescent-shaped beach with a small water-fall where Sycamore Canyon Creek emptied into the Pacific Ocean. The sound of the waterfall and the waves, the golden light sparkling and dancing over the water and the serene beach where tide pools had formed, reflecting a fiery red shimmer from the setting sun, made the scene look surreal. "I've travelled a lot, but I don't think I've ever seen some-thing so out of this world." She inched closer to Ally when Theo took off to explore the tide pools, where sea stars, sea urchins, crabs, anemones and small fish had made their homes. "And you were right about the sunset…"

"I don't remember it being quite so stunning through." Ally felt the hairs on her arms rise as her hand brushed the back of Madison's. Maybe it was her weird mood, constantly shifting between sadness because they were dropping Theo off and intense happiness to be here with Theo and Madi-son, but she felt a tear roll down her cheek as they walked along the shore in silence and watched the sunset. A double rock formation rose from the crystal-clear low tide, the sun casting beams of orange light through the naturally arched keyhole in the middle.

They sat down on a rock at the north end of the beach. The sand was purple here and it made the ocean look purple too, in places.

"Look!" Theo caught up with them and showed them a huge, orange sea star, curling over his hand. "It's a Henricia leviuscula, I think." He looked to Madison for confirmation.

"You're right, it is." Madison narrowed her eyes at him. "Also known as the..."

"Pacific blood star." Theo finished her sentence with a proud grin on his face. "I should go put it back. I just wanted to show it to you." He ran toward the tide pool to place it back in the water.

"Don't go in the water, the riptides look dangerous," Madison yelled after him.

"Don't worry, he won't. I taught him about the currents from a very young age." Ally gave her a smile and nudged her with her shoulder. "But it's very sweet of you to look after him."

Madison shrugged and shot Ally a goofy look. "I know I shouldn't worry about him, but I guess I feel responsible when I'm with him; I don't want him to get hurt." She chuckled. "I've never really had kids in my life, apart from the babysitting gigs when I was a teenager, and I honestly didn't know I was like this."

Ally laughed too. "You've obviously got a maternal streak in you. Do you want kids?"

Madison had to think about that. "I don't know. I think I would like that at some point." She bit her lip, regretting what she'd just said. The 'at some point' was probably not an option if she and Ally stayed together. "What about you?" she asked.

"I don't know either. I think I'm done with all that. Physically, I mean. I certainly wouldn't want to be pregnant when I'm over forty. It's a little too risky. I had five miscarriages before I had Theo and I wouldn't want to put myself through the risk of that happening again now." Ally paused, considering her words carefully as she continued. She didn't want to scare Madison off, yet she needed to be honest and realistic with her. "But if I was with someone who really wanted kids, I'd be open to co-parenting if, of course, that was something they really wanted. Up to a certain age."

"Of course. I get that."

Ally shifted on the rock, avoiding Madison's eyes. They were only one week into their 'dating' and already, they were running into the first potential obstacle. Madison wasn't even thinking about kids yet, and she was already past that stage. Eager to change the subject, as she didn't want to think about it right now, she focused on the sand instead. "Why is it purple?"

Madison frowned, clearly puzzled by the random shift in their conversation. "It's because of the manganese garnet rocks in the cliffs," she said, as if it was the most common thing in the world to know that. "The purple particles wash down the hillside and gather on the beach. Their dust colors the water too."

"God, you are a smartass." Ally smiled and decided to give up on her questions. The view was just too perfect to be distracted by conversations regarding their age-gap or purple sand, so she leaned in against Madison and put her head on her shoulder, simply cherishing the moment as the sun slowly disappeared, turning the sky and the ocean a deep orange. Madison put an arm around her in return and remained silent too, as they watched Theo's silhouette turn black against the glowing backdrop. Ally let out a deep sigh as she absorbed the heat that ran between them, a heat that was only growing stronger the more time they spent together, and she knew fighting her feelings was a battle she couldn't win. The sky was on fire and so was she.

44

"This is nice," Ally said, opening the door to their cabin in the Pfeiffer redwoods. "I'm glad I pre-booked it; I didn't expect so many cars upfront, considering it's basically in the middle of nowhere."

"Yeah, it seems like a popular place, but I'm not surprised. It's super cute." Madison looked around the cozy cabin. Two double beds with nightstands, a table with four chairs and a TV cabinet were the main furniture in the simple room, but the timber walls and ceiling gave it a warm glow as she switched on the lights. The nightstand lampshades and the cushions on the chairs were made of red and white checked fabric and so were the curtains in the window that overlooked the river. It was cool inside as the cabin was shaded by trees, and it was tempting to light the fireplace, even though she knew that was ridiculous in summer. There was also a small bathroom and a corner unit with a coffeemaker and a refrigerator. "I've never been in a cabin, but this is how I always pictured it. In the woods and..." She opened the TV cabinet and let out an exaggerated gasp. "They've got board games!"

"Yeah, I want to play Trivial Pursuit," Theo, said, already pulling the box from the cabinet.

"Good choice." Madison gave him a pat on his shoulder, then turned to Ally. "How about I go and get a big pizza from the camp store first? I can't think on an empty stomach and I'm terribly competitive."

"You are?" Ally laughed at that. "Seriously? I didn't think you were into board games. I guess I just assumed that ..." She grinned and stopped herself then. "Never mind."

"What, you assumed that I wasn't into them because I'm twenty-three? Are you saying these are just for children and old people?" Madison raised a brow. "Who's an ageist now?" She took the box from Theo and put it on the table. "That's right, your mom is an ageist."

"Okay, okay, I do admit I was thinking that." Ally held up a hand. "Hey, why don't I go and get the pizza to make up for being so terribly judgmental? You two set up the board."

"Yes!" Theo put the final plastic wedge into his playing piece, beating them for the second time. Madison was amazed by how much he knew, even on the most random subjects, but then he was a sponge, absorbing just about everything he saw, heard or read.

"What's the minimum age for those TV quizzes?" she joked, sitting back in defeat. "He could win you a lot of money."

Ally laughed. "I think it might be eighteen, so we'll have to wait for a while." She finished her tea and shot him a proud smile. "Just don't forget about your old mom when you win a million dollars. I'd like a holiday, please. And a new car."

"Yeah, me too," Madison joked. "My pickup's just about to fall apart."

Theo shook his head in all seriousness. "I can't because if I win a million, I'm buying the pink house so mom can keep it."

Madison saw the emotion in Ally's eyes as she put an arm around him and gave him a kiss. "Honey, I don't care about the house. You're much more important, you know that, right?" She knew Ally was pretending she didn't care that it was up for sale, at least when Theo was around, but clearly, he'd picked up on it anyway.

"I know. But I still want to buy it back for you one day, if I can." Theo wiggled himself out of Ally's grip, not wanting to be cuddled by his mom anymore. "One more round?" he asked, shooting them a challenging look as he crossed his arms in front of his chest, knowing they stood no chance.

"No, you need to go to sleep, it's way past your bedtime already." Ally looked at her phone. "It's way after ten, Theo!"

"But I can't sleep when you two are talking so I might as well stay up."

"Then we'll go to bed too," Madison said. "I'm pretty sure I can sleep after getting up at six this morning."

"Oh God, I'm so sorry, I forgot you'd already had a long day at work before we left..."

"No, it's fine. I had a great day. Really, really great," she added, lowering her voice as she looked from Ally to Theo and back.

"Yeah, me too." Ally tried not to stare at her mouth and focused on Theo instead. "Go brush your teeth. You're sharing this bed with me." She pointed to the bed nearest the window as Madison's bag was on the other bed.

"Gross, no." Theo grimaced. "I'm not sharing a bed with you."

Ally rolled her eyes as she handed him his toiletry bag. "Oh, come on, I'm your mom and the bed is big. Don't be difficult, now."

"But it's gross."

Madison laughed. "It's fine, your mom and I can share a bed together." She looked at Ally, whose cheeks had quickly turned pink and added: "What? The bed is big."

I t was strange to be in a bed with Ally, fully clothed, when all Madison wanted to do was rip off her shorts and T-shirt and roll on top of her. They were lying on their backs, both close to their respective sides of the bed as anything else seemed too intimate with Theo in the room.

Madison stared at the ceiling, feeling tired but also terribly excited. Today had given her a lot to think about and so many things were running through her mind. She'd loved being with Ally and Theo, and as weird as it seemed, it almost felt like they were a family. Thinking of the spectacular drive, the sunset, the games, the innocent teasing and the fun they'd had made her feel warm and connected in a way she'd never felt before, and all she wanted was to be close to Ally.

Unable to lie there without touching her at all, she moved her hand toward the middle of the bed. Her lips pulled into a smile when she met Ally's hand there, already waiting for hers under the cover. As if on cue, they laced their fingers together and turned their heads to face each other. When she met her gaze, Madison melted at how Ally looked at her. There wasn't just lust in her eyes anymore. There was tenderness, a dawning closeness, and a spark that seemed only there for her. Their silent exchange in that moment said more than words ever could.

45

Ally was confused to find Madison and Theo gone when she woke up. She reached for her phone and frowned when she saw it was already after eight. On her nightstand was a note that said: *'Gone out to play basketball X'*, next to a take-out coffee. She smiled as she took a sip and read the message again, noting that even Madison's handwriting made her pulse race. They'd fallen asleep hand in hand, and she hoped she hadn't tried to spoon her in her sleep.

Something had changed between them yesterday, or maybe her view of Madison had changed, she wasn't sure. It was the way she interacted with Theo, how protective she was of him, and how attentive and sweet she was toward her. Spending time together while there was no sex involved had made her see Madison in a different light, and she appreciated her way beyond their physical chemistry. In fact, she was delighted that Madison had come with them, as she had turned a rather sad occasion into a fun and memorable trip for all of them.

Ally got out of bed, put on a clean dress and a pair of

white sneakers and quickly washed her face before heading out with her coffee to find Theo and Madison. Beams of light poured through the canopies of the giant sequoias, reaching for the sun around the cabin. It felt humbling to stand between the tallest trees on earth. The redwoods were flourishing in early summer, with clumps of sword fern, moss, sorrel, rhododendrons and azaleas. She took in the sweeping views over the river and inhaled the earthy smell of the spongy redwood forest floor as she followed the signs to the recreational area. It really was quite stunning here, the picturesque trail with big old moss-covered maple trees caressed by the morning mist of the Pacific Ocean. The path grew wider until she found herself in an open area with picnic tables, a barbecue area, a small kiosk and behind it, a basketball court where she heard Theo and Madison laughing.

"Okay, now!" Madison shouted, lifting Theo up as he ran toward the hoop and dunked the ball in. "Well done, buddy!"

Theo looked over his shoulder and grinned widely when he heard Ally clapping behind him. "Did you see that, Mom?"

"I sure did." Ally smiled at him, then looked at Madison, who again, wasn't making it easy for her today, dressed in the tiny shorts she'd been sleeping in and a crop top, beads of sweat dripping down her toned body. "That was impressive. How long have you guys been out here? Why didn't you wake me up?"

"You were really fast asleep, and you looked so peaceful. I thought you might want to enjoy some time in bed for once." Madison gestured to Theo. "Kiddo here was up at seven and I was in desperate need of coffee, so we went to the kiosk and then we found the basketball court."

"Madison bought me a basketball in the store." Theo threw the ball at his mother. "Show her what you can do, Mom."

"Oh, that's very nice of Madison." Ally looked at the ball, tempted to show off but not sure if she still had the skills. She was also conscious that she was wearing a short, floral summer dress that wasn't exactly practical attire for playing on the court. Although she hadn't held a ball since college, it felt comfortable in her hands, so she threw it up and caught it, spinning it on her index finger.

"Check you out." Now it was Madison's turn to applaud, clapping her hands dramatically together with each step she took toward Ally. When they were face to face, she gave her a flirty smile that made Ally's knees buckle. "Where did you learn that?"

"Mom used to play, she's really good." Theo sounded proud of her, and Ally scrunched her nose at him before blowing him a kiss.

"You used to play? What, like on a team?" Madison snickered and held up a hand. "Sorry, no offence but you're kind of short."

"Uhuh. That was my nickname. Shorty." Ally shot her a smug look. "And Theo's right; I was pretty good. I might not be tall, but I'm fast and I've got killer skills."

"Shorty..." Madison laughed even louder now, then fell silent and tilted her head when she realized Ally was being serious. Amusement twinkled in her eyes. "Okay, in that case, I dare you to play me."

Ally knew she was both out of shape and out of practice, but Madison's cocky attitude only made her want to beat her more. "Sure. Show me what you've got." She took a wide stance before her, skillfully dribbling the ball between and around her legs without even looking at it. Madison reached out to swipe it away, but Ally was too quick for her and bounced it behind her, then turned to continue with her back against Madison. She heard Theo laughing at Madison's fruitless attempts to steal the ball and it made her more determined to demonstrate her moves. She grabbed the ball, turned and took two long and very quick steps before she threw the ball, aiming at the hoop. She managed to suppress a gasp when it actually went in; it was lucky, but Madison didn't have to know that. Grabbing the ball, she spun it on her finger again and asked: "So, do you want to play or not?"

Madison quirked a brow, clearly impressed. "I don't know, I'm suddenly not feeling so confident anymore." She inched closer, licked her lips and looked down at Ally's mouth, then reached out and slammed the ball out of her hands when Ally got distracted by her flirty body language.

"Hey!" Ally's eyes widened in surprise. She balled her hands into fists, the cheating making her old competitive streak flare up. Seducing her on the court in order to steal her ball was not fair, and she was going to teach Madison a lesson. What happened after that looked more like a battle for bragging rights rather than a game, both woman giving it everything they had to prove themselves. Ally was pleased to find that she still had it in her, and even though Madison was good, she was better, and scored point after point. Fifteen minutes later, they were both out of breath.

"I give up." Madison threw her hands in the air. "I'll admit it; I was wrong about you. You're very, very good, Shorty." She wiped her forehead, took a sip of water and handed Ally her bottle. "When did you last play?"

"Twenty-one years ago. When you were two," Ally added. Saying it out loud made their age-difference sound daunting and she immediately regretted her remark.

"What? Are you only twenty-three?" Theo asked after doing the math. "I thought you were old too."

"Thanks, buddy. I don't think anyone's ever called me old before." Amusement rang through Madison's voice, and none of it seemed to bother her. She gave Ally a fist-bump and Theo a playful tweak on his nose, then pointed to the kiosk. "Anyone hungry?"

———

46

Driving along the coast, Madison's hair was drying in the wind after a quick shower. All four windows were open, the salty breeze making her smile as it wafted over her face. The fifty miles of stunning scenery gave her energy, and even after all the physical activity, she felt like she could take on anything. After their basketball match, in which Ally had both surprised and impressed her with her hidden talents, they'd had breakfast together and walked a five-mile trail through the redwoods.

Ally was laughing next to her now, a sound so sweet she could listen to it forever, and she had pain in her abdomen from laughing so much herself. Theo's Mandarin course was playing over the speakers, and they were both practicing along with him, repeating the entirely random sentences that were highly unlikely ever to be used by anyone from this century, such as: 'How are your respectful elders faring?', and: 'May I inspect your dagger?'.

Even Theo agreed that the course structure was a little out there, but he had so far managed to connect the dots, finding patterns in the language that allowed him to form new sentences from the words he knew. The intonation was even more complicated, and Madison was glad she was able to amuse Ally with her attempts that sounded more like bad singing.

When she took a sharp bend, Ally pointed to the ocean, wiping the tears of laughter from her cheeks. "Slow down, there's a turn here soon."

"Okay, Shorty."

"I told you not to call me that." Ally gave Madison a slap on her thigh and shot her a warning smile.

"Does Devon know about your nickname?" Madison chuckled when Ally's eyes narrowed.

"Don't you dare tell him."

"We'll see," Madison teased. "Where are we going anyway?" She took the turn and drove down a hill toward a dirt lot that was used for parking halfway down. She was surprised to see at least a dozen cars there, as it had been fairly quiet on the road.

Immediately, she knew what Ally wanted to show them. "Never mind, I think I know." She smiled and shot a glance in the rearview mirror, noting that Theo's interest was sparked at the noise that welcomed them. A deep, guttural grunting, interspersed with howls, cackles, barks and roars drowned out the Mandarin course before she turned it down, and then a pungent smell hit her. "Elephant seals, right?"

"Yeah, how did you know?" Ally smiled over her shoulder when she heard Theo yell something before opening the car door.

"I guessed from the sound. Especially the males sound quite distinctive from sea lions and harbor seals." Madison switched off the engine. "And I knew there was a colony close to Ragged Point, everyone in my field knows that." She knew she looked just as excited as Theo, who was already running toward the wooden viewing platform. Unable to resist Ally, she put an arm around her and pulled her in as they followed him.

Looking down on the beach, they saw hundreds of elephant seals lazing in the sun. "This is so cool." Madison steadied her elbows on the railing, studying the big, blubbery creatures that were napping, fighting, or playing. Huge males were shuffling over the beach battling for alpha dominance with their pendulous noses, the females noticeably calmer and without the distinct elephant features.

"They look so different. The males and the females." Ally pointed at a couple.

"Yes, it's very pronounced in elephant seals; it's called sexual dimorphism. You can barely tell they're the same species. The male's nose elongates at puberty, when they start reproduction. They use it to battle for territory with other males, but they also intimidate them by making lots of noise."

"They inflate the proboscis, so their nose looks even bigger," Theo added. "And then they rear up and produce this noise that will make other males retreat." He pointed to one of the males who was rising to about six foot, throwing his head back. "Like that one."

"Maybe you two should do a presentation here too." Ally ruffled a hand through Theo's hair. "I'm sure everyone would love to know more."

Theo shrugged but Madison could tell he was proud to show off his extensive knowledge. "We'll have to come back in January or February for breeding season," she said. "There will be thousands of elephant seals here, then. Lots of pups too."

"Yeah, we should do that," Ally was quick to reply, then

curbed her enthusiasm, blushing as she shook her head. "Let's see how it goes, it's a long time away."

Madison held her gaze and could feel Ally's inner conflict. Yes, January was a long time away but that didn't mean they wouldn't still be together. Because if it was up to her, she'd be with Ally for as long as she'd let her. "No," she disagreed. "It's not a long time away. Seven or eight months is nothing when you spend time with people you care about." She stopped herself then, conscious that Theo was right next to her.

Ally's mouth pulled into a small smile, and she didn't argue but Madison could tell she wasn't convinced. What on earth did she have to do to prove to Ally she was serious? Why was it so hard to believe that they were right for each other? Because she was amazing and gorgeous, smart and funny...

"It's molting season now, right?" Theo interrupted their silent exchange, pointing at a female with only a couple of patches of fur left, some hanging off its skin like an old, dirty rag.

"It is. Just for the females though, the males start molting a month later. That's why they're all here on the beach; they mainly come to land to breed and molt." Madison pointed to the dirt path along the ridge. "Do you guys want to go for a walk, see the rest? We're not in a hurry, right?"

"Yeah, let's do that." Ally seemed grateful for the distraction. "It's only three miles. Are you up for it, Theo? Why don't you go grab your binoculars from the car?"

47

After a long walk, four-hundred feet above the ocean with a view over hundreds of elephant seals and a spectacular coastline, they stopped off at Ragged Point for a coffee and lunch before checking into their next accommodation. Madison was glad they'd left on Friday and taken their time as they didn't have to rush and could enjoy everything along the way at their leisure.

Ragged Point, the cape along the Big Sur's southernmost cliffs, was a fairly busy spot, despite there only being an inn, where they would be spending the night, a restaurant, a gas station, three stores and an ice cream stand. People came here for the scenery, the hiking trails, Young Creek Beach and for picnics and refreshments, but mostly, just to sit by the edge of the cliff and let themselves be overwhelmed by the natural beauty of the ocean and the cliffs.

"Did you know they call this the 'million-dollar view'?" Ally asked as they were seated at a picnic table, drinking coffee and eating sandwiches. Theo, who wasn't hungry as he'd been snacking in the back of the car, was walking around snapping pictures on Ally's phone. He'd documented their whole trip and Ally was looking forward to taking a look at his pictures when they got back.

"No, I didn't, but it's worth more if you ask me." Madison stretched her arms above her head and rolled her shoulders, then let out a sigh of contentment, absorbing the sapphire colored water, the black sand of the beach and the barren, steep cliffs, running into the ocean. "I could stay here for weeks and never get bored of this."

"Me too. Why don't we just relax here for the rest of the day? Maybe find the pool? Or we could go down to the beach? There's a waterfall there too." Ally shot her a wicked grin. "I assume you're done with basketball?"

Madison laughed and held up both hands. "I'm definitely not playing with you again, Shorty."

At that, Ally flicked a pickle from her sandwich into Madison's face, then ducked down under the table when Madison stood up and approached her while screwing the top off her water bottle. "Please don't," she begged, then screamed when Madison poured some of the cold water down her neck.

Madison laughed and sat down next to Ally, straddling the bench. "I'm sorry, I just couldn't resist." She looked over her shoulder, noting that Theo was distracted with Ally's phone, and cupped her cheek with her hand. "You're so cute when you scream."

"Right." Ally raised a brow and caught her hand, leaning into her touch. "Can I have a sip of your water please?" she asked in her sweetest, most manipulative tone.

"Absolutely not." Madison chuckled. "That's kind of transparent, don't you think?" She held the bottle up high when Ally tried to grab it, and flung her thigh over Ally's knee, locking her down on the bench. Unable to resist teasing her a little more, she said: "You might as well give up because you'll never be able to reach. That's the downside of being short."

"That's mean." Ally jutted out her bottom lip, but Madison could tell by the twinkle in her eyes that she liked being pinned down by her. She couldn't deny that it turned her on too, the way they were sitting so close together now. They'd only kissed once since they'd left, and she could feel the sexual tension between them growing by the minute. It was sexy as hell and frustrating at the same time, being unable to act on their needs. She let out a quiet sigh when she saw that Ally's mind was going there too. The way she looked at her mouth, the way her eyes darkened... Madison knew exactly what she was thinking.

"Beach then?" Ally asked, this time in a near whisper.

"Depends. Will you wear that skimpy turquoise bikini?"

"I might. Will you put sunscreen on my back?"

"I'll put sunscreen anywhere you want me to." Madison was about to say more but stopped herself when Theo approached them. Turning to him and swinging her leg back under the table, she smiled when she saw he was taking a picture of them. To her surprise, Ally put an arm around her and drew her in close, resting her face against her shoulder. Madison was aware that they looked like a couple, sitting like that and Ally must have realized it too when she let go, looking a little flustered.

"Want to go to the beach, Theo?" She stood up to gather their trash and took her phone back. When they walked back to their room to get towels, Madison felt her lean against her while they walked side by side, as if she was missing the contact already.

· · ·

"He's sleeping." Ally came out and sat down next to Madison around the firepit in front of their room. The yard was open, with very few trees, giving them an unobstructed view over the ocean. It was a clear night, and the moon and the fire were the only source of light, apart from some lanterns on the table.

"Will he be okay by himself?" Madison handed her one of the blankets she'd borrowed from the inn. The breeze was strong here in the vulnerable spot where they were sitting, not too far from the edge of the cliff. The view was worth it though, and the gusts of wind only added charm to the fire that was dancing wildly, casting mystic shadows over the lawn. The sound of the ocean and the endless starry sky made for such a perfect setting that she wondered why more people were not sitting out here.

"Yeah. I told him we were out here." Ally draped the blanket over her lap and reached for the hot chocolate Madison had ordered for them. Taking a careful sip of the marshmallow covered liquid, she closed her eyes and moaned dramatically. "Mmm... Thank you, this is delicious."

"It seemed fitting here." Madison winked. "That, and I really like chocolate."

"I know you do." Ally returned her flirty gaze and held it, causing a flutter to run through Madison's core. "Did you notice the beds are much smaller in this room?"

"I saw that. They're about half the size." Of course Madison had noticed. In fact, it was about all she'd been able to think of since they'd checked in. "It's going to be difficult not to reach out and wrap my arm around your waist." Her lips pulled into a smile. "It was really nice to hold your hand last night."

"So nice," Ally agreed. "This trip... I didn't think it would be so much fun. I mean, I feel sad thinking about saying goodbye to Theo tomorrow, but I've actually laughed so much, and I don't think it would have been the same without you."

"Thank you for letting me come. I'm having a great time too." Madison sunk lower in her chair and inhaled deeply. "It's not often I get to sit around a firepit on the cliffs, looking out over what is possibly the best view I've ever witnessed." She smiled. "Next to the most beautiful woman in the world."

Ally blushed. "You charmer."

"I'm not being charming, I mean it." Madison's expression grew serious. "You really are the most beautiful woman in the world to me." She reached out for Ally's hand, hesitating a moment before she continued. "I've asked Tom if I can take three days off in a couple of weeks. It's Hannah's birthday soon and I thought it would be fun to go there and catch up with everyone. The flights are reasonable, and I'll be staying with them."

"That sounds fun. Hannah's your half-sister, right? I remember you told me about her."

"Yes. She lives in Presley, Louisiana, with her fiancée Kristine." Madison paused, scared to ask the question that had been on her mind. She wasn't sure if inviting Ally to a family party was pushing it, but she couldn't help herself. "So... I was thinking that maybe it would be fun if you..." She took a deep breath, cursing herself for sounding so clumsy all of a sudden. "Since we're not casual anymore, I mean, since we're dating, I was actually wondering if you'd like to come with me."

Ally's lips parted, her eyes widening. She was either in shock, or terrified. "You want me to come along?" She continued to stare at Madison, silent for a beat before she swallowed hard and asked: "As in your date?"

"Yeah. Be my date, meet my family. I thought you could use some distraction with Theo being away and it's only for a night or two." Nerves grew in the pit of Madison's stomach. She was dreading the answer as Ally gave the impression she was about to run off, yet at the same time, she couldn't look away, in awe of how mesmerizing she looked in the flickering light of the fire. Her hair was down, messy from the drive and their activities, and her cheeks had caught the sun. Her eyes sparkled, and her lips were almost irresistible as she licked them. It was something she did subconsciously when in deep thought, and it was so sexy that Madison felt an overwhelming urge to get up and kiss her. She didn't though, giving Ally the time to think about her proposal while she fiddled with the fringe on her blanket. "I'm sorry, has that freaked you out?"

"No..." Ally finally laughed and shook her head. "Okay, maybe a little. But you're right; it's not casual anymore." She looked down at their entwined hands and lowered her voice to a near whisper. "I guess it never really felt that way in the first place if I'm being completely honest with myself. I don't know who I was fooling."

Madison let out the breath she'd been holding. "So... will you come with me? Hannah and her fiancée are really nice, and my family isn't so bad either. I mean, you've met my mom and..."

"Yes, I've met your mom," Ally interrupted her. "And she's wonderful, but you've also told me how she feels about our situation. I can only imagine the others will think the same and I don't want them to see me as that person who is making your life complicated."

"Will you please stop calling it a situation as if it's something bad that we need to solve?" Madison begged, tightening her grip on Ally's hand. "Can we just call this a relationship, because that's what it is, right? And no, my family will love you, I have no doubt about that. Hannah and Kristine and my brothers will adore you and my father is super laid-back. My mother really likes you too, she's just concerned, that's all. But we can prove her wrong, you and me." She continued when Ally didn't answer. "And just so you know, you'd never make my life complicated, only better. I'm happy when I'm with you. You make me feel alive and complete. But if it's too soon, I understand. We've only known each other for a few months, and I don't want to push you into something you're not ready for. I would never do that."

Ally tilted her head and gave her a sweet smile as her shoulders dropped, noticeably relaxing. "I know you wouldn't." She licked her lips again, looking up at Madison's mouth. "Okay, I'll come with you if you promise me that they won't mind. And only if I can get Devon or the new girl from the agency to stand in for me, it's not easy to get cover for three days."

"Really?" Madison's heart skipped a beat at her words and her face pulled into a beaming smile. "I promise you they won't mind, and I promise you won't regret it." Unable to hold back any longer, she stood up and bent over Ally, brushing their lips together. "Thank you."

Ally responded by pulling her closer, her breath quickening as she parted her lips to let Madison in. What followed was a long, lingering kiss and when they finally pulled apart, they noticed an elderly couple had sat down at one of the tables further down the lawn. Ally giggled, rolling her eyes. "Look at me. Forty years old, making out in public."

"I don't think people make out in public enough." Madison raised an eyebrow. "We should set an example, maybe we'll inspire them."

48

"So this is where you'll be holed up. I like it." Madison put an arm around Theo, who was beaming with excitement when they got out of the car.

Ally took a couple of deep breaths as she looked up at the building that suddenly felt like it was going to swallow her son alive. *It's only for eight weeks,* she told herself, although she knew deep down that it was more likely to be three years. Theo had immediately liked it here the first time they'd visited, and he seemed just as happy to be here this time around. Yes, Theo attending the summer program was going to be a test, but she was pretty confident about the outcome.

"Are you okay?" Madison asked her as they followed Theo inside.

"I'll be fine." Ally gave her a brave smile, but she knew she couldn't hide the dread she felt. Not from Madison. If only she could keep it together until she was back in the car, then she'd allow herself to break down in tears.

"You will." Madison gave her arm a squeeze and Ally

was so glad she was here with them today. "Are you sure it's okay if I come in with you guys?"

"Yeah, absolutely." She looked up and managed a smile when Mrs. Vargo welcomed them in the reception area.

"Welcome Theo, welcome Ally. It's so good to see you both again." She turned to Madison. "Hi. Are you Ally's friend, partner?"

Ally froze for a moment. It wasn't a strange question, it was LA after all, and the school was very liberal. She should have anticipated this would happen and wanted to kick herself for not discussing it with Madison first.

Madison shot a sideways glance at Theo, who was talking to a boy he recognized from last time. Ally guessed she wasn't sure how to answer as she didn't want to put her in an awkward position. Truth be told, even if Theo wasn't here, Ally wouldn't know what to say herself. She wasn't even out and admitting to a stranger that she was dating a woman was a daunting idea. "We're friends," Madison finally said, exchanging a quick glance with Ally, who nodded and gave her a grateful smile.

"Yes, she's a good friend and close to Theo." Ally stepped into the elevator Mrs. Vargo was holding and Madison stepped in too. "Theo, are you coming? Mrs. Vargo is going to show us your dorm so we can get your stuff."

"Be good, okay? Have fun, do your homework and listen to the care team. If you want to call me, or you change your mind and you want me to come and pick you up, just let them know and they'll let you call me." Ally tried to keep her voice steady as she held Theo in her arms. He usually tried to wiggle himself out of her grip, but she sensed he understood she needed it today.

"I always do my homework, you know that," he said, wrapping his arms around her neck in return.

"I know, honey. And don't forget to brush your teeth, okay? And call me on Wednesday. I'll see you again very soon."

"It's okay, Mom. I'll see you on Friday. It's only eight weeks and I'll be coming back at weekends."

Ally nodded, fighting back her tears. "I know." She finally let go of him and stepped back.

"Bye Madison." Theo walked up to Madison and gave her a hug too. When she bent down to squeeze him tight, he whispered something in her ear, and Ally saw her whisper something back at him.

"Bye buddy. I'll see you soon." Knowing Theo was fine, Madison put an arm around Ally and led them out of the building. Ally's attempt to pull herself together until they got to the car broke her heart. Because even though it was only five days until he'd be home again, she knew Ally's entire life was about to change forever. She put her hand on Ally's knee but didn't say anything, aware that she was silently crying next to her in the car.

Theo would be fine, though. While they'd been unpacking his things, he'd taken off with Tej, the boy who'd shown him around on their last visit. After that, he'd shown her around with a proud grin on his face, comfortable and in his element like he had lived there for months. She could only imagine how impressive it must be for a young boy from a small town with his intelligence to move to a boarding school with five-star facilities and kids and teachers that would inspire him.

Madison decided to take the freeway as it would be a lot quicker and as the sun began to set, Theo's words kept lingering in her mind.

"Please take care of my mom?" he'd whispered in her ear. "She's really sad." The boy's plea had made her feel emotional herself, but she'd managed not to show it. His concern about his mother was incredibly endearing but above all, she felt honored that he'd thought of her as the person to look after his mother. Not that Ally needed looking after; she was strong and independent, and she'd be fine eventually, whether Theo chose to move back home or not following the summer program. But it did strengthen the feeling that had slowly started to build over the course of their trip. That maybe they really could be a family one day.

Madison wondered what Theo would think of them if they told him they were dating. Mrs. Vargo's question had come as a surprise but she'd also felt strangely flattered.

"You'll see him again very soon," she said in a fruitless attempt to make Ally

feel better.

Ally wiped her eyes and blew her nose. "But it won't be the same. These eight weeks feel like the catalyst of something big happening in Theo's life, a signal that everything is changing and for some reason my eleven-year-old son is able to deal with it, but I'm not."

"Hey, you're going to be fine too. You just need to get used to him being away during the week. And who knows? He might change his mind and want to come back home. It's a summer program after all... He might not like being away."

"I don't think so. Did you see how excited he was?" Ally shook her head. "I shouldn't be thinking this way, it's great that he wants this. It's supposed to make it easier, not harder. I guess I just want him to miss me, you know. It just seemed really easy for him to let go."

"Maybe he was just trying to do that for you." Madison glanced at her sideways and shot her a reassuring smile. "I'm going to help you through this and it's going to be okay."

49

"Hey." Madison held up the bottle of wine in her hand. "Please tell me if you want to be alone right now. I just thought you could do with some company." She'd rushed home from work on Monday, worried about Ally, who would be alone following Theo's departure.

Ally looked at her through red-rimmed eyes and managed a smile. "You know what? I could definitely do with some distraction." She opened the door wider and led the way into the living room. "I was kind of okay this morning and afternoon because I was working, but then I came back and it was so quiet in the house..." She mustered a smile. "Actually, shall we go outside? It's a nice evening."

"Sure." Madison walked back into the hallway, grabbed the folding table and chairs and put them in front of the door. She greeted the neighbors from a couple of doors down, an elderly couple whom she'd spoken to a couple of times. By now, she'd gotten to know a lot of the locals. It was a friendly community here, and everyone seemed to know each other without interfering too much in each other's lives. "I assume you haven't heard anything from Theo?" She asked when they were both seated.

"No. But no news is good news. I'm sure he's having a great time, making new friends and learning lots of interesting stuff. I'm not going to lie though; I'm feeling a little sad right now, and I miss him already. It's just the little things; picking him up from school, cooking for him... hell, I even miss cleaning up after him." Ally swallowed hard, trying to fight back her tears. "It's a really great school, you know. So amazing. He's being assessed this week to see what subjects he's most interested in and that's what they'll focus on. It's literally tailored to his needs."

"I know. They're taking good care of him." Madison moved a little closer and put an arm around Ally's shoulder. They were sitting side by side, facing the beach. The sunset was spectacular, as always, and she soaked up the sight. Rich hues spread over the horizon, blending into a golden shimmer where the sky met the earth. "I'm here for you, and you're going to be fine."

The statement had more impact on Ally than she'd expected, because she immediately started crying. "I'm sorry, I'm just a little emotional right now. Thank you for coming over."

"Hey, come here." Madison got up, walked around Ally's chair and gave her a hug from behind.

"I feel like I've lost him." Ally sniffed. She turned, buried her face in Madison's neck, and put an arm around her in return.

Madison closed her eyes, inhaling Ally's light perfume and the scent of her shampoo. She felt for her, and she wished there was something she could do to make it better. "You haven't lost him. It's all very new and exciting to him right now, and he's just really happy at the prospect of having friends and real challenges. He'll miss you; don't you worry about that."

"You're right. This, what I'm going through right now, it's all selfish."

"There's nothing selfish about missing your kid." Madison topped up Ally's glass, noticing she'd already downed most of it. She ran a hand over her cheek to wipe her tears and Ally caught it, letting out a deep sigh.

"Thank you," she said again, closing her eyes and kissing Madison's hand. "Really, thank you."

"Anytime." Madison let go and sat back down, conscious that people were looking at them from the terrace of *Western Shores*. She suspected Ally didn't realize how intimate they looked together, and she didn't want people to gossip about her before she'd even properly come to terms with what was going on herself. Madison suspected she'd been so distracted with Theo leaving that she hadn't given it much thought yet. She might still come to the conclusion that a gay relationship wasn't for her after all; anything was possible. But she didn't want to worry about that now. In two weeks, she'd be in the Bahamas and for now, she just wanted to spend as much time with Ally as she could.

Ally composed herself and took a sip of her wine. "Let's not talk about Theo, it just upsets me, and I know he's fine. How are things in your world? How was work today?"

"It was fun. I'm starting to recognize the individual dolphins now, and I've even named them." Madison winked. "One of them is called Ally. She has a son called Theo and a she has a couple of freckles, just like you." She opened a picture on her phone and showed it to Ally. "It's a little blurry because they were so fast, but this is Ally and that's Theo."

Ally finally gave her a genuine smile, subconsciously

touching her cheek. "That's so incredibly sweet." She settled back and relaxed a little. "Do they recognize you too?"

"It's hard to be sure, but I think so. They don't mind the tagging as it doesn't frighten them or hurt them. In fact, they managed to get hold of one of the sticks today, to play with." Madison laughed. "We might have a problem because they're custom made and really pricey, and now that they've discovered it's a fun game to steal them, it's safe to assume they'll try it every time."

"They're so clever and playful. I love dolphins. Must be a lot of fun to be out on the water all day. Are you looking forward to going to the Bahamas?"

"I am, but I'm not looking forward to leaving you." Madison's face fell as she took another sip of her wine. "But it's good timing, what with you selling the house. With me gone it will be spotless during the viewings..."

"I'm so sorry about the house," Ally said. "It's not fair that I can't even give you another six months. I know you love living here."

"Ally, I understand. Don't apologize. It won't take me long to find something else, rentals come up all the time, at least in Santa Cruz. I'll be a little farther away but it's still only a short drive."

"Mmm..." Ally still looked regretful as she mumbled her agreement, then lowered her gaze to Madison's long sun-kissed legs.

Noting a sudden sparkle in her eyes, Madison raked her eyes over Ally in return, taking in her bare shoulders under the thin-strapped white sun top, and her faded denim skirt that showed off her legs and her bare feet. The silver ankle bracelet and light pink nail polish made her tanned feet look incredibly cute and she felt an urge to lift her foot onto her lap and kiss it. Ally looked away then, turning to the people on the terrace.

"What are you thinking?" Madison asked.

"Do you think they know?"

"Know what?"

Ally waved when one of her customers caught her looking, and the woman waved back. "Do you think they know we're... seeing each other?"

"I don't know," Madison answered honestly. "I think it might be quite obvious sometimes. Does it bother you?"

Ally took a moment to think about that. "I'm not sure," she said. "Maybe a little. I still have trouble letting go of the age thing. That, and admitting to myself that I'm... well, I guess I'm gay now or at least bisexual." She let out a chuckle. "Dating you is the last thing they'd expect from me and if I told just one person other than Devon or Ana, who I both trust with my life, the whole town would know within a matter of days."

"Then we need to be more careful out here." Madison resisted reaching out for her again.

"Yes, at least for now, because Theo needs to know first." Ally's lips parted as she locked her eyes with Madison's. "It's very hard to hide how much you turn me on. Very hard. Even today, when I'm not feeling great, your presence still makes me crave you so much that I can barely contain myself."

"I know how that feels." Madison chewed her lip, cursing herself for getting aroused too, while, despite her words, all Ally really needed tonight was a friend. After returning home last night, she'd gone home with Ally and held her until she fell asleep and this morning, they'd had breakfast together before they went to work. It had felt so natural to start the week together that she hadn't given it a second thought, but now, she couldn't imagine not waking up with Ally in her arms every morning. "I got some sushi on my way home," she said. "Shall I go and get it?"

"That would be nice." Ally put a hand on her belly. "I'm actually quite hungry, I haven't eaten since lunch." She paused. "You probably think I'm not in the mood tonight, but I'd love to stay over, if you don't mind. I could really do with the distraction and…" Ally shook her head. "That didn't come out right; you're not my distraction. What I meant is that despite everything, I can't stop thinking about kissing you, undressing you and…" Her voice trailed away when she saw the same heat in Madison's eyes.

"Then let's go inside." Madison grabbed the bottle and her glass and stood up, a raging fire building inside her. How did Ally do this to her? She looked over her shoulder and saw that several patrons were following them with their eyes. Maybe they'd already speculated, maybe they hadn't. As long as they kept a physical distance, they could very well just look like great friends and neighbors hanging out together. Once she'd moved away, it would be a lot more complicated. Lowering her voice, she said: "I'll make sure you're as distracted as you could possibly be."

50

"Fuck!" Ally was squirming underneath Madison as she lay on her front, her hands fisting the pillow under her head. Madison was on top of her, her knee wedged between her thighs, rubbing herself up against her ass while she fucked her so hard that the bed was shaking. A fleeting thought about surrounding neighbors and the noise they were making came and went, but she was unable to remain quiet. She felt Madison's wetness on her behind, her hot breath against her skin, her fingers filling her up. She felt her need that matched her own insatiable appetite, so powerful that she wondered if she'd ever get enough. A delicious tension was starting to build deep inside of her, and she moaned loudly, surrendering to what she knew would be a shattering orgasm.

Madison moved faster and took hold of her wrist. "I'm going to come," she whispered, breathing heavily into her ear. "Come with me."

Her words were enough to send Ally right over the edge. She held her breath, then cried out as Madison's hand clenched around hers, her muscles tightening and her thighs quivering. Madison thrust against her one last time before she tensed up, moving deeper inside Ally to feel her clenching around her fingers.

"Fuck!" Ally fell into a pool of pleasure, a roaring orgasm radiating out from her core, consuming her. Madison cried out too, before collapsing on top of her. They were breathing in sync, fast and heavily, Madison's face buried in her neck. Ally took a moment to gather herself, then let out a soft chuckle. "Good morning," she said, then groaned when her alarm went off. "That was certainly a nice way to wake up." She reached for her phone to turn it off and wrapped her arm around Madison's waist when she rolled onto her side to face her.

"I thought you might prefer this over the alarm." Madison smiled when Ally yawned, her new state of relax-ation making her sleepy all over again. "We need to get up," she said with a look of regret. "I'll make us breakfast while you jump in the shower. I'd come with you, but we both know we'd be in there way longer than our schedules would allow." She got out of bed and wrapped herself in Ally's robe. "Scrambled eggs?"

"Really?" Ally rubbed the sleep out of her eyes and gave her a smile. "That's not something I get offered every day, so I'll definitely say yes to that." She sat up in bed and marveled at how much better she felt, just by starting her day off like this. Having Madison around and being able to look at her, touch her, kiss her and talk to her was not only permanently arousing, but also comforting in a way she hadn't expected, like sinking into a warm bath. "I'll make you breakfast tomorrow..." She stopped herself and shook her head. "I mean, if you're staying over again. If you're not that's totally fine, I don't expect us to move in with each other during the week now that Theo is gone, so don't be freaked out."

"I'm not freaked out." Madison tilted her head and regarded her as she tightened the tie on her robe. "And why wouldn't we spend the nights together? We both want it. You won't feel as lonely as you otherwise would, I love being with you and besides, I'm going to miss you when I'm away, so we might as well make use of the opportunity."

A warm, fuzzy feeling rushed through Ally at hearing Madison's words. Of course she wanted to spend every possible night with her. It made her feel amazing to be desired again, to be wanted the way Madison wanted her. And it made her happy and confident, like she could take on the world.

She'd been surprised at how easy it was to be with her after she'd started to let her in. Madison wasn't the party animal Ally had assumed she was, and she wasn't naïve or immature either. Madison was captivating, fun and caring and loved taking charge as well as taking care of her. "I love being with you too," she said softly. "And I'm going to miss you too. I'd be lying if I said otherwise." She wrapped herself in the sheets and swung her legs over the end of the bed, facing Madison. "So if you want to spend our nights together, I'd like that. Just don't expect me to make any long-term promises, okay? I need some time."

"I don't expect anything." Madison stepped between her legs, bent over and kissed her. "I just want you to try, that's all. Because as far as I can tell, I think we're pretty good together."

. . .

"Did Devon say anything yesterday?" Madison asked as they were seated at the bar, having breakfast. She'd found oranges in the kitchen and made them fresh juice, coffee and scrambled eggs with tomatoes and feta on toast. "About his date?"

"No, nothing. But he was acting shifty, exactly like I was before I told him about you, and he keeps looking at his phone, so that tells me it's still going on."

"Really?" Madison smiled. "I'm a little surprised... Just because it's Devon, you know, and he's such a ladies' man. I don't know why I expected him to break it off, he just seemed like that kind of guy. He's obviously more open-minded than I pegged him for and that's amazing; I hope it works out for them." She speared the last cherry tomato onto her fork and waved it at Ally. "Chelsey is elegant and sophisticated as hell and now that I've gotten used to the idea, I can actually picture them together."

"Maybe that's what people will say about us too." Ally took a sip of her orange juice. "They'd never expect me to end up with a woman, yet here I am, having breakfast with you." She grinned, curling her lip. "After what can only be described as the best sex in history."

"Oh yeah? You like it when I take you from behind like that?" Madison laughed when Ally's cheeks turned an adorable shade of pink.

"I do." Ally looked away, well aware that she was too shy to talk about sex in everyday life, yet in bed with Madison she turned into a tiger, hardly recognizing herself. Last night, she'd made Madison come twice, and the memory of that made her glow. She shifted on her stool, still feeling the delightful aftermath of their rough sex only half an hour ago. This woman seemed to know what she wanted before she'd figured it out herself, and that was eye-opening.

"You're so cute when you're shy." Madison looked at her lovingly while finishing her coffee. "Damn it, I have to go." She kissed Ally on her cheek, stood up and started walking toward the door, then changed her mind. Crossing the room again, she shot Ally a flirty look before grabbing her face and kissing her so deep and passionately that Ally melted and thought she might slide off her stool. She held onto Madison and wrapped her legs around her hips, her thoughts fading into nothing as she sank into the kiss, moaning and grinding herself against her. When they broke apart, they were both out of breath, grinning at each other like two horny teenagers.

"What are you doing to me?" Ally could barely speak through the shock of her body's reaction. She was wet and wanting, desperate to be touched all over again.

Madison arched a brow and held her gaze. "I just want you to think of me today." She turned on her heel and left, leaving Ally speechless and longing for more.

"Don't worry, I will," Ally mumbled, more to herself, after Madison had closed the door.

51

Ally couldn't stand still at the arrivals gate, restlessly hopping from one foot to the other. Despite the airline's service for unaccompanied minors, she didn't like the idea of Theo flying alone but he had assured her he'd be fine, even sounding excited at the prospect of his newfound independence. Her heart skipped a beat when she finally saw him walking through the sliding doors with a hostess by his side. He looked so small then, especially with the enormous backpack hanging from his back.

"Mom!" his eyes lit up and he ran toward Ally, wrapping his arms around her waist.

Ally tried to swallow away her tears, not wanting Theo to see her cry. "Theo, honey, it's so good to see you." She hugged him as tight as she could and inhaled deeply against his hair. "I've missed you so much." After five days without him, she finally felt like she was whole again, and nothing could have made her day any better than holding him. "Thank you," she said, turning to the hostess, showing her I.D. "I'll take it from here, I really appreciate your help." She took his hand and miraculously managed not to cry as they made their way to the car. "Were you okay by yourself on the plane?"

Theo nodded and chuckled. "It was really cool. They let me see inside the cockpit before we took off and I made notes of all the controls. I knew some of them already because I'd read about planes before I left."

"Of course you did. I bet they were impressed by how much you knew about it."

"Uhuh. The Captain said if I remembered everything next time, he'd let me fly the plane."

Ally laughed. "Honey, I think that was a joke, but I'm sure you'll be able to fly a plane one day if that's what you want. So, how was your first week? Did you have fun? Make any friends?"

"Yeah. I told you most of it already, but Andy and I made a compass in science class yesterday and I got a merit for my biology assignment." Theo pulled his hand out of her grip, apparently deciding he was too old to hold hands with his mother now.

It was just a small thing, but it hit home hard with Ally. He was getting older and being independent would only make him grow up faster. She didn't comment on it, but instead, opened the car door for him and handed him a milkshake she'd bought on her way to the airport. "You did? I'm so proud of you."

"Mmm... chocolate banana." Theo took a long drink. "Is Madison home? Can we see her when we get home? Or can she come to the beach with us tomorrow?"

Ally took in a quick breath and made sure to keep her eyes on the road as they left the parking lot. It was hard to concentrate at the mention of Madison's name. They'd been together every night, making love for hours as if it was the last time. Just the thought of her made Ally feel weak in places she needed to function in order to get them home. "Madison's been working all week, honey. She might be tired," she said, knowing Madison was actually really looking forward to seeing him again. But she didn't want to act out of character because he couldn't know, not until she was sure.

"But she might not be tired. I can always ask, right?"

Ally didn't answer that question but started firing off others instead in the hope of distracting Theo from his latest obsession, which was of course Madison of all people. He'd asked about her three times when they last spoke on the phone on Wednesday. Their beach and skateboarding adventures, and their drive to LA had clearly made a lasting impact on Theo and once he set his mind on something, it seemed impossible for him to let it go.

"How was the food at school? Did you eat your fruits and vegetables? And what would you like for dinner? We could stop off somewhere on our way home?" She locked her eyes with Theo in the rearview mirror and smiled. "You pick."

"Really?" Theo shot her a goofy grin. "McDonald's."

Ally grimaced for comical effect. "Are you sure?"

"Yeah. I want a burger; they only serve healthy food at school."

"That's reassuring." Ally chuckled. "I'm glad they feed you well." She looked over her shoulder and winked. "We'll go get a burger, but you can't tell your teachers, okay? It will be our little secret."

.   .   .

"Can we go and see Madison now?" Ally was only just about to open the door when Theo started again. "It's seven, she'll be home now."

"Yes, she is!" Ally turned to see Madison behind them, grinning at Theo. His eyes widened and so did his smile as he ran up to her and gave her a hug. She lifted him up and spun him around, clearly equally happy to see him. "Hey buddy. I've missed you."

"Looks like he's missed you too." Ally couldn't believe Theo was still holding onto her as he wasn't very affectionate with anybody nowadays. She felt a flutter in her core and fought the urge to kiss her. "How was your day?"

"Great, thanks. Glad it's the weekend, though." Madison seemed to be struggling with refraining from intimacy too, as she kept looking at Ally with an all too familiar twinkle in her eyes that she could telepathically read by now. "You must be happy to have him back, I'll let you guys have a quiet evening together."

"No, come and watch a movie with us," Theo insisted. "Mom said I can watch a scary movie tonight."

Madison laughed. "Letting the rules slide a little now, are you?" She quirked a brow at Ally and buried her hands in the back pockets of her jeans.

Ally shrugged and put an arm around Theo as he walked back to her. "Maybe a little. I need to make the homecoming fun if I'm competing with The Seymour Institute." She winked. "Do you want to watch a movie with us? No pressure, only if you're not too tired." There was no question about Madison being tired, because Ally felt exhausted herself. After sleeping very little and being active in the best of ways at night, they'd both had long days at work.

"Sure, I love scary movies." Madison walked past Ally and Theo, letting herself in. "Will there be popcorn?"

"I can arrange that."

"And Coke," Theo added.

Ally laughed. "Don't push it now, you've already had a burger for dinner." She closed the door, went into the kitchen and put the kettle on for tea, then went to work with making popcorn while Theo and Madison picked a movie from the pay-per-view channel. She loved their chatter and laughter in the background and how the kitchen filled with the smell of popcorn while the kernels popped. Her life was changing, but maybe it wasn't so bad after all, she thought as she poured hot water into two mugs and grabbed a juice for Theo. The house felt homey and cozy tonight, and it made her want to light candles.

As if reading her mind, Madison was already on it. "We can't watch a scary movie if it's light in here," she said in all seriousness, closing the curtains and searching for matches in the kitchen drawer. "We won't get the full effect unless it's really dark." She lit the candles on the bar, took the drinks and put them on the table, then made herself at home on the couch with Theo and draped a blanket over them, explaining they would need something to hide behind.

With a huge bowl of salted popcorn, Ally walked over to the couch and sat down between them when Madison lifted the blanket for her. She let out a deep, contented sigh at feeling Theo against her. It had been months since they'd had a real movie night, and she reminded herself to do it whenever he wanted. Time was precious with him growing up so fast and it was only a matter of years before he'd prefer to spend time by himself or with friends. "What are we watching?"

"The Grudge," Theo mumbled through a mouthful of popcorn.

"Okay. Are you're sure that's not going to frighten you?"

Theo rolled his eyes. "Of course not. I'm almost twelve and it's only a movie. Tej watched it last time he was home and he's my age."

"No blood, just ghosts," Madison whispered while she pulled her legs up underneath her and scooted closer too.

"Thank you," Ally mouthed back, holding her gaze for a beat. Madison took her hand under the blanket and she sat back with an arm around Theo, overwhelmed in her contentment. She relaxed into the movie and treasured the special night with her two favorite people in the world, wondering again what Theo would think if he knew what was going on. *Don't go there yet.* Ally wanted to give in wholeheartedly. She wanted to tell Theo she was crazy about Madison before telling the whole world, but she was terrified Madison would change her mind and realize it was a mistake. Perhaps her trip to the Bahamas would make her see that what she really wanted was her freedom, and that she wanted to travel the world and go out, meet new people instead of spending her Friday nights watching movies with a woman seventeen years her senior and her son. And that was okay, she couldn't blame her for that. If this turned out to be just a passionate affair, at least it had lifted her out of her numbness and made her feel something real. Only time could tell, and for now, Ally was happy to live in the moment, because the moment felt really, really good.

52

"I can't believe I'm going to meet your family." Ally nervously fiddled with her silver bangles as they drove toward the enchanting small town along the wetlands of Louisiana. She'd gotten changed at least five times before they left for the airport that morning and had finally settled on a simple black wrap dress and a pair of strappy wedges. "Is it too late to back out?" she joked, taking in the scenery that was so different to California, yet so stunning. Spanish moss covered live oaks that lined the old main road into Presley, and she felt like they were driving onto a movie set. Whether it was a horror movie or a romantic one was yet to be determined, and she decided the landscape could very well work for both.

Madison laughed and shook her head. "Unless you want to spend the night in a creepy motel, I suggest you come along." She shot Ally a sideways look and took her hand while she was driving. "Relax, Ally. They're all very, very chilled. You're going to like them and they're going to love you, that's a given."

"Still... it feels a little official, don't you think?"

Madison had to agree with that. It felt official to her too, because she'd never taken a girlfriend to meet her family. Many had come and gone but very few had been in her life for a long period of time, and none of them had been special enough for her to want to take them home. Something life-altering had happened to her in her short time in Capitola, because even though she'd only known Ally for three months, she'd couldn't wait to introduce her to the people she loved. But she sensed Ally was nervous, and she wanted to put her at ease as much as she could. "Don't worry, it's going to be fun. Really."

"How can you be so sure?" Ally asked then.

"Because you're wonderful. It's not that hard to figure out."

"No, I mean how can you be so sure I'm the one for you? You come from a rich family, your father used to work in politics, your mom's the Mother Theresa of local charity work and you have a trust fund the size of a super yacht. I'm much older than you are, and my background is working class at best. I have a bar, but not much else, apart from a wonderful son, but despite him being the love of my life, a child isn't something people would normally accept with open arms. I don't get the music you listen to and I have no idea about the bands printed on your T-shirts. I don't go out anymore, although maybe I should and frankly, you could have much more fun with someone else. So how can you be so sure that you want to be with me to the point that you want to introduce me to your family?"

"I just know." Madison shot her a confused smile. "I've known for a while, but I didn't want to scare you." She pulled over then, and realized she'd parked next to the cemetery. "Since when is a different taste in music a problem to you? Everyone has different tastes, no matter what age. Are you okay? Do you want to go for a walk?"

Ally took a deep breath and shook her head. "No. Sorry, I'm fine."

"You're so not fine." Madison switched off the engine anyway, got out of the car and walked around to open the door for Ally. "Come on, let's go for a walk. It might seem a bit morbid, but I've been here once and it's actually really pretty."

Ally sighed. "Okay." She stepped out and took her hand. It felt natural now that she was far from home in a place where no one knew her. "I don't mean to be difficult, I guess I'm just freaking out."

"There's no need to freak out and you're not being difficult. I might have felt the same if I were in your shoes." Madison led them to the cemetery entrance, and they walked in, passing ancient graves, sunken into the ground and the most amazing old trees, their branches forming an arch over the narrow path. "If you want to go home, I'll drive you back to the airport." She put an arm around Ally and kissed her temple. "I don't want you to feel uncomfortable."

Ally rested her head on Madison's shoulder. "No, I don't want to go home, I want to be with you. It's just hard to get my head around this. You're twenty-three."

Madison sighed, "You know, if you want this to work, you're going to have to let go of the age-thing. I'm a person just like you; I'm not my age."

"I know that." Ally mustered a smile. "You're actually pretty perfect. Maybe that's what scares me."

Madison laced her fingers through Ally's as they walked along the old graves, some neglected and some wonderfully decked out with flowers and candles. "No one is perfect, but we're perfect together. I hope you will see that one day." She turned, placed her hands purposefully on Ally's shoulders and looked at her intently. "Come on, let me show you the most beautiful view of the bayou that runs alongside the cemetery. The fresh air might help, and then we can get back on the road."

53

"So this is the infamous Ally." Hannah came down the porch steps to greet them and gave Ally a hug. "It's so nice to meet you. I'm glad you guys are early; it will give us some time to talk and get to know each other a little."

"It's so nice to meet you too. Madison has told me a lot about you." Although Hannah was Madison's half-sister, and hadn't grown up with their shared father, Ally was still surprised to see that like Madison, her looks weren't exactly conventional. She hadn't known what to expect after meeting Madison's mother, but her siblings being Southern preppies from a country-club family had certainly crossed her mind. Hannah was anything but that. Tattoos covered her arms and she had the air of a British rock-chick, the way she walked and carried herself. She was dressed casually, but cool in a pair of ripped jeans and a T-shirt that could have been one of Madison's. Welcoming was the first thing that sprung to mind though, and Ally felt instantly at ease with her. "Happy birthday by the way. Are you busy with preparations? Do you need some help?" she asked.

"Thank you. And no, we don't need any help, it's all done. We made extra snacks in the restaurant kitchen yesterday so all we need to do is heat everything up." Hannah gestured to the dining table on the porch. "Please sit down. I'll go and get us drinks." She walked into the kitchen and yelled: "Babe, they're here!"

"Coming!" The woman calling back sounded Southern, and it made Ally smile. She'd never been in Louisiana, but the charm of Presley had won her over as they'd driven through the small town. "Hey! You must be Ally."

Ally held out her hand to greet her, but again, she was drawn into a tight hug. "Kristine?"

"That's me." Kristine gave her arm a squeeze. "I'm so glad you could make it." She was tall and blonde with striking blue eyes and a dazzling smile. Her simple, figure-hugging black wrap dress was almost identical to Ally's and it immediately put her at ease, as she'd been a little self-conscious about being overdressed after seeing Hannah. They gave each other a glance-over and laughed.

"Great minds think alike." Ally gestured to the long table, counting twenty-four seats. "Looks like you're expecting a lot of people."

"Yeah. we've got Hannah's family coming over, and some friends from New Orleans and you guys and some of our local friends. We could host it in the restaurant, but we like it here on the porch, so we just brought a couple of tables over." Kristine gave her a cheerful shrug. "It's a little cramped but it will be fine. We're having tapas because it's easy with lots of people. Do you like Spanish food?"

"I love it." Ally was distracted by Hannah, who came out with a large jug, filled to the brim with a red liquor and chopped up fruit. "Sangria anyone?" She put it down on the table and started filling large glasses without waiting for an answer. "Oh, sorry, I forgot to ask if you drink."

"I do, thank you." Ally took the glass and sat down when Hannah pulled out a chair for her. "You guys have the most incredible view, she said, taking in the wetlands. The sunset was stunning, and if she thought Capitola was quiet, this was a whole new level. The only sound apart from Kristine and Madison catching up behind her were frogs and crickets. The deep orange glow over the still water made the trees look like shadow puppets, and the wedge of geese flying across in a perfect 'V' pointed to the lowering sun as if announcing the end of the day.

"Yeah, it's great, right? I still take the time to appreciate it every night." Hannah took a sip of her sangria, leaning on the backrest of Ally's chair.

"Don't you miss living in the UK?" Ally asked. "Madison told me you were from London."

"No. This is my home now. But I do miss some of my friends, so I'm looking forward to catching up with them at our wedding. It's in June next year, in Norway, during summer solstice."

"That sounds amazing."

"It will be." Hannah smiled. "It's where Kristine and I met during a Christmas vacation, so it only made sense to return to where it all started." She smiled dreamily before sitting down next to Ally. "So, tell me about yourself. I know you have an adorable son called Theo who is very clever..."

Ally felt herself relax as she talked to Hannah, telling her about her life in Capitola and how she'd met Madison and Edie. Kristine and Madison joined them at the table, and it wasn't long before she was laughing along with them, feeling entirely at ease. Hannah was funny and interesting, and Kristine was adorable and super sweet. Their golden retriever Belle had her own seat at the head of the table; a high bench that Hannah had made for her with a thick, fluffy cushion.

"What about your family? She asked Kristine. "Are they joining us?"

Kristine exchanged an amused glance with Hannah. "My family are not exactly the social kind. They came over for coffee this morning so they wouldn't have to put up with a bunch of lesbians tonight." She laughed. "It's fine, they're fairly accepting of me and Hannah but with you guys being a couple, and our friends Kate and Felicia coming too, my dad might have an aneurism. They're the complete opposite of Hannah's family. My mom doesn't talk, but you've met Edie, she's always the queen of the party."

"Yes, I've met Edie. She's quite the extrovert. But a lovely woman, I like her."

"Does she know about the two of you?" Hannah asked.

"She knows." Ally looked at Madison. "She's a little worried about our age-difference, which I can understand."

"Nonsense. She'll come around. Seventeen years difference is nothing. You're just two people who are attracted to each other, and that's beautiful." Kristine chuckled, then lowered her voice. "Besides, if anyone's got age issues, it's Edie. The plastic surgery is getting a little out of hand; I've been having trouble figuring out her mood lately because her face is so frozen." She held up a hand. "Sorry Madison, no offence to your mom."

Madison laughed. "It's fine, I've noticed that too." She blew a kiss at Ally over the table. "And you're right; she'll come around."

"I take it she doesn't know about Chuck then?" Hannah said, and again, her eyes met Kristine's with a hint of amusement. Ally loved how they were so entuned that they seemed to communicate without words.

"What are you talking about?" Madison asked.

Kristine gave Hannah a questioning look and Hannah laughed and nodded.

"Go on, I know you like to impart the gossip." She nudged Kristine. "She's such a Southerner."

"Oh come on darlin', I'm not that bad, but it's funny, right?"

"Seriously, what's so funny about Chuck?"

"You really have no idea?" Kristine asked, her eyes widening with excitement when Madison shook her head. "Do you remember New Year's Eve, when Chuck was talking to Jolene the whole night?"

"Your friend Jolene... the one with the Grease outfit and crazy hair?"

"I'm not sure if you have the right to call someone else's hair crazy, since yours is pink," Kristine retorted. "But yes, that's her. Anyway, Chuck was smitten by her. They were seeing each other for about three weeks until Jolene decided he was too young for her."

Madison stared at Kristine, trying to figure out if she was joking or not. "But she's close to sixty, right? And Chuck is only twenty."

"Exactly." Kristine slammed a hand on the table. "See? Compared to them, your age-difference is nothing. If Edie knew, she wouldn't even blink an eye at your relationship. But wait, that's not all of it because there's a pattern here." She paused for effect, clearly enjoying herself.

"Really? Chuck and Jolene?" Madison grinned and shook her head. "And there's more?"

"Yes, it's only just getting good," Hannah said. "But you have to promise this stays between us."

Kristine straightened her back and narrowed her eyes. "So, Chuck recently moved, into that serviced building where Edie's friend Darla lives, right? We've been to his apartment to take a look and it's really swanky. There's a lovely yard with a pond, a gym, they have cleaners, you name it."

"So?" Madison's brain was working full speed now, trying to figure out where Kristine was going with this.

"So... Darla is the youngest there. I'm not sure how old she is but my guess is mid-sixties. It's not officially a seniors' complex, but most of the people living there are retired."

"I know. That's why I was so surprised that Chuck agreed to mom's plan to move in there. I get that it's a good investment for them and he pays them rent, but still, it's an odd choice and Chuck's not the kind of guy to live a quiet life. I don't even think he's allowed to play loud music in there."

"Exactly!" Kristine exclaimed again, a blush of excitement rising to her cheeks. "That's what we were saying too. So last week, Chuck's car was at the garage to be serviced and when he came into work, he told us that a friend had dropped him off. But when he left at night, I saw it was Darla who picked him up."

"Okay. That's unusual, and I have to compliment you on your story-telling abilities, but I've already told mom he took her to dinner, he told me himself on the phone. I still don't see where you're going with this." Madison's mouth fell open then, and she stared at Kristine over the rim of her glass. "Wait... are you telling me that..."

Kristine nodded dramatically. "I saw him kiss Darla in her flashy BMW, and as Hannah said to me, I'm pretty sure he's banging her." She mimicked Hannah's English accent with a smirk on her face, holding up her glass in a triumphant toast.

Madison broke out into a coughing fit as the sip she'd just taken went straight up her nose. Ally laughed too, more out of sheer amusement at Madison's reaction as she didn't know who Darla was. She held up her glass too and cheered with the others, deciding she was having a good time.

54

Madison shot Ally an endearing smile and felt incredibly happy at seeing her so animated with her friends and family. The fact that she was having a good time was a great sign. Hannah kept bringing food out while people arrived. Artichokes with a parmesan-butter dip, albondigas, grilled Padron peppers, tortillas, mussels, croquettes, crispy squid with capers and sautéed chorizo along with breads and dips. She loved coming here, and besides the great company, the food was certainly one of the other reasons.

Hannah and Kristine's friends had arrived too, and it was fun catching up with them. She'd studied Jolene with interest when she'd walked up the porch steps in all her glory, wearing a pink mini dress and shiny black killer heels. The bow in her high blonde perm and her lipstick matched the pink color of her dress, and Madison had serious trouble imagining Chuck and her together.

It was an eclectic mix of people who were either extremely dressed up or extremely dressed down, apart from Ally and Kristine, who looked effortlessly elegant.

They'd never been in a social situation together before and she found it hard to tear her attention away from Ally so she could talk to other people. Ally looked beautiful as always, but tonight, she had a glow to her that told Madison she was genuinely at ease and it was incredibly attractive.

"Hey sis."

Madison turned when she felt a hand on her shoulder and stood up to give Chuck a hug. "Chuck! You look good." She scanned the drive for her parents. "I thought you were driving with mom and dad?" Chuck looked unusually dapper in dark jeans, a checked shirt and a navy blazer. His hair was normally messy, but he'd combed it back to add to his sophisticated look.

"No, a friend dropped me off." He shot a tense glance at Jolene and gave her a quick nod and a wave. "So, are you going to introduce me to Ally?"

Ally looked up when she heard her name and smiled up at them. "Chuck?"

"Yes, this is my younger brother Chuck. Chuck, this is Ally." Madison watched them hug and introduce them-selves, rolling her eyes when Chuck gave her a thumbs-up, mouthing the word 'hot'. "Oh, and I think that's the rest of the family."

Her parents arrived too, along with her older brother Mason and his girlfriend Brittany. Madison wasn't nervous herself, but she felt a little uncomfortable because she knew Ally would be. At least her mother would be sitting at the other end of the table, since their side was occupied.

It was getting dark, and Kristine had lit the torches that lined the driveway up to the house. Candles were flickering on the table, casting a cozy glow over the immaculately presented food.

"Sorry we're late," Edie said as she walked up to Hannah

and handed her a small wrapped present. "Happy birthday, honey." She looked over the table, adjusting her cream-colored cape. She was wearing a white pant suit, set off with a pearl necklace and high heels. "Well this looks like a delicious feast as always." Then her gaze turned to Madison and Chuck, greeting them in turn before focusing her attention on Ally. "Hi." She pulled her into a hug too and held onto her shoulders as she stepped back. "It's really nice to see you again." If her mother had a problem with Ally being there, she didn't let on, her acceptance allowing Madison to slowly let out the breath she'd been holding.

"It's good to see you too, Edie." Ally was about to sit back down when Edie stopped her.

"Wait Ally, why don't you come and sit at the other end with us, so we can catch up?"

Madison narrowed her eyes at her mother, who blatantly ignored her. "I'll join you too," she said, getting up. She didn't want Ally to feel cornered or risk her being pressured by her mother in any way. Now that Ally was finally here to meet her family, she was not going to let her mother ruin things between them.

"Sure, honey." Edie walked ahead to the end of the table and pulled out a seat for Ally and herself. "And this is Madison's father, my husband Ben. Ben, this is Ally."

Madison took a seat next to Ally and watched Ally and her father exchange small talk. Her father was in a great mood as always since his retirement and seemed excited to meet her. He immediately topped up Ally's glass before pouring himself a glass of sangria and held it up as he looked over at Hannah. "Happy birthday, sweetie." Then he turned to Madison, his eyes lowering to her hand as she took hold of Ally's in an attempt to put her at ease. "You look happy."

"I am happy, Dad."

"That's what I like to hear." He helped himself to some of the food and passed the plates on to Edie. "So Ally, tell me about yourself..."

Ally kicked off her shoes and slumped down with a coffee next to Hannah after everyone had said their goodbyes. She was exhausted from engaging with Madison's parents, her brothers and Mason's girlfriend but all in all, it had been fun and fairly comfortable. "It's so quiet here now," she whispered, almost scared to ruin the blissful silence by talking.

"Yeah, sometimes it feels like we're at the end of the world after a busy night." Hannah put her feet up on the table. "Kristine and I always take twenty minutes after we've closed down the restaurant to just sit here and enjoy the silence." She turned to Ally and put a hand on her arm. "I hope Edie behaved. She seemed pretty persistent about you moving to the other side of the table."

Ally nodded. "She was fine. Nice, actually. She admitted she had a little trouble with our age difference when we had a quiet moment. But she also said that she could see how happy Madison was, and that she would do her best to be more understanding."

"Oh God, I still can't believe she's making a deal out of it." Hannah rolled her eyes. "But you know what? Edie means well, and she'll get over it. She's fine with having a gay daughter and a gay step-daughter, so I'm sure she'll get used to you and Madison being a couple too."

"I hope so. I don't want her to worry about Madison because she's with me." Even though Edie had practically given Ally her blessing to date her daughter, it still stung that she wasn't entirely on board. But Hannah was right; she'd get used to it. After all, Ally had needed time to get used to it herself. Maybe they could change her mind eventually, maybe they couldn't. Either way, it was their business and no one else's. "Your dad seems lovely," she said, changing the subject. "Not what I'd expected from a political strategist at all."

"That's what I thought too when I first met him," Hannah said. "It's strange how people can grow to feel like family in such a short time. I feel very lucky to have them."

"You and Madison seem pretty close too."

"We are. We spent quite a bit of time together while Madison was back living at home after graduation. She used to come up here on weekends whenever she needed some time to herself, so it gave us the chance to get to know each other better." Hannah blew Kristine a kiss when she and Madison sat down opposite them. "Anyway, enough about Madison, let's talk about Chuck again. What's the verdict, gossip queen?"

"Shut up." Kristine laughed. "You're making me look like an old scuttlebutt in front of Ally."

"That's because you are," Hannah teased. "At least you've become one since you moved in here with me." She stood up, leaned over the table and gave Kristine a kiss. "I'm only joking, darling. But seriously, what's the gossip? I know you've been watching Chuck and Jolene."

Kristine laughed even harder now. "Okay, I'll admit that I've been keeping an eye on them. I thought it was my duty since you were both distracted with your parents and Hannah was the birthday girl and had to talk to everyone." She composed herself, then continued with an amused look. "It was a little uncomfortable at first. Chuck nodded at her and she smiled back and that was that for the first two hours. Then, after Jolene had a couple to drink, she went to sit next to him, and they talked. It didn't look flirty so I'm not going to make more of this than it was. It seems like Chuck really has moved on and that they cleared the air." She grinned. "But guess who came to pick him up in the parking lot behind *The Radley* when everyone was distracted by the cake at the end of the night?"

"Darla!" Madison, Hannah and Ally exclaimed simultaneously.

"Bloody hell, that's a bit bold, don't you think?" Hannah said with a chuckle. "Edie was right here on the porch."

Madison shook her head in disbelief. "Mom's never going to get over this if she finds out they're screwing." She smiled when Ally raised her now bare feet to her lap, and she started rubbing them. "But then neither am I," she continued. "Darla's gone through six husbands, dyes her dogs pink, thinks exercise is bad for you..."

"She drives the same car as Barbie, hasn't touched a carb in the past twenty years and is in no way in touch with reality," Hannah chipped in. "I don't get it either."

"And then there's Chuck, the high school dropout and beer enthusiast, who usually looks like he's just come back from three months backpacking, although I have to give it to him, he looked super dapper tonight," Madison said. "And he also prides himself on being able to produce extremely loud farts."

"Maybe we're being too harsh on them." Kristine's expression turned a little more serious after the laughter had subsided. "What if they really are crazy about each other? Then who are we to judge?"

"I suppose you're right." Hannah smiled at her. "And no one needs to know, apart from us. If it's serious, he'll tell us eventually."

Madison stood up. "Good. End of conversation, then. Thinking of my brother and Darla together is making me nauseous and I'm so tired that I'm about to fall asleep right here," she said, yawning.

"Tired or drunk?" Hannah tilted her head and grinned, regarding her.

"Both." Madison laughed and held out a hand for Ally. "Are you coming to bed or do you want to stay out here?"

"No, I'm coming." Ally put an arm around her waist instead and smiled over her shoulder. "Thank you so much, guys. Good night."

55

"Good morning. Can I help you with anything?" Ally was up early and saw Kristine busying herself in the kitchen. She laughed when Belle jumped up at her and started licking her face. "And hello to you too, Belle."

"Hey there." Kristine gave her a warm smile, looking fresh as a daisy. "No, I'm fine. Just tidying up before I head over to *The Radley* to start the prep for lunch. Aspirin?" She filled a glass with water and handed Ally a packet of painkillers.

"Thank you, you're a lifesaver." Ally took one. "I'm not used to drinking much these days, but I had a really great time last night, so the headache is totally worth it. Your friends and family are lovely."

"Yeah it was fun, wasn't it?" Kristine gave the counter one last swipe with a dishrag and pointed to their restaurant through the kitchen window. "Want to come over to *The Radley* with me and have a coffee? The machine is way better than the one here and I'm in no rush."

"Oh, I don't want to distract you from your work, and..."

"Nonsense." Kristine walked to the door and held it open for Ally. "Hannah has gone to work, and I assume Madison is still sleeping? She'll know where to find us. Come on, Belle. You too."

"Sure, I'd love a coffee." Ally followed her across the drive as there was clearly no arguing with Kristine, and was thoroughly impressed when she saw the cute, white building with blue window frames behind a delectable patio, shaded by a linen pergola. Roses were growing up against the walls and baskets with little blue flowers were hanging under the windows. "It's so picturesque."

Kristine's face lit up at the compliment. "Thank you. Hannah and I did everything ourselves. It was pretty dated and neglected but we managed to make it look nice on a shoestring budget. Hannah inherited the house and *The Radley* from her mother, who gave her up for adoption at birth," she explained, opening the door and walking ahead of Ally. She switched on the coffee machine and the coffee bean grinder behind the bar, spreading a delicious aroma throughout the light space that was stylishly decorated with white-washed wooden tables and chairs, lots of plants and an old pool table that they'd turned into an herb garden. "I'm curious to see your bar in Capitola." Kristine said.

"Then you guys should come visit. I did it all up myself too. It's very small compared to this but it's right by the beach and next door to our house, so it's convenient when I have to work at night because Theo can call me from his bedroom window."

"That sounds perfect. Madison told me she loves living there." Kristine laughed. "But I think you might have something to do with that too."

Ally felt herself blush as she leaned over the bar. "Well, the pleasure is mutual."

"I can tell. You two seem pretty smitten with each other." Kristine held up a cup. "What are you having?"

"Double expresso, please."

"Good choice." Kristine winked. "I'll throw some croissants in the oven too; it will help with the hangover."

Ten minutes later they were sitting outside with coffee, a large jug of ice water and croissants with homemade strawberry jam. The sun was out and the view gorgeous. Ally inhaled the smell of fresh hay from the surrounding farmland, and imagined it was comforting to Kristine the way the smell of the ocean was to her. "You've built something truly amazing together," she said.

Kristine let out a deep sigh of contentment. "It's been really good since Hannah came back into my life. Love is just the most amazing thing; it gives you such energy and inspiration. I would have never had the courage to quit my job and do this if I hadn't met her." She quirked a brow. "I'm sure you know what I mean."

"I do, Madison inspires me too. I feel alive when I'm with her, and she makes me laugh all the time." Ally looked down at her hands resting in her lap. "But it's hard for me to get past the fact that she's so young, especially since I have Theo. I think I'm falling in love with her and I'm terrified because it's been over a decade since I've felt something so strong about someone. And on top of that, I've never been in a relationship with a woman before so there's a lot to think about."

"I'd say you need to do the opposite and stop thinking. Go with your gut." Kristine looked at Ally over the brim of her cup. "I get that you're cautious because of your son but remember that all he wants is for you to be happy. And dating a man of your own age, instead guarantee the future of your relationship or your happiness. You simply can't fight attraction." She reached over the table and put a hand on Ally's arm. "Don't be put off by your age difference because Madison is very mature for her age; anyone can see that. She's not the kind of woman to bring someone over to meet her family either, so you must be very special to her. And the way she talks about Theo... Isn't that what any mother would want? She works for both of you, makes both of you happy."

"Yeah, she does." Ally looked up to meet Kristine's eyes. She was such a lovely, warm woman, that she hadn't even realized she was opening up to her. "If I'm entirely honest, the problem is with me – I'm worried mostly that as I get older we may not work the same way as we do now. It's maddening because on the one hand, Madison makes me feel desired and confident about myself, but thinking long-term, I get really insecure."

"I understand that, but life is unpredictable, and anything could happen." Kristine ran her hands through her long, blonde hair, hesitating for a moment before she continued. "You must know that more than anyone, and I can't even begin to imagine how losing your husband must have broken you. But that doesn't mean you're going to lose Madison too, so take every day as it comes and enjoy having her in your life. But you have to have faith that it's going to work, because without faith, it won't. Love is love, it's as simple as that."

"I know." Ally sank a little further down in her seat, cherishing the sun on her face. "Thank you, Kristine. It's been really great to get to know you and Hannah and it's good to talk to someone." She gave her a grateful look and nodded. "You're right, I need to have faith."

56

"I'll see you in eight weeks, then." Madison tried not to get emotional as they were saying goodbye. She'd sneaked behind the bar like she had so many times lately, to give Ally a long hug, but the warm feeling of the physical closeness made it almost impossible to peel herself away from her. She inhaled her light floral perfume, wanting to hold onto the scent of her hair and her skin for as long as she'd be away. She knew she was being a little mellow-dramatic; her assignment was only for two months after all, and time would fly by. By the time she returned, Theo would be back from the summer program, and everything would be normal again. But still, the thought of not seeing Ally until then saddened her to the point that she almost felt like crying and she seriously wondered how they'd gotten here so fast. No matter how exciting the coming weeks would be, she didn't want to leave her. "I'll miss you so much," she mumbled against Ally's neck.

"I'm going to miss you too." Ally tightened her grip on Madison, wallowing in their closeness. "Will you call me?" she whispered.

"Every day." Madison let go of her and managed a smile as she looked into Ally's eyes. "Will you call me too?"

"Of course." Ally swallowed away her tears, then shook her head and laughed. "Look at us. This is ridiculous."

"I know. But it's not going to be any easier, ridiculous or not." Madison paused. "The thing is, it doesn't feel right at all to be away from you."

Ally shook her head. "It will be fine. It's your career, it's important and besides, it won't be the last time you'll be working away. Right now, we're kind of obsessed with each other, but it will get easier over time," she joked. "Trust me, I've been here before." She cursed herself for pulling Marcos into this, but Madison didn't seem to mind.

"Glad one of us has their head screwed on," she said, moving to the other side of the bar again when two customers walked in. "Well, I'll see you soon, Ally. Take care and I'll call you as soon as I get there."

Ally waved and couldn't resist blowing her a kiss, despite the regulars following their exchange.

"How long will she be gone for?" Ana asked as she sat on her regular stool at the bar after Ally had served everyone.

"Two months."

"Hmm." Ana narrowed her eyes, studying her. "You seem upset."

"I'm fine." Ally kept a brave face as she flicked the dish towel she was holding over her shoulder, resting a hand on her hip. "That's the thing with her line of work. It won't be the last time, so we'll just have to get used to it."

"You're saying that as if you're thinking long-term." Ana

sounded surprised. "But Madison will be moving out soon, right? After you've sold the house?"

"Yeah, but that doesn't mean we won't be seeing each other." Ally stared at Ana, a little irritated that she wasn't taking her feelings for Madison seriously. "She's my girl-friend," she continued, lowering her voice. "And it's getting serious, so we're going to tell Theo when she's back from Bimini."

"You're going to do what?" Ana pursed her lips and blew out a deep breath. "Why would you tell him? The whole town will know you're dating a young girl with pink hair."

Ally gritted her teeth. "Madison is not a young girl. She's a very responsible, caring woman with a heart of gold and she's great with Theo. Why is it such a problem to you?"

"It's not a problem, but I assumed it was just a phase," Ana retorted defensively. "I was happy for you that she made you smile, but I never thought it would last."

"You were the one who always told me to move on," Ally said with a sharp edge to her voice. "Well, I'm moving on."

"But..." Ana frowned and shook her head. "Don't you worry about what people are going to think of you? How Theo is going to react?"

"No, I don't, and I need you to be supportive, because you're the closest person in my life. Yes, the whole town will know in a couple of months' time. But you know what? I don't think it's going to be a scandal. People will talk, sure. But they'll get used to the idea soon enough, because Capitola is a pretty open-minded place."

"Well, it may not even get to that."

"What's that supposed to mean?" Ally asked.

Ana sighed. "What do you think Madison will be doing in Bimini? Partying? Flirting with girls of her own age? She might not come back at all..." She immediately looked like she regretted what she'd said, but it was too late.

Ally's expression grew cold, and she picked up her notepad to go outside, deciding Ana could make her own coffee. She was supposed to comfort her now that Madison had left, not make it worse. "I'm done with this conversation."

57

Madison was on her way home from the port in North Bimini, where the Marine Life Research Center and its dock was located. She took a shuttle bus to the nearest beach, glad to get away from the noise of the new cruise pier they were building, then started walking the three miles of pristine beach toward her apartment complex. It had been another hectic but successful day out on the boat, and the tropical climate and lush surroundings made her smile each morning she woke up. Besides the pod of dolphins they'd been tracking, she'd seen hammerhead sharks, blacktip sharks, grand triggerfish and stingrays among many other tropical fish from the boat. The diverse eco system of the Bahamas was simply astonishing and every marine biologist's dream. At night, she continued to work, but none of that mattered as she was enjoying what she did. Her balcony, where she'd placed a small desk, had a stunning view so she overlooked the Caribbean Sea while she worked and, in the morning, she drank coffee there, waking up to birdsong and the sound of the ocean.

Slowing her pace, Madison took off her shoes as she strolled past resorts and beach clubs with cushioned cabanas and sun loungers facing the ocean for sunset views. A little farther down, small shacks were serving conch fritters and frozen cocktails, and casual restaurants offered amazing freshly fried fish.

It was Saturday and she was in a great mood, not only because she'd have her first day off tomorrow and was looking forward to exploring the island, but also because she knew Ally would be with Theo right now. She could picture them on the beach together and it made her smile knowing Ally would be happy today. Because that was all she wanted; for Ally to be happy. Despite being in paradise, Madison felt lonely without her. She wasn't used to feeling lonely. In fact, she'd always enjoyed her own company. But Ally had found her way into her heart and now it was hard to think of anything other than her. *Only seven more weeks,* she told herself, but that thought made her even more restless. They'd called each other every day and talked for hours. Hearing Ally's voice had become addictive and she subconsciously reached for the phone in her pocket as she sat down at one of the wooden picnic tables in the shade of a palm tree. Feeling hungry, she ordered grilled snapper with a salad and a frozen margarita before dialing Ally's number.

"Hey," Ally said, picking up at the first ring. "Perfect timing, Theo and I have just finished dinner."

"Great." Madison closed her eyes, cherishing the soothing sound of Ally's voice as she imagined her smile. "Where are you and how's the little man?"

"We're at home. We had dinner outside and we're just clearing everything away before we go and see a movie on the cliff with Ana. They're screening a comedy there tonight. I don't remember the title, but Theo was keen on seeing it."

"That sounds fun. I wish I was there."

"Yeah, me too. Ana's been a pain in my ass this week and I think she's trying to make up for it by taking us out."

"That sucks. What happened?"

Ally sighed. "It's nothing." She didn't want to bring it up because it would only ruin her good mood again. "How was your day?"

Madison could hear Theo in the background, then the front door closing and the sound of the wind blowing. "It was good. I'm tired though, glad I've got tomorrow off." She thanked the waiter, who brought over her drink, then continued: "It sounds stormy. I hope the screen doesn't blow away."

Ally laughed. "We were just saying the same thing, but I'm sure they've prepared for it." There was a pause while Theo interrupted. "Hang on a minute, Theo wants to talk to you."

"Madison!"

Madison's lips pulled into a wide smile at the sound of his voice. "Theo, buddy. How are you? How's the summer program?"

"It's ace. I showed my biology teacher the pictures of the algal bloom and he said I could do a project on it."

"That's exciting. It's a shame I can't help you with it right now."

"Yeah, but I think I can manage; I've done a ton of research already. Have you seen any sharks?"

Madison chuckled. "I have. Hammerheads and black-tips. They're everywhere. I'll send some pictures to your mom so you can see them. How are your teachers? Are they smart?"

"Yeah. They know everything."

"Everything, huh? That's pretty cool."

"Not every, everything," Theo corrected himself with a chuckle. "I asked them about God and heaven and stuff, and they didn't know about that, but they seem to know about all the other things, or they show me where to find out about them. Because I have my own laptop now to do my homework on and to look things up." He paused. "Do you miss mom?"

Madison was surprised at his question that came out of nowhere. "Yeah, I do. Do you miss her when you're in LA?"

"I do. But not so much," he added with the honesty only a child his age could display. "Because I know I'll always see her on Friday again and I'm really busy."

"Keeping busy is good, buddy." Madison heard Ally talk to him before she came back on the phone.

"Hey again." Ally laughed and lowered her voice. "Glad to hear you miss me. I miss you too."

"Good." Madison smiled. "Because I was actually thinking... well, I just had an idea. How about you come over here and visit me?" Take a couple of days off work? You'd love it and I'll have two days off in week three so we could chill out together. I'll book you a flight if you can make it, it's during the week so you can still be with Theo on the weekend."

"Really? I'd love that but I'm not sure if I can get away from the bar again." Ally let out a soft sigh. "I'll try, of course."

"Great." Madison looked around to make sure no one saw the big grin on her face. "Let me know and I'll make arrangements."

"I will." Ally cleared her throat and suddenly sounded a bit more businesslike. "Ana is here with the car, so I've got to go. Talk later?"

Yeah, I'll talk to you later." Madison hung up and took a slow sip of her cocktail, cherishing the deliciously cold and tangy liquid on her tongue. It immediately relaxed her, and she sank into a dreamy haze, thinking about Ally being here with her. It would be perfect.

58

"Thank you for having me over so late, I can imagine it's not very convenient for you." Mira, the woman who had just viewed the pink house gave Ally a grateful smile. "I've been held up at a building site all day and just couldn't get away any earlier." She looked up at the house once again as they stepped outside and Ally locked the door behind them.

"It's not a problem." Ally did her best to sound cheerful. "I work next door so I'm usually around."

"Well, thank you again." Mira shook her hand. "I know the realtor didn't like me coming here without her so please apologize from me. I love this place and I'd be delighted to add it to my portfolio. The location sells itself and it's got great potential." She looked at the bar and then at Ally's house. "Do you own *Western Shores* too?"

Ally nodded. "I do, and that one." She pointed to her own house.

"Interesting." Mira gave the block of houses another good glance-over. "Would you be interested in selling all three properties? I'd be happy to do a deal on the other two directly."

"No," Ally was quick to say. "Of course not, it's my home." She held up a hand. "I'm sorry, that sounded a bit harsh, but no, I have no intention of selling my home or *Western Shores*."

"Of course. I understand and I apologize." Mira studied her with interest. "But you're aware that you could buy a very nice six-bedroom property elsewhere if you did, right?"

"I'm aware," Ally admitted. "I just love my home."

"Of course. Don't we all?" Mira handed Ally her card and smiled before she walked off. "Don't hesitate to call me if you change your mind. In the meantime, I'll call the realtor about the pink house tomorrow."

"What's the matter? Did she hate how small it was?" Devon jutted out his bottom lip when Ally came back into the bar, looking deflated. "Don't worry; there will be lots of other people viewing it, right? I'm sure one of them will feel like they're meant to live there."

Ally sighed, not liking Devon's words of comfort. If anyone was meant to live there, it was Madison, and now that she was gone, she realized it more than ever. "No, it's not that. In fact, she loved it and I'm pretty sure she'll put an offer in. Mira's a local investor with lots of properties along the coast, and she's itching to get her hands on it. It's just that..."

"You hate the thought of selling it..." Devon finished her sentence and gave her an understanding nod. "This must be difficult for you. I know you had plans with Marcos to convert the properties..." He paused. "Or perhaps it's not even about him anymore."

"It is and it isn't." Ally shrugged. "I mean, it felt wrong selling it because of him initially, but I've also come to realize that I don't want Madison to leave." She sat down on a barstool while Devon finished washing the last glasses. "We haven't even known each other that long but the three months she's been here have been so intense that it feels a lot longer. Is that weird?"

"Not at all. You have a teenage crush on her, and you want her to stay next door so you can sneak in for a quick..." he stopped when Ally flicked a beer mat at him and laughed. "Come on, Ally. You know I'm right."

Ally rolled her eyes and laughed too. "Okay, you've got a point. But it's not just sex anymore. I like her and I have genuine feelings for her."

"I know. I was just trying to make you laugh." Devon put away the glasses, poured them both a beer and sat down next to her.

"Don't you have somewhere to go?" Ally asked, taking a sip. "You've been sneaking out straight after work every night lately." She made sure not to give away what she knew. "I assume you've been seeing the woman you were talking about?"

Devon gave her a fearful glance. "No, I've been home mostly, but we've been messaging. She's working tonight."

"Want to tell me about her?" Ally asked. "It seems that you really like her."

"I think I do." Devon fell quiet for a beat. "But it's..." He shook his head. "Never mind."

"It's what?" Ally placed a hand on his and tilted her head. "You can tell me anything, Devon. Even if you think you can't. Anything." She realized she'd gone too far at the second 'anything' as Devon narrowed his eyes and gave her a long, uncomfortable stare. Sweat was pearling on his brow and he shifted on his stool, looking like he was about to leave any second.

"What do you mean by that?"

Ally felt her cheeks turn bright red, and she shrugged. God, she was such a bad liar. "Just that I'm here for you if you want to talk."

"No, I don't buy that. Normally you'd be making fun of me for being a sucker but you're not." He frowned. "You saw me with her, didn't you?"

Ally hesitated, then bit her lip and nodded slowly. "I did."

"Then why didn't you say anything? It's unlike you not to mention it. Unless..." Devon stared into his beer, avoiding her eyes. "Unless you know."

Ally contemplated denying everything, but she figured she might as well confess now that they were talking. "That time Madison took me out on a date... We went out on a boat, and so we came off at the pier instead of the road and saw you two sitting at the bar together. We didn't mention we saw you because, well..." She paused. "I wasn't sure if you had a problem with me knowing since Madison recognized her and knew she was trans. I assume this is new to you and I thought maybe you'd rather tell me when you were ready, so I waited."

"So you *do* know. You both know." Devon downed his beer in one go, then refilled his glass. There was a long silence, in which he continued to avoid eye-contact, tapping his foot on the footrest of the stool. Ally could almost hear his brain churning as the panic of his secret being exposed kicked in. "Fuck," he finally said. "I don't know what to do, Ally. You can't tell anyone; do you hear me?"

"I won't. And Madison won't either, you can trust her." Ally took a long drink and refilled her own beer. If Devon was going through a hard time, then they might as well get drunk together. It wasn't like she had to be home for Theo, and Madison was away. She felt a sharp pang to her stomach just thinking about her. Even though they'd called each other almost daily, she missed her like crazy and not having her here was much harder than she'd expected.

"She kept cancelling on me," Devon said, almost in a whisper. "We were matched up on this dating app and I asked her out, but she kept coming up with excuses. I think it intrigued me that she wasn't as keen as most women I date." He sighed. "I thought she was playing hard to get, but I know better now."

"But it meant you guys talked a lot, right? Maybe more than you normally would with a woman you like."

"Yeah, way more. We messaged for hours each day; it was all I wanted to do when I got home. She wouldn't tell me where she worked, but apart from that, I felt like I knew everything about her. Everything apart from that one major thing." Devon took another long drink before continuing. "When we finally did meet up, I didn't even realize she was trans until she told me. I was shocked and angry and behaved like an asshole; I took off and ignored her messages and calls for a week, but I couldn't stop thinking about her." He turned, meeting Ally's eyes. "So, I finally called to apologize, and she came over to *Western Shores* after I closed up because I didn't want to meet in public and I didn't feel comfortable inviting her to my place. And again, we talked for hours. We must have been there until three in the morning. It's so easy to talk to her and somehow we just click, you know?"

"I get that." Ally gave him a sweet smile. "And you understand why she didn't tell you right away?"

"I do now." Devon shrugged. "She told me men used to

block her as soon as they found out, so she waited with telling me. She hasn't had the surgery yet and it's... I don't know. It's hard not to think about that when I'm with her." He rubbed his temple as a rash spread across his face, and Ally knew he was beyond nervous. "But then she kissed me."

Ally nodded. "And it felt right."

"Yeah." Devon swallowed hard. "And I have no idea what to do now. I haven't called her since because I can't stop overthinking it and I feel so conflicted..."

Ally put an arm around him in an attempt to put him at ease. "Devon, you fell for a person, just like I did. A wonderful, beautiful, charming person, no matter what sex." She paused. "Try to remember that if you really care about her. Own it, don't be ashamed. Whatever body she was born in and whatever she plans to do with it, she is a woman inside, so if this is difficult for you, then imagine what it's like for her."

"I'm trying to do that." Devon raised a brow. "But I don't see you owning your relationship with Madison. You've been hiding it for months." He shook his head. "I'm sorry, that wasn't fair. I know it's because of Theo."

"No, it's not all about Theo," Ally admitted. "It was more my own problem, but I think I'm ready for people to know soon. Ever since Madison left, I've missed her so much that I just don't feel complete without her. So yeah, I think she's worth the risk, and if we're still okay after she comes back, then we'll tell Theo together."

"Why would you not be okay? She's crazy about you, don't you see that?"

"I know she is." Ally smiled. "She asked if I wanted to come and visit her in Bimini."

"Then you should go." Devon refilled his glass again, looking relieved that they'd changed the subject.

"It's not that simple with the bar." Ally was feeling light-headed but gave in anyway when Devon pulled her a third beer. She had no intention of leaving now that he was opening up to her like this and told herself she would just have to suffer through the headache tomorrow morning.

"Nonsense. I'll take care of things here." He managed a grin. "I could do with the extra cash after seeing Chelsey's designer purse. That woman's got expensive taste."

Ally laughed at his joke, glad that he was relaxing. "Okay, in that case, I'd be very grateful." She held up her glass before taking a sip. "So, you're going to call her, right?"

"I think so." Devon smiled at her and she was surprised to see a glimmer of emotion in his eyes. Devon was a stereo-typical manly man and prided himself on being a ladies' man. The fact that he was not only showing his emotions but considering dating someone out of his comfort zone was touching and inspiring. "Thank you, Ally. You make it sound so easy."

"Come here." Ally stood up from her stool and gave him a hug. "It's not easy, but it can be simple if you allow it to be. Love is love after all; a very wise woman recently told me that."

59

The Bimini ferry port was packed with people coming and going, the island being popular among day trippers. Behind the wharf, the fast ferry from Miami was docking, soon releasing locals and tourists who had come to enjoy the island with its white sand beaches and crystal-clear azure shores. Ally would be one of them, and Madison felt herself shiver in anticipation.

Twenty-five days had passed since they'd seen each other. Twenty-five days that had been interesting, fascinating even, as she'd been blessed by blue waters and the tropical coastline where she resided, a team that made her smile and the opportunity of stepping up in her job. But without Ally, she wasn't able to enjoy it as much as she normally would have, her mind constantly drifting back to the woman who had captured her thoughts and her heart. Madison had longed to kiss her, hold her and see her incredible smile again. She'd expected to miss her sure, but not to this extent, like a part of her was missing.

The first people came off the ferry, most of them dressed for a beach club or a fancy lunch. Her heart started racing when Ally appeared among them, looking dazzling in a long navy off-the-shoulder summer dress and simple leather sandals. The light clinking of the bangles around her wrist made all other noise fade into the background and when she spotted Madison close by in the crowd, she quickened her pace and flew around her neck.

"Finally! God, I've missed you," she said, sinking into the embrace.

"Hi beautiful, I've missed you too. Like you have no idea." Madison lifted her up and held her so tight that Ally gasped. It felt incredibly right to have her in her arms again.

"Hey, be careful, you're going to crush me, I'm only small." Ally laughed, then let out a long sigh. "You smell great. I've been indulging in your pictures on my phone and believe me, Theo took many during our trip to LA, but it's just not the same."

"I know exactly what you mean." Madison put her back down and took her duffel bag. "The past weeks have seemed like a lifetime. How is that even possible?" She cupped Ally's cheek and met her gaze. "I really want to kiss you right now, but I might get carried away so maybe it's better if we wait until we get to my apartment."

"Yeah, that might be best." Ally's gaze lowered to her mouth, and she licked her lips as she flicked her hair to one side and ran a hand through it.

The unconscious gesture was so sexy that Madison felt a twitch of arousal, and she shifted on the spot, eager to take Ally to her home. "Come on then." She took Ally's hand. "Is this okay?" She looked around, noting there were lots of people around.

"Yes." Ally gave her hand a squeeze. "It's perfect."

Madison was unable to wipe the silly smirk off her face as they walked toward the port's parking lot. She was so proud to have Ally by her side and the restlessness she'd felt was finally gone, now that she was here with her. "My transport is a little unconventional, but I think you'll like it."

"I have no doubt. I like everything about this so far, especially you." Ally looked up at her and fluttered her eyelashes. "I'm glad I came. Two months without seeing you would have been torture."

"I know. I've thought about you every day, all day." Madison wasn't embarrassed to admit it; she wanted Ally to know the distance hadn't changed a thing about how she felt. "I see you're already wearing your bikini," she said, glancing at the turquoise strings around Ally's neck. "My favorite one."

"I know it is." Ally shot her a mischievous smile. "I wasn't sure if you wanted to go to the beach right away, but I'd really prefer to see your apartment first. It's mind-blowing how much pent up sexual energy one can culminate when constantly fantasizing."

"Tell me about it." Madison looked Ally up and down, imagining how easy she could pull off her dress. It was almost too much to handle, knowing they would be alone soon. "I can't wait to have you naked for hours and hours." Her eyes settled on the curve of her breasts. "And tomorrow, I'll take you to a really quiet beach. Unless you're tired of course..."

"Tired? I'm bouncing off the walls." Ally chuckled. "Do you know how long it's been since I've been away with some time to myself? Twelve years! Believe me when I say that I intend to do a lot of things but sleeping is not one of them." She paused for a moment, her eyes narrowing. "So, a quiet beach, huh? How quiet are we talking?"

"Let's just say you won't be needing that bikini."

"Hmm. I like the sound of that. The kind of quiet were

we could go skinny dipping?" Ally's lips parted, telling Madison she was just as turned on as she was.

"Yes, exactly." They'd reached the small parking strip and Madison walked up to the golf cart she'd rented, gesturing to the passenger's seat as there was no door to open for Ally. She was delighted to hear the sound of her laughter ringing through the air like her favorite song.

"Are you kidding me?" Ally looked both amused and highly impressed by the shiny white golf cart.

"I'm not. There aren't many cars on the island and Bimini is very small, so this is what most people drive. You can rent them everywhere and it's great to be in an open vehicle where you can enjoy the sea breeze and the stunning scenery."

"Hey, I have no problem with it, I love it." Ally got in, then grinned as she turned to Madison. "Can I drive?"

"Sure." Madison laughed as Ally got into the driver's seat. She took off her flip-flops, put her feet up on the dashboard and directed her toward her apartment that was a very slow twenty-minute drive from the ferry terminal.

"Welcome to my castle," Madison joked as she let Ally in. Her studio apartment was tiny, but she was barely ever there and having lived in the pink house, she wasn't used to much space in the first place. "Almost like home, right?"

Although it was a two-storey apartment complex, rather than small houses, the individual apartments were painted in the same color scheme as the houses on Capitola beach. The pink, yellow, turquoise, green, blue and orange fronted apartments in sun-bleached shades, with small balconies that overlooked the ocean, stood on a commercial strip of beach, right next to a row of small restaurants and a hotel.

"I'm surprised they didn't assign you the pink one," Ally said as she put her bag in the corner of the studio. "But green is nice too. And I see they continued the color scheme in the interior décor."

It was pretty basic; a bed made up with olive green bed linens, a wooden table and chairs for two, painted in apple green, a, worn-out green rug and a small kitchenette. Even the artworks on the walls were green.

"I know, it's an odd choice for an interior, and it's a little garish, but it's grown on me." Madison laughed and opened the sliding doors to the balcony. The view was to die for, and she knew Ally would love it too.

"Now we're talking," Ally said, stepping outside. The modest balcony with a desk and two deck chairs overlooked a white sandy beach, rows of palm trees and the ocean behind it. She leaned over the balcony railing and took a deep breath, closing her eyes as her senses absorbed the smell of the ocean.

"Glad you approve." Madison came up behind her, brushed her hair to one side and nuzzled against her neck. "You're so sexy, you make me crazy," she whispered against her ear, making the hairs on Ally's arms rise. Her hand instinctively reached for the hem of Ally's dress and she pulled it up on one side to run her fingers over her thigh and her behind, resting her hand there as she wiggled a teasing finger under the edge of Ally's panties. "And your skin..."

Ally straightened herself and leaned back against her as Madison roamed her hands farther up over her stomach, then pulled at the bow of her bikini, freeing her breasts. A soft moan passed her lips, and she held her breath as

Madison continued the exploration of her body, cupping both breasts and pulling her against her.

"This dress needs to come off," she whispered, smiling against Ally's ear.

Ally turned around, arousal flaring up in her eyes. She tugged at Madison's T-shirt. "This needs to come off too." She pulled it up and Madison lifted her arms. "You're not wearing a bra," she whispered with a mischievous look, trailing her fingers over Madison's skin before leaning in and taking a nipple into her mouth.

Madison moaned and threw her head back, then stopped her before they got totally lost in each other and pulled Ally inside. "Wait. Not out here."

Ally laughed. "I'm so desperate for you, I forgot where we were." She slid her dress back down and stepped out of it, leaving her in her half-dismantled bikini.

"That looks so good on you." Madison gave her an approving glance-over, twitching at the sight of Ally's petite body in the tiny bikini. "But as much as I like it, it needs to come off too."

Ally looked at her as she pulled at the side strings of the bottom half, then at the dangling back and neck strings of the top, making it fall down like a house of cards. "Your turn," she whispered, pressing her breasts against Madison's ribcage. She brushed her lips while she unbuttoned the shorts and slipped her thumbs under the waistband, pulling down her panties along with her shorts. Her eyes raked over Madison like a hungry beast. "Lie down."

Madison's pulse raced as she looked around, trying to decide on the bed or the rug. She wasn't used to Ally being so assertive and knowing she'd been lusting after her for weeks made her wild with desire. She went to her knees and fell back on the rug, too impatient to even cross the three steps to the bed.

Ally was quick to straddle her, lowering herself onto Madison's aching center. She shot her a seductive smile that told Madison she knew exactly what she wanted, reached between them and spread her open before grinding herself into her, hard.

"Fuck, Ally!" Madison moaned at the sensation of Ally's heated wetness hitting her clit. She grabbed Ally's hips and rolled her own, looking up at her as she moved seductively, arching her back, clutching Madison's thighs behind her. She'd never witnessed anything so sexy, so utterly pure and raw. The slow rotation of Ally's hips, her legs spread wide, her hazy eyes, half closed now, and her dark hair hanging down in streaks, caressing her breasts, was turning her on like nothing else. Her ribcage was heaving up and down, her nipples hard like pebbles. "If you don't stop, you're going to make me come right now," Madison panted, her toes curling from the pressure that was building as Ally rode her throbbing clit. She indulged in the sight of her naked form, unable to look away despite the building climax that threatened to force her eyes closed.

"I want to make you come," Ally whispered, her moans in sync with her thrusts, each thrust changing her breathing until she was clinging on the edge too, every nerve in her body electrified. Utterly drunk with lust, and insatiably craving each other's flesh, they moved faster. A giant pulse raced through them both, connecting them as one. They cried out, shaking, taking each other's hands and locking them tight. Ally fell forward over Madison, multiple after-shocks making her both gasp and sigh in post-orgasmic delight. It didn't stop until they'd crumbled like sand and were spent and still. She rolled off Madison and turned on her side to face her.

Madison lay there sucking in much needed lungfuls of air, noticing the fire in Ally's eyes still hadn't subsided. She ran a hand through her hair, then watched it fall as she let go. "You make me ravenous for you," she said again, lowering her gaze to Ally's plump and glistening lips that were calling her.

Ally smiled, took her hand and kissed it. "I think it's safe to say you do the same to me. It's like I turn into someone else, I get completely carried away." She chuckled. "I just want you so much, it's insane."

"That's good." Madison inched closer and kissed Ally, unable to resist her inviting mouth. "Because I want you again..." she mumbled against her lips, "...and again and again." Her hand trailed up Ally's leg toward her center as she parted her lips and kissed her deeply, groaning at the wetness she felt. She turned and shifted, so she was half on top of Ally and wedged her thigh between her legs. With slow strokes and circles, she teased her opening until she was languid in her arms, moaning as she eagerly parted her legs and bucked her hips to meet Madison's fingers.

"Yes..."

"Yeah? Is that good?" Madison pulled out of the kiss and looked down at her, licking her lips.

"So... good..." Ally stammered, biting her lip as she turned her head from side to side.

"What do you want, Ally?" Madison smiled as she quickened her strokes, pushing down on Ally's clit, making her squirm. "Do you want me to fuck you?" she whispered against her ear.

Her words clearly did something to Ally, as she bucked her hips again and reached for her face to pull her down.

Madison grabbed her hands and pinned them above her head, holding them in place as she entered her without warning. She'd been longing to be inside Ally again, to feel how wet she was, how willing. The pool of desire she found instantly aroused her again, and needing more, she shifted, covering Ally with her body.

Ally moaned loudly now, delirious with pleasure as Madison went deeper, pumping her fingers in and out as Ally's desire accelerated. Knowing she was almost at the point of no return Madison released Ally's hands and moved swiftly to lie between her legs, replacing her probing fingers with her tongue, lapping at Ally's hardening clit until she threw her head back and screamed her name.

60

"Where are we going?" Ally searched for a tissue in her purse to dab her forehead and her neck. It was dark, but the temperatures were still high when Madison parked the golf cart next to the pier and she wasn't used to the humidity.

"I'm taking you for a night cap in Alice Town." Madison gestured to the few bars, shops and restaurants on the main strip. "I bet it's been a while since you've been to a bar other than your own."

"You're right, it's been forever." Ally smiled as she followed Madison into the dark recesses of the Sand Bar, a spot where locals and tourists were sipping rum and playing dominoes at the long tables. It was more like a shack than a bar and there was no floor, so they were walking on sand. The ceiling looked like it was about to cave in, but then the straw wouldn't do much damage if it came falling down on them. Reggae music was blasting through the speakers and people were dancing in any available space in the room, which at the moment seemed to be between the tables and on the patio overlooking the boat slips of the harbor and

Browns Marina. "I love this place already." She swayed to the music as they made their way to the bar, feeling a little tipsy after the cocktails they'd had over dinner.

Madison ordered them both a margarita and brought them outside to the patio where they took off their shoes and danced under the stars with their toes in the sand. The mood was friendly and mellow, and Ally was having fun. The short break felt like a breath of fresh air from her daily routine, and she'd almost forgotten how much she loved dancing until she fully submerged herself in the music and in Madison who was moving along with her, pulling her in for a kiss now and then. The crowd wasn't paying attention to them and even if they were, no one seemed to care, so Ally wrapped her arms around Madison's neck and inched closer. Desire flared up inside her as their bodies came together, and she wondered if she'd ever get enough of her. Despite making love for hours before dinner, she wanted her all over again.

"You're a good dancer," Madison said, shooting Ally a flirty grin.

"So are you." Ally met her gaze, fire spreading through her core. "And dancing with you is making me want you again."

"Oh yeah?" Madison pulled Ally even closer against her. "Is it turning you on?"

Ally felt her cheeks flush. "I think you know it is."

"Then what about this?" Madison lowered her hands down to Ally's ass and squeezed her cheeks, lifting her up in the process.

Ally laughed, wiggled herself out of her grip and slapped a hand against her chest. "Not here." She stepped back, creating some distance between them. "It's the first time I've ever been 'out' with a woman, so don't push it."

Madison laughed too. "I'm sorry, I keep forgetting that. You're doing pretty well though for a newbie. Not uncomfortable?"

"Not if you refrain from groping my ass." Ally reached for her drink on the high table next to them. "It's been a while since I've done this. You know, just having a drink and dancing. I'm having fun." She looked around and felt immensely happy at seeing all the cheerful faces, people of all ages partying together like it was all they wanted to do, and she realized she didn't do this enough. Being with Madison was exciting and liberating, and it made her feel like she was getting the most out of life again.

"Me too." Madison took a sip of her own drink and spilled most of it over her hand. "Oh God, I think I might have had enough to drink for tonight." She wiped her hands on her shorts and licked her fingers with a grin. "But you have to agree that those glasses are impossible to handle without the drink ending up anywhere but in your mouth."

"Yeah, I think I might have some margarita in my hair." Ally instinctively reached for her hand, wanting to lick the sugary drink off Madison's fingers, then stopped herself, reminding herself they were in a public place. "Maybe we should head back and get cleaned up." She gave Madison a mischievous smile. "As much as I like your tiny shower at the pink house, it's also an appealing prospect to have access to a slightly bigger one tonight."

Madison didn't have to think about that twice. "Okay. Home. Shower. You and me." They ran out to the golf cart when it suddenly started raining. "Do you want me to put the cover on?" she asked. "I didn't see this coming and it's really slow, so we'll be wet through by the time we get back."

Ally laughed and shook her head. "No, it's fine. Might get rid of some of the stickiness." She sat shotgun to

Madison and laughed even harder when it started to pour. She knew tropical storms were unpredictable, but she'd never witnessed anything like this.

"Hey, what are you doing?" Madison looked up in amusement when Ally stood up on her seat and held onto the roof framework. She tried not to get distracted by the fact that she could see under her dress and forced herself to keep her eyes on the road.

"Don't worry; I'll be careful." Ally raised her face to the sky and closed her eyes as the heavy rain hit her like a lukewarm shower. It felt nice and cool on her skin after the warm and humid afternoon, and she didn't care about getting soaked. Today, she was simply living, not worrying about a thing and that felt amazingly liberating.

B y the time they arrived at Madison's apartment, there wasn't a dry patch on either of them. Especially Ally who was literally dripping, since she'd been standing the whole way. Lightning flashed over the Atlantic, lighting up the beach and Madison took her hand when she got out, leading them there. "Incredible," she whispered as she carried her shoes in her hand.

"It's stunning." Ally hadn't bothered putting her sandals back on either and she sighed as her feet sank into the wet sand, cooling her feet.

They sat down and held hands as they watched the spectacular lightning show. Ally rested her head on Madison's shoulder and Madison pulled her in and put an arm around her in return. As the rumbles got louder and the flashes more frequent, she couldn't think of a better place to be right now. Fork lightning crashed into the sea, lighting up the dark sky as the thunderstorm lashed the coast. The tall, thin palm trees on the beach all swayed in one direction, their crowns blowing to the east. Each time lightning struck their dark silhouettes, their trunks looked dauntingly crooked against the white of the flash, yet they never broke.

"How can something so potentially destructive be so addictive? I feel like lightning could strike me any minute, yet I'm still loving it," Ally said.

Madison nodded in agreement. "It's contradicting to enjoy something so dangerous, but we're unable to look away." She paused as she looked up at the sky where a pattern of bright white light spread like blood through veins. "Have you ever heard of the love bridge experiment?"

"No, I don't think I have." Ally turned to her. "Tell me about it. In simple language, please," she added with a chuckle.

Madison thought for a moment. "Well, for this experiment, scientists picked two bridges. The first bridge had low handrails and hung two-hundred-and-thirty feet over a river. It was swinging and unsteady. The second bridge was way lower, only a few feet above a stream, and sturdy, with normal handrails. They also picked two groups of men who were heterosexual and slightly anxious. On both bridges, the men crossing were approached by a cute, female researcher half-way across. She gave them her number and asked them to call her if they had any questions about the experiment. As far as the men were aware, everything had been laid out in detail, so there wasn't really any reason for them to call her unless they felt attracted to her. Out of the men crossing on the sturdy bridge, two out of sixteen gave the woman a call. Out of the men crossing on the high, unstable bridge, nine out of eighteen called. In other words; if we are in danger, our senses are heightened, and we get a buzz. So basically, we find each other more attractive in perilous moments rather than safe ones." She grinned. "Although I'm not sure if that's possible with you."

"No, I don't think it is either." Ally smiled as she leaned in, drawn to Madison's mouth like a magnet. Raindrops were dripping down their faces as their lips locked, the wet touch filling her with warmth and arousal. She ran a hand through Madison's hair and moaned softly, parting her lips to entwine their tongues. The kiss was slow and lazy at first, then hungrier as they got carried away, loosing themselves in each other. A sudden loud bang of thunder made Ally shriek and they broke apart. She laughed, holding onto her chest. "Fuck."

Madison laughed too and stood up. "Want to go inside? I'm a little shaken myself and that storm is getting closer."

"Yeah, that might be best." Ally got up too and put an arm around her as they headed to the apartment building. "And anyway, I'm looking forward to that shower now."

61

"You certainly made good on the beach promise." Ally sighed in delight as Madison rubbed sunscreen over her back. Although the towel they were sharing was more than big enough for them both to fit on, they'd mainly been lying on top of each other, making out in the shade of a palm tree. The small beach they'd walked to from Madison's apartment was deserted, but they'd kept their swimwear on in case locals decided to come for a swim.

If there was such a thing as paradise, this would be it, Ally thought. Sheltered by rock formations and heavy vegetation, the short strip of perfectly clean white sand was still and incredibly quiet, and the deep turquoise of the water like no other place she'd ever seen. She was enjoying herself in perfect bliss as Madison's hands roamed over her back, occasionally sneaking down to her ass. It was amazing to just relax and not worry about anything.

"Have you had any viewings on the house yet?" Madison asked, squirting some lotion onto Ally's shoulders before straddling her.

"Many." Ally groaned, not sounding too enthusiastic, but loving Madison's weight on top of her. She hadn't brought it up because she didn't like thinking about it, but it was important that Madison knew the situation. "There's a particular investor who's super keen, but so were most of the other viewers. I think there might be a bidding war soon." She shook her head. "It's hard to believe that such a small place can be so inspiring and iconic architecturally to strangers. I almost think they love it as much as I do."

"Well, it's a special place and the area has become significantly more popular over the past years." If Madison was disappointed to hear the house would most likely be sold in the coming weeks, she didn't let on. "The location is prime and if a cute little pink house is your thing, it's unlikely you'll find a more perfect one elsewhere."

"I know. I should be happy about it because I need the money for Theo's schooling. And it really is a lot of money," Ally added. "But it's still sad."

"Yeah, it is." Madison moved her hands to Ally's sides, making her shiver as she grazed her breasts.

"Do you have any idea where you'll be looking yet?"

Madison shrugged. "I've kept an eye out for rentals in Santa Cruz. They seem to come up quite frequently, so I'll probably get something there. Although I'd love to stay in Capitola, it isn't exactly riddled with available rentals." She paused. "If I get a two-bedroom apartment in Santa Cruz, I'll make my mom very happy and you and Theo can come and stay whenever you want. He likes the boardwalk, right?"

"Yeah, he loves it." Ally looked over her shoulder and smiled. "And you can stay with me until you've found an apartment. On the weekends too, of course... It will be a bit cramped and there might not be enough space for your stuff, but Ana's got a storage room if you need a place to put some boxes."

Madison dried her hands off on the towel and lay down beside Ally, facing her. She propped herself up on her elbow and rested her cheek in the palm of her hand, giving her a quizzical look. "What about Theo?"

Ally turned on her side too, her expression growing serious. "I've been thinking that maybe we should tell him when you get back."

"You think we should tell him?" Madison could hardly believe what Ally was saying. She'd been fighting to keep a distance for months and now she was suddenly doing the exact opposite. "What made you change your mind?"

Ally scooted a little closer. "Honestly, it's pretty simple; I missed you. Way more than I expected. I had some time on my hands in the evenings and I took up painting again, but I found myself painting your face... It's probably the best work I've ever created in a long time." She grimaced. "Sorry, does that freak you out?"

"Not at all, it's incredibly endearing." Madison trailed a finger from Ally's shoulder down to her wrist, then took her hand. "I'm happy that you want to tell Theo about us."

"Good." Ally shot her a grateful look. "I found myself looking at your front door every morning while I was opening the bar. Even before I realized I liked you I used to love it when you came in for a coffee and I have to admit, I used to wait for you to come home too. The thing is, I've lived more intensely and felt more in touch with myself in the months that you lived next door than I have in the past ten years combined. I love to listen to music now, food tastes better, things smell nicer and it's almost like my senses are sharper; I'm noticing the small things around me too, like a smile on a stranger's face, laughter in the background or a flower in bloom. Awareness, you know?" She flicked her hair to one side and twirled a finger around a dark lock. "Looking back, I think I was attracted to you from the moment I met you, I just didn't want to admit it because a relationship with you seemed so implausible."

"But you don't believe that anymore, right?" Madison asked. She smiled at Ally's hair-flick that she found so irresistible.

"No, not at all." Ally laced their fingers together. "It makes sense now. Something that makes me feel so good can't possibly be wrong. Things won't be the same after you move out and even though you won't be far away, it's still going to be different from having you next door." She pursed her lips and hesitated before she continued. "So, if you'd like to stay with me for a while until you find something that's perfect for you, I would like that."

"Thank you, I would like that too." Madison felt tears well up and she swallowed them away, inching closer until her lips were almost on Ally's. "But we need to see how Theo reacts first." A warm glow enveloped her as she studied Ally's face; her delicate features, the few freckles on her cheeks, her big, brown eyes and her long lashes. Her future was with Ally and Theo, and she could see it as clear as day.

"Yeah, we do. But let's worry about that when the time comes. For now, I just want to enjoy my time with you because another four weeks is a long time." Ally took a deep breath as she looked into the sun, then got up and pulled Madison with her. "Come on, let's go for a swim, I'm frying here." She walked up to the edge of the still water of the bay that was so clear she could see the grains of sand between her toes as they waded in deeper.

"Make sure to shuffle your feet," Madison warned. "Just

so you don't step on something and hurt yourself. Camouflaged creatures will detect the shifting sand and move out of the way."

Ally grimaced. "Damn, I forgot we're not in the safe waters of Monterey Bay. Oh my God, is that a stingray? Should we be worried?" she asked, a little apprehensive when she saw a big, flat fish flying around their legs.

"Yeah, it's a stingray, but it won't hurt you. They only use their venomous spine as a last resort. Like bees." Madison lifted Ally up when she sensed her nervousness, and Ally gratefully wrapped her arms and legs tightly around her. "Seriously, you're safe. Stingrays are one of the most majestic creatures of the ocean. So elegant and totally misunderstood." She looked down at the brown, diamond-shaped creature as it flew past them. "Just don't swim over them or grab their tail and you'll be fine."

"I'll make sure to remember that." Ally grinned and dipped her head into the water. "But I think I'll just permanently attach myself to you while we're out here."

"I have no problem with that." Madison lifted her higher and kissed her, tasting the saltwater on Ally's lips. She looked happy, and that made Madison incredibly happy too. Calm ripples formed around them and the droplets on Ally's tanned skin reflected the sunlight, shimmering as they waded farther out until they were almost submerged. "God, you've got me," she whispered, out of her mind with passion for Ally. "You own, me, all of me." Ally's breasts were pressed against her chest, their hearts beating in sync, and she felt both strong and vulnerable at the same time – confident everything was right and meant to be, yet terrified of losing her. She felt a lump in her throat and knew then, that for the first time, she was falling in love.

62

'*I'm going to accept the bid.*' Madison narrowed her eyes as she read the message from Ally again, then shook her head and sighed. She was happy for Ally, but it didn't feel right. From the moment she'd set foot on the beach in Capitola, she'd known the pink house was a special place. The news of the house going up for sale had been unexpected, but understandable considering Ally's circumstances. She didn't like the idea of anyone else buying it though, because it felt like her home already.

'*Congratulations! Is it the developer?*' she typed back, knowing Ally was at work and might not be able to take a call.

'*Thanks. Yes, it's her. The good news for you is that she's not going to start fixing it up until December so she's willing to rent it out to you for a little longer.*'

Madison smiled at that, but it still didn't make her feel much better. Soon, the pink house would be occupied by tourists coming and going, possibly giving Ally a hard time about the noise from the bar or leaving trash on the beach.

It would be turned into a sleek, modern studio; warm and colorful on the outside, but cold and soulless on the inside, erasing every trace of Ally's hard work to make it feel and look like a real home despite the lack of space. But it was what it was, so trying to sound positive, she typed: *'That's great news. If you're happy, I'm happy.'*

She knew Ally was far from happy either. Theo's future was important though, and she didn't want to put a downer on Ally's day by sounding dramatic. Just when she was about to send another message, her mother called. She thought about ignoring it as she was already in bed, then picked up anyway.

"Hey Mom."

"Hi honey. How are you?"

"I'm okay. How are you?"

Her mother was silent for a beat, then said: "You don't sound okay. Is everything alright?"

Madison rolled her eyes. Her mother could always tell her mood by her voice, no matter how hard she tried to hide it. "Ally has agreed on the sale of the pink house," she finally said.

"Oh dear, I'm sorry to hear that." There was a pause. "I know you love that silly little house."

"It's not silly, Mom. It's charming and just right for me. The location is perfect, the views are breathtaking, and I feel at home there." She sighed, then added: "And most importantly, it's next door to Ally and Theo."

"Right. Of course," Edie said. There was a scratching noise, and then the popping of a cork. "I know you like being close to them, but you'll be able to find something else a short drive away." Madison could tell by the sizzling sound that her mother was pouring herself a glass of Champagne. "Or perhaps you and Ally might want to look for something together eventually?"

Madison frowned. "Since when are you encouraging me to move in with her? I recall you had a serious problem with me and Ally dating not too long ago."

"Yes, well that was then, and this is now. I may still not be sold on the idea, but I saw you two together at Hannah's birthday dinner and I could tell you were smitten with each other. And in the end, I just want you to be happy, so I've decided I'm going to be supportive. I really like Ally and your father adores her too."

"Dad said that?"

"Yes, he did. Maybe you could bring her over next time you come home? Theo is welcome too, of course." Her mother's tone indicated she wasn't entirely comfortable with the idea yet, but Madison was grateful that she was trying. "So, the house. How much is it going for?" she asked, changing the subject.

"Eight-hundred-and-fifty-thousand."

Her mother gasped. "Christ. That's insane for a miniature house without a decent bathroom."

Madison shrugged. "Yeah, well... it's in a prime location and no one can build in front of it. The views are guaranteed for a lifetime so it's unlikely to ever go down in value. Prices around there have actually gone up twenty percent in the past ten years alone. It's the right time to sell for Ally, and I know she needs the money, but I just wish I could stay."

"You'll find another place that you love and as I already said before, your father and I are happy to help you out. We've done the same for Mason and Chuck and, as long as it's a good investment for us and you pay us rent, we're open to ideas. There is your trust fund too, of course. You have a significant amount in the account, thanks to your grandmother."

Madison let out a chuckle at hearing the sour undertone in her mother's voice as she uttered the word 'grandmother'. Madison had never met her grandmother from her father's side, as she'd passed away before she was born, but from what she'd heard, the woman was a witch who had made her parents' life very difficult at times. "I know," she said, refusing to get involved. Witch or not, she'd set up a very generous trust fund for Madison and her brothers, and she was grateful for that. "I think I might be ready to buy something now, since I know I want to stay in the area. And thank you for your offer to help, but my trust fund should be more than enough for a nice two-bedroom apartment by the coast." She chuckled. "Unless you and dad are interested in investing in a tiny house in Capitola?"

Her mother laughed too. "I was kind of waiting for that question, but I don't think we could scrape that much together. And you know your father prefers to invest in new builds."

"I know." Madison felt her pulse race as possibilities started forming in her head. Although she wasn't exactly on board, her mother didn't sound completely against the idea either. Her father had a soft spot for her, so she might have a small chance with him too. "I have about four-hundred-and-fifty though, right? And I could probably get a mortgage for two-hundred-and-fifty max, now that I have a job, and..."

"That still leaves a significant sum to find honey," her mother interrupted her. "And anyway, it's probably too late now since Ally has accepted the offer." She cleared her throat. "It's very early days with you and Ally and buying a house is a big decision. What if it doesn't work out? I won't go through all the doomsday scenarios with you again because I know you don't want to hear about them, but even if you'd manage to buy it somehow, it's a huge risk. What if you split up and you're stuck in that house right next door to her?"

"But it will work out, Mom. I love her." As Madison heard herself say it, she knew it was true. She loved Ally.

63

The deep-fried squid with aioli that Devon had made for her tasted amazing, and Ally moaned as she took a bite, then drizzled more lemon over it. "So good," she mumbled, helping herself to another one. She hadn't had time to eat lunch, as a group of thirty cyclists, including Jack, had come in, all wanting snacks and drinks. Devon had been in the kitchen most of the time while she'd served them, running in and out with extra chairs and pillows to create more seating space on the wall in front of the bar. Now that she was finally standing still, hunched over the bar, tiredness took over, and she felt how clammy her T-shirt was against her back.

"Good to know that your friend Jack doesn't hold a grudge after you let him down easy," Devon said, emptying the bin. "He's been bringing in a lot of new customers lately."

"Yeah, Jack is great. Not the type of person to get funny after being turned down. We actually had a really nice conversation this afternoon, and I've invited him over for dinner next week to thank him for all his help with Theo."

Ally stretched her arms over her head and bent to one side, then the other, relieving her sore muscles. "God, I'm tired."

"Why don't you go and sit outside with a drink while I close up? You've been here since seven this morning and I only started at four." Devon gave her a little push, nudging her away from the bar. Then he opened a cold bottle of beer and handed it to her, along with the plate of food. "Shoot. Out of my way."

Ally looked at her phone and saw she had a missed call from Madison. It was a few minutes after ten, and she was pretty sure Madison would be asleep by now, after calculating the time difference. Still, she really wanted to hear her voice. "Thanks. I'll give Madison a call, then." Ally gave him a grateful look and wobbled out to the terrace where she slumped down at a table. The phone only rang once before she heard Madison's voice, warming her heart and making her pulse race.

"Hey beautiful."

"Hey. Sorry I didn't call you back sooner, it's been super busy here."

"That's okay. It's been a little crazy here too. It's really good to hear your voice."

"Same." Ally frowned when she heard a woman yelling something about mosquito repellent. "Wait... is that your mother I hear in the background?"

"Ehm..." Madison's voice suddenly had a tremble to it.

"I could have sworn I heard your mom," she continued when Madison didn't answer. "That voice and the Southern accent are hard to miss... are you at home?"

"Yeah, I'm in Lafayette," Madison admitted. "I had to take care of a couple of urgent last-minute things, so they gave me two days off. I've been traveling through the night."

"Is everything okay? Is your family alright?"

"They're all fine, I'll explain everything to you when I get back." Madison paused. "I miss you."

Ally smiled, the sincerity in Madison's voice putting her at ease. "I miss you too. Not long now." She kept her voice down in case Theo was awake. "Fifteen days."

"Seventeen, actually. They weren't happy with me leaving, so I'll have to stay for another two days to round things up there. But what's another two days, huh? We'll have all the time in the world. And Theo will be home very soon," she added. "I bet you're looking forward to having him back."

"You have no idea." Ally chuckled. "I'll be making the most of our time together during his holiday, because he's got his mind set on attending that school now. But it will be easier when he starts his first semester, knowing he's happy there and comfortable with traveling back and forth. And that I'll have the money to pay for it, of course." She peeled at the label on her beer bottle, wedging the phone between her shoulder and her ear. "Mira is signing for the house tomorrow."

"She is? That's great. So you're on a first-name basis with her now?"

"Yeah, she was quite personable from the beginning and she came over for a coffee at *Western Shores* today. She asked me if I was seeing someone and I told her about you. I figured she was practically a stranger so it's not like she'd tell anyone." Ally bit her lip and smiled. "It felt really nice to talk about you and she thought it was super romantic how the girl with the pink hair moved into my pink house and won my heart." She felt herself blush, not sure if she was sounding too sappy, but the truth was, she really did love talking about Madison, and she couldn't wait to tell the world. Somehow being with Madison had made her confident with herself and with her sexuality. She was proud to be with her and excited for what lay ahead.

"That's so cute," Madison said, and Ally could picture her face as she talked to her on the phone. Her smile, her icy-blue eyes, her tanned skin and those irresistible lips. "I love that you told them about me. Do you feel better about it now that you know her?"

"A little. She's still going to rent it out to tourists, so I'll never know who will be staying next door, but she seems very reasonable in case I get noise complaints."

"That's good. What are you doing right now?"

Ally couldn't help but smile at the flirty tone in Madison's voice. "If you're asking me if I'm alone, I'm not. I'm drinking a beer in front of the bar. Devon is closing up." She took a moment to absorb the scene in front of her, feeling truly appreciative of what she had. "There are so many stars tonight..." She lowered her voice when Devon switched off the music. "And it's so quiet and peaceful."

"I miss being there with you," Madison said.

"You'll be back soon enough." A longing tugged deep in Ally's gut when she imagined Madison's return. "What are you doing?"

"I'm in my parents' back yard, lying in my hammock. I expected them to remove it after I left since my mother hates it. She claims it's for lazy hippies." Madison chuckled. "But I'm glad it's still hanging, and I might sleep out here tonight, it's a lovely evening."

"I like that image," Ally twirled a lock of hair around her finger. "I can picture you lying there, looking all..."

"Sexy talk?" Devon interrupted her as he sat down too, opening his own beer. He shot her a teasing grin and took a long drink, then burped really loud, making Ally flinch.

"Sorry, Devon's just come to kill the mood. Talk tomorrow?"

"Sure." Madison sounded amused. "Say hi to Devon from me, I'll call you from the airport on my way back."

"Thanks for that," Ally said as she rolled her eyes at him.

"You're welcome." He winked. "Everything still fine on the lover's front?"

"Better than ever." Ally turned to him. "What about you and Chelsey?"

Devon shrugged, but she could see a small smile playing around his lips. "I called her, and we went for a coffee. It was nice but also a little strange to be in a public place together. Made it feel real, you know?" He looked down at his beer. "And I'm taking her out for dinner this week, when we both have an evening off."

"That's great." Ally gave him a surprised stare. "I'm so proud of you, Devon. I didn't expect you to be so comfortable so soon. Not that there's any reason you shouldn't be, it's just that knowing you..."

"I'm not entirely comfortable to be honest," Devon interrupted her. "In fact, I'm really scared. This is all new to me and I'm still not sure how I'll feel if we get intimate, but the thing is, I'm really into her. She's captivating and funny..." He sighed. "It's the strangest thing but I just want to be around her."

"Maybe you've never been in love before."

"Maybe. Despite the long string of women I've dated, I've never felt the need to be in a relationship and I've certainly never felt like this before. So confused, happy, terrified and excited, all at the same time." He raised his gaze to look Ally in the eyes. "But seeing you with Madison has taught me that being open to a non-traditional relationship can be a beautiful thing, and I think it's inspiring how you've accepted it."

Ally gave him a warm smile and reached out to run a hand through his hair. "That's really sweet of you," she said, swallowing down the lump in her throat. "I fought against it at first, but I had no other choice than to embrace it because in the end..." She hesitated, a little shocked by what she was about to say. "In the end, I love her."

64

The taxi drive to Capitola from the airport had Madison all excited today, even though they were driving most of it over the freeway. It was a lot warmer than when she'd left, and she could really feel the heat in the air now. Leaning out of the window, she smiled as they took the exit to Capitola. It felt like a warm bath, and she knew she'd made the right decision when the smell of the ocean hit her as they drove into the quaint town that she now called home. They drove past the museum and underneath the old train tracks, then passed Ally's mural on the side of the fire station. There was a lazy vibe this Sunday, most people still indoors at nine am. The promenade was busier though, with cyclists and tourists sitting on the benches, enjoying the sunshine with an ice cream or a take-out coffee.

"Thank you, you can drop me off here." She tipped the taxi driver, rushing to get her luggage out of the trunk, juggling her three bags and the giant bunch of roses she'd bought for Ally on the way. It would have been a lot easier to go via the bridge, she realized as she trudged heavily through the sand, but she'd been looking forward to that first glimpse of the row of colorful houses behind the creek, and as always, it didn't disappoint. The tables in front of *Western Shores* were occupied, and Ally was standing at one of them, talking to two women before she disappeared back inside.

Madison felt a flutter at seeing her, and a pull so strong that she wanted to run. By the time she got to the bar, she was out of breath and sat down on the stone wall, dropping everything apart from the roses. For the first time, she heard reggae music was playing through the speakers, and it touched her, knowing Ally's visit to Bimini had inspired her.

"There you are!" Ally yelled as she came back outside with two coffees. She put them down, then flew around Madison's neck as she stood up.

"Hey, you." Madison hugged her back, overwhelmed with warm feelings as she felt Ally's body press up against her own. She was home, reunited with the woman she loved, and it felt right and so, so good. Aware of their audience, she let go and stepped back, then handed Ally the roses.

"Thank you, how romantic." Ally closed her eyes and inhaled deeply against the red petals, then looked up at Madison's mouth.

Madison gave her an amused and almost invisible shake of the head. Kissing each other right here and now would be a bad idea, as she was already worried the roses were giving them away. "Want me to help you put those in water?" she asked instead.

"Sure," Ally said softly, unable to keep the emotion out of her voice.

Madison left her bags outside and walked through the bar to the back, searching for a bucket in the storage cupboard, then turned around and held it up when she felt Ally's presence behind her. "This one okay?"

Ally ignored the bucket, her eyes fixed on Madison's lips. "I want you."

"I want you too. But we can't kiss each other out here," she whispered. "Not yet."

"I know." Ally looked over her shoulder to check that no one was watching them, then dragged Madison farther into the room, closed the door and pushed her against the freezer until she sat down on it. "But this works." She stepped between her legs and laced her fingers through Madison's hair before kissing her so passionately that Madison felt dizzy with arousal as their lips parted. Ally's warm breath, her tongue, the touch of her hands and her soft, sweet moans made her twitch.

In a frenzy of raging lust, she got off the freezer and continued to kiss Ally as she backed her up against the wall. Fantasies had occupied her mind for weeks and the longing for Ally had physically tortured her. Her hands crept under Ally's T-shirt until she found her bra, cupping her breasts as she ground her hips against hers.

Ally gasped against her mouth when her fingers raked over her hard nipples, the sound of her pleasure pulling Madison back into reality.

"Jesus, Ally." She noticed Ally looked just as bewildered as she felt and ran a hand through her tousled hair, her eyes full of wild desire. "Are you sure no one is going to come in here?"

"No, I'm not sure." Ally sighed and straightened her T-shirt, then tucked it back into her waistband. "Theo is with Ana and I don't know when they'll be back." She pulled Madison's hair behind her ears and wiped away a mascara stain from underneath her eye. "Fuck. I should probably go back out there, it's also kind of busy today. But we could meet here later tonight? When Theo's in bed?" Her dark eyes and the way she kept pressing her body against Madison's told her it would be hard for Ally to wait that long.

"That sounds like a plan. I'll be right here, ready to tear your clothes off and make you scream." Madison shot her a flirty look and took her hand. "But I need to tell you something before you go. Check the card in the flowers."

"Okay." Ally reached for the red envelope wedged between the stems and opened it. "What's this?" She pulled out a single key attached to a small heart-shaped silver key chain with the letter 'A' engraved in the middle.

Madison took a deep breath, feeling way more nervous than she thought she'd be. "It's the key to my new house," she said, noting she didn't sound so confident anymore. Her palms suddenly felt clammy as she dug her nails into them. "So you or Theo can let yourselves in whenever you want."

Ally frowned as she studied it, then raised her gaze to Madison, her lips parting in surprise. "What? How did you manage to find something new so fast? Does that mean you're moving out already?"

"No, I'm not moving out, I'm never moving out." Madison hesitated. "I bought the pink house."

There was a long silence while Ally processed her words. Madison shuffled on the spot as she waited for her to say something, terrified of her reaction. "But that's not possible, I sold it to Mira..."

"And I bought if from Mira, right after your exchange. There's not a single developer who doesn't like to turn a quick profit." Madison gave Ally a hopeful smile, still unable to gauge her reaction. "She's also not as feisty and businesslike as she comes across on her website; I explained the situation and told her about you. She called me after you'd had coffee together to tell me the deal was on."

"So you really own the house now?" Ally shook her head in disbelief, then gave her a tight hug. She buried her face in Madison's neck, quietly crying. "I can't believe it... Why didn't you tell me you wanted to buy it?"

"I didn't realize I wanted to buy it until it was too late, and I wasn't even sure if I could pull it off. It's not exactly a bargain; I was worried my interest would jeopardize your sale if I told you I wanted to buy it." Madison rested her hands on Ally's shoulders and studied her. "I hope those are happy tears..."

Ally bit her trembling lip as she nodded, tears trickling down her face. "You have no idea how happy it makes me that the house is yours. As long as you didn't do it for me..."

"I did it because I wanted to." Madison's heart was beating in her throat as she cupped Ally's cheek because what she was about to say would change everything. "I love you, Ally, and I want to stay here in Capitola with you and Theo. I want us to be there for each other, to be a family." She waited for an answer, but again, Ally was too stunned to speak. "I love you so much," she said again, this time in a whisper.

Ally sniffed, wiped her tears and gave her a smile that sent a warm shiver down Madison's spine, finally relaxing her after worrying for days. "I love you too," She said, swallowing hard as she took Madison's hand, fisting the key in her other. "I really do." Her voice broke as she continued. "I didn't think I could ever love someone again after Marcos died. I think that deep down, I always felt safe, knowing no one could ever take his place. And that's true. No one can take his place because he's Theo's father and my first love. But you somehow managed to tear down this perfect front of false contentment I'd created, and I don't know how you did it, but I feel like I need you now. I love you and I need you."

Something warm hit Madison's cheek, and when Ally wiped away the falling tear, she captured her hand against her face and kissed it. So much passed between them in the moments that followed but talking didn't seem the right thing to do, so she leaned in and kissed Ally softly, knowing life would never be the same again.

65

"Theo, honey, can we talk to you?" Ally moved over, making space for him to come and sit between her and Madison on the picnic blanket. They were on the beach, eating dinner from the containers Madison had brought from home. She felt sick with nerves but waiting would only make it harder in the long run. He'd changed so much after only two months away. Perhaps not physically, but he was a lot more independent now and didn't want to be treated like a child anymore, so it was only fair that he got the grown-up talk he deserved.

"What's wrong?" Theo narrowed his eyes. "You look scared."

Ally put her food to the side and managed a smile. "Well, to be honest with you, I am a little scared. We've been wondering how to tell you this but there's no right or wrong way, so I'm just going to say it and then we'd like to talk to you about it." She took a deep breath and braced herself, feeling her hands shaking in her lap "Madison and I are dating."

Theo's face flushed, and he averted his eyes, focusing on his dinner instead. "I know," he said. "I saw you kissing."

Ally's eyes widened. "Oh God... when did you see that?"

"On our way to LA, outside the room at Ragged Point."

"Oh..." Ally flinched. "You weren't really meant to see that. I'm sorry." She looked to Madison for help.

"You know there's nothing wrong with two women kissing, right?" Madison tried. "Your mom and I... we're in love and we'd like to be together. But we want to know how you feel about that first."

Theo looked up at Madison and she could swear she saw a glimmer of excitement in his eyes. "Are you coming to live with us?"

"Next door first, but eventually yes, if you're okay with that." Madison smiled at him.

"So you're not moving out?"

"Madison bought the pink house," Ally explained. "We were thinking it might be a nice idea to make one big house, so we'll have more space."

"Okay..." Theo looked over his shoulder, eyeing the pink and the blue houses. "Does that mean I'll get a bigger bedroom?"

"We can talk about that," Ally said, relief washing over her. This was going a lot easier than she'd expected, but then again, he'd obviously known for a while. "Why didn't you tell us you knew?"

Theo shrugged. "I don't know. I forgot, I guess."

Madison tried to suppress a chuckle. They'd been having sleepless nights over this but apparently it wasn't a big deal to Theo. "Are you okay if your mom and I sleep in the same room?"

"Gross." He grimaced, then finally looked up at Ally. "Sure. Whatever."

"Thank you, honey. I'm very glad you understand." Ally was so happy she had to fight back her tears. She took Theo in her arms and squeezed him tight against her, then laughed when he tried to wriggle his way out of her grip. "Okay, okay, I know you don't like hugs anymore."

Madison felt emotional at seeing Ally's big smile, and she wiped at her own eyes, not wanting Theo to see her cry. "So, do you have any questions, buddy?" She asked, trying to keep her voice steady.

"Does grandma know?"

"Yes, grandma knows," Ally said. "And Devon knows too. Do you mind if people know about us?"

Theo took a moment to think about that. "No. Amelia at school has two moms and she doesn't mind." He rolled his eyes. "Not that Madison would be my mom..."

"No, I wouldn't," Madison agreed with him. "Your father was and always will be your father and I will never replace him. But I want to be here for you and your mom. Help you when you need help and listen when you need someone to talk to." She smiled. "And I want to be your friend, above all."

"We're already friends." Theo dug his fingers into the sand, avoiding Madison's eyes that were welling up now.

"Of course we are," she said, composing herself and turning to Ally, begging her to take over.

"So, Amelia..." Ally frowned, digging through the conversations she'd had with Theo. "She's a friend from school, right?"

"She's not my friend. Just a girl." Madison and Ally exchanged glances when they noticed his face flush again.

"Just a girl, huh?" Ally teased, running a hand through his hair.

"Mom, stop it!" Theo ducked away and stood up. "I don't

want to talk anymore." He handed the empty food container to Ally and turned to Madison. "Can we go looking for shells now?"

"You bet." Madison put her own food aside and leaned in to give Ally a kiss on her cheek. She laughed when she saw Theo's face pull into another grimace and nudged him. "Get used to it, buddy. Come on, let's go find some cool stuff."

66

Ally beamed with joy as she watched Madison and Theo walk off together, pointing to the sand and bending down now and then to pick something up. In only five months, her life had changed so much that she could hardly believe where she was now. Soon, the days would become shorter and colder, a time of the year she always used to dread. Being alone in the dark with too much time on her hands to think about the past had been difficult for her, but she had a feeling that things would be very different this winter. Cozy, warm, exciting...

"Mind if I sit down?" Ana had snuck up behind her, pulling her out of her thoughts.

"No, of course not."

Ana followed Ally's gaze to Madison and Theo, now both sitting cross-legged by the shore, engrossed in an animated conversation. "Maybe I was wrong," she said, out of the blue. "About Madison."

Ally nodded, not arguing with the statement.

"And I need to apologize," Ana continued. "I didn't know what to think when you told me. It seemed so implausible, so ..." she shook her head. "Never mind. Looking at the three of you, I was clearly wrong. You look happy, and I want that for you." She let out a soft sigh as she paused to look at Ally. "I've always encouraged you to move on but when I actually saw you opening up to someone else other than my son, I guess... well I guess it was hard somehow."

"Thank you for saying that." Ally looked at her intently. "Madison is not replacing Marcos. He will always be Theo's father."

"I know. I'll need some time to get used to this, though." Ana shrugged. "It's unconventional, to me at least, but I'll try to keep an open mind about it." She put a hand on Ally's arm. "Why don't you let Theo stay with me tonight? Take your girl out on a date?"

"My girl?" Ally couldn't help but chuckle because nothing could have surprised her more, coming from Ana.

"Girlfriend, partner, whatever they call it nowadays." Ana's cheeks turned red. "Take some time to yourselves, have fun."

"Okay... That would be great, thank you." Ally pulled her knees up and rested her chin on her forearms. She'd always believed that there was only one true love for everyone, and that she'd had her shot a long time ago, but Madison had proven her wrong. She'd surprised Ally time after time, and somehow settled into their lives naturally, like she'd always belonged there. The beautiful disaster Ally had expected her to be was nowhere to be found, and instead, she was filled with love, warmth, desire, but most of all hope.

· · ·

Madison and Ally walked back toward the house after Ana had left with Theo. *Western Shores* was still abnormally busy long after the sea lion incident, and food bloggers had tempted hordes of tourists to come and taste their signature tempura anchovies. Devon and a new girl Ally had hired were busy serving food and drinks to at least fifty people, and curious glances from locals were cast their way as they walked hand in hand, speculative whispers undoubtedly being exchanged.

"Enough with the secrecy," Ally said, waving at a couple of people she knew, just to make her point.

Madison arched a brow, taken aback by Ally's sudden decisiveness. "Are you sure?"

"Absolutely. I'm tired of keeping you a secret." Ally looked up at her and smiled. "I'm proud to be with you and frankly, I don't care what anyone thinks as long as Theo is okay with it." She turned to Madison, got up on her tiptoes and kissed her softly on the lips. It wasn't inappropriate or even sexual, but there was no doubt that they were more than friends now, as the crowd fell still.

Madison smiled against her mouth, hearing a low gasp and some muted murmurs. "I think that did the job," she whispered. The awkward silence that suddenly settled over the terrace was broken by a loud whistle, coming from Devon. He started clapping, and for no reason other than that people generally instinctively followed, everyone else started clapping and whooping too.

Ally laughed and gave them a theatrical bow. "Thought we might as well get it out of the way and it will give them something to talk about." She took Madison's hand again and looked up at her with a beaming smile.

"I have no doubt we'll be the talk of the town tomorrow."

Madison laughed too, baffled by Ally's bravery and total lack of concern. "Your place or mine?" she asked, glancing up at their homes that looked perfect together: Ally's serene blue a balanced contrast against her edgy pink.

"Hmm... hard to decide. My bed is bigger, but I seem to have a thing for your shower." Ally tilted her head and narrowed her eyes. "Do you think we should paint all three properties one color?"

Madison searched for her key in her pockets as she thought about it, then shook her head. No, I like it exactly as it is," she said as she opened the door. "It's a nice reminder, don't you think?"

Ally stepped inside with her and nodded in agreement. "Yeah. And a great story of the girl with the pink hair who rented my pink house." She pushed Madison against the wall and grinned. "It will live on forever."

EPILOGUE

"**M**om, Dad!" Madison spread her arms to welcome her parents when they got out of the car. She hugged her mother first, then her father, ruffling up his hair in the process, just to wind him up.

"Cut it out, Madison." Her father laughed and fixed his hair in the side-view mirror, then took in his surroundings. "So, this is your new home... Looks pretty neat to me." A smile crept on his face when he spotted the bay and the village behind it.

"Neat?" Madison shot him a quizzical look. "Who have you been hanging out with?"

"He went camping with Chuck." Her mother rolled her eyes. "Came back looking like a caveman, smelling like a sewer and talking like... well, like Chuck."

"Right. That explains it. Where is Chuck anyway? I thought he'd be coming along."

"He's coming." Her mother had a quiver to her voice. "With Darla. She'd never seen the West Coast so they're driving together. You don't mind Darla coming, do you?"

"No… of course not." Madison didn't know what to say, "I just didn't know they were such close friends," she lied.

"Those two have been spending an unhealthy amount of time together if you ask me," her father said, shooting Madison a knowing look. "But maybe he just likes her car."

"Maybe." Madison pointed to her mother's shoes, changing the subject. "How on earth can you walk so fast in those, Mom?" If Edie had any trouble conquering the cobbled roads in her stiletto heels, she did not let on, walking so fast that Madison and her father had trouble keeping up.

"Oh it's easy, sweetie. I've walked in worse places than this. Plus, my legs are really strong now, with all the yoga I've been doing."

"Her mind is pretty strong too," Madison's father joked. "She's been meditating so much that I've had to check her pulse from time to time." He cleared his throat, casting her a sideways glance. "Well, I'm looking forward to meeting your new… I mean I'm looking forward to meeting Theo," he corrected himself. "And seeing Ally again, of course."

Madison looked at him in amusement. During their phone conversations, Chuck kept referring to Ally and Theo as 'her new family', as if she'd gotten married and given birth over the course of eight months, and she had a suspicion the running joke had rubbed off on her father during their camping trip. "Theo's great, you'll love him." Speeding up their pace, they followed Edie, who was heading for *Western Shores* where Ally was waiting for them.

"Ally!" Edie shrieked with genuine enthusiasm. "It's so great to see you again."

Her father greeted Ally too, complimenting her on her bar and the beautiful location that apparently was 'neat' too. Once again, he seemed completely at ease with her, but then he didn't care much for anything but golf these days unlike her mother, who was obsessively throwing herself from one hobby to the other, trying to keep as busy as she possibly could. "And that's the house?" He looked up at the pink house and grinned. "Your mother was right. It does suit you." He pointed to the blue one. "And that's yours, Ally?"

"Yes, that's mine and Theo's, but soon to be ours." Ally smiled at him. "We've already knocked through a doorway, so Theo has my bedroom now when he comes home at the weekends and we sleep in Madison's room. There's still a lot to do but we're not in any rush."

"So I've heard." Ben sat down and rubbed Madison's shoulder when she took a seat next to him. "We'll have to come back to see the results."

"You should. There will be a decent spare room by that time, in the tower." Madison said, pouring them all a glass of wine from the bottle in the cooler. "We're making the bathroom on the blue side bigger, and the extended kitchen will be on the pink side." She waved at Theo, who came running up to them from the beach. "But so far, only this guy's room is done. He's an expert at anything ocean related, and he's created his own ecosystem in there. I'm sure Ally and I will be spending a lot of time maintaining it while he's away during the week," she added with a joke.

"Hi Theo," Edie said, looking a little emotional. "It's nice to see you again."

"Do you remember my mom, Theo?" Madison realized then that it was a big thing for her mother to see Theo again. He would be in her life from now on, and that meant he would also be in her mother's life. Of course, Edie wouldn't be his grandmother in that sense of the word, but she adored kids, and Madison was positive she'd jump at any opportunity to bond with him.

"Hey Edie." Theo studied her outfit with interest. "You look nice."

Edie laughed. "Thank you, sweetie. I've heard you have an amazing new bedroom."

Theo nodded with a grin. "I've got an aquarium wall. Madison helped build and design it for me."

"Seriously? I didn't know Madison could do that." A look of surprise and endearment settled over Edie's face as she watched Theo lean in against Madison, his elbow resting on her shoulder.

Madison shrugged. "Not by myself of course, I'm not a builder. But I managed to get the pump, the heaters and the light working, and we filled it together, didn't we, Theo? It took us eight full days and ten trips to different beaches." She laughed. "I even had to use my diving equipment to find some of the rocks and kelp but it all seems to be surviving."

"Do you want to see it?" Theo looked up at Edie who was even taller than Madison in her high heels.

"Absolutely, I'd love that."

"Can I come too?" Ben asked, joining his wife.

Ally gave Madison's hand a squeeze as Ben and Edie went inside with Theo. "They seem so excited," she said, surprise lingering in her voice.

"I told you, it's a big deal for them. Theo will be their family too, now." She gave Ally a soft kiss on her cheek. "And so will you."

Ally smiled and let out a deep sigh. "I'm glad we arranged this housewarming dinner. It's going to be fun for everyone to get to know each other." She got up and stuck her head around the door of *Western Shores*. "I'll go see if Devon's got things under control."

"Okay." Madison checked the time. "Then I'll set up the tables. More people will be arriving soon."

. . .

The long table, shaded by a gazebo, was set up for a late lunch on the beach just in front of *Western Shores*. Madison was at one end with Ally and Theo, and in front of them were their friends and family. The table was laid out with wine and fresh seafood, served in abalone shells, and Ally's new part-timer was serving after Devon and Ally had finished the preparations.

Western Shores was closed for the day, as Ally had wanted Devon there too. He was sitting next to Chelsey, who looked incredibly elegant in a navy and white striped boatneck dress and he was barely able to keep his hands off her. Hannah and Kristine were here too, along with Ana, Ally's father and his girlfriend, Ben and Edie, Mason and his girlfriend and finally, Chuck and Darla, who were trying their best to keep a low profile at the other end of the table, pretending to be just friends. The way her brother looked at Darla touched Madison, and she felt a little ashamed for not taking his relationship seriously. Whatever was going on between them, it was clear that they had feelings for each other, and if they were happy, she wasn't going to question it.

Feeling incredibly grateful for everyone who had come all the way here to celebrate them officially moving in together, she stood up and held up her glass in a toast. "Thank you for coming to our housewarming party," she said, looking at each and every one of them as she pointed at the three small houses. "I apologize to those of you who've had long journeys for putting you up in a hotel but I'm sure you'll understand it's a little cramped for thirteen people in there.

At that, laughter broke out, and Madison continued with

a beaming smile. "It's far from done yet, but we really wanted you all here while we can still sit outside and enjoy the weather. I know weekends are difficult for some of you, but as Theo is in LA during the week, we really appreciate you making the time." She paused and looked down on him, resting a hand on his shoulder. "This highly gifted guy turned twelve this summer and he also started a new school. We're so proud of him for doing so well and honestly, it's been amazing to get to know him. Most of all though, it's an honor to call him my friend." She locked eyes with her mother for a beat, and seeing a glimmer in her eyes, she knew her words had touched her. "Thank you, Mom and Dad, for being so generous and helping me out with my dream of staying here with these two amazing people who I'm so proud to call my family." Her father – modest as always – gave her a small smile and a nod, and her mother's eyes were welling up now. Swallowing down the lump in her throat, Madison turned to Ally and took her hand. "I'd also like to raise a glass to my beautiful and amazing girlfriend Ally, who makes me the happiest woman in the world every single day."

Ally looked up at her and blew her a kiss. The love in her captivating brown eyes, her dark hair blowing in the wind along with her silk kaftan and her smile that told Madison she was hers and only hers, made her want to kiss her right there and then. She didn't though, as she needed Ally to hear her say what she had to say in front of everyone.

"Theo once asked me to take care of you and I promised him that I would." She felt a tear trickle town her cheek when Ally squeezed her hand, her lip trembling with emotion. "And I will," she said, her voice breaking. "For as long as you'll let me. I love you, Ally."

"I love you too." Ally stood up, wrapped her arms

around Madison and kissed her so sweet and tenderly that Madison almost dropped her glass.

"Gross, stop it," Theo said, making everyone laugh and pulling them out of their moment.

Madison shook her head at him and laughed too. Eight months ago, she'd come here with the plan of settling down for a while until she found a place to call home. Since then, those eight months had become the most meaningful and precious in her life, changing her course forever. Perhaps some things were meant to be, or perhaps things just fell into place naturally. What she knew for sure was that her time here had changed her in the best of ways and made her realize what was important.

She put an arm around Ally and turned to the ocean, truly appreciating the breathtaking view that called to her each morning. The old wharf where seagulls and pelicans were perched on the railing, lined up like soldiers. The golden sand and the clear water, the small creek with restaurants and coffeehouses behind it. The sun-bleached cliffs, rising from the ocean, the lush hills around the village and the iconic colored houses that people came to see from afar. She was a part of it now, and if there was such a thing as perfection, she had no doubt that it was right here, with Ally and Theo. Her family.

AFTERWORD

I hope you've loved reading *Western Shores* as much as I've loved writing it. If you've enjoyed this book, would you consider rating it and reviewing it on www.amazon.com? Reviews are very important to authors and I'd be really grateful!

ACKNOWLEDGMENTS

As always, first and foremost, thank you Claire Jarrett, my editor! I've deleted a total of 45.000 words on this manuscript and practically started over, but you helped me through it. Western Shores is now a worthy book 4 in The Compass Series and I couldn't have done this without your help and encouragement.

Thank you to Laure Dherbècourt, my main beta reader, for being so thorough and precise, and to Ro Fetterman for hunting down my Britishisms.

Dr Shawn Noren, I really appreciate you taking the time to tell me about life of a Marine Biologist. I knew absolutely nothing about the subject and it's been super interesting to meet you. You're truly an inspiring woman.

Serena J Bishop, thank you for explaining academia to a novice, and for your insight into the world of gifted children. You're my favourite nerd! :)

Carol Allen, it was fun to hear about your gifted grandchild. I can see why you're so proud and I'm looking forward to seeing you again this summer!

ABOUT THE AUTHOR

Lise Gold is an author of lesbian romance. Her romantic attitude, enthusiasm for travel and love for feel good stories form the heartland of her writing. Born in London to a Norwegian mother and English father, and growing up between the UK, Norway, Zambia and the Netherlands, she feels at home pretty much everywhere and has an unending curiosity for new destinations. She goes by 'write what you know' and is often found in exotic locations doing research or getting inspired for her next novel.

Working as a designer for fifteen years and singing semi-professionally, Lise has always been a creative at heart. Her novels are the result of a quest for a new passion after resigning from her design job in 2018. Since the launch of Lily's Fire in 2017, she has written several romantic novels and is currently working on 'The Compass Series'.

When not writing from her kitchen table, Lise can be found cooking, at the gym or singing her heart out some-where, preferably country or blues. After living in Amsterdam and Hong Kong together and getting married in Spain, she and her wife have finally settled in the UK with their dogs El Comandante and Bubba, and their cats Kanye and Lil' Tittie.

ALSO BY LISE GOLD

Lily's Fire

Beyond the Skyline

The Cruise

French Summer

Fireflies

Northern Lights

Southern Roots

Eastern Nights

Living

Printed in Great Britain
by Amazon

59729600R00251